Bend of Honor

Bend of Honor

Tom Hansen

2021

Bend of Honor is a work of fiction. All incidents, dialogue, and all characters except some well-known professional sports figures are products of the author's imagination and are not to be construed as real. Some locations, businesses, and organizations are real but are used only to support this novel's fictitious nature. In all other respects, any resemblance to actual persons living or dead, events, or locales is entirely coincidental.

Cultural Unity Publishing
4106 N. St. Elias
Mesa, AZ 85215

Cultural Unity Publishing is a division of Educational Video Training Concepts, LLC.

ISBN: 978-1-7328182-5-5

Printed in the United States of America

Cover Design by Luke Hansen

The main setting for this novel takes place in my hometown. With that, I dedicate this book to my friends and classmates from New Richmond, Wisconsin. We always have and always will walk together through this game of life. To those who have passed, we will meet again someday.

In Memoriam (NRHS Class of 1973):

Mary Jo (Donahue) Day
Dennis Branstad
Wally Cox
Bob Hansen
Alan Sylte
Jane (Helling) Cohn
Renee (Emerson) Jones
Sue (Anderson) Thompson
Cindy (Bethke) Cody
Colleen (Moore) Fisher
Pete McKeon
Gregg Espersen
Pat Driscoll
Sandy (Larson) Green
Tom Dowd
John Bazille

For your reading pleasure and reference,
a cast of characters chart is included in the appendix.

"I would prefer even to fail with honor than to win by cheating."

Sophocles

Chapter 1

Not a day goes by that Carl West doesn't think about his dad. The last day of his father's life was his finest—an epoch in a career filled with glory and success. But Billy West's fame and fortune never supplanted his humility nor his honor. Carl loved and respected his father, not because Billy was an NFL quarterback, but because he taught Carl the true meaning of life, none of which had anything to do with football.

The video of his dad's final play was replayed on ESPN for years afterward and now sits in the film room at the Hall of Fame in Canton, Ohio, along with his jersey stenciled on the back with the number two. The Reno Mountaineers offered him number one; however, he turned them down with four quick words: "God is number one."

Carl's grandpa Syd could have been an NFL star himself. He still holds rushing records at Oklahoma during the glory years of the Wishbone offense; instead, he chose to make it big in the business world after graduation. *Big in the business world* could be the most significant understatement of our time. The company he founded, West Enterprises, became the most extensive sports marketing firm on the planet, and the year after Carl's grandma passed, Syd won a bid to bring an NFL expansion team to Nevada.

He and West Enterprise's board of directors wanted to start up the franchise in Las Vegas; however, the Raiders had been approved to move to Sin City from Oakland, and now the sparsely populated Silver State would have two NFL teams. The doubters said the Mountaineers would not last because there was no TV market in Reno to support the massive expenses needed to run the organization. Syd replied by telling the naysayers that if the Packers could survive in Green Bay, a city half the size of Reno, then the

Mountaineers could be profitable in their municipality east of the Sierra Nevada's.

Signing Billy West during their expansion draft was a spectacular strategic move. He had been the NFL's leading passer every year since being selected as the first overall pick in the 1995 expansion draft for the Jacksonville Jaguars. Billy had shattered NCAA passing records during his four years of college football at Arkansas, and for the past twenty years, he crushed many NFL records too. At age forty-two, the Mountaineers believed that he was still a long way from being washed up.

Before the games began in September of 2014, their first year in the NFL, oddsmakers gave Reno a 400 to one chance to win the Super Bowl. But after Billy West led them to fourteen regular-season victories and the top seed in the playoffs, the Mountaineers became considerable favorites to win it all. So, the long bomb with no time left on the clock was Billy's last-ditch effort to make sure that the dream of an NFL championship became a reality.

Sun Life Stadium in Miami Gardens had been rocking all afternoon, and the roar of the Super Bowl crowd could be heard ten miles away at the racetrack in Hialeah. The Carolina Panthers scored what looked to be the icing on the cake with eight seconds to go putting the Reno Mountaineers down thirty-one to twenty-seven. The fans dressed in black, blue, and silver were screaming like crazy and had begun singing the dreaded *Na Na Hey Hey Kiss Him Goodbye* song in celebration of their beloved team's first world championship. The ensuing kickoff was returned only to the Mountaineer's sixteen-yard line, leaving only four seconds for Billy West to overcome the impossible. He called a trick play in the huddle instead of the coach's wish for a Hail Mary.

The Panthers brought in eight defensive backs and set up in a prevent defense. The three rushers applied pressure as Billy rolled right, was tripped up but didn't fall, then turned and ran the opposite direction and pointed at Jerome Gregory. The veteran playmaker was streaking down the left side with two other wide receivers nearby. The entire core of defensive backs took the bait and swarmed the receivers after West pump-faked to them. Then Billy stopped on a dime, turned, set, and launched a fifty-three-yard pass to fullback Cory Simes as he sprinted down the right sideline with no one near him. The pigskin was placed precisely in Simes' outstretched arms as Billy was crushed to the ground by Star Lotulelei. The Panthers' fans became eerily silent as they watched their world championship fade away in what seemed like slow motion. Lotulelei rolled off Billy and sat in stunned silence next to him as the Mountaineers' fans stormed the field and tore down the goalpost. West patted the All-Pro defensive tackle on the helmet, offered condolences, pointed toward heaven, then jogged slowly to the players who were celebrating madly in the end zone.

During the postgame interview, Billy humbly credited God, his coaches and teammates, the fans, and his family for the win, never once mentioning his own incredible performance. He even acknowledged his son Carl as his biggest fan and his motivation to be the best he could be. Months later, Billy West would be an early selection for enshrinement in the Hall of Fame next to his idols Johnny Unitas, Brett Favre, and Joe Montana.

Unfortunately, Billy wasn't around to see his name permanently fixed to the wall in Canton. He and his wife died in an accident only hours after the end of the game.

*****

Carl resolved that the West family name would not carry on for generations to come. He had no desire to marry and raise kids in the wake of the tragedy that had occurred following the Super Bowl. His mom and dad's closed-casket memorial service was a joint affair, which Carl regretted ever since. Hundreds of NFL players, coaches, and sports reporters packed the church to glorify their fallen hero, while his mom's mourners stood in the back of the balcony behind the choir. The Jaguars' and Mountaineers' owners paid tribute by announcing that both teams would retire Billy's jersey on the same day. All NFL players would wear commemorative patches on their sleeves for the entire following season. At the funeral, Carl decided that, like Billy's jersey, the West surname would be retired from the family to honor his father's greatness. No, sir, there would be no wife or kids in his future.

There was no excuse nor explanation of how Carl's parents perished from this earth. After two hours of postgame madness, locker room celebrations, and interviews, they had hopped in a taxi to take them to the Miami airport. The other players hired limousines, but Billy didn't believe in wasting money when so many people in the world had so little.

Meanwhile, Carl had decided to stay in Florida for a couple of days and relax on the beach. He had turned eighteen two weeks before, and this was his chance to be on his own without the shadow of his mom and pop following him around. The drinking age in Florida was twenty-one, but Carl was sure that any bartender who enjoyed football would allow the son of Billy West a beer without any questions asked. Probably a free one at that! He had only four months before he graduated from high school, but if he missed a few more days in the classroom to lie on the beach, his teachers wouldn't care. His father had just won the Super Bowl almost singlehandedly!

The camera drone that rammed into the windshield of Billy and Carol's taxi on the way to the airport belonged to WMIA, the Gold Coast's flagship news station. They wanted exclusive footage of the MVP's exit from their city. The driver, thinking his cab had been struck by a giant bird, instinctively tried to cover his face with his hands and lost control of the vehicle. It veered across the median and struck a semi-truck head on. The taxi driver died along with Carl's parents.

WMIA denied that it was their drone; however, the video camera was recovered, and it was registered to the news agency. Lawyers blew up Carl's phone, begging to represent the West family in what could have been the most significant civil suit in American history. But Carl didn't need the money—after losing his dad, he just needed a new best friend.

Chapter 2

Carl lived in a lakeside mansion with his grandpa, Syd, for the remainder of the school year. His grandma had passed three years earlier from an unexpected heart attack, and Syd looked forward to the company of his grandson. The final four months of his senior year were a big waste of time. First and foremost, depression had taken a devastating toll on Carl. Secondly, the commute from his grandfather's house to school took forty minutes in good traffic, much slower when snow flurries whitened the Lake Tahoe countryside. In the minimal days that Carl attended, he had no desire to read, complete worksheets, or study for tests. And his teachers didn't seem to care. They passed him with C's and B's out of empathy for the loss of his parents.

Grandpa Syd was a big donator to his alma mater, so Oklahoma accepted Carl without considering his low grade-point average. Like his father and grandfather, Carl had excelled in football, albeit as a wide receiver. From the time he could first remember playing in a Pop Warner game, he had hoped one day that he would catch an NFL touchdown pass from his dad. That dream ended abruptly on the streets of Miami.

The Sooners' head coach had offered him a scholarship, but Carl turned it down. After Billy's death, he had no desire to be a football player. Actually, he had no desire to do anything. Carl was set for life thanks to his grandfather's wealth and the inheritance of his parent's estate.

Because he eventually had to select a major, Carl picked Mass Media. After two years of eschewing his studies and sulking through college undergraduate classes, he met Molly Anderson one night at a frat party. Molly wanted to be a sportswriter, and soon she and

Carl became best friends. He decided that he, too, would enjoy that same profession. Carl had suddenly found a new purpose for living.

The first two years of college had tanked his chances of graduating with honors or achieving a 3.0 grade point average. On the other hand, Molly finished second in her class of 302 students who received a bachelor's degree in Mass Media. Following graduation in May of 2020, she was offered a sports reporter position with the *Oklahoman* without even applying. But Carl had no offers in Oklahoma, so he sent his resume to over a thousand news organizations nationwide, only to receive about the same number of turndown letters. The companies that were courteous enough to respond indicated that Carl's GPA was unacceptable for their organization.

Grandpa Syd wanted Carl to come back home to Nevada and work for his company, but Carl had little interest in sports marketing. The memories of his dad would eat at his heart day and night. Syd told him to give it some time, and he said the job offer would stand anytime Carl wanted it.

Molly's big brother, Curt, was ten years her senior. Their mother never mentioned why there was such a big gap of time between siblings, and she would change the subject when they asked. Curt became a psychiatrist in Eau Claire, Wisconsin, a small city only a few miles from Colfax, where he and Molly grew up. They barely spoke to one another since she left for college; however, when Curt heard that Molly was dating the son of superstar quarterback Billy West, he would call her once or twice a week to get the "inside scoop" on the NFL. Curt was a heavy online bettor and made more money gambling than he did in psychiatry.

Curt finally got to meet who he hoped was his future brother-in-law the summer after graduation when Molly and Carl visited Western Wisconsin. Curt was an avid fisherman, and he wanted to teach Carl the finer points of freshwater angling. Carl had loved saltwater fishing with his dad off Florida's coast when they lived in Jacksonville, and he was an enthusiastic fly fisherman in the mountain streams that fed into Lake Tahoe. He bragged that the trout never stood a chance.

Carl and Curt hit it off immediately after Carl landed a fifty-two-inch musky on the Chippewa River flowage downstream from the dam. Carl had been skeptical that anything in a river could swallow the sixteen-inch gold Suzy Sucker lure attached to his eighty-pound braided test line. After a violent fight with the massive creature, Carl almost swamped the small aluminum boat while hauling the lunker onboard. Back on shore, he beamed with pride as he lifted the musky to his chest with both hands. Curt snapped pictures from every angle, and the new friendship was solidified.

After a few beers while sitting on the couch in Curt's den watching the Brewers beat up on the Twins, Curt blurted out, "So, are you two getting hitched?" Curt never hesitated to speak his mind after a few beers!

Molly looked at Carl with a sparkle in her eye, and Carl glanced at Molly with a sheepish grin. Then he dropped his head and watched his hands nervously perform a splendid twiddling of thumbs. He had vowed never to marry or procreate a male child to continue the West name after his father died. But now, Molly was making him have second thoughts.

"I don't think it's the best time for marriage," replied Carl quietly. "I'm unemployed and trying to find a job with a newspaper but haven't had much luck."

"I did a little Google research," said the alcohol-influenced Curt. "Sounds like you have a ton of money that you inherited. Why bother working, bro?"

Carl couldn't believe his new friend would say something so offensive. He stared at Curt with an evil eye. "You Googled me? What the hell is that all about?"

"Relax! If you're going to be my brother-in-law, I need to make sure my baby sis is getting a fine guy, that's all."

Now it was time for Molly to give her brother the evil eye. "That's BS, Curt! There's got to be something in this for you. You never phoned me the entire four years I was in college. Why do you suddenly want to be the brother-of-the-year?!"

"Hey, the guy's good-looking, pretty well built, has a great personality, and, well, can break a musky's neck with an eighty-pound test line! Sounds like a marriage made in heaven if you ask me!"

"I need to get a job," said Carl bluntly. "I have other plans for my inheritance that don't involve me getting rich."

With that statement, both Molly and Curt gave a puzzled look at Carl. They were too stunned to ask what he meant. After a few moments of silence, thinking about the elephant in the room, Curt said, "I have a friend who works in human resources at the *Eau Claire Gazette*. I think I can help you land a job right here in God's country."

"I appreciate the offer, but I'm not one to take handouts. Thanks anyway."

Molly reached over and took Carl's hand in hers, then looked him in the eyes. "Carl, it's not a handout. It's a start. That's all you need right now—a start. Once you show the readers that you are a fabulous writer, you will build your resume, and you can move on to bigger and better things."

"A fabulous writer—who are you kidding?" asked Carl while shaking his head. "And what about you? What if the Gazette doesn't have a position for you? You're a hundred times better writer than me, and you know it! You need to follow your career dreams, too!"

"I'll find a job somewhere. I guess what I'm saying is I think we should, you know, think about getting married." Molly moved closer and kissed Carl.

Curt jumped up from the couch and clapped his hands. "Well, there you have it. A marriage proposal made in heaven right from the lips of my sweet little sister! That doesn't happen too often to men, Carl, so I strongly urge you to accept her offer!"

Embarrassed, Molly rose and gave her brother a love punch on the arm, then headed for the kitchen. It was time for another beer, or maybe something more potent.

Chapter 3

George Markins played soccer in college with Curt Anderson at the University of Wisconsin-Eau Claire. Both were enrolled in the Bachelor of Psychology program, but even though there was an extensive library on campus, they did most of their studying at She-Nannigan's tavern down on Water Street. Professors complained to Coach Max Rivers that George and Curt just weren't cutting it in the classroom because their homework was either pathetic or nonexistent.

Coach Rivers was an ex-marine drill sergeant who had little patience for whiny professors and even less for people telling him what to do. However, the university president ordered him to address his athletes' academic performance issues or look elsewhere for a job next year. Knowing Curt and George as he did, Rivers expected a humdinger of an excuse from his two stars. But what he got floored him!

Using his best gruff voice, Coach Rivers said, "Boys, I've had numerous complaints from colleagues about your poor effort in their classes. They tell me that you are spending too much time at the bars downtown when instead, you should be spending that time in the library. What do you have to say for yourselves?"

The soccer buddies had rehearsed their response. "No, Coach, that's not it," replied Curt, tongue in cheek. "When we go to She-Nannigan's or Lucky's, we're there for active research, not for drinking or partying. Right, George?"

"Absolutely, Coach!" responded George, trying to keep a straight face. "We just go there to interact with classmates in an intimate setting to build a solid foundation for our studies of human learning, emotions, and behaviors. Really, Coach!"

Coach Rivers canceled their athletic scholarships but allowed them to remain on the team. If they improved in the classroom, the funding would be reinstated. Shortly after that, George dropped his psychology classes and switched his major to Human Resources. Curt received his bachelor's in Psychology at UW-Eau Claire, then obtained an online master's and a doctorate in Clinical Psychiatry from the University of Barbados. UOB was a small college in the Caribbean that was accredited by the Council of International Schools.

Wisconsin was one of only two states that accepted COIS accreditation as part of a psychiatry certification. Curt completed his required 1,500 hours of a supervised clinical internship with Doc Morgan in the tiny town of Withee, an hour's drive from Eau Claire. The population of Withee was 427. Doc Morgan had one patient, Eve Smith, an octogenarian widow who paid Morgan handsomely for his services. The doctor happened to be a UW-Eau Claire Blugold's soccer fan; thus, he was thrilled when Curt wanted to complete his residency with him.

Curt spent most of the 1,500 hours gambling on the Internet, a hobby he acquired while meeting the University of Barbados' online obligations. Browser tabs allowed him to quickly switch back and forth between professor chats and the International Sports Gaming website, which just so happened to be registered in the West Indies island of Antigua, not far from Barbados.

Meanwhile, George's father threatened to pull him from the soccer team and take his car away if he didn't apply himself one hundred percent in the classroom. His father also strongly suggested that he end his friendship with Curt and begin focusing all his energies on getting good grades instead of hangovers.

After graduation, Curt couldn't find employment, most likely due to his mediocre grade point average compiled with a doctoral degree from an unheard of college in the Caribbean. So, he rented an office in a strip mall near campus and set up a psychiatry shop of his own. When Doc Morgan passed away, he made housecall visits to widow Smith back in Withee. As she had done with Morgan, Eve paid Curt generously for his appointments.

Curt stopped by local schools and left his card with overworked and underpaid psychologists. Their workload was immense due to the number of struggling teachers who wanted low-performing and misbehaving students out of their classrooms. Because Curt charged minimal fees, the school psychologists were thrilled to refer students with unruly parents directly to him. The district's Special Services department gladly picked up the cost of Curt's compensation so they wouldn't have to deal with the recalcitrant parents and their obnoxious advocates who continually demanded meetings and threatened lawsuits.

Although his clientele numbers were low, Curt didn't worry too much about it because Internet gambling was becoming very prosperous. On the other hand, George landed a job in human resources at the Eau Claire Gazette, thanks to a referral from a friend of a friend of his father's. As usual, it's not what you know—it's who you know.

Once George was on his own and needing only a little assistance from his dad, he began to meet Curt at She-Nannigans again. Tuesdays were *Girl's Night Out* at the bar, and women received either shots or draft beers for a buck until closing time. The friends became expert beer pongers on those nights! Reminiscing about the good ol' days, Curt and George wondered why they had bothered to sweat out soccer practices during their college career. Shoot, they could have applied their newfound bar game skills at She-Nannigan's arena every afternoon instead!

So, when it was time to help Carl West, his future brother-in-law, find a job in mass communications, Curt called on his buddy George at the local newspaper. Fortunately, George's boss, the human resources director, was on vacation that week and had placed George in charge. He wasn't supposed to make any official hiring while the director was gone, but George played stupid for his friend and brought Carl on board anyway. It was easier to ask for forgiveness than to ask for permission.

The only opening at the Gazette was for an obituary consultant. The previous consultant, Jim Bowman, had been diagnosed with malignant cancer at a noticeably young age and succumbed to the carcinoma faster than the doctors thought it would happen. His lifelong dream was to travel and see the world, but unfortunately, he never got the chance to leave the USA.

Carl's job would entail receiving phone calls from a deceased person's family or a funeral director and advising them on how to write a death notice with a biography. If the client approved of Carl's suggested obituary, Carl would fax a copy to his editor, who in turn passed it on to digital typesetters that would layout the newsprint. The job opening was listed as part-time, and Carl would be paid on an hourly basis. His territory was from Black River Falls to Hudson, but he could choose to live anywhere in the region. It wasn't exactly a glamorous newspaper position, but it was a start.

As soon as Carl was hired, Molly applied to be a sportswriter at the *Minneapolis Dispatch*. Minnesota's largest news organization had no posted openings at the time, but mysteriously, Molly was hired two days later. She would become a columnist for professional sports in the state. Her job was to provide critical opinions on the Vikings, Twins, Timberwolves, and the Wild.

Carl and Molly chose to live halfway between Eau Claire and Minneapolis in the small Western Wisconsin town of New Richmond. Molly's commute would be an hour each way to the Twin Cities. The winters would be horrible, but that would be an adaptive process. Even though Molly grew up in the Midwest, neither she nor Carl had any idea of how to put chains on automobile tires.

*****

Two months later, the wedding was held in Molly's mother's backyard gazebo overlooking the Mississippi River on a cliff outside of Pepin. Molly and Curt Anderson's father had passed several years ago, and their mom had remarried Burt Merriman. Burt was an entrepreneur who owned several expensive restaurants throughout the United States and a few other countries. Their home was a contemporary, two-story, 6,000-square-foot estate situated on fifteen acres, with its own private nine-hole golf course strung along the bluffs.

Grandpa Syd made the trip from Nevada for the wedding. Carl had phoned and told him not to worry if he couldn't make it. "I know you're very busy with the business, Grandpa, and there's no one here that could keep you company."

"Carl, you're the only grandkid that I have," replied Syd. "I wouldn't miss it for the world!"

Syd was on the brink of loneliness. His wife was deceased, and his son Billy had been an only child who died way too young. His grandson Carl had no siblings either. Syd had a brother and sister who had both passed, but he had no idea where his nieces and nephews lived. They neither called nor wrote, not even a Christmas card during the holiday season. Thus, the only folks at the wedding on Carl's side of the altar were a handful of buddies from college. Molly's brother Curt was his best man.

Carl had been worried that his grandfather was going to be isolated and bored. But during the wedding reception, Carl was downright baffled. Grandpa Syd appeared to be chummy with Molly's stepdad, Burt Merriman. It was as if they had been lifelong friends.

During a dance with his new wife, Carl whispered to Molly, "How does Grandpa Syd know Burt?"

Molly smiled but didn't say a word.

Chapter 4

Carl didn't know where to start. He learned absolutely nothing about writing obituaries in college, nor did he want to at the time. And to top it off, he thought he could work from home. Instead, George had set up an office for Carl in the back of the *New Richmond News* building. The entry was off the alley behind the newspaper's printing area, just a stone's throw from the Sweet Beet Bakery's garbage bin. The office itself was eight-by-eight feet of concrete with a rollup steel door, previously used to store sheets of newsprint paper. After renting it, the Gazette installed a landline phone and provided a tiny melamine desk from Ikea, then completed the room décor with an uncomfortable rolling chair, a cheap filing cabinet, and a tacky throw rug. Carl hoped he wouldn't have any customers come a calling!

But the strangest thing was the computer system that was installed for Carl. After setting up everything else on the cheap, the technology he was supplied was top of the line. Internet technicians wired the computer, the digital phone, and a separate fax machine from a communications box attached to the wall using three fiber optic cables. Someone taped a note to the phone advising Carl that lines one and two were the only ones allowed for incoming and outgoing business calls. The third line was off-limits. Carl was ordered never to even pick up on that line when it rang. The note contained bold print, underlined words, and exclamation marks, remarkably similar to the markings his college professors used to write when they returned his assignments. Carl was baffled that he couldn't even touch the blinking button if it rang. However, being a newbie, he didn't bother to ask his superiors for the rationale behind such an idiotic request.

George told Carl to limit his hours of work to twenty per week, which was all that was in the budget. The company would reimburse mileage at the rate of fifty cents per mile, quite a bit lower than the government rate; however, Carl could write off the excess when he filed his taxes. No matter, really, because Grandpa Syd bought him an electric Tesla Model S sedan for graduation. Carl had concerns about parking in the alley next to his office because the area was a bit sketchy. But New Richmond had that small town, safe and secure feeling to it, so he didn't give the parking situation a second thought.

Molly convinced Carl to work four, five-hour days each week so he could play in a golf league on Friday afternoons. She wanted him to make new friends, and most lawyers and doctors in town played in the league. Molly thought that making social connections in the legal and medical world would pay off for them in the long run.

But here it was, the first day of work, and Carl sat at his cheap desk and stared at his expensive phone, wondering if it would ever ring. Somebody was bound to die soon, right? Not that he was looking forward to taking a call from a heartbroken new widow, but he was anxious to start writing. Carl decided to call Molly, who had begun her new career at the Minneapolis Dispatch last week. Seeing the caller ID, she picked up on the second ring.

"Hey, what's up, Hon?" asked Molly. "How's your first day on the job going?"

"Wonderful! I'm all caught up. You know me; efficiency is my middle name!"

"Okay, I detect some sarcasm in your voice. Let me guess—you're bored, right?"

"Let's just say I have no idea where to start. I'm just waiting patiently for someone to die, that's all."

"Okay, I get it. George didn't give you much training, did he?"

"Nope, not exactly."

"Then I suggest that you make a list of all the funeral homes, senior centers, and hospitals in the area and drop off your card. Let them know you are the new obit consultant for the Gazette."

"My card?"

"Yes, your business card, silly! What did you think I meant?"

"Hmmm. Didn't get any business cards yet."

"Well, I'm sure they are being printed. Why don't you start with some research that might help you understand your new field?"

"What kind of new research?" asked Carl, half puzzled and half not wanting to do anything that sounded like college.

"Start reading some of the obituaries that your predecessor wrote to get a feel for the writing style."

"Most of the obits are written by a family member or funeral director. Why do I need to study those? I'm beginning to think that this is a pretty mindless job."

"Absolutely not, Carl! You're considered a consultant, which is like a writing advisor. Your job is to give feedback and writing suggestions to help the bereaved in their time of loss. That's not mindless! Why don't you start by finding your predecessor's obit and compare that with some obits he wrote? See if you can detect a certain style. The man had terminal cancer. Do you think he wrote his own obituary before he passed, or did someone else write it for him? Analyze the writing, that kind of stuff. Make a game of it or something. It will get you started."

"My God, you sound like my composition professor at OU! That's why I never went to his office for help. I was afraid of the extra work he would throw at me!"

"Hey, you called me, not the other way around."

"You're right. I need to be more careful about that the next time," chuckled Carl. "See you tonight! Have a great day!"

"Okay, you too! Love you, Carl!" Molly smiled and hung up the phone, shaking her head.

*****

George told Carl that his obituary-writing predecessor was Jim Bowman. He had an office about the same size as Carl's in a converted storage area next to the golf course locker rooms in nearby Hammond, Wisconsin. Carl decided to meet the golf club staff to see if anyone had been friends with Jim. The Heritage Court assisted living facility was across the street, so Carl planned to introduce himself to the manager on the same visit and kill two birds with one stone—figuratively speaking, of course.

The Independence Day celebration in Hammond would be coming up on Friday the fourth and last through the weekend. Because of that, every business in the small community of 2,000 souls was engaged in the preparation efforts. The golf course would be hosting its annual tournament; thus, the manager didn't have time to chat with Carl about Jim Bowman.

"I didn't know him well," said the manager hastily. "Too damn young to die from cancer! He seemed like a good guy. He would play a round of golf now and then after work. Pretty high handicap. Is there anything else, Mr. West? I'm kind of busy here."

"No," replied Carl. "Thanks. Is there any chance I could see his office?"

"That's not a problem, but you won't find much. Folks from the Gazette cleared it out yesterday. They even ripped out the telephone cables, patched the walls, and painted it."

"They came out on a Sunday to do that?" asked Carl. He was a bit stunned. What was the rush? Couldn't they have waited until Monday, or even a bit later?

"Yep, that surprised me, too. Their lease was year-to-year, and they had paid the rent in full through December."

"Okay, well, thanks!" said Carl. "I'll be back to shoot a round sometime soon."

"Great! See you then."

Carl left the golf course and walked across Davis Street to the Heritage Court across the road. It was a typical end-of-June day in Western Wisconsin. The weather was a perfect seventy-eight degrees with puffy cumulus clouds smattering the light blue sky. Soon, the humidity and higher temps would pierce the area, and the mosquitoes would be buzzing in the ears of young and old alike. Carl gazed around the countryside at the corn that was beyond knee-high, which was the measuring stick for the Fourth of July. It appeared the farmers had a successful spring planting season with plenty of rain.

Marla Owens was the day manager at Heritage Court, but she was too busy assisting nurses with the daily tasks of caring for the elderly and the impaired to speak to Carl. She asked him to leave his card, and Carl said he would mail one to her as soon as he got them. He walked across the street, got back into his Tesla, and backed up to pull out of the parking lot. He shifted into first gear, crept the sportscar forward a few feet, then slammed on his brakes. Something was very strange.

Carl adjusted the rearview mirror and focused on an SUV that had been a few yards down from where he had parked. A golfer was putting his clubs in the back of a black Chevy Tahoe. Seeing he was at a golf course, that wouldn't be out of the norm; however, the same man had been taking out his clubs at the exact time Carl had arrived, about a half-hour earlier. The driving range was closed, so a golfer's only option was to play at least nine holes. There was no way that man could have finished a round in thirty minutes. So, what had he been doing? You wouldn't take out your clubs if you were just going inside for a bite to eat. And to top it off, Carl could swear he saw the same vehicle parked in front of Caribou Coffee in New Richmond when he had stopped for his morning java on the way to work.

Carl shrugged it off and drove away. He turned left onto Davis Street and headed for downtown Hammond. Carl had visited much of the United States, mainly when he traveled to the Jacksonville Jaguars road games to watch his dad play. But in the short amount of time he had been here, Carl believed that most of the small towns that dotted much of the Wisconsin map, including Hammond, seemed to be rural America at its finest. Hot dogs, apple pie, Chevrolet, corn, cheese, beer, and the Green Bay Packers—what more could you ask for?!

Davis Street was Hammond's main street, but most locals called it County Road T. The downtown area was less than a mile in distance, but along the way, Carl saw a library, a bank, a school, and several taverns. Farmers in their denim overalls were chatting it up outside the coffee shop, slapping each other on the back and shaking hands to say goodbye. A sheriff's deputy was laughing right along with them. In tiny communities, everyone seemed to know everybody.

Carl pulled into a parking stall next to the post office and went inside. He knew the chances were slim that a postal clerk would give him any information, but he thought he would give it a try. What did he have to lose? Carl waited in line for five minutes and then approached the counter.

"Hi, sir," said Carl with a voice that lacked confidence. "My name is Carl West, and I'm trying to find an old friend of my parents who lives around here. See, my parents died in a traffic accident, and I didn't have an address or phone for this man. I wondered if you could help me?" Carl thought if he told a partial truth, he would feel better about lying to the man. His parents did perish in an accident, after all.

The postal clerk gave Carl an inquisitive stare, then replied, "What's his name—this friend of your folks?"

"Jim Bowman. He worked for the Eau Claire Gazette and had an office at the golf course."

"Yeah, I know who Jim is, or was I should say." The clerk paused for a moment. He wasn't sure how much information to give this man. The guy didn't even know that Jim had passed. "Why don't you go to the golf course and ask them?"

"I tried that, but they didn't seem to know Jim all that well."

"Well, they should've known that Jim was deceased, by God!"

"Oh my God, Jim is dead?" asked Carl with his best-surprised tone. He was never an actor, so this pretense wasn't easy for him. "How did he die?"

"Cancer, just like a lot of folks around here. Now, you best be moving along. Other customers need some assistance."

"If you could tell me where he lived, I could stop by and give my condolences to his next of kin or friends that might be watching his place."

The postal clerk was annoyed, and he wanted to end the conversation with Carl, so he said something he shouldn't have, "Jim lived out in the country somewhere north of town. All I'm going to tell you is his post office box number was sixteen. As of yet, there hasn't been anyone come along to forward the mail, so we keep the box active for ninety days. Now, go on. I'm the only one here working, and I've got other customers, you know!"

"Okay, I'm sorry. Thanks for your help!"

Carl left the counter area and went to the half bronze and half glass mailboxes just off the lobby. He found number sixteen and peered inside. The letter on top was difficult to read, but Carl saw that the address was labeled *P.O. Box 16, 7706 N. Davis Street, Hammond, WI 54015*. Carl took a dollar bill out of his wallet and wrote down the street address.

As he turned to go to his car, Carl noticed that the mail sorting room's door was open. He nonchalantly shuffled to the entrance and glanced inside. No one was working! Was this a one-person show? Now he understood why the postal clerk was a bit testy. The man must oversee all the indoor operations at the post office, including sorting mail and greeting customers.

Carl then defied all the teachings of his parents, and perhaps one or two of the Ten Commandments. He slid inside the doorway, quickly spotted mailbox sixteen, grabbed the envelopes that were in it, and hightailed it out of the building and into his Tesla. He peeked back at the front entry to see if anyone was moving towards him to give chase but only saw the elderly women who had been waiting behind him in line. She walked out the door with a package in her hands.

Carl punched Jim Bowman's address into his GPS and headed back north on the main drag. Just past the golf course, Madam GPS announced, "The destination is on your right—7706 North Davis Street." Carl didn't see a road, so he drove a few hundred yards, then pulled over onto the shoulder and muttered to the GPS, "Huh? There's no driveway around here!" The GPS responded by flashing *recalculating* on the screen.

Looking out the window, Carl saw rows of dark green cornstalks, red barns next to white two-story houses, brick silos, and hayfields littered with black and white Holstein cows. As the residents called it—God's country. Carl made a U-turn and headed back towards Hammond.

Once again, Carl missed his turn. He wondered if Madam GPS was playing a nasty game with him. Carl pulled into the golf course parking lot and stopped. He picked up the envelope that he grabbed from the post office and rechecked the address. Yep, this was the right place. But how could that be?

Carl flipped through the other envelopes left in Jim Bowman's mailbox, but none indicated a physical address, just the post office box number. Jim had received mainly junk mail; however, there was a utility bill that most likely went unpaid following his death. Carl knew he shouldn't do it, but he decided to open the St. Croix Electric Cooperative invoice. ***PAST DUE NOTICE*** had been stamped on the envelope in dark red ink.

According to the bill, St. Croix Electric had attempted to deduct the monthly payment directly from Jim's bank automatically, but it had been closed. The account was most likely frozen until Jim's estate could be probated. But the service address on the bill was the same location that was on the other envelope.

Carl was now determined to track down where Jim lived. This time he drove north slowly along the shoulder of the road so cars behind could pass. As he got to the end of the golf course property line, the friendly GPS lady once again told him he had reached his destination. And once again, Carl stared out the passenger window and muttered, "Huh?!"

There was a road—if you could call it that. It was two worn down wheel tracks that had been carved by tractors. Carl decided he had nothing to lose, so he drove down the bumpy path that paralleled the sixth hole on the other side of a barb-wired fence. Just past the tee box was another forest covered with pines. It wasn't until he was several trees into the woods that he noticed an attractive one-story log cabin lying serenely underneath a canopy of pines. A detached garage was around the back, but the tractor tracks ended fifty feet from the cabin's front door and were replaced by a gravel driveway.

The home wasn't a mansion by any means; however, the cabin had an air of class to it. Stone accents were placed perfectly alongside the long Swedish Cope beams. Substantial double-pane windows were on both sides of the main entry door, and a mahogany deck encircled the entire cabin. You would never have to get your feet muddy to go from the front to the back.

Carl knocked on the door to see if anyone answered. No luck there, but he didn't expect to find someone residing in the house. Carl assumed Jim was single and had few relatives—as witnessed by the mail accumulating in his post office box. However, the windows were all shuttered, meaning someone had been here since Jim died. He wouldn't have tightly closed up the place every day when he went to work. But then again, the last time Jim left home, he may have been going on vacation for an extended period. Knowing he had terminal cancer, seeing the world would be an exciting way to go. Carl made a mental note to ask George where Jim was when he died.

Carl walked around the property's perimeter and checked the garage door to see if it was unlocked. No again. Obviously, he couldn't see the inside of the cabin or garage without breaking and entering, but the thought did occur. Curiosity was killing him, and he didn't even know the reason. Carl thought about all the strange events that had happened today. Why did the Gazette dismantle Jim's office on a Sunday? Why did the golfer in the SUV who had coffee in New Richmond pretend to golf in Hammond? And how could Jim afford to live in this hidden, expensive home at the end of a tractor path on a part-time salary?

Carl shook his head and decided he had read too many mystery novels. This was all bizarre, but he guessed he was overthinking the situation. He got in his Tesla and returned to New Richmond. It was time to get back to work, whatever that might entail. Perhaps now would be a good time to find Jim Bowman's obituary and see if he wrote it himself before he passed.

As he turned left on Second Street from Knowles Avenue in New Richmond, Carl saw the same black Chevy Tahoe that was at the Hammond Golf Course. It was parked in front of the Indulge Salon Studios. Now things were getting even more peculiar. The man at the golf course was bald. What would a hairless man be doing at a beauty parlor?!

Chapter 5

Carl slid his office door open, raising it from the ground up. He shook his head in disbelief. "Ah, alley entryways and roll-up doors that enter into a closet workspace—the glamourous part of a newspaper reporter's job that they don't teach you about in college," he whispered sarcastically to himself.

Carl sat down and fired up the computer. It started so quickly that it startled him. To satisfy his curiosity about the speed, he clicked on the settings button and opened the systems tab. Sure enough, the device specifications indicated the computer was running at 4.2 gigahertz with sixty-four gigabytes of random-access memory. Wow! If Carl ever got really bored, he could play video games all day and become a grandmaster!

The computer screen appeared with the Gazette logo on a blue background. He would have to change that. Perhaps a wedding picture of him and Molly on the cliffs overlooking the Mississippi River would be more appealing. The only app buttons on the desktop were Adobe Creative Studio, Microsoft Word, and Chrome Internet. Then, of course, there was the recycle bin, one Carl was sure he would often use as he tried to figure out how to write a quality obituary.

Carl began by doing what all great researchers do—he Googled. "Whoever this Google fella is, he ought to try his luck at Jeopardy!" muttered Carl to himself as he typed in *Jim Bowman*. In his lonely environs, sarcasm was getting the best of him.

And sure enough, Google pulled through again. The first item to appear was Jim's obituary on the Gazette website. It read:

Jim W. Bowman, 32, of Hammond, Wisconsin, died at 12:46 a.m., Sunday, June 14, 2020, after a short battle with leukemia.

Jim was born December 10, 1987, in McLean, Virginia, where he lived his entire life before moving to Wisconsin in 2015. He worked as a blackjack dealer during the summers at Bally's Casino in Atlantic City while putting himself through school at Old Dominion, where he graduated in 2009 with a bachelor's degree in Journalism. Jim was a member of the Monarch's soccer team. He worked in advertising with the Virginia-Pilot newspaper in Norfolk before starting a new career with the Eau Claire Gazette.

Jim is survived by his brother, John, of Prudhoe Bay, Alaska, and his father, Jack, of Fairfax, Virginia. He is preceded in death by his mother, Kelly Bowman, paternal grandparents, Ken and Connie Bowman, and maternal grandparents, Kizer and Gladys Milton.

Services will be held privately for Jim, and he will be buried in the Mudhen Lake Cemetery near Siren, Wisconsin.

Contributions in Jim's memory may be made to the American Cancer Society and sent to the Eau Claire Gazette, 701 Farwell Street, Eau Claire, Wisconsin 54701.

Carl was no obituary connoisseur, at least not yet, but he could tell immediately that Jim hadn't written his own obit. Obviously, someone else would have written the first sentence unless Jim had connections with a spiritual fortune-teller. But the rest of the obituary was too basic and straightforward with no degree of elegance. Even Carl could do better than that.

What caught Carl's attention was that Jim had only two surviving relatives: a brother who was tucked away in the northernmost part of Alaska, and a father somewhere in Virginia. That was probably why Jim's mailbox in Hammond was full, and no one was forwarding the letters. Could it be that his brother and father didn't even know that Jim had passed? Why would he be buried in Wisconsin when he spent most of his life in Virginia? Clearly, someone knew the whereabouts of Jim's next of kin, or they wouldn't have written it in the eulogy. Carl wondered who wrote the obituary. If he knew who submitted it to the newspaper, that person might be able to answer a lot more of his questions.

With nothing better to do, Carl decided to Google Jim's brother and see if he could find an address or phone number for him in Alaska. He would then call him to find out if he knew about Jim's death. Carl typed *John Bowman, Prudhoe Bay, Alaska*, into the Google search box.

Within seconds, the first posted headline read ***John Bowman sentenced to 30 years in prison***. Carl clicked on the hyperlink that took him to an article written four years earlier in the *Fairbanks Daily News-Miner.*

> *John Bowman, a petroleum engineer for Conoco-Phillips based in Prudhoe Bay, was sentenced to thirty years in prison on organized racketeering charges. He will serve his time at the Federal Correctional Institute in Sheridan, Oregon.*
>
> *Details of the case were sealed after a bomb threat was called into the courtroom during Bowman's trial. The hearing was postponed for a week, and when it resumed, the room was cleared of all*

nonessential personnel. Jury members were moved to an unidentified location where they could watch the proceedings via video feed.

Bowman will be eligible for parole in twenty years.

"Huh? Give me a break!" shouted Carl at his computer screen. "That's all the information that damn newspaper could write?! What kind of racketeering was he involved in, for God's sake?!"

Curiosity was now getting the best of him. He picked up the letters he had stolen from Jim's mailbox and shuffled through them. One envelope had no return address; however, it was postmarked from Las Vegas, Nevada, on June 29th, two weeks after Jim's death. Carl knew he was crossing the line, but he decided to open it. What he saw was absolutely baffling.

Inside the envelope was a recipe card with a note from someone named Milton Shrum who was requesting a "redo":

Can't reach you by email. Why has your account been suspended?

Redo
Milton Shrum
913ATF4L@CAP

"What the heck is that?!" Now Carl was talking to a piece of paper. This was going to be a lonely job!

Carl flipped the card around to see if anything was written on the back. Nothing! He rechecked the inside of the envelope to see if there was something he had missed. Nothing!

Carl was determined to figure this puzzle out. He opened his email and typed ***913ATF4L@CAP.COM*** into the address box and then wrote a short note in the text box:

Dear Mr. Shrum,

I work for the Eau Claire Gazette. I have replaced Jim Bowman, who unfortunately died from cancer not long ago. Your name and email address were sent anonymously, and I was hoping you could shed some light on its purpose.

Your response would be much appreciated!

Sincerely,
Carl West

Carl clicked on *SEND.* Seconds later, he heard a ding and checked his inbox. There was only one item, and its title was perplexing:

Message Undeliverable

Carl thought that whoever wrote the note had written the wrong domain. He tried the same address using ***NET*** and ***ORG*** after CAP. Same result—undeliverable. "I don't get it!" he exclaimed, hoping the computer would chat with him and help him understand.

Carl sorted through the rest of the letters, but all were either overdue bills or junk mail. He folded up the recipe card, tucked it in his wallet, and then walked across the street to the Next Door Café for lunch.

The bald man who drove a Chevy Tahoe sat down in a booth a few feet from Carl.

Chapter 6

"Wow, one day on the job, and you have a strong case of paranoia!" giggled Molly.

"I know it sounds that way, but I swear the guy was following me. First, Caribou Coffee, then the golf course, then the hair salon, and finally the café. It's got to be more than just a coincidence. I mean, the guy has no hair, so why was he in the salon?"

"Well, men do get manicures and pedicures, and I think that place also provides those services."

Carl and Molly were feasting on fried onion burgers, something they had become addicted to while living in Oklahoma. After trying to explain his thoughts about the bald man in the Chevy Tahoe, Carl decided not to tell Molly about the cryptic note in Jim Bowman's mailbox. In fact, he figured it was best not even to mention his Hammond Post Office thievery. He didn't want his darling new wife to think he had a bad case of the crazies!

"So, how was your day?" Carl asked while grease dripped down his chin. He picked up a napkin to wipe it off, and his face turned red. Molly smiled at his embarrassment.

"It was awesome!" exclaimed Molly. "I like working for the Dispatch. They've assigned me to be their lead columnist for the Vikings this year."

"Why you?" asked Carl musingly. When Molly gave him an angry glare, he apologized. "I'm sorry, that wasn't meant to be demeaning. I know you are incredibly talented, but I was curious why the newspaper wouldn't assign a veteran writer to handle their top client. That could become a stressful assignment for you, especially if the Vikings aren't winning."

"No, they'll win this year." Molly got up to clear the table. She was still upset by Carl's comment.

Carl wanted to ask how she could be so confident, especially considering that oddsmakers had given them only a fifty to one chance to win the NFC North, and *Sports Illustrated* picked them to finish in the cellar of their division. But he decided to let it go and change the subject.

"Well, anyway, George contacted me and said a few people have called the Gazette about submitting an obituary. He had them type up the basics of their deceased relative's death and then told them to email it to me for advice and submission. So, I will find out tomorrow if I can cut it writing obits."

"Type up the 'basics' of someone who's passed on?" inquired Molly. "Now that sounds quite morbid!"

"Yeah, well, that's what happens when you're in a dying business!" Carl winked, and Molly smiled back. It seemed she was no longer angry about his earlier slip of the tongue.

*****

Carl couldn't sleep. He was very apprehensive about writing his first obituary. Someone's love one had just gone to the great beyond, and Carl would be advising a grieving widow, son, daughter, brother, sister, or whoever on how to word this person's life. He would have only one chance to ennoble the dead man or woman and dignify his or her life for eternity. Carl had never felt this kind of stress before. He got out of bed and padded to the kitchen for some milk.

Molly had brought home the Dispatch with her, so Carl opened it to the obituary section. He wanted to see how a major newspaper wrote them. When he finished studying the obits, he glanced at the sports section to see how the Twins were doing in the standings near their season's midway point. All the MLB teams would soon be on All-Star break, and the NFL teams would begin their preseason.

Carl was about to lay the paper down when he noticed a short article that caught his attention:

> *The Dispatch has appointed Molly West as the lead columnist for the Vikings this season. Molly is the daughter-in-law of Hall of Famer Billy West. She graduated Summa Cum Laude from the University of Oklahoma and is a member of the Kappa Tau Alpha honorary journalism society. Viking fans will be pleased with Molly's in-depth NFL insight and tell-it-like-it-is writing flair.*
>
> *Molly replaces Hugh Cicero, who will leave the Twin Cities to become a sports columnist for the Las Vegas Review-Journal. His new assignment will be to cover the Las Vegas Raiders football organization.*

Carl thought it was a nice gesture for the Dispatch to do a brief blurb about his wife, but it was the last paragraph about Hugh Cicero that sparked a synapse in his brain.

For the last time today, he decided to have a chat with himself. "Today's theme must be Las Vegas," he mused. "The anonymous letter in Jim Bowman's mailbox was sent from Sin City, and now Hugh Cicero is moving there. Well, everything happens in threes, so I'm sure I'll hear about Las Vegas one more time this week!"

The voice inside his head said nothing back.

Chapter 7

The newlywed couple leased a four-bedroom, two-bath home on Lincoln Road in an established section of New Richmond near the hospital. The house was recently purchased by an investor specializing in refurbishing older homes and renting them out to young families. The landlord had sodded the front lawn, landscaped the backyard, and renovated the basement. Gone were the old oil furnace and window air conditioners—they were replaced with central air and heat. The investor then painted the home a two-tone beige and chestnut brown. The upgrade beautified the entire neighborhood, and Carl and Molly West were now affectionately known by residents of the community as Westsiders . . . no pun intended.

Neither Carl nor Molly was much good at making coffee, so they ditched their automatic drip machine and opted for the expensive brands made by professional baristas. Well, that may be a stretch as most of the chains actually employed high school and college students, especially during the summer months, and retirees when the kids were back in school. Fortunately, the expensive espresso machines could make a great cup of coffee on their own.

Carl's favorite, Caribou Coffee, was located inside the Family Fresh Market on the corner of Knowles Avenue and Highway 64. Molly preferred to support her caffeine fix at a Starbucks a block from the Minneapolis Dispatch headquarters. Today, Carl noticed the bald man with the Chevy Tahoe checking out the blackberries in the produce section of Family Fresh while he ordered his latte. Was it time to finally confront the man, or was running into him at every turn merely a coincidence?

Carl had a better idea. He put a cover on his paper coffee cup, walked outside, and then glanced around the parking lot until he noticed the Tahoe parked under a light post. He looked back to Family Fresh's entrance and was glad to see the bald man wasn't following him. Carl pulled out his cell phone, took a picture of the SUV's license plate, and then quickly moved to his Tesla and hopped in. He drove the alley for two blocks and parked in his spot next to the office, or whatever that concrete hole was where he worked.

Carl sat at his desk and studied the snapshot of the license plate. Then he Googled the Wisconsin Department of Transportation and found out that they have an online license plate search. He pulled up the web page, found the box, entered the plate number, and voila, the information appeared on the screen. But it wasn't what he hoped to find. There was no name or address, or any personal information that Carl had expected to see. Just a registration expiration date, renewal reference number, vehicle make, and vehicle year.

Carl pounded the desk in frustration and moved the mouse to close the screen when he noticed something. The vehicle listed on the Wisconsin DOT website indicated the SUV was a 2020 Chevy Suburban. Carl could swear it had been a 2020 Tahoe, but maybe he was mistaken. Both cars were virtually identical; however, the Suburban was slightly longer.

Carl shook his head and decided he was wrong. It probably was a Suburban. But he needed more information, specifically the driver's name and address. IntelSearch would do that for $20 and provide the owner's name, contact information, traffic court citations, and arrest records. The peace of mind was worth twenty bucks!

George had forwarded emails from bereaved widows of three deceased husbands who wanted an obituary placed in the Gazette. Carl glanced at the messages quickly, but the obits would just have to wait until his vehicle search was finished. This would be the last time that personal business trumped his duties to the Gazette.

Five minutes later, Carl was much more confused than he ever had been. According to IntelSearch, the car was registered to Vance

McCoy of Fairfax County, Virginia. But it had a Wisconsin plate! Carl guessed that the man owned two residences, one in Virginia and one in Wisconsin. It must be cheaper to register and insure a car here. What else could it be?

IntelSearch supplied no street address, phone number, traffic court, or arrest records. Carl assumed he had just wasted $20 until he noticed two items that may have proved something fishy was happening. First, the vehicle listed on IntelSearch was a Chevy Traverse, not a Suburban, and certainly not a Tahoe. Second, Vance McCoy's date of birth was January the first of 2000. He was a new millennium baby. But that meant he would be twenty years old, and the bald man following him is at least sixty years old, perhaps even more. Now what?

Carl decided that after work, he would drive around town and try to find the SUV. He planned to jot down the vehicle identification number fastened to the dashboard. That might not be easy to do quickly and without being seen. Also, trying to explain to Molly how he spent the first hour of his morning at the office would send another red flag of paranoia to her brain. He couldn't tell her, at least until he had some proof, that the bald man's mysterious actions were not merely a coincidence.

Carl peeked at his watch and took a deep breath. It was time to get to work. Somehow, Carl needed to clear his mind from all the distractions and focus on doing what he was being paid to do—write obituaries. He read each of George's three emails from the widows who had written biographical accounts of their seemingly wonderful dead husbands. Then he reread each one. And then again.

All three obits sounded acceptable to Carl. He brainstormed but couldn't think of any suggestions to give the ladies. How was he ever going to last in this job? Carl called each of the widows, and lucky for him, reached their voicemail. He feared to speak directly to them when he had no advice to offer.

Carl left the same message on each recording: "I'm so deeply sorry for your loss. Your well-written eulogy will appear in tomorrow's newspaper. If you have any questions, please call me at 715-246-8888. God bless you!"

He copied the words directly from the emails to an official Gazette submission form and faxed them to his editor. For the first time in his life, Carl felt like a loser. This was not a job well done!

Also, his great and glorious father, a Hall of Famer and superhero to many, had taught him to never, ever give up. Billy West made sure that Vince Lombardi's motto was drilled into Carl's head since he was old enough to understand sentences: "Winners never quit, and quitters never win!"

But today, Carl quit. He couldn't think of any constructive words or phrases to enhance the obituaries, so he simply copied, pasted, and faxed. Carl didn't even think to use Spellcheck.

He sat back in his chair and sipped the last of the now lukewarm coffee. He thought about how his dad would watch endless game films to find ways to become better. Could Carl even be a smidgeon like Billy West when his new career was so insignificant compared to playing football in the NFL? Then he remembered another one of his father's mottos: "No matter what you do for a living, be the very best at it that you can be."

Carl tossed the paper cup into the wastebasket and was now determined to live up to his dad's standards. Whatever it took, Carl would observe, research, and drive himself to improve his articulation and journalistic skills. Like Molly, someday he could be a sportswriter for a major newspaper if he put his mind to it.

Then the phone rang.

Chapter 8

The phone buzzed just once, a sharp, piercing tone similar to a fax machine without the squiggly static at the end. The red light inside the third line blinked five times, then stopped. Carl was told never to answer that line, so he sat dumbfounded, staring at the phone. Why was he not allowed to pick up when he was the only person working in this office? It didn't make sense!

Curiosity may have killed the cat, but Carl was no feline. What's the worst that could happen? It was improbable that he would be electrocuted, and chances were nil that lightning could penetrate the steel-reinforced cement block structure that surrounded him. Perhaps the Gazette would know somehow if he answered it, but it was doubtful they would fire him. He forgot, right? Rookie mistake!

The light was no longer blinking, meaning the call had ended. Carl picked up the receiver and punched the button. Nothing. No dial tone or busy signal or anything else. It was silent—a dead connection. Okay, so his bosses figured out how to keep Carl from making outbound calls, but what about inbound? He pulled out his cell phone and planned to place a call until it dawned on him that he didn't know the private direct line number. The main office business number was printed on a tiny slip-in card attached to the phone, but that was all. The fax number wasn't even listed.

Carl called his own office, hoping he could hit the pound key and the number three after the answering machine connected. That might transfer him to the third line. After five rings, an automated voice apologized for "missing his call" and to "please leave a message." Carl punched the ***#*** button, followed by ***3***, but the landline did nothing. The called disconnected. He tried two more times with the same result.

Carl was about to throw the office phone against the wall when it buzzed, and the third line started blinking. He quickly picked up the receiver and pushed the number three. The call went dead immediately, and the line was once again completely silent.

"Damn it!" yelled Carl. Now he was faced with two enigmas—a bald man following him in a Chevy Tahoe, Suburban, or Traverse, and a business phone system from another galaxy!

*****

Carl returned to the office after literally running to Caribou for another cup of java. He needed to work off some anxiety, so he jogged the short distance in his work clothes. Fortunately, the company's dress code was a notch less than business casual unless the employee met with customers. Carl had on khaki pants and a red Polo that was given to him after being hired. The Gazette logo was stitched on the pocket. His Docker's shoes were so worn down that they were as comfortable as his tennies.

Carl opened the pull-up door and entered his office as the phone rang. Yes, it rang this time—not buzzed, meaning it was the first line, and he could actually speak to someone! It was George. He debated asking him what was going on with the third line but decided not to stir things up this early in his employment.

"So, how are things on your second day, my friend?" asked George cheerfully. Carl guessed it was George's duty to uplift his workers' spirits.

"Just plain wonderful!" lied Carl. He wasn't about to play Negative Nelly after slightly over one day on the job.

"That's great! Well, anyway, you need to check your secondary email each day."

"My secondary email? What's that?"

"Oh, it's an automated system that sends you obits to look over and edit, if necessary. Don't change any of the words. Just do a spelling and grammar check, then forward them to us like you do the regular call-ins. They are usually sent by funeral directors who have customers without a next of kin to write the obituary. And because funeral directors are terribly busy, they don't always write the best, if you know what I mean. But, once again, do not change any of the wording, okay?"

"Sure, George, you're the boss! I won't mess with them. So, what's that email address, and how do I access it?" Carl was now completely perplexed. None of this was making sense to him.

"It's the first letter of your first name, followed by your last name at Rankins.com. All small letters. In other words, ***cwest@rankins.com***. Go on the Rankins's website and login to set up your account. Your login is ***CW5050***, and your password is ***Obitman***. I made that up for you!" George laughed at his own creative humor.

"What the heck is Rankins, George? I've never heard of that Internet host."

"Oh, Rankins is our holding company, that's all. They own several newspapers around the world."

"I've never heard of them. I thought Adams Publishing out of Minneapolis owned the Gazette. I read that on a sign in your office, George."

"Yeah, well, that's correct. But Rankins owns Adams. Hey, it's all corporate crap that you don't need to worry about. Just make sure you check the email address and forward the obits to us, okay?"

Carl could tell that George was getting perturbed, so he agreed and ended the call. Then he did as he was told and pulled up the Rankins's website, which was bizarre, to say the least.

The web page simply read "Rankins" with nothing around it. Just Rankins in blue letters on a white background with no graphics or pictures or anything that would appeal to a customer. The only word on the entire homepage, other than Rankins, was a login button. Carl clicked it and was taken to another drab web page with two boxes—login and password. There wasn't even a hyperlink for new people to register. That meant the customer had to have an existing login and password given to him to see what the company had to offer, or in Carl's case, to set up and access his email. Wouldn't you think a publishing company could hire a better web designer?

Carl logged in using the words George had given him, but what he saw then was even more peculiar. Once again, there was no marketing or company information anywhere, but his email page opened, and sure enough, he had mail.

It was from Sam Diggins, the assistant funeral director at Holmes Mortuary. Seems Joy Smith, age eighty-six, had died at the Woodlawn Cliffs Rest Home in Hudson. According to her short bio, Joy graduated decades ago from the University of Wisconsin at Green Bay, but no field of study was indicated, nor was her chosen career. She evidently never married because there was no mention of a husband or kids. She had only one surviving relative—a sister in Denver, Colorado, who lived near Empower Field at Mile High Stadium on Mortland Drive. Why a surviving family member living near anywhere mattered in a eulogy was perplexing to Carl.

Carl reread the obituary that Sam had written and thought it was extremely minimal for a lady who had endured eighty-six years of life on this earth! After all, Joy had beheld the ups and downs of the Great Depression, World War II, the Vietnam War, the Cold War, the battle for Civil Rights, and the terrorist attack on the World Trade Center. With all that experience, couldn't Sam have written more than three paragraphs for a eulogy?! But George had cautioned Carl not to make any additions, and he really had no suggestions on how to improve grammar. And just like yesterday, that frustrated Carl to no end! He wanted to be better than that and be able to offer some advice! But in the end, Carl copied and pasted Sam's obituary of Joy Smith onto the Gazette form and emailed it to his editor.

"What a mindless job," whispered Carl to himself. "They're actually paying me for this. What a joke."

Carl Googled a list of funeral directors in the area. He compiled their names and addresses into an Excel mailing list and then sent them a group message with his bio. Carl asked them to call him before writing an obituary for the deceased, and he would be happy to relieve them of that task—free of charge, of course!

That simple gesture made him feel much better. Hopefully, they would phone him with the specifics of the death, and Carl could do what he was paid to do—write obituaries. He was about to shut down the computer and go out for lunch when something occurred to him.

Carl scrolled down the list of names and noticed that Holmes Mortuary was not on it. He didn't expect to find Sam Diggins because he knew Sam was the assistant, not the funeral director. But why didn't Holmes Mortuary come up with the director's name when he did the Google search?

Carl then Googled Holmes Mortuary, and there were twelve marketing ads displayed. His computer's search engine had cookies turned off and location disabled, which meant the addresses listed were from all over the United States. Each one claimed to be the perfect funeral parlor to call when a loved one died. All would provide the ultimate in care as they prepared the family member for his or her final resting place.

Carl scrutinized each Holmes Mortuary location but found none listed anywhere near Hudson, Wisconsin, where Joy Smith had died. The closest Holmes was in Milwaukee. Carl guessed it could have been possible that their funeral home handled Joy's arrangements, but that would have been difficult.

He was about to give up. It didn't really matter that Holmes Mortuary was not on the list. He accomplished what he set out to do, which was to alert funeral directors in the area that he would be there to provide obituary writing services and place their notices in the Gazette.

For a second time, Carl was about to shut down the computer when he noticed something weird in the Googled ads for Holmes Mortuary. One of the twelve locations was on Sag River Road in Prudhoe Bay, Alaska. He tried to remember where he had recently heard of something associated with Prudhoe Bay, but he couldn't place it.

But as soon as he had rolled down the office door, it struck him like a brick falling on his head. Jim Bowman's brother, John, worked as a petroleum engineer in Prudhoe Bay before being sent to an Oregon federal prison for racketeering charges. Was this all just another wild coincidence?

Chapter 9

Molly convinced Carl that he needed to relax and enjoy his job rather than get all worked up about things he had no control over. Carl agreed that he would try not to think about the bald man and his Chevy whatever-model SUV. Nor would he wonder how Jim Bowman could afford a private luxury cabin hidden in the Hammond Golf Course woods. And he wouldn't think twice that Jim's brother, John, was serving a lengthy prison term for racketeering in Oregon. And it had to be merely a coincidence that John resided way up north of the Arctic Circle, where there just so happened to be a Holmes Mortuary, even though a mortuary with the same name didn't exist in Hudson but still claimed to prepare final arrangements for Joy Smith. Then there was the blasted buzzer phone line in his office that couldn't be answered.

As the summer rolled on, Carl did give it his best effort to focus on the job at hand. He read obituaries in every major newspaper in America, looking for creative writing examples. Funeral directors became comfortable letting Carl do their eulogies for them. However, Carl continued to not mess with the obits generated on the secondary email address that he accessed off the Rankins's website. As George had requested, he simply copied, pasted, and forwarded them to his editor.

Carl and Molly were enjoying life in New Richmond. July had turned hot and muggy with a few days in the low nineties. But in Wisconsin, there was always a nice, cold beer waiting for you after work and on weekends. The Fun Fest in Cyclone Park was a great place to meet new folks, although most of New Richmond's lifelong residents preferred the old days when Second Street closed between Minnesota and Arch avenues for the three-day event. They missed the carnival attractions (Octopus, Tilt-A-Whirl, Rock-O-Plane, and game tents) being downtown and the street dance next to the First National Bank. Local rock groups would blast songs through the humid night air while the smell of charcoal-grilled chicken and brats wafted through the city. The parade was on Sunday, with high school bands from around the area showing off their stuff, and Miss Thistown and Miss Thattown queens all perched high on their floral floats waving to the crowd.

Carl was recruited to join a local softball team. They played in weekend tournaments in such infamous places as Webster, Connorsville, and Boardman, where the emphasis was more on winning the beer trophy than the championship. As July turned to August, Molly's workload had expanded, and she was commuting to the Twin Cities six days a week. But when Carl's team wasn't playing on Sundays, they rented two old patched-up rubber innertubes from the River's Edge. Then they floated lazily down the Apple River to Somerset, complete with a cooler full of Miller Lite for him, and a bottle of Boone's Farm Strawberry Hill wine for her.

Carl didn't see the bald man for the rest of the summer, nor did he see the black Chevy SUV. Eventually, Carl assumed that Molly was right, and he had suffered from momentary paranoia. He was busy at his job—providing consulting and editing services for clients on his primary email and simply copying and pasting death notices from his secondary email. Carl wished he knew why the Gazette didn't use just one system, but he really didn't care because the paychecks were coming in every other week. His self-esteem improved each time he gave writing advice to a funeral director or even a grieving widow or widower.

One day in mid-August, an obituary was sent to his Rankins's secondary email account. He looked it over for typographical errors, which was the only editing he was allowed to do with those eulogies. He was about to copy, paste, and forward it on company letterhead to the Gazette when he noticed something that sparked his curiosity. It was the person who had died. Carl knew him.

Wally Roseberg was his best friend growing up in Florida, but the two never communicated much after Carl moved to Reno for his senior year in high school. Both were stars on the same school and club teams. Wally excelled as a running back in football, a point guard in basketball, and a baseball shortstop. The obituary hit Carl like a punch in the gut. He sat back in his chair and reread what was written. It had to be his old friend! How many Wally Rosebergs that were the same age as Carl and who lived in Jacksonville could there be?

The obituary read:

> *Wally Roseberg, age 23 of Jacksonville, Florida, went home to see his maker on August 2nd. He is survived by his half-brother Keith, a musician in Overland River, Tennessee.*
>
> *Wally will be remembered for his great sense of humor and loving ways.*
>
> *A celebration of life will be held at 4:30 pm on Sunday, September 13th, at the Kramer Funeral Home in Jacksonville. It is advised that friends arrive early as a large crowd is expected.*

Once again, Carl was disturbed that the obituary was so brief. All the obits from the Rankins's emails were short, and he hated that, but he was told just to glance them over and send them onward. But this time, it was personal! Wally had been his best friend, and he deserved a better eulogy than that!

Carl decided that he would attend Wally's memorial service on September thirteenth. It was the least he could do, and maybe he would find some of his old buddies to hang out with on the same visit. He didn't remember Wally had a half-brother, and he was shocked Wally must have lost both his parents somehow in the past few years. How ironic was that? Both he and Wally no longer had either of their moms or dads around. Pretty sad!

Molly threw a fit when Carl told her his plans to go to Florida for the memorial service, but her motives seemed awfully weak. She said she didn't want to be left alone, but she was working six days a week, and he wasn't going to be gone too long. Then she said he shouldn't be taking days off from his job so soon because he might be fired. However, he was being paid hourly and limited to only twenty hours per week anyway. The Gazette gave him no vacation days, so he didn't have that option. Carl told Molly that he would make up the hours he missed once he returned to New Richmond. Molly finally put her hands on her waist, and with an angry red face, shouted, "Just don't go, okay?!" She then stormed off to the bedroom.

Molly and Carl barely spoke to each other for the next couple of weeks. Meanwhile, Carl bought a non-refundable roundtrip ticket to Jacksonville. He still didn't know what the big deal was with Molly's complaints. Wally had been his best friend, and going to his memorial certainly seemed to be the right thing to do.

On Friday, September eleventh, Molly dropped Carl off at the Minneapolis airport on her way to work. She tried one last plea to have him stay home. He could go with her to the office and see how the Dispatch organization was run, then dine at the Spoonriver Restaurant and take in a Broadway play at the Guthrie Theater.

"Sorry, Hon," replied Carl, shaking his head. "I've got to do this." He leaned over and kissed her, then got out and closed the passenger door.

An hour later, he boarded his Delta flight for Atlanta. After a short layover at Hartsfield International, he connected to Jacksonville, then rented a car and drove to the Red Roof Inn at the corner of Airport Road and Interstate 95. It was only $53 a night, a great bargain for any traveling man.

Carl and the two cockroaches both enjoyed the shower tub that evening.

Chapter 10

Early Saturday morning, Carl drove from the motel to his old stomping grounds in Montclair. He stopped at the gate to his house, situated in a prestigious neighborhood south of downtown. Carl peered past the cobblestone driveway and Mediterranean-style mansion to the backyard. He could barely see the long dock that he and his dad fished from on the St. Johns River.

On Sunday mornings, when the Jaguars were at home during the NFL season, to ease his nerves, Billy West would get up at dawn for an hour of undisturbed relaxation. He and Carl would take the Nitro Z21 and cruise a short distance down the river to cast for bass in the estuary. Carl loved that bonding time with his father, a time of peace and solitude only hours before Billy would be revving up the crowds at the site of the old Gator Bowl.

Carl wiped away tears on his t-shirt as he reminisced about his youth and the fun he had with Wally Roseberg. Then he drove past the Bolles complex, a private educational campus where he attended elementary, junior, and senior high schools. Although Carl commuted each day, Bolles was a boarding school for many international students. He and Wally had been the "big men on campus," premier athletes who dominated three sports.

Carl parked the car and roamed around the grounds. It was a Saturday, so only the boarders were out and about. Most were enjoying the early morning air—tossing Frisbees, sipping iced lattes, or lying on the thick St. Augustine grass reading a novel. Most would head back to their air-conditioned dorms before the hot, humid Florida sunshine beat down on them. Like clockwork, September brought late afternoon rainstorms that would soak everything in sight for precisely one hour before the sun lit up the sky once again.

But the cool water drops were a welcome relief during football practice, maybe not for the coaches, but certainly for the players!

The school building looked like a Spanish Colonial estate home for the rich and famous, perched on the banks of the St. Johns. The gym entrance was open, so Carl entered and admired the vast trophy case that filled the lobby. He found the All-State football plaque from his junior year that featured Wally and him. There was an etched picture on a metal plate with them in their uniforms, and they had the deepest of grins on their faces. It was almost unheard of that two players from the same school would achieve first-team honors in the same year. How sad it was that they would never see each other again in this world. Carl wished he could have stayed for his senior year instead of moving to Reno.

Carl wandered around, hoping to find a teacher or administrator from the good old days. No luck—the office and classroom doors were locked, so Carl started heading back to the parking lot.

After he was a few steps out of the gymnasium door, someone shouted, "Carl West, how's my main man?"

Carl turned and saw the familiar face of a tall, older, African-American gent with short gray hair and weathered, leathery skin. He recognized him at once. "Well, if it isn't Henry Ellis in the flesh!" retorted Carl. He jaunted over and gave the lead custodian a warm embrace.

"First, I'm real sorry about your mom and dad, son." Henry paused and hugged Carl one more time. "They were good people, they were! Yes, sir, your daddy was a hell of a football player, but he was even a better person, an honorable man to be sure! But I don't need to tell you cuz you already know that!"

"Yeah, I do, Henry, and thanks for mentioning it. I miss them both like crazy." Both men dropped their heads for a moment. Then Carl continued, "So, it doesn't appear you're about to retire anytime soon. I thought you'd be out living on your Bayliner and hauling in striped bass from sunup to sundown by now!"

"Wish I could, but Maw won't let me. We're putting the three grandkids through college these days. Their mama up and left them, and their daddy can't find a job."

"Sorry to hear that, Henry. Is there anything I can do to help? Dad left me plenty of money to get by on, and you're one of my all-time favorite friends."

"Naw, but thanks, Carl. I've lived eighty-two years without charity, so I'm not about to start now. But the offer is much appreciated! So, what are you doing back in good ol' Jackson town?"

"Well, I'm sure you heard that Wally Roseberg passed away. I'm here for his memorial service. I have no idea how he died, though. Have you heard, by any chance?"

"What?! Wally died, you say! That's a shock, it is! I just saw him a couple of weeks ago. He stopped by to give the football team a motivational talk. He looked good then. Was it some sort of disease?"

"I'm not sure. But you said you saw Wally just two weeks ago? Are you sure?"

"Yep, very sure. It was the night of August twenty-eighth. That was the first football game. He did an awesome job getting the boys all fired up, you know!"

Carl felt sorry for Henry. It was clear that he had some sort of dementia. The obituary said Wally had passed on August second. Carl was sure that whoever gave the speech to the football team did an excellent job; however, it wasn't Wally!

Carl bid farewell to Henry and said he would come back to Florida someday to go fishing with him. They embraced once more.

Carl thought about driving by Wally's house but remembered from his obituary that his parents were no longer living. Instead, he opted to try and find some old high school buddies. Phone calls to Mac Johnson, Keith Barnes, and Joe Ramer proved fruitless. The stored numbers for them in Carl's iPhone were no longer in service. Why should they be? Since leaving Jacksonville six years earlier, he hadn't called his friends, and Carl had heard they all attended college out of state. Chances were high that they were beginning new jobs in new places, just like him.

Carl decided to relax and blow off the rest of the day at the Bearded Pig barbeque joint across the river from downtown. He ordered his favorite—the San Marco Platter, which was filled with enough red meat to make a vegetarian's hair stand on end! Carl washed the tender ribs, chicken, pulled pork, and brisket down with several pints of the award-winning Adalwolf, a slow-pour German pilsner made at the local Aardwolf Brewery, just a little over a block away.

By mid-afternoon, Carl was stuffed and feeling a bit woozy. He knew better than to test the Florida DUI laws, so he called an Uber to take him back to the Red Roof Inn. He laid on his bed, flipping through the channels to try and find a college football game that interested him; however, it was too early in the season for teams to be playing fierce competitors. It was the time of year that the best Division One schools scheduled games against "cupcakes" to build up their records and maintain a spot in the Associated Press Top Twenty-five. Those that couldn't crack that list could at least hope to win six and be eligible for a bowl game come December. Carl fell asleep during the third quarter of the Florida Gators home contest versus Tulane. The score was sixty-three to zero!

He woke up at 5:00 a.m. the next morning with a throbbing headache and a huge case of bad breath. Molly had left him six messages, all worried about his health and welfare. It was 4:00 in Wisconsin, so Carl decided to wait a few hours to call.

The Red Roof Inn had placed mini-Cuisinart brewers in each room with a small wicker basket of coffee, powdered creamer, and sugar. Carl grabbed a packet from some obscure java company and made a pot while he ducked under a hot shower. The steady water and steam were a Godsend, and Carl vowed never to drink again. And he decided to limit his future barbeque portions to one meat only, instead of a massive helping of fat-laced pork, beef, and chicken. But the mac and cheese on the side would have to stay.

Carl wrapped himself in a towel, poured a cup of coffee, and sat in a ratty armchair as he watched ESPN's Game Day Vegas Insider Report. On Sundays in the fall, the sports television mogul would provide final predictions for the upcoming NFL games that day. The guest host was Ken Peterson, a professional oddsmaker from Las Vegas. He would give the latest moneylines, point spreads, and over/under for each contest. The show started at 6:00 a.m. on the east coast, which meant it was in the wee hours of the morning on the west coast. But that didn't matter to hardened gamblers who earned a living by betting on NFL winners and losers each week. They stayed up late on Saturday or woke up early Sunday to listen intently and take notes as Ken analyzed each game. Vegas oddsmakers seemed to have a supernatural mystique to make spot-on predictions for every sport they examined.

Today marked the 101st anniversary of the American Professional Football Association, which was renamed the National Football League in 1922. Carl had other things on his mind and was only half-listening until Peterson began analyzing a game that interested him. Carl selfishly wished that Wally Roseberg's funeral wasn't on opening day. He would have eagerly attended the game at TIAA Bank Field to watch his dad's old team take on the Tennessee Titans in what appeared to be a defensive contest, at least according to oddsmaker Ken Peterson:

> *"The Jaguars and Titans are without their starting quarterbacks as both were injured during the preseason. Add that to the fact that they just may be the two best defensive teams in football; we expect a very low-scoring game. The over/ under is an unheard of twenty-three points, and Jacksonville remains a four-and-a-half-point favorite. I'm predicting a low-scoring affair, but I think the Jags will cover the spread. I'm going to say thirteen to seven, Jacksonville. Sorry Titans' fans!"*

"Well, this would be a good game to miss," stated Carl aloud to the TV set. "I'm not into boring games. Dad never played on a Jacksonville team that couldn't even score two touchdowns!" Carl looked at Ken Peterson through the television screen, thinking he might have heard him and would soon reply.

Carl skipped breakfast, not because of the slim offerings in the room off the lobby, but because he wasn't hungry. No surprises there. He could still taste the smoky barbeque flavoring from yesterday's feast, and his stomach felt bloated.

At 9:00 a.m., he called Molly, who was getting ready for church and didn't have much time to speak. The five-minute conversation was your basic chitchat.

"How are you?" asked Molly flatly.

"Fine. How 'bout you?"

"Great. Why didn't you return any of my calls?"

"Phone problems," lied Carl. "I forgot to bring my charger. I had to borrow one from the front desk."

"Did you see any friends?"

"Nope, I don't think any still live around here. Oh, but I stopped at Bolles to make sure all my trophies were being polished!" Carl laughed but got no reaction from Molly. "Anyway, I ran into Henry Ellis, my old custodian friend, and had a nice talk."

"Oh yeah, well, that's nice."

"Yep, but I'm kind of sad. Henry has dementia. He said he saw Wally Roseberg just a couple of weeks ago. Says he was at Bolles to give a motivational speech to the football team. Poor guy, I feel horrible about Henry!"

Molly was in a hurry to sign off and abruptly ended the call. "Got to go! Love you! Call me later."

Carl was about to say something in reply, but the phone went silent. He had never known Molly to be in such a rush to get to church. He decided to head out to a sports bar and watch some games before the memorial service. Carl was startled when he didn't see his rental car in the hotel parking lot. Then he remembered that he had taken an Uber back from the Bearded Pig. There was a taxi out front, so he hopped in and rode back to the barbeque joint to retrieve his car.

The weather was typical for a mid-September day in Florida—blazing hot with stifling humidity. Carl dressed in a blue short-sleeve shirt with a striped tie and white dress pants. He no doubt would have gotten a few stares and chuckles had he been strolling down Fifth Avenue in Manhattan wearing that outfit after Labor Day, but this was the semi-tropics. By the end of the memorial service, even his light clothes would be drenched with sweat.

Sports Madness was Carl's go-to place for watching NFL games. The sports bar and restaurant was a franchise located in a handful of major cities around the US. They sectioned off fourteen areas with a corral, and every section had a sixty-five-inch QLED television hanging down from the ceiling. Each game was broadcast somewhere in the massive 25,000 square-foot building. On Sundays, customers dressed in their favorite team jerseys and spent the next three hours hootin' and hollerin' for great plays by their favorite players or booing referees for every call that didn't go their way.

Carl sat down in the Atlanta Falcons and Carolina Panthers corral, not because the game was an intense rivalry, but because the Jags and Titans clash was in the neighboring section. He could watch both games easily by sitting at a table in the back. Two brothers, one wearing the red and black Falcons' jersey and the other a powder blue Panthers' shirt, invited Carl to join them. They both were airline pilots. The Falcons' fan lived in Norcross, Georgia, and flew for Delta, while his brother was from Charlotte and worked for American. They both had the day off in Jacksonville, a coincidence that had never happened to them before.

Carl had planned on drinking a Coke and nibbling on a few parmesan-garlic wings, but when he accidentally let it slip that he was Billy West's son, the two pilots each bought him a draft beer. Here we go again, thought Carl. Soon the folks at the nearby tables overheard the conversation, and they slid their chairs close to hear what Carl had to say about his infamous hero father. Three shoved their greasy napkins over to him for an autograph.

Friendly verbal sparring was the main talk inside the Falcons-Panthers' section before the game started. Atlanta was six-point favorites when betting began early in the summer, but that had dropped to four-and-a-half points by game time. The Falcons were heavy preseason favorites to win the NFC South, and on paper, they should have an easy time beating the Panthers. However, it was the season opener, and the game was in Charlotte, so anything could happen. During the coin toss, the banter became a bit ugly. The draught beer caused uncontrolled tongues to throw out a few cuss words, and moms coming from church covered their kids' ears with their hands while dads hurried to find an empty table. Carl smiled and shook his head. Passionate fans and their love of suds—a combination best to be avoided with young children!

Carl bid farewell to his new friends at the end of the third quarter. By that time, the entire section was engrossed in the contest, and personal anxieties were mounting. The game was tied at twenty-one. Although it was a long season, an early loss to a division opponent could be perilous to a team's playoff chances. Atlanta seemed to be firing on all cylinders, but three touchdown passes had already been called back on penalties. The Falcons' fans were beside themselves with anger at the "hometown" officials. The Panthers' fans thought the officiating was amazingly exceptional.

After he exited the corral, Carl rolled his eyes, then paused to see what the score was between the Jags and Titans. Well, so much for the defensive battle. The Jags were up 24 to 21, with a minute left in the third quarter. Carl walked briskly to his rental car, set the GPS for the Kramer Funeral Home, then turned on the radio to listen to the Jags-Titans finish.

Kramer was located east of the city on Joeandy Road, two miles from the Atlantic Boulevard bridge that crossed to the beach. Carl wanted to arrive early to see if he could find someone he knew. He pulled into the parking lot at 4:10, and his heart skipped a beat.

There wasn't a car in sight.

Chapter 11

Carl waited alone at the mortuary until 5:00 p.m. He was positive he had read the obituary correctly. It said there would be a celebration of life today at 4:30; he was sure of that. He grabbed his cell phone from the passenger seat and Googled "Kramer Funeral Home." Yes, it was the only one in town.

But then a weird thought hit Carl like a slap in the face. Wally Roseberg was a devout Jew. According to Judaism's traditions and customs, a Jewish funeral usually takes place within one day following someone's death. It's a very solemn service where mourners reflect upon their loved one's life.

If his obituary was correct, Wally was survived only by a half-brother who lived in Tennessee. He would have gathered family and friends the next afternoon for seven days of Shiva. While mourning Wally, they would have stayed at home to pray, and they wouldn't have held a celebration of life later. That would only have served as a distraction to their religious healing process. Even if there were a memorial later, it would be at a synagogue, not a funeral home!

Carl was confused. What was going on? Now it dawned on him that something else didn't make sense. Why was Wally's obituary even posted in the Gazette? Did he have relatives who lived in the Eau Claire area? Carl was almost sure Wally had no connection to Wisconsin whatsoever. How could he not have thought of that before?!

He remembered what Henry Ellis told him. Henry claimed Wally gave a motivational speech to the Bolles High School football team just two weeks ago. Maybe Henry doesn't have dementia after all, and perhaps he did see Wally. If that's true, then Wally is still alive.

Carl remembered that the obituary was sent to him on the private Rankins's email line and not some random call. It claimed Wally had passed on August second. Carl was supposed to fly back to Minneapolis the next day on an early morning flight, but he decided to stay in Jacksonville another day or two until he figured this puzzle out. In the morning, he would call George to see if his boss could shed some light on who posted the obituary in the first place. Molly would not be happy!

Carl drove back to the Red Roof Inn and did something he hadn't done in ages—he searched a thick phone book for a name. He was sure that many trees had been destroyed just to stock each room in the hotel with the massive directory of yellow and white pages. But an online search would end up costing him at least $20 to "unlock" the person's number along with other informational tidbits of a personal nature. Carl didn't care about Wally Roseberg's financial records or who he may have married, which were included in the fee. He just wanted his phone number.

Interestingly, Wally was not in the Jacksonville area white pages; however, his mother and father were listed: Gershom and Batya Roseberg. They were Hebrew names that Carl easily remembered because they were not common. But how could that be? He distinctly recalled the obituary had said that Wally's only surviving relative was a half-brother.

Carl placed the call on his cell phone while he sat at the edge of the bed. After one ring, a recorded voice came on and said, "You have reached a number that is no longer in service." Carl ended the call, laid down on the mattress, and stared at the ceiling with his hands tucked behind his head. He still couldn't make sense of anything. Had he misread something?

Carl thought for a moment, then decided to recheck Wally's obituary. He opened the *Safari* browser, then Googled "Eau Claire Gazette obituaries." His company's website appeared, and the obituary page was displayed. In the search box, Carl typed "Wally Roseberg," and his friend's obit materialized.

Sure enough, everything Carl thought he remembered was correct. Wally had died on August second. The celebration of life was today at Kramer Funeral Home, and he was survived by only one relative—Keith, a half-brother from Overland River, Tennessee.

Carl bit the bullet and shelled out twenty bucks to try to locate Keith using the online Whitepages. After fifteen seconds of searching, a baffling response was posted. There was no Keith Roseberg, which didn't surprise Carl because a half-brother might not have the same last name. However, what was flabbergasting to Carl was that there was no city, town, or municipality in Tennessee called Overland River. It simply did not exist.

Chapter 12

Molly hung up on Carl as soon as he told her he was staying a few more days in Jacksonville. She had no hypothetical response as to why a false obituary was placed in the Gazette, but she didn't believe Carl's life mission was to become a private detective. They were newlyweds, and Molly needed him to be around the house instead of partaking in a wild goose chase. He understood why she was angry, but he needed closure to this mystery if he was ever going to focus on his work.

Unable to sleep, Carl switched on the Sunday Night Game-of-the Week between the Patriots and the Jets. Now that Tom Brady was playing for Tampa Bay, he was pulling for the Jets. It was unconscionable that New England would let Brady walk after what he had done for the organization. Carl knew Tom well because the future Hall-Of-Famer and Billy West were good friends, and they would include Carl on deep-sea fishing excursions off the Florida coast. Tom Brady had been in tears as he eulogized Billy West at his funeral.

For Carl, the most enjoyable part of watching a Sunday night game was the halftime recap of that day's contests. Tonight's show did not disappoint. Al Michaels and Cris Collinsworth spent most of their limited time crucifying the officiating at the Atlanta Falcons and Carolina Panthers game. First, the three touchdown passes that had been called back due to holding penalties were on display for the millions of viewers to see and determine their validity. Head linesman Jake Shrum was shown taking an enormous amount of heat from Atlanta head coach, Dan Quinn, as he had thrown the flag on all three nullified touchdowns. One holding call could have been justified, but the other two appeared to be mistaken. Replays from every angle showed no hands grabbing any part of the defensive jerseys or impeding the quarterback's rush.

The game went to overtime tied at twenty-four, and what happened on the first play from scrimmage had everyone's head shaking, including Carolina Panthers' fans who thought an act of God had given them another chance at victory after it was snatched from them. Atlanta cornerback Desmond Trufant intercepted a Teddy Bridgewater pass at the Carolina forty-five-yard line and returned it for what appeared to be a game-winning touchdown. Visiting Falcons' fans who were high-fiving and hugging in the stands suddenly stopped their cheering when a roar from the home crowd bellowed through the air. Back judge, Miles Milton, was waving his arms, indicating that Trufant was down by contact at the forty-five. The slow-motion replays from every angle clearly showed no Panther had touched him. But what was even more perplexing was that the automatic review of a turnover did not change the call.

Cris Collinsworth stated that the NFL needs to figure the officiating system out quickly before it ruins the season. Al Michaels was less critical and blamed the miscalls on first game jitters. Neither was overly condemnatory because Atlanta placekicker Younghoe Koo blasted a sixty-yard field goal a few minutes later, and the Falcons held on to win twenty-seven to twenty-four.

Meanwhile, the Jaguars beat the Titans twenty-four to twenty-one, and Collinsworth chuckled and claimed that officials in Jacksonville must have been prone to the same first game jitters that took place in Charlotte. There was only time for one replay to prove his point. Jags' quarterback Gardner Minshew tossed a completed screen pass to Dare Ogunbowale. Ogunbowale galloped sixty-five yards with two minutes to play for a TD that would have virtually ended all hopes for a Tennessee comeback. The play was called back for a false start, one which none of the replay cameras happened to catch. So, the Jags ended up winning by three points instead of ten. Al Michaels shrugged it off by saying, "Well, no harm, no foul, I guess. Jacksonville won the game anyway!"

*****

Carl tossed and turned in bed for a couple of hours, then rolled on his back and stared at the ceiling again. Something was bothering him, but he couldn't put his finger on what it was exactly. He felt bad about his argument with Molly, but that wasn't what was causing his insomnia. It had to do with something either Cris Collinsworth or Al Michaels had mentioned during the halftime show.

By 3:00 a.m., Carl figured he wasn't going to be able to sleep, so he dressed and headed out to his rental car. He thought it was possible that if Wally was still alive, perhaps his parents might be living too. He would drive to Roseberg's house and see if Gershom and Batya were still residing there. The phone number was no longer in service, but maybe they had succumbed to disconnecting the landline in lieu of a cell phone or two.

Carl arrived at 4:00 a.m. and parked the car on the street outside of the Roseberg's long driveway. He wasn't going to disturb anyone at this time of day, but if for some reason someone left early for somewhere, he would follow them to their destination and have a chat. Even if he or she wasn't Gershom or Batya, the person might know where they could be.

After the sun rose and the humidity began infiltrating the breathable air, Carl decided to approach the house and knock on the door. Unlike the house that he grew up in, Roseberg's didn't have a gate or any security system that he could see. Well, except for the German Shepherd that appeared in the large picture window and barked like there was no tomorrow when Carl neared the front steps.

Carl paused for a moment and smiled. That was his old friend, Jazz, who he had known since the dog was a pup. Carl and Wally jogged many miles with Jazz back in the day. There was no need to ring the doorbell or knock—Batya had opened the door and covered her mouth with her hands in surprise. Jazz jumped up on his hind legs and started licking Carl's face. His tail was wagging faster than Ringo Starr could pound a drum!

Chapter 13

"Gershom! Get down here right now!" shouted Batya at the staircase leading up to three bedrooms, including the master. "You'll never guess who just showed up on our doorstep! It's Carl West!"

"Carl West?" replied Gershom, who was in the middle of shaving in the bathroom. All the walls muffled the sound. "My God, Carl's here?! I'll be right down!"

Carl was escorted to the den—the same room that he and Wally watched every pro sport imaginable on the fifty-six-inch TV as they would wind down from an intense workout. Both boys were campus VIPs, and they wanted to maintain the coolness that the label afforded them. Thus, they practiced hard during high school sports, lifted weights four times a week after practice, and ran ten miles every weekend. Batya and Carol West, Carl's mom, were also close friends, and they insisted on enforcing a rule that the boys must shower before watching television. Jazz agreed!

Before Carl sat down on the couch, Batya squeezed him so hard that he thought his eyeballs were about to pop. A grizzly bear's hug would have been much gentler.

"My dear boy, what have you been up to?" asked Batya. Carl didn't have a chance to answer because Batya had taken her hands and pulled his face to hers for a big, juicy smooch—right on the lips.

Carl's cheeks turned various shades of red before he could respond. "I'm married now to a sweet gal I met in college at Oklahoma, and we live in New Richmond, Wisconsin. It's a small town near the Minnesota border. Molly, my wife, is a sports columnist for the Minneapolis Dispatch, and I work for the Eau Claire Gazette."

Gershom bounded down the stairs and scurried to the den. Carl stood up to greet him, and for the second time that morning, he was embraced to the max! And kissed again—this time on the forehead.

"Carl, my boy, how are you, son?" asked Gershom, now shaking Carl's hand with ferocity.

"Very well, Mr. Roseberg, thanks!"

"No 'Mr. Roseberg' in this house! It's Bat and Gersh to our friends! You know that!" Gershom gave Carl another squeeze for good measure. He sat back down on the couch.

"Carl was just telling me that he's married now, and he's working for a newspaper in Wisconsin," said Batya.

"Let me guess. I bet you're a sportswriter, aren't you, Carl?" asked Gershom, still beaming with pride at his son's best friend.

"Well, no, Gersh, actually, I write obituaries." Gershom and Batya's smile diminished. Carl guessed they were a little disappointed. They would expect more from their second son!

"Obituaries, huh?" asked Gershom before cracking a slight smile. "I would assume that's a dying business." Gershom laughed at his own wittiness, and Carl grinned.

"Yep, well, I've heard that one before."

"Oh, Gershom, you're just horrible!" stated Batya sternly. Then she slid over to Carl and patted him on the knee. "We're very proud of you, Carl, and don't you ever forget it!"

"It's okay; I'm not offended. But my being an obituary writer is why I'm here. Please, don't take this wrong, but is Wally still alive?"

Batya and Gershom smiled and replied in unison, "Are you joking?!"

"No, I'm not." Carl was immensely relieved by their response. His best friend must still be roaming this beautiful earth! "Let me show you something."

He opened the Safari browser on his iPhone, pulled up the Gazette web page, then showed Gershom and Batya their son's obituary:

Wally Roseberg, age 23 of Jacksonville, Florida,
went home to see his maker on August 2nd. He is

survived by his half-brother Keith, a musician in Overland River, Tennessee.

Wally will be remembered for his great sense of humor and loving ways.

A celebration of life will be held at 4:30 pm on Sunday, September 13th, at the Kramer Funeral Home in Jacksonville. It is advised that friends arrive early as a large crowd is expected.

"Oh my God," muttered Batya softly. She glanced back at Gershom, who was reading the obituary over her shoulder. "Is this freaky, or what?"

"Well, we can assure you, Carl, that our Wally is very much alive and well!" exclaimed Gershom. "He came up from his home yesterday, and we all went to the Jaguars game. Had dinner downtown, then he dropped us off before heading back to Tequesta, which is right there next to Palm Beach."

"What does Wally do in Tequesta?" asked Carl.

Gershom thought about it a minute, then said, "He's an architectural drafter or draftsman or something like that. He says he does CAD drawings for a company called InterPlan. I have no idea what CAD is, but I don't want to appear stupid and ask him, you know!"

"Computer-aided design," stated Carl. "That's what CAD is, Mr. Roseberg."

"Gersh! I told you to call me Gersh."

"Okay, sorry, Gersh. Where did Wally end up going to college?"

"He had a full ride to play football at the University of Nevada—Las Vegas. Started two years and broke a few records. He sent us clippings from the newspaper. A sportswriter claimed Wally was the best back to ever play in the Mountain West Conference! Then for some dumb reason, he quit after two years and took the job in Tequesta. You know, Carl, Wally had originally signed a letter of intent to play for the Miami Hurricanes but backed out and went to Vegas. He never really told us why. We wish he would have stayed in Florida so we could've watched him play, but, oh well."

"Did he have to sit out a year for breaking his letter of intent?"

"No, and I'm not sure why. Miami just released him, that's all."

Batya had been scrutinizing the obituary while Gershom and Carl were talking. Finally, she interjected, "What's weird about this obituary, other than it's the shortest eulogy I've ever read, is that the Wally in the article is the same age as our Wally, and he lived in Jacksonville. But I can tell you for certain, unless Gersh is hiding something from me, he has no half-brother or any relative living in Tennessee!"

"Well, what I find even more curious is the bit about a celebration of life taking place yesterday at the Kramer Funeral Home, which is a legit business, by the way. I was there at 4:30, and not another soul was in the parking lot."

"We would never have done that, Carl," said Batya matter-of-factly. "We're Jewish. Had Wally died on August second, we would have buried him the next day and held Shiva for a week right here in this house."

"Yes, I thought about that while I was sitting alone in the Kramer parking lot. Well, I'm just glad Wally is alive and well! Do you think he'd like a visitor from his past? I'll be in Florida for a couple more days, and I could drive down to Tequesta and see him."

Batya grabbed Carl's face again with both hands and plopped another kiss on the lips. "Oh, would you, Carl?! He would be so happy to see you. Oh, you're such a good boy! And you always have been!"

Embarrassed but not flinching, Carl slowly backed away. "Where does he live down there on the Gold Coast?"

Gershom put his arms around Carl and replied, "He's in a condo right on the beach at a place called *Juno By The Sea.* Juno Beach, you know. Batya, write down Wally's address and cell phone number for Carl."

Carl stayed to chat for a few minutes. He talked of old times while Jazz laid at his feet, still wagging his tail. After saying goodbyes, complete with more hugs and kisses, Carl made his way to the door.

Gershom wanted to have the last of the morning pleasantries, so as Carl turned to go, he said, "You missed a great game yesterday, son. Wish you could have joined us. Jags looked good. Officials kind of sucked, you know. We should have won by ten instead of three. It would have been much less nerve-racking, you know!"

Carl nodded and smiled. "Yeah, I heard. Take care, you two!"

As Carl got into his car, something Gershom said bothered him, but he couldn't quite place it. He fired up the engine and headed for I-95. If the traffic were kind to him, he could be in Juno Beach in time for a late lunch with his old friend.

Chapter 14

"I'm sorry," said InterPlan receptionist, Ann Colter, smiling. "Mr. Roseberg is not in today. What did you say your name was again?"

Carl had tried to phone Wally's cell number while cruising down the freeway, but a recorded voice said that his mailbox was full. So, unfortunately, Carl couldn't leave a message. The GPS guided him to Wally's condo in Juno Beach, but no one was home. He remembered Gershom said Wally was a draftsman at InterPlan Architectural firm in Tequesta. Carl assumed Wally was working on a Monday afternoon. His office was a short distance away.

"Carl West. I'm an old high school friend. Just thought I'd stop and say 'hi.' When do you expect him back?"

"I'm not sure. He went to—"

Just then, Ann was interrupted by a tall man with silver hair and wire-rimmed glasses who stormed out of an office next to the reception area. He was grinning and approached Carl with his arm extended, ready for a handshake.

"Hello sir, I'm the owner of this firm. Did I hear you say your name was Carl West?"

"Yes, you heard correctly. And you are who?"

"Randy Hansen. It's so great to meet you. I was a huge fan of your dad's! And I'm so sorry—that was an awful way for your parents to die. Please accept my condolences, Mr. West."

"Thank you. And you may call me Carl. So, I was trying to find my friend Wally Roseberg. I understand that he works here, is that right?"

"Uh, well, yes, he does, Carl. He's a drafter."

Carl wasn't sure why Randy hesitated. Either he worked at InterPlan, or he didn't. Why would the owner shillyshally with a simple question like that?

"Will he be back in the office sometime today?" asked Carl.

"Hmmm. Not sure. He's out with a client."

Again, Carl was confused as to why Randy was dithering. Perhaps he didn't want Wally's personal life to interfere with company business. "Okay, well, if you don't mind, could I leave my phone number?"

"Yes, of course! Ann, please give Carl something to write on."

"Sure thing," replied Ann. She tore off a Post-It note and handed it to Carl along with a pen. Carl jotted down his cell number and gave it back.

Carl shook hands with Ann and Randy, then said goodbye. He walked out to the parking lot, opened the car door, and glanced back at the InterPlan building. Strangely, Randy was standing at his office window, watching him get into his rental.

"Here we go again—another attack of paranoia," thought Carl. "I ain't mentioning this to Molly!"

*****

Carl stopped at Hog Snappers Shack and Sushi a half-mile from InterPlan on South Dixie Highway. He ordered the crab-crusted snapper with a side of deep-fried clams and washed it down with Googan Kook, a draft beer from nearby Civil Society Brewing Company. Googan Kook was a double-IPA with eight percent alcohol by volume, and during mid-afternoon in the squelching Florida heat, was most assuredly a sedative that would force a siesta upon any victim who had little sleep the night before.

Carl walked across the street to the Dollar Tree and bought a beach towel and umbrella for twenty bucks. He hoped both items would last long enough for a few hours of rest and relaxation. Carl then drove a short distance to Coral Cove Park, propped his cheap umbrella into the sand, and laid down the fragile beach towel thirty yards from the water so that the afternoon tide didn't wash him away. Five minutes later, he fell sound asleep listening to the waves crashing onto the shore.

Eventually, Carl was awakened by the dreamy sound of the Righteous Brothers singing *Unchained Melody*. It was his and Molly's unique ringtone for each other on their iPhones. Carl shook off the cobwebs and tried to catch his bearings as dusk unfolded around him. His iPhone read 7:31 p.m. He had been sleeping for about four hours. Carl's cell phone would automatically go to voice mail on the eighth ring. He picked up on the seventh.

"Hey, Mol, how are you, Hon?"

"Could be better—thanks for asking. My newlywed hubby abandoned me here in Cheeseworld for a romp through paradise, then didn't even bother to call me today." Molly's tone was respectfully sarcastic, which was frightfully oxymoronic to Carl!

"Sorry, Mol, that was my bad. To make a long story short, I saw Gershom and Batya Roseberg today at their home. Just like them, Wally is alive and well! He's living in Juno Beach. I showed them his obituary, and they guessed it must be quite a coincidence—some guy with the same name who lives in Jacksonville and is the same age."

"Wally's alive?! Oh, thank God, Carl! That's just fantastic news! I'm so happy for you!"

"Thanks, I guess," replied Carl softly.

"What do you mean you guess? Your best friend didn't die. I think that's a great reason to be happy! So, where are you right now? Will you be coming home tonight or tomorrow?"

Carl didn't have the guts to tell her that he'd been hanging out at the beach all afternoon. "Ah, let's see. I'm stuck in traffic somewhere on I-95." Just then, a wave broke, and the surf crashed loudly over the craggy limestone rocks jutting out from the shore. The Atlantic Ocean wasn't about to put up with Carl's blatant lie, nor was it going to take the blame for the unavoidable lover's spat that would follow.

"You're on the freeway, you say?" asked Molly suspiciously. "I didn't realize that I-95 ran so close to the beach that you could hear the ocean."

"Okay, so I'm on the beach. I was just killing some time to give Wally a chance to get home from work, that's all."

"You said Wally lives in Juno Beach. Is that where you are?"

"Close. I'm at Coral Cove Park in Jupiter."

"So, you're planning to see Wally tonight? You drove all the way down there from Jacksonville?"

"Yes, of course, I drove here," replied Carl defensively. "He's still my friend, and I wanted to see him while I had the chance."

"Well, you could have run that by me, don't you think?! Just so you know, George Markins called and wanted to know where you were. He said he tried your cell phone but didn't get an answer. That sounds familiar! He's a little frustrated that you are AWOL from your job, Carl."

"AWOL! Well, that's bull crap! I'm just a part-time employee and make my own hours. They can hire me full-time if they need me there so badly! And how did George get your number anyway?"

"I'm assuming that I'm your emergency contact." Molly paused for a moment, took a deep breath, then continued. "Okay, let's both calm down. When are you coming home, Carl? Don't you get it? I need you here now."

Carl began to feel terrible. He couldn't just leave Molly alone in Wisconsin with no idea how long he would be away. It wasn't fair to her.

"Okay, Mol, I'll be home tomorrow for sure. I'll see Wally tonight and catch an early flight home from West Palm Beach in the morning."

"Text me your flight number, and I'll pick you up at the Minneapolis Airport. Can't wait to see you!"

"Alright, will do. I love you, Molly."

"I love you, too."

Molly hung up and sent a text to George Markins: *I'll have him back at work by tomorrow afternoon.*

Chapter 15

The Juno By The Sea condominium complex had one unique feature Carl had never seen before—residents' names painted on the parking area's curb. Carl found Wally's reserved spot in front of his condo and pulled his car in. To ensure he wouldn't miss him, Carl waited there for Wally to come home. It never happened.

Carl slept lightly for perhaps an hour before the sun began to rise in the east. Twice during the night, he tried to call Wally's cell phone, but both times he received the same frustrating recorded message stating Wally's mailbox was full. The flight to Minneapolis via Atlanta would leave at 9:00 a.m. It was now 7:10, and the drive to Palm Beach International took about thirty minutes. Carl pounded the dash in frustration, then gunned it out of the parking lot.

By the time he dropped off the rental car and entered the terminal, it was 8:05. Carl upgraded to first class so he could go through the TSA Precheck line and save valuable minutes. Molly would never forgive him if he missed the flight. As the Delta jet taxied to the runway, Carl guzzled down a Bloody Mary. That was just what the doctor ordered to ease his nerves.

The plane touched down in Minneapolis at 2:10 p.m. Molly's mood seemed to have improved as she gave him a hug and a big kiss. They walked hand-in-hand to the parking lot, then Molly got into the driver's seat while Carl sat and leaned his head on the passenger-side glass. He was tired, yes, but also rooted in thought. Something was bugging him, and once again, he couldn't put his finger on it.

"What's the matter, Babe?" asked Molly as she exited onto I-494, heading east.

Carl perked up and stared out the window. "Nothing. Where are we going? Your office is the other way."

"I'm taking you back to New Richmond."

"Why? Don't you have to work this afternoon? I thought I was going to hang out with you until you finished."

"I'll drop you off and then come back. I'll need to make up the hours, so it will be a long night. Probably won't be home until after ten."

"So, then don't take me home. Take me to your office, and I'll come home with you."

"Well, that wouldn't be good for your job situation. George Markins said that there are a few obits on the Rankins's email account that need to be sent in today. You need to go to your office."

"No way! Screw him! Today's Tuesday. I'll work ten hours tomorrow and Thursday, and that will max out my week. That's my call, damn it!"

Molly paused for a few moments to give Carl a chance to cool off. "I think it's best that you get those obits done today, then go home and relax. You don't want to lose your job. I know it doesn't seem like much of a job now, but it will affect your career if you quit or get fired. You need a good reference from George if you want to be a sportswriter somewhere down the road."

"Okay, you may be right," said Carl. "Sorry, I'm just tired. It was a long, frustrating weekend."

"I understand," replied Molly smiling. She dropped him off at home to get his car, then hightailed it back to the Twin Cities. In an upset, the Bears had beaten the Vikings at US Bank Stadium on *Monday Night Football.* Molly's deadline for her column was in five hours. She couldn't wait to polish it up and submit it to her editor. The column would be the first one published since the preseason ended.

If she worded it correctly, it would be a game-changer. Literally.

*****

Carl stopped at Caribou Coffee for a late afternoon latte with a triple shot of espresso. He desperately needed the caffeine boost to flow through his bloodstream. Carl pulled out a twenty-dollar bill to pay for the coffee, and as he did, the folded recipe card he had tucked in his wallet a few days ago fell to the floor.

Carl couldn't remember what was on the recipe card, so he opened it up. It read:

Can't reach you by email. Why has your account been suspended?

Redo
Milton Shrum
913ATF4L@CAP

It was the card that had been in the letter addressed to Jim Bowman. Carl had tried to reach Milton Shrum by emailing him at ***913ATF41@CAP.com*** and ***.org*** and ***.net***, but with no luck. Every message had come back ***Undeliverable***.

But now, Carl studied the words, and a chill went up his spine. He handed the barista the twenty-dollar bill and told him to keep the change. He ran to the Tesla, spilling the latte on the sidewalk and his shirt. Carl got into the car, fired it up, then looked at the recipe card once again.

This time goosebumps covered his entire body.

Chapter 16

The obituaries sent to Carl on the private Rankins's email account would just have to wait. Instead, Carl opened up ESPN on his web browser and searched for the Atlanta versus Carolina game that he had watched in the sports bar on Sunday. Seconds later, the recap appeared, and Carl was intrigued by the headline:

Falcons Nip Panthers in OT Despite Questionable Calls

The game summary included highlights and lowlights, great plays and mistakes, and every sort of statistic imaginable. But the main focus was on the terrible officiating calls, and the online video replays proved the refs were having a bad day!

Two officials were singled out as having a particularly awful game. Jake Shrum was the head linesman who threw his flag for holding on three occasions, and each of those penalties resulted in an Atlanta touchdown pass being called back. Only one of those holds might be valid, even though the ESPN analysts suggested that particular call, too, was sketchy.

But the biggest head-scratcher was when back judge Miles Milton claimed that Falcons' cornerback, Desmond Trufant, was down by contact after intercepting a pass in overtime and running it back for what should have been the game-winning touchdown. Video replay clearly showed that no one touched Trufant after the turnover.

Carl watched the four questionable calls on his computer several times, and he noticed something that the announcers never mentioned. All three holding penalties had one thing in common—

a delayed toss of the flag. It was as if head linesman Shrum wanted to see how the play might end before making the call.

Carl placed the recipe card on the table and pounded his fist. This was absolutely not a coincidence! It couldn't be!

Can't reach you by email. Why has your account been suspended?

Redo
Milton Shrum
913ATF4L@CAP

Carl wasn't sure what the word "Redo" or the "4L" before the "@" symbol meant. Other than that, in his mind, the rest was obvious. Milton was not Shrum's first name, as he believed when he initially read it and attempted to send an email to him. Milton and Shrum were the last names of the two officials who made horrible calls on Sunday. And, "913" must mean "September thirteenth" while "ATF" is the "Atlanta Falcons" and "CAP" is the "Carolina Panthers."

Why would someone mail Jim Bowman a recipe card with the names of two officials who would be reffing the Atlanta versus Carolina game on September thirteenth? And why would those same referees make four dreadful calls that may have influenced the game's outcome? Then Carl remembered something else about the letter sent to Jim Bowman—the envelope was postmarked in Las Vegas.

Sports corruption! It had to be! But what part did Jim Bowman play, and how did he ever get involved in something so monumental as fixing an NFL football game? Carl thought about Jim's hidden, gorgeous home in the woods, and it dawned on him that he might have been part of a large-scale illicit gaming operation, perhaps with some sort of crime syndicate in Las Vegas. Did he moonlight in illegal gambling, or was his job at the Gazette just a cover? Who would suspect that a part-time obituary consultant would have fixed NFL games?!

By now, Molly would be back in her office in Minneapolis. Carl wanted to tell her about Jim Bowman and the recipe card. He punched in her number on his cell phone but hung up after one ring. Molly already thought he was paranoid, so now wasn't the time to add fuel to the fire.

Carl picked up the recipe card again and studied it. What did "redo" and "4L" mean? It must be part of the code. He watched the Atlanta-Carolina recap again on the ESPN website, replaying it another five times. Whatever that code was didn't make sense to him.

But something else was now beginning to make sense. Jim's brother John was in prison for racketeering. Could it be that Jim and John were partners in crime? A four-by-six-foot cork bulletin board was on the office wall that the Gazette had hung for him. When he first noticed it, Carl thought it would just gather dust because he had no plans to decorate the room like some sort of elementary teacher. But now he had second thoughts. Carl grabbed a pad of Post-Its from his desk to take notes and create a bubble chart to organize and connect his findings.

First, Carl brainstormed all the people he thought may be involved in an illegal gaming plot. He placed their names on separate Post-Its: Jim Bowman, John Bowman, Referee Jake Shrum, and Referee Miles Milton.

But there had to be others. Something else had bothered Carl since he began working for the Gazette. Seeing he was doing the same job as Jim Bowman, could there be a connection to anyone he had come in contact with since starting the position?

Carl thought about his first days and weeks back in July. A possible link popped into his mind, but he couldn't remember the details. He checked his saved email file, and there it was! Holmes Mortuary!

The email sent via the Rankins's account contained an obituary for an elderly lady who had died. It was written by Sam Diggins, supposedly an employee of Holmes Mortuary in Hudson. But Sam's name was not on a list of funeral home directors, nor was there even a Holmes Mortuary in Hudson! However, a Holmes Mortuary did exist in Prudhoe Bay, Alaska, where John Bowman had been a petroleum engineer!

Carl covered the bulletin board with paper so he could draw lines that intersected his Post-Its. He wrote Sam Diggins on a Post-It, as well as Holmes Mortuary. Then Carl decided to add one for Wally Roseberg. Not his close friend, but the fake Wally from Jacksonville, whoever he was. Could that be a connection, too?

Carl was brainstorming who else might be involved when a thought enveloped him like a bad dream. He jotted it down on a Post-It and stuck it on the bulletin board. Goosebumps reappeared, sending shivers down his back.

The bald man who drives a Chevy SUV.

*****

Carl's phone rang, which startled him out of a deep trance. It was George Markins. He was all business—not even a hello.

"Carl, so you're finally back to work. There are two obits on your Rankins's email that need to be submitted in one hour. Can you make that happen?"

"How did you know I was back at work, George?"

"Oh, I spoke with Molly, that's all. Don't worry about it. We just need those obituaries pronto, okay? Thanks, Carl!"

George hung up before Carl could ask why his boss seemed to have a pipeline to Molly. Right now, he didn't give two hoots about the Rankins's obits when he knew they would have already been written publisher-ready. He couldn't understand why he even needed to submit them. Why weren't they simply sent directly to the Gazette?

Carl opened up his Rankins's email account. Sure enough, two obituaries were there waiting to be actioned. Carl was too wrapped up in the mystery surrounding Jim Bowman to even care about reviewing them. He copied the first eulogy onto a Gazette form without even reading it:

> *Jalmer Peters, age 51 of Dallas, Texas, passed away unexpectedly on September 11th. He is survived by his wife Gail, sons Kevin and Keith, mother Ruth, and father, Clyde Peters. Jalmer was raised and attended school in Lesterville, New York.*
>
> *Jalmer will be remembered for being friends with everyone he knew. His kindness was incomparable. Jalmer always seemed to be high on life.*
>
> *Funeral services will be held at 9:30 a.m. on Sunday, September 20th, at the Bramer Funeral Home on Thunder Lane in Dallas.*

Carl then copied the second eulogy onto another Gazette form, once again, without reading it:

> *Arnie Kilton, age 42 of Los Angeles, California, died following a lingering illness on September 10th. He is survived by his brother George, and sister Myna of Moore Lake, a small community near Seattle, Washington.*
>
> *Arnie was a young man whom heaven claimed much too early. He was bright, articulate, and very creative. Arnie will be deeply missed by friends and family alike.*
>
> *A memorial service will be held at 1:30 p.m. on Sunday, September 20th, at the Odella Funeral*

Home in Seattle. Odella is located on the east end of Tover Road.

Before Carl faxed the forms to his editor, he quickly skimmed both obituaries. His only job on the Rankins's submissions was to peruse for spelling and grammar errors. He found none but shook his head in disgust.

"These are terribly written," Carl mumbled to himself. "Two more obits with only three paragraphs each. How pathetic! This is an embarrassment to the deceased's family and me!"

Something was gnawing at his conscious while he punched in the fax number and hit send. Carl wasn't sure why he even cared because he didn't know the dead men. Both Jalmer Peters and Arnie Kilton were from faraway places, so what was bugging him?

After faxing them, Carl was about to toss the originals in the wastebasket when three things that each dead man had in common piqued his curiosity. The first was that the deceased were young, just like Wally. The second was that they didn't have many surviving relatives, similar to Wally's bio. And the third was the same question Carl had about Wally's obituary: Why were they printed in the Gazette anyway? There didn't appear to be any connection to relatives living anywhere in the Midwest. It just didn't make sense!

Carl's thoughts returned to Jim Bowman. He wrote "Alaska" on one Post-It and "Holmes Mortuary" on another. But Carl was still confused about how they were connected, so he didn't draw any lines between the bulletin board's notes. He began to do what a lonely guy does quite frequently—he muttered to himself.

"Okay, so what do I know? Sam Diggins was the assistant funeral director for Holmes Mortuary in Hudson; however, there is no dang Holmes Mortuary there! But there is one in Prudhoe Bay, Alaska, where Jim Bowman's racketeer brother lived! Strange!"

Carl started to pace around his tiny office, rubbing his temples. His internal clock was still on Florida time, which was an hour later, and he didn't have much sleep the past few days. Carl knew he had a bad habit of talking to himself, but he couldn't control it.

"Hey, wait a minute. What was the dead lady's name for that first obituary I sent in? I need a Post-It for her, too, because her final arrangements were at a nonexistent Holmes Mortuary in Hudson. It was Jane or Jill, something with a J."

Carl checked the email from Sam Diggins again. There it was. Sure enough, the deceased's name started with a J. Her name was Joy Smith. He wrote it on a Post-It, stuck it on the bulletin board, then drew a line from Joy to Holmes Mortuary.

It was a start. But would he ever reach the end? Carl sat down again and laid his head on the desk for a short rest to clear his mind. Five minutes later, he was sound asleep, dreaming that he was locked up in prison in the same cell with Jim and John Bowman.

His cell phone rang precisely at midnight.

Chapter 17

Carl groggily lifted his head off the desk, grabbed the cell phone, and saw that the caller ID read *Molly*. He reluctantly pushed the *accept* button.

"Hi, Mol," he said in a weary voice. "What's up?"

"What's up?!" Molly responded angrily. "It's midnight, and you're not home. That's what's up!"

"Sorry, Babe. I must have dozed off at my desk. I'll wrap up and be home soon."

"Okay. I was just worried about you! Did you get the obituaries sent off to George? I mean to your editor?"

Puzzled by the question, Carl hesitated for a moment. "Yep, got it done. I'll be there in a few minutes. Bye." He ended the call before Molly could say anything, then thought again about what she had asked. Why would Molly care if he had submitted the damn obituaries anyway? And why a slip of the tongue—George instead of the editor? Molly didn't seem too distressed about whether he was alive or dead as long as he had taken care of business!

Driving the short distance home, Carl decided not to say a word to Molly about Jim Bowman. She would have him committed to a psychiatric hospital for paranoia, insanity, and impersonating Columbo! But, he should report what he knows, or thinks he knows, to the FBI, right? Or would they believe he was loony, too?

To Carl, the recipe card's code seemed to be fairly obvious evidence pointing to Jim Bowman's involvement in an illegal sports gaming operation. But why he chose to cover his criminal activity by being an obituary consultant was bewildering. Why not be a barista at Caribou Coffee instead? That job would be fun, and you could spend your days sampling all sorts of tasty java! Carl chuckled at the thought. It was late, and he was fed up with the stress. If this kept up, he would need to be treated for an anxiety disorder!

He wouldn't have far to go to find a psychiatrist. His brother-in-law Curt was parked in the driveway.

*****

Carl tapped on the driver's side window with his fist. Curt had reclined the seat and was sound asleep, his snoring loud enough to keep the raccoons from checking out the neighborhood garbage cans. Carl tried the door. It was unlocked, so he opened it. Carl ducked in and grabbed Curt's shoulder with both hands and shook him. He could smell beer on his breath, and there were six or eight empty bottles of Miller Lite on the passenger-side floor.

Curt woke up and was startled at the two eyes that were only inches away from his own. "Wha, wha, what? Where am I?"

Carl backed off and stood up in front of the open door. "Where are you—that's what you want to know?! Perhaps you should ask yourself why you are sleeping in my driveway. Your sister Molly's inside. I'm guessing she would gladly provide a pillow and a throw rug for you to doze on down on the basement floor. There's a slightly used cat box for you to do your business, too!"

"Very funny," replied Curt dully. He propped the seat forward, exited the car, and hugged his brother-in-law. Carl didn't hug back.

"So, seriously, why are you in New Richmond, and why didn't you go inside with Molly?"

"Okay, I was worried about you. I had lunch today with George Markins, and he was concerned that you aren't doing your job. He said you flew down to Florida for an old friend's funeral but didn't return to the office on Monday. I have a keen interest in the quality of your work. Remember, I'm the one who recommended you for the position. My reputation's at stake, Dude!

"As for Molly, well, I had a few beers to keep me awake during the drive from Eau Claire. She wouldn't have been pleased, so I figured I would sleep in your driveway until morning. I assumed that you were home, too. And that begs the question—what are you doing out so late?"

"Well, you and George will be happy to know that I've been toiling away at my job," said Carl sarcastically. "What's up with George anyway? He's the guy that hired me, but he ain't my boss! The editor is my boss. So why does he always seem to have a bug up his butt about my work ethic?"

"I'm guessing it's the same reason I just told you about. He hired you, so his job is on the line if you don't meet the company's expectations."

Carl led Curt to the porch door. "Company's expectations? What kind of expectations do they have for a part-time obituary consultant that offers no advice? I'm just a damn peon, Curt!"

"What do you mean? I thought you invoked your unique literary skills into designing marvelous eulogies for the recently deceased." Curt smiled and slapped Carl affectionately on the back. Carl unlocked the side entry door and gave Curt a friendly push into the kitchen.

"I'm too tired for your lame humor." Carl showed Curt the guestroom, then headed to his room at the end of the hallway. Molly was out like a light. Five minutes later, so was Carl.

Molly awoke at 5:00 a.m. sharp, as she did every workday, but this morning was a bit different. She sat up in bed and smelled the distinctly magnificent aroma of bacon frying in the kitchen, which was on the other side of the house. Carl was snoring next to her, so Molly wondered who was cooking. She slipped on a robe and padded down the hallway. She stopped suddenly in semi-shock when she saw her brother, Curt, cracking eggs in a pan on the stove.

Curt glanced at Molly and smiled. "Hey, sis, how's it going?"

"When did you get here? And more importantly, what are you doing here?" asked Molly.

"Arrived in the middle of the night. I was planning on just sleeping in the driveway, but Carl came home and woke me up. I knew you would be leaving for work early, so I thought I'd cook up a little protein splash to invigorate your day!"

"You didn't answer the other part of my question—what are you doing here?"

Curt put down the cooking utensils and walked around the corner into the living room. He stared down the hallway to make sure Carl wasn't awake, then stepped back into the kitchen. He placed his forefinger over his lips to indicate that Molly needed to keep her voice down.

"You know why I'm here," whispered Curt. "And if you don't, then stop and think a minute."

Quietly, Molly replied, "You better tell me, Curt. I'm not about to assume anything."

"George wasn't sure Carl would get back to Wisconsin in time to send in the obituaries that needed to be submitted, so he asked if I could do it for him. Well, I hadn't seen your new house, so I thought if I traveled to Carl's office in New Richmond, that would give me a good chance to take a peek at your abode. Kill two birds with one stone, sort of. George gave me a copy of the key to Carl's office. But obviously, your hubby made it back okay, so instead, I'm just going to dine on a superfine homemade breakfast created by yours truly, then head back to Eau Claire."

"The deadline for submitting for today's paper was last night at ten o'clock. If you arrived as you said in the middle of the night, then you didn't get here in time. So, why did you bother making the drive?"

"Well, actually, I did get here before ten. I saw Carl's car parked in the alley by his office, so I figured he had arrived alive. I walked over to Glover Park and had a beer, then drove to your house."

"A beer? Like, just one beer? Come on, Curt, you've never drunk only one beer!"

"Okay, well, what I meant was one six-pack. I worked out before I left Eau Claire, and I was a tiny bit thirsty. Cut me some slack, sis!"

Molly rolled her eyes and shook her head in disgust. "I need to get ready for work. If you left now, I'm sure you could make it safely back to Eau Claire for your own work," she said sarcastically.

"Well, now, isn't that hospitable of you?" Curt winked at his baby sister.

"Okay, sorry! I'm not trying to be mean. Why not come back this weekend and take Carl fishing on the St. Croix River? We'd have more time for fun and chit-chat."

"You know I'm not going to do that. It's football season, and now is when I make the big bucks for the year. I'm at my computer every Saturday and Sunday." Curt and Molly stared at each other for a few tense moments, neither one wanting to say something he or she would regret. Finally, Curt turned off the stove, dished the bacon and eggs, then moved to the kitchen table and sat down. "I'll eat and clean up, then hit the road. But this can't happen again. Carl needs to do his job."

"You didn't need to drive down here," said Molly, hoping to get the last word. "A phone call to me would have sufficed."

Without saying goodbye, Molly abruptly turned away to head to the bathroom and ran smack dab into Carl. Her husband was groggily making his way into the kitchen after a few hours of sleep and stumbled backward after the head-on collision. He stood up and rubbed his eyes with his fists.

The sound of laughter emanated from the table a few feet away. "Hey, you both appear to be in bad need of some caffeine," chuckled Curt. "But first, you really should invest in a coffee pot and act like the downhome married folks that you desire to be!"

With a wide grin, Curt walked over and gave his sister and brother-in-law an affectionate hug. Molly didn't smile back.

*****

Carl showered and dressed while Curt cleaned up the kitchen. Thinking about homonyms, he remembered he was rather curt with Curt last night. Because of that, Carl offered to buy his brother-in-law a latte at Caribou Coffee on his way to the office. Curt opted for a strong, black cup of java with a shot of espresso instead. The bacon and eggs had done nothing for his hangover.

The conversation wavered from planning another fishing excursion, or perhaps duck hunting when the season opened in a couple of weeks, to when Curt would be blessed with his first niece or nephew. Carl was all for the fishing and hunting but deferred to Curt's sister for the last question. Then the topic of online gaming came up.

"So, are you still gambling on games from your computer?" asked Carl.

"You bet—no pun intended!" smirked Curt. "In fact, I did very well last weekend."

"No kidding. Who did you bet on?"

"Well, I didn't dare tell Molly, but I picked the Bears straight up over the Vikings on Monday. Won a bunch!"

"Why do you think Molly would care?" asked Carl sincerely.

"Well, with her writing columns for the Vikes, I thought I should support her efforts. But even though I picked "da Bears" this week, I did put a $1,000 down on the Vikes to win the NFC North. The odds are fifty to one, so I could pick up an easy fifty grand!"

"Okay, so I'm not a gambler, but I don't get it. You bet $1,000 on the Vikings to win the NFC North, but you bet against them in week one?! Huh?!"

"Just had a hunch that the Bears would bring their "A" game this week, that's all. But I almost blew it on the Atlanta-Carolina game. I took the Panthers and the point spread, which was four and a half at game time. I'm not sure if you saw it, but it went into overtime, and Desmond Trufant picked off Bridgewater's pass for a touchdown. Fortunately for me, he was ruled down by contact. The Falcons had to settle for a field goal and only won by three."

"So what you're saying is if the TD had stood, the Falcons would have won by six, and you'd be out the money, right?"

"Yep, that's how it works!"

"Well, I did see the recap, including the play you're talking about, and I'd have to say that I didn't see Trufant being touched after the interception. I think the refs got that one wrong, but yes, that was fortunate for you!"

"No way, Carl. Trufant was definitely touched. I can't figure out why people didn't see it."

"Okay, so I beg to differ. How much did you win on that game?"

"I put down five grand and won $4,550! Not bad, eh?!"

"You bet $5,000 on that game and $1,000 on the Bears?! Your psychiatry business must be booming!"

"Actually, I'm a pretty damn good gambler, that's all. I also won $4,350 on the Jacksonville game. Bet another $5,000 on that one, too. The over/under seemed pretty low, so I took the over. Ended up being a high-scoring game, so I got lucky."

"Yeah, I know. It was supposed to be a defensive battle, considering both starting quarterbacks were on the disabled list. Why don't you win $5,000 if you bet $5,000?"

"The bookies get their cut, my friend. They need to put food on the table, too, you know. Hey, I got to get back to Eau Claire, so I'll be signing off. Let's plan on duck hunting in a couple of weeks. There's a pond the mallards like to hang out on County Road K east of New Richmond. When we've bagged our limit, we'll drink a few cold ones at Rooster's Roadhouse."

Curt and Carl fist-bumped their goodbyes, then headed to their expensive cars. As he opened the door to his Tesla, Carl glanced over to Curt, who was unlocking his BMW convertible. Parked next to Curt was a bald guy sitting in the front seat of a black Chevy Tahoe. Carl did a double-take. He hadn't seen the man since last July.

Chapter 18

As Curt drove off, Carl slammed his door and started jogging towards the Chevy Tahoe. The man saw him approaching and gunned the SUV out of the parking spot, then turned south on Knowles Avenue, squealing his tires and drawing the attention of surprised pedestrians. Carl stopped and placed his hands on his hips in frustration.

Five minutes later, he was in his Post-It note decorated office trying to make sense of everything. But Jim Bowman and the bald man in the Chevy Tahoe were of no concern at the moment. Now what was bothering him was his conversation with Curt. How did his brother-in-law get involved in big-time gambling? Where did he get the money? Molly had told him that Curt's psychiatry practice was mediocre at best.

What was troubling Carl the most was that one of Curt's recent winnings came from a game that Carl was almost sure was fixed. He picked the recipe card off his desk and stared at it again.

Can't reach you by email. Why has your account been suspended?

Redo
Milton Shrum
913ATF4L@CAP

Milton and Shrum were definitely referees who were involved in the outcome of the game. Had to be! "913" meant September thirteenth, the date of the game, and "ATF @ CAP" indicated the

Atlanta Falcons at Carolina Panthers. So what was "4L" and "Redo" all about? It was driving him crazy!

Then a thought occurred. Curt said the point spread was four and a half at game time in favor of Atlanta. If the refs had been told what the outcome needed to be, then they would have tried to keep the Atlanta margin of victory at four or less. That was it! Of course! The "4L" was a code for the officials to keep the Falcons from winning by no more than four points! And that's why Desmond Trufant's interception was considered "down by contact." If the touchdown had stood, they would have won by six points and covered the spread.

Carl wondered if "redo" meant that Miles Milton and Jake Shrum were supposed to replace two previously scheduled referees for that game. Or did "redo" tell that the winning margin needed to be adjusted. Somehow, he would investigate and see if Milton and Shrum were initially assigned to the Atlanta-Carolina game or were replacements. Carl knew the answer would have him treading on thin ice—if they were substitutes hired to fix the game, then there was a chance that someone in the NFL executive headquarters was part of this scheme! And if Carl was caught sticking his nose into something this huge, he would be looking over his shoulder for mob hitmen the rest of his life!

Perhaps it was time to end his probe before it became too dangerous. Most likely, Jim and John Bowman were deeply involved in illegal gaming. John went to prison for racketeering, and Jim is dead. Is it possible that Jim didn't die from cancer and he was killed? Maybe he messed up somewhere along the way and did something his crime bosses disapproved of!

Carl had to make a decision. He either continues down a treacherous path or simply ignores what he knows and focuses on his work as an obituary consultant. He was about to tear down the Post-Its from the bulletin board when chills went up his spine, and the goosebumps covered his body once again.

Was it possible that his brother-in-law had been tipped off on which games to bet? Curt knew Jim Bowman because of the working relationship between Jim and George Markins. He bet five grand on the rigged Atlanta contest and even turned a blind eye to the "down by contact" play that virtually won it for him. Carl sat down and finished his coffee, then crumbled up the paper cup and threw it at the wall.

He leaned back and stared at the ceiling, trying desperately to organize his thoughts. Strangely, a feeling of peace began to surround him. If Curt was involved in illegal gaming, Carl's decision to ignore the whole situation was confirmed. There was no way he could turn over the recipe card to the feds and save his marriage. Molly would leave him if he implicated her brother, and he ended up in prison.

Carl took a deep breath and tried to relax and forget about the fixing of NFL games. For all he knew, the Atlanta-Carolina game may have been the only one that had been fixed. It was doubtful that even the most sophisticated crime syndicate could alter the outcome of more than one or two games a year. Right? That type of corruption would require the involvement of an enormous amount of unscrupulous people.

Carl decided that he would focus on writing and helping others to write obituaries and nothing more! But his desire to become a sportswriter had just changed. How could he have written an unbiased article on the Atlanta victory knowing what he knew? Carl's mixed-up thoughts were eating at him. He had to concentrate only on his job! To avoid George Markins' wrath, Carl would check his Rankins's email account first thing each morning. Then he would make phone calls to funeral directors and nursing homes to offer his assistance for writing obits. That was that! Nothing more!

The Rankins's email was empty, as was his other business account. He searched and located the phone numbers for several nursing homes and wrote them down on a scratchpad. He picked up his office phone and began to punch in the first number on the list, then hung up before it connected.

"I can't do this," he muttered to himself. "If Dad had found out about a possible point-shaving scheme in pro football, or any sport for that matter, he would have called the feds. Why? Because it was the honorable thing to do, regardless of who got hurt."

Carl wished he had someone to talk to besides himself. But, if a crime syndicate was involved, he didn't want to drag Molly in on something that could prove lethal. And besides, she probably wouldn't believe him anyway. Obviously, calling Curt was out of the question, too.

What about Wally Roseberg? Carl could trust his old friend if he only knew how to find him. But the call to InterPlan Architecture in Tequesta yielded the same results—Wally wasn't in the office, and the receptionist had no idea when he would return. It was a broken record!

It was no use trying to immerse himself in drumming up obituaries. Carl needed another break. Wednesday, better known as "hump day" in office lingo, was rapidly slipping away. He needed both a coffee and a beer, the former to keep him awake, and the latter to mellow him out. Carl chose the latter.

Champs Sports Bar was across Knowles Avenue and had great food and even better drinks. The only games playing on the big screens inside were soccer matches in Europe, which were of no interest to Carl. So, he climbed the steps and sat down at a table on the roof. The weather was perfect for mid-September—sixty-eight degrees and sunny, and the view of the city was impressive. Carl passed on the food and beer. Instead, he ordered an *Angry Ball*, a specialty drink consisting of Angry Orchard Hard Cider and Fireball Cinnamon Whiskey. That ought to do the trick to pull him out of his funk!

On the table, tucked underneath the condiment holder so it wouldn't blow away, was today's Minneapolis Dispatch. Carl had been so wrapped up in his own doings that he hadn't read Molly's column for a few weeks. He pulled the newspaper out and extracted the sports section. Molly's column was on the first page—you couldn't miss it.

Molly was very critical of the Vikings for their loss at home to the division-rival Chicago Bears. It was the first time that Kirk

Cousins had completed less than half of his thrown passes in a football game—dating back to his college days at Michigan State. Rookie wide receiver, Justin Jefferson, didn't seem to run the right routes, and Molly blamed the coaches for not having the team prepared for the season opener. She did manage to take a shot at the officiating, but Carl thought that was just a half-hearted way to appease the diehard fans and give them hope for next week.

Carl took another sip of his Angry Ball and stared at the blue water tower over by the fire station. Another thought popped into his sedated mind that he couldn't seem to shake. Why in the world would Curt bet $1,000 on the Bears straight up after he already bet $1,000 that the Vikings would win the NFC North? Somewhat contradictory, wouldn't you say? Curt told him that he "had a hunch."

Remembering something curious that he just read, Carl picked up the sports section and skimmed Molly's column again. Sure enough, Molly had crucified two referees that had blown several calls. Could it be that the Vikings-Bears contest was "fixed" as well? And could Curt have known about it? But still, wouldn't Curt be upset that a loss to the Bears might prevent the Vikings from winning the NFC North, which he had already bet on? You can't have it both ways in gambling—you either win or lose. There's no in-between.

Carl remembered the other game that Curt said he bet $5,000. It was the Jacksonville versus Tennessee game, and he took the over/under wager. Oddsmakers set the total at twenty-three points, which was very low. However, considering both teams had staunch defenses and injured quarterbacks, it was probably an accurate estimate. Curt took the "over" and won big.

Carl was hoping this was all a nasty coincidence. Curt was now a close relative and good friend. But if the three games he wagered on were all compromised by some sort of crime syndicate, and Curt knew about it, then Carl had to take a stand. He had to tell the feds and hope they would offer protection for Molly and him. Carl was sure that his father would have done the same thing.

But first, Carl needed to know exactly how Jim Bowman had died. Was it really cancer like everyone in Hammond told him and had been written on his obituary? There must be official records of his death. Carl paid the bill and hurried back to his office. He wished that he would have consumed one more Angry Ball.

Chapter 19

Carl was certain that Jim Bowman moonlighted in illegal gaming. How did that come to be? He wasn't sure, but he assumed Jim's brother got him involved. Why take the risk? That question was much simpler to answer—it's difficult to make a living as a part-time obituary writer. Carl feared that Jim messed up somewhere along the way, and a criminal organization had him killed.

Carl sat at his desk and doodled on a notepad. It was how he had survived the multitude of boring lectures in college. But doodling had always been an effective way for him to arrange his jumbled thoughts. His scribbles bordered on artistic, and Carl considered changing his career to comic book writing.

As he changed his esses into human caricatures, a synapse finally connected two nerve cells in his brain. Carl had a possible lead. According to Jim's obituary, he had died following a short bout with leukemia in June. If that were true, he would have been treated by a doctor somewhere in the area. Carl Googled "cancer treatment centers nearby" on his computer.

Several hospitals appeared on the list, most in the Twin Cities area, as well as the *Mayo Clinic* in Rochester. The only facility in St. Croix County was located inside the *General Hospital* in New Richmond. Named *The Cancer Treatment Center of Western Wisconsin*, it was a stone's throw from the backyard of Carl's house. He would stop there on his way home.

The head of the cancer center was Dr. Mike Kohlrusch, who also doubled as the county's assistant medical examiner. Carl was surprised Dr. Kohlrusch offered to see him without an appointment. But that astonishment ended abruptly after they greeted one another with a firm handshake.

"So you're Carl West, the great Billy West's son, right?" asked Kohlrusch with a grin from ear to ear, still wildly shaking Carl's hand.

"How did you know that, Dr. Kohlrusch?"

"Mike. Please just call me Mike, okay?" Carl nodded, then Mike continued. "I heard rumors that you had moved here. There's a lot of football fans in this area, you know. Then I read your wife's column in the Dispatch and guessed that you had to be living somewhere close to the Twin Cities. I sure like her writing style, by the way. So, I understand that you played softball all summer in town and are in a league out at the golf course, but you never mentioned to anyone that you were Billy West's son. Why not?"

Carl's first impression was that Mike was affable and most likely very well respected in the community. He was friends with the younger softball players, the older golfers, and the multigenerational crowd that started rumors! No doubt, Mike was a good doctor, but he talked a mile a minute! Carl wondered how often he paused to breathe.

"Let's just say that I want to be known as Carl West and leave it at that. My dad was an incredible human being, both on the field and off. I'm very proud of his accomplishments, but I am my own self."

"I understand and certainly can appreciate that," said Mike, still smiling. "So, how may I help you today?"

"By any chance did you know Jim Bowman? I replaced him at the Eau Claire Gazette."

Mike's smile diminished for a few seconds, and he looked away momentarily. Carl could read in Mike's eyes that he did know Jim and that his simple question struck a nerve. Carl was about to apologize when Mike responded with a serious tone in his voice.

"Yes, I knew Jim fairly well. He was a patient of mine. Why do you ask?"

"I'm not sure, really. I just had some free time on my hands, and I was reading over his obituary. I felt bad that he died from leukemia and hoped to get a little more information to know the guy. That's all." Carl said it with a straight face. He wasn't about to reveal to Dr. Kohlrusch that he thought Jim was dabbling in illegal gambling.

"Carl, I can't give you any details about his death. I would be violating the Health Insurance Portability and Accountability Act, which you may know as HIPAA."

"Yes, I know what HIPAA is. But, seeing Jim's deceased, can't you release his information?"

"The HIPAA agreement runs for fifty years following someone's death. Sorry, Carl, I can't divulge any information about Jim."

"Did you know Jim personally, or just as a patient?" Carl wasn't about to give up that easily.

"I knew him first as a patient, but I guess you would say that we became friends. However, it was only for a short time. He died a couple of months later."

"Yes, his obit said it was a brief illness," said Carl.

"Yeah, I know. I wrote the obit."

"You wrote the obit?" asked Carl as he raised his eyebrow in astonishment. "Why did you write it? From what I read, he still has a father living in Virginia somewhere."

"Jim asked me to write it when he knew he didn't have much time left. I couldn't locate his father, and the only other surviving family member was a brother who was in prison. He only told me about his brother so I wouldn't try to contact him."

This was Carl's chance. He had to twist the truth a bit to get the answers he wanted. "He had a brother in prison? What for? From what I've heard from his colleagues at the Gazette, Jim was an upstanding and well-respected person. Hard to believe he would have a lawless brother!"

"I know I shouldn't have because it wasn't any of my business, but I asked Jim about his brother. He wouldn't tell me anything about why he was sent to prison. The whole thing is kind of strange if you ask me. His brother had a great job as an engineer in Prudhoe Bay, Alaska. I can't imagine what he did to break the law in that tiny, freezing town up there by the Arctic Circle!"

"Yeah, I agree," replied Carl, and both he and Mike nodded at each other. "So, going back to the obituary, why did he have you write it? He wrote obits for a living, and he knew he was going to die, so why didn't he write one up and give it to you?"

Mike stared at Carl in amazement. "Jim wrote obituaries for the Gazette?!" asked Mike with a perplexed tone. He walked over to the window and gazed out at the traffic on Somerset Road. "I could swear Jim told me he was a sportswriter for the Gazette. Are you sure he wrote obituaries? Seems a rather menial occupation, if you ask me."

Carl's face turned a bright red. Mike saw his embarrassment, then thought about what he just said. He remembered Carl was Jim's replacement at the Gazette. Mike had assumed Carl was a sportswriter, too.

"Sorry, Carl," said Mike somberly. "I didn't mean to offend you. I forgot you were Jim's successor. Writing obituaries certainly requires a great deal of talent!"

Carl blurted out a rather long laugh. "Bullcrap, Mike. You are right—it is a menial occupation. But I'm hoping it's a stepping stone to becoming a sportswriter someday, that's all. Rookies do what it takes in this profession, too!"

Mike grinned back. He was thankful Carl wasn't upset by his comment. "Well, anyway, Jim never mentioned writing his own obituary. He gave me a few facts, and I wrote it up. As the county's assistant medical examiner, it's one of my duties if the next of kin can't be reached. Usually, the funeral director will relieve me of the task, though."

Carl perked up. He didn't realize Mike doubled as one of St. Croix County's coroners. If Mike suspected something other than leukemia was the cause of Jim's death, he probably performed an autopsy. Perhaps that's why Mike acted strangely when Carl first asked him if he knew Jim. Carl wanted to find out.

"Did you do an autopsy on Jim?" asked Carl nonchalantly.

Mike paused again, and his smile turned into a frown. He was beginning to think that Carl was playing him.

"The obituary said he died from leukemia, my friend," stated Mike bluntly. "Why would I perform an autopsy? I was the doctor who treated him for his cancer. Don't you think I knew what killed him?"

Mike was becoming testy. Carl wanted to end the conversation on a positive note, but he could tell how Mike was acting the good doctor was hiding something.

The tending physician's records and coroner's report for Jim Bowman were most likely right here in Dr. Kohlrusch's office. The clinic's administrative offices closed at 7:00 p.m. Those offices were only a three-minute walk from Carl's backyard.

Once Molly was sound asleep, Carl would take a midnight stroll.

*****

Molly didn't return to New Richmond until 8:00 p.m. She stopped at Wu Fung's in Woodbury for pork chow mein and shrimp fried rice take out. Cooking wasn't much fun after ten-hour workdays and long commutes. She didn't feel like talking either, so she and Carl ate in virtual silence, then Molly headed for the bedroom and crashed.

Carl watched ESPN's *Sportscenter*, the ten o'clock news, and *The Tonight Show with Jimmy Fallon* to kill time. At midnight, he laced up a pair of tennies, strapped on a backpack, and pretended he was out for a late stroll on Hospital Road. In the backpack was his most recent purchase from Walmart.

Earlier, after leaving Mike's office, Carl drove to the Supercenter on the edge of town. Walmart had every intention of being the first store to sell Halloween costumes, even though it was over a month away. Sure enough, Carl found precisely what he was looking for—a complete surgeon's outfit. Along with a stethoscope and rubber gloves, it contained a long white coat and light blue scrubs so you could dress formally or for surgery. There was a name tag with "Dr. James Kildare" imprinted on it just for laughs. Carl debated wearing the badge, but in the end, he decided to impersonate the famous fictional TV character from the early sixties. Why not? Most nurses and night crew hospital staffers were too young to know about the black and white television series. Carl only knew about Dr. Kildare because now and then, he would watch reruns with his mother when his dad was out of town.

One concern he had with the costume was his tennis shoes. Carl wasn't sure if surgeons wore them, but he would just take the chance. His major worry was getting into Mike's office. The hospital waiting room was open twenty-four hours, so Carl planned to walk in and go directly to the restroom and change into his garb. If he could get past the nurses' station, how would he break into the room? Carl decided to deal with that problem when the time came.

The first part of the plan went smoothly. No one in the reception and waiting area gave him more than a glance. The men's room was only a few feet away. Carl entered and walked into a stall, then hung the backpack on a coat hook attached to the door. He opted to wear the scrub cap, gown, and face mask so he would be covered up almost entirely, thus unrecognizable from the security cameras planted in every room and hallway. Carl pulled on rubber gloves, not to disguise himself any further, but so he wouldn't leave fingerprints in Mike's office. Lastly, he pinned the name badge to his gown, then rolled up the backpack and shoved it into the garbage can.

Carl opened the door a tiny bit and peeked out into the waiting area. Three elderly women were sleeping on leather chairs, and a young man was pacing nervously around the room. Carl hoped the man would have good news soon.

Getting past the nurses' station would be a challenge. Fortunately, only one nurse, Betty Johnson, was on duty. Unfortunately, Betty looked like the hospital sheriff—chubby cheeks, muscular build, piercing black eyes, and an angry scowl on her face. Carl didn't think he could slip by her very easily, scrubs or no scrubs.

An idea came to him, although it was a shot in the dark. Nurse Johnson was checking a chart, so Carl slipped out of the bathroom and walked over to the pacing young man.

"Hi, my name is Dr. Kildare. You appear to be a bit nervous. Is there something I can do for you?"

The young man stopped in his tracks and smiled at Carl. "Thanks, Doc. I'm Tom Yary. My wife went into labor, and they don't have a room available for her yet. As soon as they find one, I can go in."

"Oh, I see," said Carl. "What's your wife's name?"

"Ann Yary," replied her husband. Then he let out a big grin. "This is my first baby, you know."

"Well, good luck, Tom! I'm sure you will have a wonderful, happy, healthy addition to your family very soon!"

"Thanks! By the way, you look awfully young to be a doctor. That's a compliment, you know!"

"Yes, and I'm much obliged. I think I'm the only doctor in America who gets carded going into a bar!" Carl let out his best fake laugh, then turned and walked back into the restroom. Nurse Johnson never saw him. Tom Yary wondered why a doctor would use the lobby restroom, but he didn't give it much thought. He was still thinking about his wife and wished the hospital would find a labor room soon.

Carl found the hospital's main office number on Google and called it on his cell phone. He hoped it would ring into the receptionist's line next to the lobby. He peeked out from the door and held his breath. Sure enough, the call was picked up by Nurse Johnson.

"General Hospital," she announced in a gruff voice. If Carl wasn't looking right at her, he would have thought she was a guy. "May I help you?"

"Yes, this is Dr. Kildare. I need you to check on Ann Yary. She's waiting for a labor room and is all alone in the maternity hallway."

The nurse didn't even flinch at the doctor's name. Betty only knew a handful of the medical staff and didn't care to know more.

Many doctors were using the small-town hospital as a career starting block so they could later transfer to Minneapolis or St. Paul. But Betty was a bit peeved that a doctor would order her away from the front desk.

"There's no one down in maternity who can check on her?" asked Nurse Johnson in a low, husky voice. She glanced up at Ann's husband, who was pacing in the lobby. Betty had checked Ann in an hour earlier and knew the hospital was prepping a room for her. They had placed her temporarily in an unused one that was up for a remodel. How could it be that the young pregnant mom wound up in a hallway, for God's sake! "Let me call down there and find someone, Doctor—. I'm sorry, what did you say your name was?"

Carl panicked. Would this ruse work? Well, what did he have to lose? He was in the restroom, and if push came to shove, he could just put his clothes back on and leave. "Kildare. Hey, it's late, and I'm sorry if I was a bit snippy. I'm just concerned, that's all. It won't do much good to call down to the maternity station because the nurses are all involved in deliveries right now." Carl crossed his fingers on his free hand. Could Nurse Betty be duped into believing his lies?

Through the crack in the door, Carl could see the nurse roll her eyes and shake her head in disgust. But in the end, she did what he asked. "Okay, Doctor Kildare, I'll check it out."

As soon as Betty left the reception area, Carl dashed from the restroom and entered the hospital hallway in his scrubs. The stethoscope swung like an elephant's trunk at his chest. Tom Yary thought something looked strange, but he had too many other things on his mind at the moment.

Carl glanced around at the signs and found one that pointed to the administrative offices. He nodded at the medical staff he passed in the hallway. They all did a double-take, wondering why the surgeon was wearing a facemask while not in the surgical center. Carl found Mike Kohlrusch's office and waited for the hall to clear before checking the door. He knew the chances were slim that the door would be unlocked, and he guessed right. Carl needed to find a way to get inside. He had to think quickly.

At the end of the hallway was the custodial office. Carl pondered his next move for a split second, then jogged in that direction. If anyone saw him running, he hoped they wouldn't think twice—just another surgeon hurrying to save a life. He was about to knock on the door when it opened.

Jalen Biggs was one of three night custodians. He was the youngest and least senior, and he desperately needed this job. Jalen's seventeen-year-old girlfriend was pregnant and living with him since her parents found out and kicked her out of the house. They lived in an efficiency apartment in the back of Huey's Bar on the northside of town. Jalen's wife cleaned the tavern in exchange for free rent and a bottle of Crown Royal each month. The young couple couldn't afford a car, so Jalen walked the mile and a half distance to General four nights a week.

The Crown Royal was Carl's saving grace. Jalen was late returning to his cleaning area after his break, and he bumped smack dab into Carl as he tried to exit the room in a hurry. There was a distinct smell of whiskey on his breath. Carl thought that might work in his favor.

"Oh, excuse me, Dr.—." Jalen glanced down at Carl's name badge. "Uh, Kildare, is it?" He was quite perplexed as to why the physician was wearing his facemask and rubber gloves, but he knew it wasn't any of his business!

"Yes, son, it is, and I'm in quite a rush! I'm needed back in surgery, but I must get some paperwork from Dr. Kohlrusch's office. He gave me his key, but I accidentally left it at home. Would you mind opening his room up for me?"

Jalen immediately shook his head no. "Uh, sorry, Dr. Kildare. I'm not allowed to do that. I could get in a bunch of trouble, you know."

Time was of the essence, so Carl decided to play his poker hand right now. "How much trouble would you be in if your boss knew you were toking whiskey on your break?"

Jalen was speechless. His cheeks turned five shades of red as he looked into Carl's eyes, hoping for sympathy. "Please, sir," pleaded Jalen. "I would be fired on the spot. My girlfriend's pregnant, and I really, really need this job!"

"And I really, really need to get into Dr. Kohlrusch's office. Open it up, and your secret is safe with me."

Jalen looked left and right down the hallway, then ducked back into the custodial office and grabbed a master key inside a desk. He motioned for Carl to come into the room so they wouldn't be seen.

"Here. This is the master for the entire hospital, Dr. Kildare. There are security cameras in the hallway, and I don't want to be caught opening up the room. Please lock the office when you leave, okay?"

Carl nodded and patted Jalen on the back. "No worries. I'll give the key to Dr. Kohlrusch when I see him."

Jalen's eyelids widened to the max, and he shook his head furiously. "No, please don't do that. I don't want him asking questions about where you got the key! And don't bring it back here because one of my co-workers might be around. Is there any chance you could drop it off at my apartment some time? I live in the back of Huey's Bar, which is just a block up from the Dairy Queen. I work nights from midnight to five-thirty, so I'm home most days."

Undoubtedly, the kid was in fear of losing his job and not thinking straight. Carl had no plans to return the key, but he needed to end this conversation right away. "Okay, sure. Not a problem. I'm tied up for the next few days, so it might be a while before I can get over to Huey's. I've got to go now! Thanks!"

Carl dashed down the hallway and entered Dr. Kohlrusch's office. He noticed the security camera overhead, but he was still covered up with his facemask, cap, and gown. Doubtful anyone would be able to decipher who he was, and he didn't plan to leave any evidence of his breaking and entering anyway. Carl didn't need to flip the light switch because every room in the hospital had emergency fluorescent bulbs affixed to the ceiling that automatically turned on at dusk. They provided sufficient illuminance for Carl to take pictures of the files with his cell phone and put everything back the way he found it.

Dr. Kohlrusch had two, three-drawer oak Stonegate designer file cabinets that matched his traditional Amish desk and bookcase. One cabinet was labeled ***PATIENTS,*** and the other labeled ***MEDICAL EXAMINER REPORTS***. Both would be his personal copies because the official documents were stored in the hospital records room in the north wing or at the St. Croix County Government Center in Hudson.

Not surprisingly, both cabinets were locked. But evidently, Dr. Kohlrusch wasn't a stickler for uncompromised security because he left the keys attached to a wooden stick in the pen holder. Carl had noticed them earlier. He grabbed the keys and opened the patient file first.

The folder tabs had been typed, and the records were arranged in alphabetical order. That was the last of anything that could be considered neat and orderly. The data was scrawled haphazardly and was barely legible. Kohlrusch would have flunked third-grade cursive writing had he turned in those scribbles to his teacher! Carl felt terrible for the administrative assistant who had to decipher his notes and transcribe them for archival purposes with a word processor.

Using his iPhone, Carl snapped pictures of every page in Jim Bowman's patient file, then opened the medical examiner's cabinet and did the same. He placed everything he had touched back where he found it, then walked to the door. Opening it a crack, he looked both ways down the corridor. It was empty.

Carl hustled down the hallway and followed the signs for the emergency room. He didn't want to pass Nurse Betty, the reception area, or Tom Yary again. Hopefully, someone found a labor and delivery room for his wife by now.

Nearing the ER, Carl passed two interns who were also dressed in scrubs. He nodded at them, and they could only assume the doctor hustling past them was immediately going into surgery. Why else would he be wearing his facemask and rubber gloves?!

Carl ducked into an empty room, quickly removed his scrubs, tossed them in a garbage can, and then walked through the ER waiting room and out the door. He kept his head down to avoid the cameras that were attached to the walls. As soon as he got to Hospital Road, he jogged the short distance to his backyard.

Through the porch, Carl entered the house, plopped down on his favorite leather recliner, and sat in the dark to try and catch his breath. His heart just about jumped out of his chest cavity when Molly turned on the light. She had been waiting for him on the couch.

Chapter 20

"Well?!" asked Molly angrily.

Carl was sure that was a question. He wasn't sure he had an answer, so he just stared at her for what seemed to be the most prolonged moment of his life. He wanted to tell her about the illegal gaming theory and how Jim Bowman had been involved, but not in the middle of the night. And he certainly didn't want her to know that for the last hour or so he had impersonated a surgeon and broke into the medical examiner's office at the hospital.

"Well?" repeated Molly in an even more vexing tone. "Where were you?"

"I couldn't sleep, so I went out for a jog," lied Carl, but his voice was cracking, and Molly knew he wasn't telling the truth.

"You went out for a jog in long pants, is that right? Since when have you exercised in anything but athletic shorts and a t-shirt? Were you with someone?" Molly was becoming more incensed, and Carl couldn't get a word in edgewise.

"No!" inserted Carl firmly. "I was just going to take a walk but decided to run instead. And no one was with me!"

Molly and Carl sat quietly staring at each other. You could cut the air with a knife. Finally, Carl took a deep breath and said calmly, "Look, there's something I need to tell you, but I'm too tired to start a long conversation tonight. I promise we'll chat tomorrow. Okay?"

Molly paused several seconds as tears flowed into her eyes. "Is there another girl?"

Immediately, Carl jumped up, moved next to her on the couch, and hugged her. "Absolutely not! That's not it, and it's not even close. I love you, Molly."

They embraced for several minutes, then Molly stood and tugged at Carl's hand. "Come on, let's get some sleep."

He needed one more tiny white lie to get through the night. "I'll be there in a few minutes. I need to take a quick shower first."

Carl went into the bathroom and turned on the faucet, but he didn't enter the shower. He let the water run for a few minutes to make noise, then peeked in to check and see if Molly was asleep. Sure enough, Molly had been out like a light as soon as her head hit the pillow.

Carl turned off the faucet and went to the kitchen. He poured a glass of milk, pulled out his iPhone, and began shuffling through the pictures he had taken from Jim Bowman's files. This couldn't wait until morning. He had to know now.

*****

Carl started reading the patient reports first:

DATE: 4/17/2020
PATIENT: James William Bowman
AGE: 33 years/4 months
SYMPTOMS: Patient complains of fatigue, weakness, and dizziness
SUMMARY: Results of bone marrow aspiration, biopsy, and complete blood count indicate a red blood cell level of 3.6 million cells per microliter and a white cell level of 2.8 mcL. Peripheral blood smear results indicate refractory anemia with ring sideroblasts. Details of the blood chemistry study and cytogenetic analysis are attached.

Patient diagnosis: Stage Two Myelodysplastic Syndrome
Prognosis: Treatable (preleukemic)
Success Rate: 70% curable; 30% acute myeloid leukemia

Carl stopped reading after he read the prognosis and success rate. According to Dr. Kohlrusch's reports, Jim Bowman did not have leukemia, at least not at the time following the preliminary lab tests. So why did Dr. Kohlrusch tell me he did, and why did the good doctor also write leukemia as the reason Jim died in his obituary?

Carl scanned the attached lab test results, but they were Greek to him. No use wasting his time trying to decode medical jargon. Preluekemic, with a 70% cure rate, was all Carl needed to know. Now he wanted to see what Kohlrusch had written in the medical examiner's report as the cause of death.

Carl scrolled slowly until he found what he was looking for:

> DETERMINATION: *Acute arsenic poisoning by self-induced ingestion.*
> SUMMARY: *James William Bowman was transferred by an unidentified male and admitted to General Emergency Room on June 13, 2020, at 5:37 p.m. He was unconscious, unresponsive, and appeared to suffer from severe gastroenteritis and hypersalivation. George Cowan, MD, ordered bowel irrigation, and at 6:03 p.m, the rectal catheter was in place, and the procedure began. At the request of Dr. Cowan, Michael Kohlrusch, MD, arrived at 6:58 p.m to assist with diagnosis and treatment. Dr. Kohlrusch ordered a group-specific blood transfusion (Type O-Rh Negative) to remove suspected arsenic from the circulatory system. Transfusion commenced at 7:46 p.m and was completed at 9:38 p.m. Mr. Bowman suffered a sequence of multi-organ failures: Hypoxemia (10:14 p.m.); Acute Respiratory Distress Syndrome (11:24 p.m.); acute renal dysfunction (12:16 a.m.); and cardiac arrest (12:38 a.m.).*
> TIME OF DEATH: *12:46 a.m., June 14, 2020.*

The procedures to try and save Jim Bowman appeared to be medically correct and sufficient. Carl would never attempt to dispute something for which he had no clue. Perhaps running this by a different physician would determine if Kohlrusch and Cowan had made the right decisions on June 13th; however, explaining to a doctor how he had obtained a HIPAA confidential report would be problematic. But two things in the medical examiner's report made Carl stand up and take notice.

First, "self-induced ingestion" indicated that Jim poisoned himself, either accidentally or on purpose. If it was not accidental, then it was suicide. Second, an unidentified man dropped Jim off at the emergency room. Who was this man? Did anyone report him to the authorities? Seeing that Jim died from arsenic poisoning, wouldn't it be expected that hospital security personnel would attempt to identify that person?

Carl needed sleep so he could think things through with a clear mind. He climbed into bed but tossed and turned for the rest of the night. He couldn't stop thinking about his meeting with Dr. Kohlrusch. The man seemed to be incredibly nice, but he was not truthful about Jim Bowman's death. Was it because Carl was a new acquaintance, and the doctor didn't feel like opening up to him? Still, why did he write in Jim's obituary that he had died from leukemia when it was really arsenic poisoning. Perhaps it was because when you hear "arsenic poisoning," you think of murder. Or at least that's what you think of when you hear it in the movies!

Before dawn seized the morning sky, Carl rolled out of bed, washed his face, and hurried to his car. After a quick stop at Caribou to grab a large coffee with a double shot of espresso, he gunned it to his office. No one was out on the streets this early in the morning except for the paperboys riding their bikes to deliver today's news.

He rolled up the office door and didn't bother to close it. Carl wasn't going to be there long. He grabbed the Post-It note with Jim Bowman's name from the bulletin board. In tiny print, he wrote that Jim died from arsenic poisoning, and Dr. Kohlrusch had tried to hide that information. He put the Post-It back where it came from and took down the note with Joy Smith's name on it.

Now was the time to find out if Joy was a real person, and if so, where her body was taken after she died. Carl knew it wasn't Holmes

Mortuary like it had said in her obituary because there was no funeral home with that name in Hudson. She supposedly passed away at Woodlawn Cliffs Rest Home, which was a legit nursing home. Her obituary was submitted via the Rankins's email account by Sam Diggins, who claimed to be the assistant funeral director at Holmes. A fake funeral home with a real associate director—that just didn't jive. Carl guessed Joy Smith and Sam Diggins were both false names. The mystery surrounding Joy, Holmes Mortuary, and whoever wrote the obituary using the disguised name of Sam Diggins was next up on his detective list.

Carl printed Joy Smith's obituary, then grabbed his coffee and headed back to the Tesla. His destination was Woodlawn Cliffs Rest Home in Hudson. He sped down Somerset Road past the hospital, turned on County Road A, and floored the accelerator.

After failing to slow down through the tiny town of Boardman, he saw red lights flashing in his rearview mirror. Seems more than just paperboys were out and about early this morning!

Chapter 21

The St. Croix County deputy sheriff stood at an angle behind the passenger door with both hands on his pistol. The gun was aimed directly at Carl's skull. Carl had rolled down the window after pulling off the road, and the rookie patrolman was shaking from head to foot.

"Step out of the car!" yelled the officer loudly. Carl could tell the man was nervous. They were about the same age. "Keep your hands where I can see them!"

Carl opened the door and immediately raised his hands above his head. With no arms to assist his movement, climbing out of the driver's seat was somewhat awkward, and Carl stumbled clumsily. The officer assumed he had been drinking.

"Turn around and put your hands on top of the car!" ordered the deputy. Carl did as he was told.

"Licence and registration!" shouted the officer.

"How exactly would you like me to do that?" replied Carl. He wasn't trying to be sarcastic—he just didn't know.

"Are you disrespecting me, sir?!"

"Absolutely not! But with my hands on the roof, I can't give you what you want. My license is in my wallet. You can remove it if you wish. The registration is in the glove compartment. I'll get it if you allow me to."

The deputy inched close to Carl and placed the gun's barrel on the back of his neck. Then he reached in Carl's back pocket and pulled out his wallet. Carl was praying that the rookie officer wouldn't accidentally pull the trigger.

The deputy holstered his gun to find Carl's license, but his eyes moved quickly back and forth between the wallet and Carl. "If you take your hands off the roof, you will be shot!"

Carl couldn't help himself following that remark. "I know I was speeding, officer, but why do you need to threaten me with a deadly weapon?"

"Speeding?!" the deputy shouted in the form of a question. "That's an understatement! You were going 102 in a thirty-five zone, for God's sake!"

"Okay, I'm sorry. But there is no need for a gun. I'm harmless, really I am!"

There was enough sincerity in Carl's voice that the deputy tended to believe him. With the gun still in his holster, he ordered Carl to turn around and keep his back resting on the car. Carl gladly obliged. Then the officer took out a flashlight from his belt and shined it in Carl's face.

"Have you been drinking, sir? Your eyes are bloodshot."

"No! I just haven't slept for the past couple of days, that's all."

The deputy couldn't smell alcohol on Carl's breath, and he appeared to be coherent. "Okay, go around your car slowly to the passenger door and get your registration out of the glove compartment."

While Carl did as ordered, the officer looked at his driver's license and did a double-take. When Carl returned with the registration certificate, the deputy smiled.

"You're Carl West? Your dad was Billy West, the quarterback, right? I heard you lived around here."

This was the second time in the past day that Carl was happy to be the son of the greatest NFL quarterback in modern times. He hit it off with Dr. Kohlrusch earlier, and now he thought he might have a chance to keep this traffic stop to just a hefty fine. He was pleasantly wrong.

"Yes, sir," replied Carl politely. "I am his son."

The deputy was grinning from ear to ear, then reached his arm out to give Carl a handshake. "Well then, Carl, you don't mind if I call you by your first name, do you?" Carl smiled and shook his head no.

"I think I'll just let you go with a warning this time. How does that sound? But you really should slow down a bit, okay?"

Carl was shocked. Just a warning?! No fine for going sixty-seven miles per hour over the limit?! "Yeah, sure will! I don't know what I was thinking. I'll definitely slow it down!"

"Great!" beamed the deputy. "Hey, by any chance, could you swing some Packer-Viking tickets for me? In Minneapolis or at Lambeau Field, either one is fine with me!"

Carl saw where this was going and didn't want to upset the officer. He figured Molly could find seats for those games, so he said, "Yes, sure can. If you write down your name and address for me, I'll put two tickets in the mail for you."

"I have a better idea. How about you and me meet down at the Smilin' Moose bar in Hudson for a beer sometime? You can give me the tickets then, and I'll introduce you to some of my cop buddies."

Carl didn't want to, but he also didn't want to offend the man who just let him off of a major traffic offense scot-free. "Yep, that sounds perfect. What's your name?"

"Bruce Merriman." Carl snickered, then Bruce asked, "What's so funny?"

"Oh nothing, sorry! No offense, Bruce. I was just thinking that my wife's stepfather's name is Merriman, that's all. Nothing funny, so I'm not sure why I laughed. I'm sure there's a lot of Merrimans around here."

Bruce lowered his head and muttered quietly, "Wish I wasn't a damn Merriman."

"Why not?"

"Dad left my mom and me when I was six. Haven't seen or heard from him since. Guess he owns a few high-class restaurants that are doing really well, but he hasn't given us a cent. Quite a jerk if you ask me."

Carl thought about it for a moment but didn't say anything. With legions of peculiar events happening in his life, could it be possible that Bruce Merriman's father was Burt Merriman? If so, that would make his new deputy friend Molly's stepbrother.

What were the chances of that?

*****

Dawn was breaking over the eastern skies as Carl pulled into the parking lot at Woodlawn Cliffs Rest Home. He was exhausted. He had only a few hours of quality sleep since returning from Florida two days ago, and his mind was a wreck. Carl inclined the driver's seat to its max to take a thirty-minute nap. A young gal wearing a nurse's uniform tapped on the window and woke him up. His watch read high noon.

"Sir, please open your window," yelled the girl as her fist continued to pound on the glass.

Carl opened the window and uttered groggily, "Oh, hi. Is there something wrong?"

"No, sir. I mean, yes, sir, there is. You're not allowed to sleep in this parking lot. A resident's daughter saw you out here when she came to visit and was afraid that you might be dangerous."

"Oh, sorry! I really am sorry. I arrived early and hadn't had much sleep, so I must have dozed off. I'm here to speak to an administrator."

"Well, okay then. Come with me, and I'll introduce you to Linda Schultz. She runs this place."

"Thanks!" Carl followed the nurse into the building and to Linda's office. Most of the residents were eating lunch in the dining area centrally located in a glass-covered atrium. Many stopped and stared at Carl when he entered. They all wondered who in the rest home raised this terrific specimen of a man.

Carl sat in a comfortable chair inside a beautifully decorated office. Linda Schultz wanted to impress prospective residents' families to sign on the dotted line before leaving the property. The building itself was perched on a cliff overlooking the St. Croix River, an added attraction. Five wings radiated off the atrium: senior center, memory care, assisted living, skilled nursing care, and hospice. The facility was a perfect option for those nearing the end of life—as long as they had the money to afford the luxury. It wasn't cheap!

Linda walked up to Carl with a broad smile and firmly shook his hand. "My name is Linda Schultz. How may I help you? Are you looking for a home for a parent or a grandparent? You've come to the right place, I guarantee it!"

Carl smiled back, then shook his head. "My name is Carl West. Sorry, Ms. Schultz. I'm here inquiring about a resident of yours who recently died." Linda's smile vanished. This wasn't going to be a sale. "I write obituaries for the Eau Claire Gazette."

"Newspapers actually hire people to write obituaries?" asked Linda sarcastically. "I thought loved ones did that. Even I write obits for our residents who don't have family members around. Sounds like you've got a job made in heaven!"

Carl couldn't argue her point, nor could he defend his own career. He had no idea why the Gazette needed him! "Yes, I believe I do. Anyway, I'm inquiring about Joy Smith, who passed away last July."

Linda giggled and grinned, and Carl was baffled why she would think a person's death was funny.

"Joy Smith isn't dead," stated Linda. "In fact, she's having lunch in the dining room as we speak."

Carl's mouth dropped open, and he couldn't think of a reply. He pulled Joy's obituary out of his pants pocket and handed it to Linda. As she read it, a scowl formed on her face.

"Well, all I can say is that you and your newspaper have made a culpable mistake! I hope you have good lawyers!"

"I didn't write it," responded Carl defensively. "However, the Gazette published it. Sam Diggins wrote the obituary. He's the assistant funeral director at Holmes Mortuary here in Hudson."

"There's no Holmes Mortuary in Hudson or anywhere else around this area. So, even if Joy had died, and I assure you she hasn't, we would never have sent her body there."

Carl waited a moment for Linda to cool down. "I know that there is no Holmes Mortuary in the Hudson area. I just wanted to hear what you would say and how you would react to the obituary. I didn't know Joy was still alive. That's a shock to me, it really is! I was hoping you could lead me to Sam Diggins and Holmes Mortuary, but now it appears that there is more to this story. I need to do some more investigating!"

"And if you're smart, you better prepare a retraction for the newspaper. And you better hope that Joy's husband doesn't' read it. He has enough money to hire the best legal team around! He would put the Gazette out of business!"

Carl was astounded. "Wait a minute, are you saying that Joy has a husband who is still alive?! According to her obit Sam Diggins wrote, she was never married."

Linda shook her head and stared into Carl's eyes. How could this seemingly intelligent, good-looking man be so ignorant? "Carl, there are several items in your version of Joy's biography that are incorrect. Yes, she has a husband. And she has four children who are scattered around the United States. But she doesn't have a sister, nor does she have any sibling or relative that lives anywhere close to Denver, Colorado. And lastly, she never graduated from the University of Wisconsin-Green Bay. In fact, she never went to college!"

*****

"Well, that meeting didn't exactly go as planned," thought Carl as he opened the door to his Tesla. "Now what?"

Linda wouldn't allow Carl to speak to Joy, and quite frankly, Carl had no desire to chat with the elderly lady after his conversation with Ms. Schultz. He needed to find Sam Diggins but didn't know where to start. It certainly wouldn't be at the fictitious Holmes Mortuary!

As he started the car, Carl noticed an unread text on his iPhone sent at 6:00 a.m. It contained three simple words—and four dreaded exclamation marks: ***Where are you?!!!!***

In frustration, Carl slapped his temples with his open hands. How could he have forgotten to leave a note for Molly letting her know where he was going? Sleep deprivation, anxiety, and confusion were becoming lethal to his marriage.

Carl glanced at his watch. It was 1:00 p.m. He would stop at a florist and buy a dozen roses, then drive to the Twin Cities and surprise Molly at work. Roasted seafood dinner with wine at Martina's, and she wouldn't even remember why she was mad at him!

Carl had a few hours to kill before heading to Minneapolis. He was halfway between St. Paul and New Richmond, so going back to his office made no sense. To clear his mind from all its troubles, Carl drove to Lakefront Park for a scenic stroll along the St. Croix River and the Hudson pier. He sat on a park bench and gazed out at the luxurious sailboats adrift in the autumn wind. Soon ice would be forming, and the boats would be dry-docked until the following April.

Carl had forgotten about Jim Bowman for the moment. His mind was now focused on Holmes Mortuary and Sam Diggins—a fake funeral parlor run by a fake assistant director. What was up with that?!

Then a thought occurred—Wally Roseberg and Joy Smith shared something in common. Both had obituaries published in the Gazette, yet, neither had died. What were the chances that this was merely a coincidence? Both biographies were sent to Carl on his private Rankins's email account. Was there something to that, as well? Carl wrote a note to himself to compare Wally's and Joy's obituaries when he got back to the office.

Then miraculously, Carl's anxiety suddenly shut down. His mind switched to thoughts of Molly. Carl Googled "florists near me" on his iPhone and found one within walking distance only a few blocks away. He stood up and inhaled a deep breath of fresh air, then exhaled slowly. The riverside walk had provided a mild attitude adjustment that swayed towards a positive outlook on life. Carl looked up at the blue sky painted with puffy white clouds and smiled as a flock of geese cruised by in their symbolic V-formation. They were migrating south to spend the winter in Florida or Arizona. Soon, flocks of retired snowbirds in expensive motorhomes would be following them down Interstate 35 and 65.

Next door to the Hudson Flower Shop was Knoke's Chocolate and Nuts. Carl popped in and bought his wife a box of St. Croix Critters, a Western Wisconsin treat loaded with delicious caramel-coated pecans smothered in dark chocolate. Then he meandered into the flower shop and purchased two dozen roses instead of just one. This was turning into a great day!

Alas, Carl's newfound exhilaration would soon diminish.

Chapter 22

Molly was assigned two reserved parking spots in the SP Plus lot behind the Dispatch headquarters in Minneapolis. Because she was a writer who frequently interviewed sports personalities in her office, the Dispatch didn't want celebrities to be required to search for parking when they were visiting. You simply punched a code into the receptacle to enter the lot, which could be traced back to the Dispatch employee if necessary. Molly had eagerly given Carl the six-digit number, hoping he would stop by and see her occasionally on his days off.

A white Toyota Land Cruiser with deeply tinted windows was parked in Molly's guest spot when Carl arrived. No problem; she must be interviewing someone famous in the Vikings' organization. Maybe it was Head Coach Mike Zimmer. He and Carl's dad became friends in a very unusual way while Mike was the Dallas Cowboys' defensive coordinator. They met for the first time after Billy West made perhaps the worst game decision of his career. Playing in Texas Stadium in late November of 2002, the Jacksonville Jaguars were leading the Dallas Cowboys by a score of nineteen to fourteen with less than three minutes to go. The Jags had the football, a first down at the fifty-yard line, and a ton of momentum heading into the final minutes of the game. Dallas had only one time out and the two-minute warning to work with in regulation. Jacksonville Head Coach Tom Coughlin chose to eat up the clock by running the football.

Fred Taylor rushed for six yards on the first play from scrimmage, and Dallas used their final timeout. Taylor then ran the ball up the gut for three yards, and the clock stopped at the two-minute warning. Taylor had gained 158 yards that afternoon and was virtually unstoppable, so Coughlin called for one last running play to end the game with a first down. If Taylor didn't get the one yard he needed, the clock would run down to about a minute, and a good punt could pin the Cowboys inside their ten-yard line with no time outs remaining. The call was a no-brainer!

Following the two-minute warning, Billy West lined up under center and scanned the defense. Dallas shifted to fill the gaps and brought their cornerbacks and safety into linebacker positions. Billy was confident he read a run blitz coming by the Cowboys' defense, so he stepped back and called an audible. Instead of giving the ball to Taylor, Billy faked a handoff, rolled left, and looked for wide receiver Jimmy "Lightning" Smith to be sprinting unnoticed towards the end zone. But Dallas had only simulated a run blitz, guessing West might read it and do just what he had done. Smith was covered, so Billy tried to run the ball himself from ten yards behind the scrimmage line but failed miserably. As he squirmed from the grasp of defensive end Peppi Zellner, Billy was blindsided by linebacker Dexter Coakley and fumbled the ball. Mario Edwards picked up the pigskin and ran it back 47 yards for a Dallas touchdown. The Cowboys were victorious, and their fans were delirious! Tom Coughlin stood on the sidelines with his hands on his hips and glared at his all-star quarterback. Billy knew he messed up, so Tom didn't need to add insult to injury with a rhetorical comment.

Billy apologized to his coaches and teammates in the locker room. "You boys didn't deserve to lose, and you didn't. This one's on me, fellas. My bad, but I promise I'll make it up to you!"

Then Billy did something unprecedented in professional sports. He went to the Cowboy's locker room and asked to see Defensive Coordinator Mike Zimmer. With a sincere voice, Billy smiled and shook his hand.

"I want to commend you, Coach Zimmer, on your playcalling today! Your defensive strategies were excellent, and your preparation was top-notch! Hat's off to you and your players. Excellent coaching, sir!"

And that was the beginning of a lifelong friendship, albeit from a distance. Billy and Mike phoned each other frequently and met up now and then for a golf outing during the offseason. Unfortunately, Carl never got the chance to meet Mike. Perhaps today would be his lucky day. Could it be Coach Zimmer is the owner of the Land Cruiser parked next to Molly? Carl hoped Mike was the celebrity who Molly was interviewing.

Carl parked the Tesla a few feet away in a loading zone. If he got a ticket, well, so be it. Carl left the chocolates in the car because he needed both hands to carry the flowers and the crystal vase into the building. He was excited to surprise Molly and make up for all of his un-newlywed actions of the past week. The flowers would be conciliatory, the dinner at Martina's would be majestic, and the chocolates would be the icing on the cake!

Carl's grandiose love plan ended when he walked past Molly's car, glanced at the Land Cruiser, and then did a double-take. Goosebumps covered his body, and the crystal vase and beautiful arrangement of roses accidentally slipped out of his hands, shattering glass all over the cement parking lot. Carl's mouth opened wide as he gawked at the words stenciled in small letters on the back gate of the Land Cruiser:

Holmes Mortuary

Carl's eyes moved slightly downward and focused on the license that was affixed just below Holmes Mortuary. It was an Alaskan plate. There were no numbers, merely letters. But those letters made Carl's body go numb:

Diggins

*****

Carl left the flowers and broken glass in a mess on the concrete, then sprinted to the Dispatch's private entrance for employees and VIPs. The security guard knew he was Molly's husband and let him in without question. Carl entered Molly's office, sat down, and nervously jittered his legs. Molly's secretary saw him and followed him into the room.

"Hi Carl," said Jan Willows politely. "How are you? Molly is in a meeting with her boss and a client but should be out shortly."

Carl was desperate for answers. Perhaps Jan could help. In his sweetest voice, Carl asked, "Oh, that's no problem. Who is she meeting with?"

Jan smiled and winked, "Well, I'm not supposed to tell you, but I'm sure Molly will let you know when she gets home, so I might as well spill the beans. Do you promise not to tell her that I told you?"

Carl nodded and returned the smile. "Of course not! I'm a champion at keeping a secret, you know!"

"Well, okay. He's an investor who is looking to buy the Minnesota Vikings. Can you believe that?"

Carl was astounded. "Are you saying that Zygi Wilf is looking to sell?!"

"Well, he wasn't. But from what I understand, this investor guy is offering double what the Vikings are worth. Hard to say no to that, right?" A ringing could be heard from Jan's desk in the lobby. "Oh, that's my phone. Got to go! Nice to see you again, Carl!"

Carl didn't respond. He was becoming more agitated by the minute. His weary and worn out mind was ready to explode. Why did Sam Diggins email a fake obituary for a lady who was very much alive and well?! And why did he say that Holmes Mortuary was the funeral home handling the arrangements when there were no Holmes Mortuaries within several hundred miles of Hudson? Why is he pretending to be an assistant funeral director? Is Sam Diggins his real name?! The guy had to be involved in illegal gaming with Jim Bowman—there was no doubt about it! But again, why did he submit a fake obituary to the Gazette? What was the purpose of that?!

Molly was going to break the news to the Vikings' fans that a man named Sam Diggins would be buying the franchise. Carl needed to tell his wife that Diggins was an imposter before she embarrassed herself and the Dispatch. But, could he rationalize his theories to

Molly about Sam and illegal gaming in a way that didn't sound unhinged?

A few minutes later, Molly walked to her office with a tall, good-looking black-haired man, probably in his mid-forties, wearing a gray Kiton herringbone two-piece suit. He was definitely dressed for success. A pang of jealously ripped through Carl's already fragile emotional state. He stood up quickly when Molly entered the room.

"Oh, hi, Carl," voiced Molly with a subtle tone. She was still upset he was gone when she woke up this morning and left without a note. But she didn't want to cause a scene with her guest standing next to her."What are you doing here, Babe?"

Carl looked at the visitor and then back at Molly. Now wasn't the time to apologize while the man could hear every word. "Well, I was just in the area and thought I'd stop by," replied Carl unconvincingly. Molly and her guest could both tell he was lying.

Molly took control. "Sam, I would like you to meet my husband, Carl West. Carl, this is Sam Diggins. He's here for an interview." Sam beamed with an air of confidence, stepped forward, and reached out his arm for a handshake. Carl wasn't going to be outdone with a lack of self-assurance. He gripped Sam's hand, squeezed hard, and smiled back. He hoped he was inflicting severe pain!

"And very nice to meet you, too, Mr. Diggins." Carl held on tightly for a few awkward seconds, then let go. Then Carl decided it was now or never. "Haven't I met you before? Your name sounds quite familiar."

"Please call me Sam. No, I don't believe we've met. However, I knew your father very well."

Carl opened his mouth to respond, but nothing came out. He was overcome with stunned muteness! How the hell could Sam Diggins, who poses as a fake assistant funeral director from a fake mortuary, possibly know his dad?! Should he tell Molly about this guy? But then again, Molly didn't even look surprised that Sam Diggins knew Billy West.

Carl decided that it was time to probe. "So, you were friends with my father? Where did you meet him?"

"No, Carl, I didn't say we were friends. Just acquaintances, that's all."

"Oh, sorry. I thought you said you knew him 'very' well. I was assuming you were friends. So, are you a friend of a friend of his? How did you meet him?"

Molly glared at Carl with eyes that pierced right through his body. This conversation was no longer just chitchat. She could tell by his tone that Carl was grilling Sam. Was he jealous? Molly needed to end the discussion before it got out of hand.

"Excuse me, Carl, but I need to get on with Sam's interview. I'm sure he has a busy schedule. Do you think you could wait for me in the lobby?" If looks could kill, Carl was a dead man!

Carl got the hint, but he wasn't finished with Sam Diggins. "Oh, yes, for sure! I just got carried away, that's all!" He smiled and shook hands again, then walked to the lobby. But instead of waiting there for Molly, Carl had other plans. He stepped over to the receptionist's desk and asked if she would leave a message for his wife. He wanted to let her know he would see her at home. So much for his big night out at Martina's!

Carl hustled down to the parking lot and was surprised to see a garage maintenance crew cleaning up the broken glass and flowers. Wow, that was fast! He tried to play dumb, but it didn't work so well.

"Hi, gentlemen," said Carl. "You've got quite the mess on your hands."

"I guess you should know, dude. You're the one who made it!"

Carl was flabbergasted. How did they know it was him? Well, there was no use denying it. "So, how did you know it was me?"

"Security cameras everywhere," replied the apparent leader of the three. "How did you think we knew?"

Carl looked up and noticed video devices attached to the rafters every one hundred feet. "Yep, that makes sense. Hey, I'm sorry I didn't clean up. I was in a big hurry at the time. I'd be happy to help you now, though."

The crew leader laughed. "No problem, dude. This is our job. It's what we get paid to do. You seem like a nice guy. The man who got out of the Land Cruiser was nasty, though."

Carl perked up. "Oh yeah, in what way?"

"He was on his cell phone yelling at someone when he got out of the car. Got so mad he threw the phone to the other end of the parking lot, then just left it there! We were watching the security footage at the time, but we couldn't hear what he was saying. Anyway, we picked it up and dropped it into our lost and found box. Figured he would come back and get it when he was done doing whatever he was doing."

"Say, you know something—I know that dude pretty well. I'll be seeing him shortly. Can you give me the phone, and I'll make sure he gets it?" Carl's mind was spinning with sinister thoughts. If he could get a hold of Sam Diggins's phone, perhaps he could see who the man calls or what websites he visits. But he was doubtful the crew leader would give it to him. He was wrong.

"Okay, I guess there's no problem with that, seeing you all know each other. Hey, I'm sorry I called your friend nasty. I didn't mean no judgment, you know. He was probably just having a bad day or something."

"Aw, don't sweat it, my friend," said Carl, playing up to the crew leader. "You're right. Knowing him as I do, he can get a little testy when he's stressed out. So I'm sure he was having a bad day."

The maintenance workers, who doubled as parking lot security, swept the glass and flowers into a cardboard box, then headed for their tiny office. The crew leader handed Carl the phone. Carl thanked him and hustled to his car. He had no plans to give Sam the phone, so he hoped the maintenance workers would not be watching on camera and wonder why he didn't return it.

Carl sat in the driver's seat of his Tesla and looked closely at Sam's phone, then tossed it in the passenger seat and pounded his fists on the steering wheel. "It's a dang burner!" exclaimed Carl to precisely no one. He still had the weird habit of talking to himself.

"There's no Internet access and no contacts! What am I supposed to do with that worthless thing?!"

Carl decided to follow Sam Diggins instead of confronting him. He exited the lot, crossed Second Avenue, and pulled into the Northstar Hotel's dropoff area. He explained to the bellman that he was picking up a hotel guest, and the bellman gave him the thumbs-up sign—it was okay to park there for a few minutes. Fourteen minutes later, Sam Diggins strutted out of the SP Plus parking lot and onto the sidewalk. Carl never anticipated that Sam would be walking!

Carl pulled a hundred-dollar bill out of his billfold and hurried to the bellman. He wrapped the money around his key fob and offered it to the attendant in exchange for letting him park there for an hour. The overjoyed porter gladly accepted the cash and remarked, "Yes, sir, of course! Stay two hours, if you like!"

Carl watched as Sam turned the corner onto Seventh Street. He jogged lightly to catch up, then kept an even pace several yards behind him. Sam sauntered a block to Marquette Avenue, turned right onto Eighth Street, then entered the IDS Center. The fifty-seven-story building was the trademark of the Minneapolis skyline.

Sam walked briskly to the elevators. Carl didn't dare follow because Sam would recognize him and wonder what he was doing. Carl stepped back and watched the digital readout above the doors. The elevator stopped on floors eighteen, twenty-six, twenty-seven, and forty-one.

Carl trotted to the corporate listing chart on the wall. Bank of America and a small investment firm were the only companies on the eighteenth floor. Charles Schwab rented both the twenty-sixth and twenty-seventh floors. A company named SOTO appeared to have leased the entire forty-first floor. Knowing Sam would need a large sum of money if he were going to buy the Vikings, Carl guessed that Diggins was either going to the bank on the eighteenth floor or visiting Charles Schwab to check on his investments. Carl decided to start with the bank.

The IDS Center's Bank of America was a full-service financial establishment. There were departments for mortgages, investments, savings, loans, and commercial banking. Carl searched every possible location inside the bank but did not see Sam anywhere. He quickly exited and headed back to the elevators. Next, he would try Charles Schwab.

The reception area was on the twenty-sixth floor, where an attractive young lady greeted customers. Carl guessed she was right out of high school, or close to it. He was hoping she might make a rookie mistake.

"Hi, my name is Larry Smith," said Carl with a straight face. "I'm an attorney who represents Sam Diggins. We're here for a meeting, and I was wondering if Sam had shown up yet. Would you be so kind as to check for me?"

Not wanting to mess with a lawyer, the receptionist glanced at her sign-in sheet. "No, sir, it doesn't look like a Sam Diggins has come in. Would you like to wait for him?"

"Is there any chance he may have gotten off the elevator on the twenty-seventh floor?"

"Oh, no sir, absolutely not. That is a private entrance. A security guard would have directed him back down here."

"Okay, thanks. I think I'll run down to Starbucks and grab a cup of coffee. I'll be back."

The receptionist smiled and nodded. "I will tell Mr. Diggins where you are."

Carl simpered, waved, and headed back to the elevator. Sam must be on the forty-first floor. SOTO was the company name. What could that acronym stand for? Carl had never heard of it. He pushed the up button outside the elevator door.

Carl was greeted by a tall, gray-haired, elderly security guard wearing a holster with a small revolver tucked inside. He needed to think quickly. Whatever SOTO was, why did they need an armed guard? A little white lie worked with the Charles Schwab receptionist; perhaps another would work with this man.

"Hi! My name is John Diggins. I'm Sam's brother. He forgot his cell phone in the car, and I know he needs it. Any chance I could run it to him. I'll be back in a minute—promise!"

"Yeah, sure, what the heck. I wouldn't want Sam to be upset with me!" The guard pointed down the hallway. "He's down in Fornasiere's office, third one on the left."

Carl couldn't believe his luck. "Hey, thanks! I'll let my brother know you're a good man!"

"Thanks, John. Take your time. They'll probably be in there for a while. Rob Fornasiere usually burns the midnight oil. He's a workaholic!"

Carl ambled down the hallway, trying to figure out what SOTO stood for. The logo was pasted on every wall, but he didn't know what the letters meant. Clearly, Sam Diggins, who poses as an assistant funeral director, was a VIP here. But how could that be?! His license plate said he was from Alaska! As he neared Fornasiere's office, Carl knew the next step was critical. He could feel the security guard's eyes watching him. How could he talk his way into Fornasiere's office? Once again, he would need to improvise!

Carl knocked and waited a few anxious seconds that seemed like an hour. Rob Fornasiere opened the door and gave a puzzled look at Carl. "May I help you?" bemused Fornasiere. "Who are you?"

Before Carl had a chance to respond, a voice inside Fornasiere's office did it for him. "Well, Rob, that man standing in front of you is none other than the son of the greatest quarterback who ever played the game!"

Chapter 23

WMIA news anchor, Drew Cullens, tried not to appear giddy while on the air, but he certainly felt rapturous inside when he kicked off the six o'clock news segment with words no fans in the sports world wanted to hear:

> *"Good evening. Today is Thursday, September 17th, 2020. I'm your host, Drew Cullens.*
>
> *"Our top story comes from right here in sunny Miami, and more specifically, right here in our WMIA corporate headquarters. Earlier today, the United States District Court for the Southern District of Florida dismissed the most substantial civil lawsuit in history involving a sports personality. Sydney West, owner of the Reno Mountaineers NFL franchise, had sued WMIA for damages amounting to $500,000,000 in the wrongful death case involving his son, Hall of Famer Billy West, and his daughter-in-law Carol.*
>
> *"After nearly five years of investigations, the FAA and the FBI determined the camera drone that caused the accident when it struck a Yellow Cab taxi's windshield following the conclusion of the 2015 Super Bowl was not owned by Miami's flagship television station. According to expert testimony, the serial number registered to WMIA*

had been forged on a metal plate and attached to the pilotless aircraft. The FBI has now initiated a criminal investigation to determine who was remotely flying the drone. However, I need to reiterate that WMLA did not own the aircraft, nor did a reporter or any other employee of WMLA fly the drone.

"Sydney West disagrees with the ruling, stating there is no proof the serial number was forged, and the preponderance of evidence still points to WMLA ownership of the drone. He plans to appeal the outcome.

"In other news . . ."

*****

"I know Syd West," said Wally Roseberg as he clicked off the remote control for the twenty-seven-inch television in Randy Hansen's office. "Right now, he must be in the beginning phases of throwing a two-month temper tantrum!"

"He can take his temper tantrum to the grave for all I care," replied Randy. "Let the devil deal with that cocky ambulance chaser for a few years, like eternity, perhaps!"

"You realize every NFL fan is on his side, don't you? I mean, he is the father of their fallen hero."

"Yeah, right." Randy shuffled some drawings around on his desk while Wally checked his iPhone messages. Changing the subject, Randy yawned and uttered, "It's been a long day, and I need some rest. What's the plan now? The house is in the final phase. All that's left is an aesthetic touchup."

"Could you slow that down so we make sure we have everything right?"

"You understand, Wally, that our client is building a 100,000-square foot home on his own private island in the Caymans, and he didn't blink an eye at the $600 per square foot cost. Our fee is $6 million. Let's complete this project, and I'll take you to dinner at NAOE."

Wally chuckled. He could see where Randy was going with this. "I didn't know you were into Japanese food." Then he paused and put on a straight face. "Okay, one more trip should do it for me. The house will require two to four hours, but his private airport control tower might need a couple of days to complete. I wish he wasn't living in the guest house. Things would be simpler if he wasn't around. When is he leaving for Vegas?"

"I think he said tomorrow."

"I'll take the Learjet and try to finish up by Sunday night."

"You want my pilot, or are you going to fly it yourself?"

"Hey, I got my pilot's license so I could mix a little business with pleasure, Randy. So, of course, I'm definitely flying your baby to the Caymans!"

"How long did it take you to certify to fly a Learjet anyway? I'm thinking about getting certified myself."

Wally laughed. "Why don't you start with a single-engine plane like a Cessna? I've ridden with you at warp speed down I-95 in your Vette. I'd hate to think how tight I would need to buckle up in a Learjet flown by you!"

"Funny man." Randy stacked his papers and drawings neatly on his desk, then headed for the door. "Well, I'm out of here."

*****

"I'm taking the InterPlan Learjet to Vegas in a few minutes," said Wally into his iPhone. "I need to make sure Randy doesn't catch wind of the flight plan. After Vegas, I'll be heading to the Caymans."

"What about Carl?" asked the voice on the other end of the line. What have you found out?"

"It appears everything is as you believe, but I will need to meet with him soon."

"What's taking so long?! I want this to end!"

"We all do," responded Wally. "I'm pulling into Palm Beach International, so I've got to go. Make sure you expunge the burner."

"Give me a break! I know the routine."

The voice ended the call, ripped out the SIM card, and pounded the casing with a hammer. He walked out to the backyard and tossed the smashed burner phone into a hole he had dug and re-dug many times. Then, he covered it with dirt along with the other fifty-four previously destroyed phones.

Chapter 24

"I want in," exclaimed Carl in his best self-assured voice. He never enrolled in drama classes, nor had he ever dreamed of being an actor. But now, he was delivering an extempore speech to two men whom he considered extremely dangerous. Failure could mean his life.

Sitting at a quiet table in the Capitol Grille, Carl, Rob Fornasiere, and Sam Diggins were drinking a $6,000 bottle of Chateau Petrus Pomerol red wine from the Bordeaux region of southern France. They had walked two blocks from the IDS Center to the expensive Hennepin Avenue restaurant shortly after Carl had introduced himself to Rob and reintroduced himself to Sam Diggins. Sam couldn't forget Carl's impertinence during their brief yet agitated encounter in Molly's office. His hand was still aching from Carl's powerful handshake!

When Rob had opened the door to see who was knocking, Carl had to think fast. He had followed Sam Diggins to learn more about the man pretending to be an assistant funeral director who was now planning on purchasing the Minnesota Vikings. Carl was sure Sam was somehow involved in fixing NFL games, but he had no idea how he did it. Why was Diggins at a company named SOTO?

Then, as if a bolt of lightning struck Carl in the brain, he finally understood the connection between Sam and SOTO. On the wall behind Rob's desk was an enlarged logo of SOTO with the acronym spelled out next to it: Sports Officials Training Organization. Carl had heard of that corporation but never gave it much thought, which was why he couldn't remember what the acronym stood for earlier. Rob Fornasiere was the director of a company that trained referees and umpires, then placed them in professional and collegiate sports contests. Carl was sure that Rob's biggest client was the National

Football League, but he assumed that Rob also acted as an agent for other sports. Reflecting upon the illegal gaming operation, Carl guessed that SOTO was training the corrupt officials. Was Sam Diggins in cahoots with them? Realizing that professional sports fixing of this magnitude could only be accomplished from a highly-organized crime syndicate, he was now walking on eggshells.

Thinking quickly, Carl said he had a business proposition for Sam Diggins, which was why he had followed him to the IDS Center. Lying prodigiously, he explained that he had been working with lawyers and accountants in the hopes of purchasing the Minnesota Vikings when he found out from Molly's secretary that Sam was ready to make an offer to Zygi Wilf. That was the reason for his irritability when he first met him in Molly's office. Sam's face showed signs of skepticism, but Carl thought he might be buying the story.

It was Rob who suggested moving the discussion to the Capitol Grille. Carl wasn't sure how things would play out. He mused that with a quality performance, he could convince Sam his lies were genuine. But to fool both Rob and Sam into believing his pretense, well, that might prove to be extraordinarily arduous for a rookie Thespian! Enter the bottle of Chateau Petrus Pomerol—center stage!

Carl told Rob and Sam the dinner was on him. He waved the waiter over to the table and asked for the most expensive red wine in the house. Carl presumed the luxury might cost him around sixty dollars. Needless to say, he had no concept of the value of vin cher! Fortunately, his father left him a great deal of wealth.

"So, let's get right down to the point," said Sam matter-of-factly. "What exactly is your so-called business proposition?"

"I want in," replied Carl. "I would like to partner with you in your quest to purchase the Minnesota Vikings. It's a dream of mine to own a professional sports team, and now that Molly is working in the Twin Cities, the Vikes seem like the likely team to target."

Rob and Sam glanced at each other and took another sip of wine. Neither said a word. Carl's anxiety level hit the roof, but he wasn't going to say more until Sam replied. His thoughts were scrambled and contradictory, but what was driving him crazy was Rob's presence at this meeting. Why was he here? Why did he tag along when he knew the discussion was going to be about buying the Vikings? Yes, he was the person responsible for training crooked referees and placing them in NFL games, presumably at Sam's request, but why would he risk being part of this type of transaction? If the NFL suspected Rob was pursuing a financial interest in one of their teams, that would constitute a significant conflict, and his contract would be terminated! The maître d and waiters all seemed to know both Sam and Rob superlatively, and someone would likely say something about seeing them together only a few days before the transfer of ownership was completed. If the word got out to the wrong person and the NFL found out, Rob's career could be in jeopardy.

"I already have a business plan, Carl, and unfortunately, you're not part of it." Sam smiled sarcastically at Carl, and Rob just dropped his head. Sam's reply was rude, and Carl could tell Rob agreed. But he didn't care. Carl didn't want to purchase the Vikings anyway. This was all just a ruse. However, if he gave in too easily, his deception might be unraveled.

Carl decided to proceed with more formality. "I'm sure you do have a strategy for success, Mr. Diggins. But don't you think if the son of Billy West were a major investor, your marketing plan would be enhanced, and your profits skyrocket?"

"He's got a point, Sam," interjected Rob. Carl was dumbstruck that Rob even spoke.

"What's your offer?" asked Sam.

Oh, oh. Carl had no idea what the Vikings were worth. He needed to be spot on with his proffer, or Sam would know Carl hadn't done his homework. And that could blow everything and put him in a precarious position. He had read Zygi Wilf was a billionaire, so he guessed the team's value was somewhere in the billions.

"I can invest one billion," fibbed Carl. "What share of the partnership would that get me?"

Rob and Sam glanced at each other once again. Rob nodded, and Sam smiled. Carl couldn't read their faces. What were they thinking? Why was Rob acting like he was part of this investment? Now he needed a strategy for backing away if, by chance, Sam accepted his offer.

"How do you plan to come up with a billion dollars?" asked Sam cynically. "I know your dad made millions, but I doubt that he reached the billion level."

"Let's just say we have plenty of money in the family and leave it at that!" Carl pretended to be offended by Sam's remark. But now was the time to make an exit plan. He wished he had more sleep this week to clear his mind. His brain was on overload!

There was another long and tense moment of silence. Finally, Sam spoke up. "We need a day or two to think about your offer. Could I get your cell phone number? We'll call you as soon as we've made a decision."

"We? We'll? We've?" This was Carl's chance. Before he left, he wanted answers. That was the purpose of this charade. "Is Mr. Fornasiere an investor, too? Is that not a conflict of interest seeing he acts as an agent for the NFL?"

Sam realized he had made a slip of the tongue. "Yes, you're right. I didn't mean to use a plural pronoun—please forgive me. Rob is just a close friend who I use to seek advice, that's all. He's not going to be an investor."

It was Carl who paused this time. Thus far, his lies had worked. Sam and Rob believed Carl's story about going in with them on the Vikings' deal. But he still didn't know why Sam emailed fake obits for him to publish. Based on everything discussed, he guessed Sam had no idea Carl was the obituary writer for the Gazette. Molly must not have told him, nor did George Markins, the man who hired him. Sam probably didn't care who submitted the fake eulogies to the editor, just as long as they were published. Or did he know and was just toying with him? But what was the purpose of the damn obits anyway?!

Carl tried to shake off the contradictory thoughts but was unsuccessful. His mind was traveling through a maze, and he had difficulty focusing on the purpose of the meeting. Sam must have known Jim Bowman was dead, right? But what had Jim done that got him killed? Or was his death self-induced? There's no evidence that Sam had anything to do with the poisoning, right? Regardless, he clearly hadn't found out Carl had replaced Jim.

Now was the time to call the FBI and let them take over from here. First, Carl needed to retract his offer, and he had an idea. With an air of confidence he inherited from his father, Carl stated, "One more thing must take place to seal this deal. I plan to be a hands-on owner. I want to assume the role of general manager. Are you good with that? If not, I'm afraid I will need to walk."

One last time, Rob and Sam glanced at each other. But now they weren't smirking. After another long pause, Sam declared, "Once again, we will need to talk about this. Please give me your cell number, and we'll call in a day or two."

That wasn't the response Carl desired. Now what? He reluctantly gave Sam his phone number, then Rob and Sam shook hands with him and departed.

When the waiter delivered the bill, Carl nearly passed out. He handed the man his credit card, then muttered to himself, "$6,000 for a bottle of wine! Are you kidding me?!"

*****

"Zygi won't take less than $4,000,000,000," stated Rob from his desk. He and Sam were back in his office at the IDS Center. Sam was pacing the room nervously. Ordinarily cool, calm, and collected, the anxiety flowing through his veins was new to him. "Why not take the billion and make Carl a one-quarter owner."

"That's not it!" shouted Sam. Rob waited for an explanation, but nothing more came.

"So, what's the problem?" asked Rob gently. "Are you opposed to letting him be the GM?"

"No, damn it!" Rob waited again, yet Sam added nothing. He lifted a coffee mug off a table and threw it against the wall, shattering the ceramic cup into hundreds of pieces and leaving a sizable dent in the drywall.

"Calm down, Sam," offered Rob softly. "What's bugging you?"

Rob Fornasiere was mild-mannered, intelligent, and knew how to handle difficult people with kid gloves. He had been the ace of the University of Minnesota baseball team for four years, compiling a forty-one and five won-loss record and sporting an ERA of 1.82. Rob was the top pitching prospect in the 1978 MLB draft until he suffered a severe rotator cuff injury in Omaha's final College World Series game that year. The relatively new Tommy John surgery was unsuccessful, ending Rob's career before it even began.

But Rob couldn't give up the thrill of sports. He set his sights on officiating, starting with high school football, volleyball, basketball, and baseball. His knack for remaining poised and levelheaded under pressure served him well.

In 1982, the Big Ten Conference hired him for basketball and football, and five years later, he was refereeing NFL games every Sunday. But the pay was minimal, considering Rob only worked once a week. He continued to ref college basketball and umpire baseball games on his off days to make ends meet.

Rob loved his jobs, but he didn't have a personal life. Between traveling and officiating, he worked twelve to fourteen hours each day. Facetime became the norm for keeping in touch with his wife, kids, and grandchildren. So in 2012, he decided it was time for a change.

Rob founded SOTO (the Sports Officials Training Organization) to train eager prospects who desired to referee or umpire at the college or professional level. His staff consisted of retired officials who, at one time, were the best in the business. The tuition was high, but so was the quality of skill training. He paid himself an average salary and was able to sleep at home every night.

Rob hit paydirt in 2014 when the NFL asked him to work as their agent in finding and placing first-rate officials. They offered him a six-figure contract in addition to what he brought home as the owner of SOTO. Rob was ecstatic! He was on top of the world!

Then he met "the boss."

Chapter 25

"If I knew what was bugging me, I'd tell you!" barked Sam. "Maybe it goes back to last July when I heard that Carl had taken over Jim Bowman's job at the Gazette, and his wife Molly had replaced Hugh Cicero at the Dispatch. No one told me, damn it! Sure, the boss can do as he pleases, but I don't appreciate people in our organization keeping information from me. And, to top it off, I had no idea that Jim Bowman was poisoned until two weeks after his death! Why wait so long to have him killed anyway?! Bowman screwed us way back in December! I thought the boss had changed his mind and let him live! A second chance or something like that!"

Rob was stunned. He thought Jim Bowman had died from cancer. But he wanted Sam to believe he knew about the poisoning, so he asked nonchalantly, "How did you find out that Jim died?"

"Well, thinking Jim was still our agent, I emailed him a note about an upcoming game. But I kept getting a message that my email never went through. So I snail-mailed him a note from Las Vegas, which, by the way, I never got back. Then George Markins tells me in July that Jim is dead and he found someone new! Wouldn't you think I would have been the first to know?!"

"I'm sure it just slipped through the cracks. Don't sweat it. But that has nothing to do with our dinner with Carl. What else is bothering you?"

"Something is not Kosher about our meeting with Carl. Somehow I get the feeling he understands more than he's telling. Do you think he may know about our operation?"

Rob shuffled to a small bar in his office between two bookshelves and pulled out a bottle of Johnnie Walker Blue Label.

He scooped two ice cubes into a tumbler, splashed in the rare malt whiskey, then handed it to his friend.

"Relax, Sam. If he knew anything about you, he would have brought it up. I believe he does want to purchase the Vikes. Carl's the son of perhaps the greatest athlete of modern times. He's been surrounded by football his entire life. And his grandfather owns a highly successful and very profitable sports marketing company. I can see why Carl is longing to own an NFL team, and even though he's just a part-time obituary writer, I'm sure he has access to the funds. His inheritance had to be quite hefty."

Sam quaffed a long sip of whiskey, then nodded his head. He took a deep breath and began to unwind. Lifting his glass in a semi-toast, Sam announced, "Perhaps psychologists should be prescribing Johnnie Walker for anxiety instead of all those blasted drugs! But anyway, you're right. I'm over-reacting, aren't I? I'm sure Carl has a ton of connections that could help us."

"And if we make him GM, that could be an added benefit."

"I wonder if Molly has any idea what he is planning. If she does, she sure didn't show her cards today at the Dispatch."

"A good reporter never shows her cards, you know." Rob poured Sam another glass of whiskey, which he gulped down with no degree of elegance.

"Speaking of the Dispatch, I left my car in their parking lot, so I need to get moving."

"Do you want a ride?" offered Rob.

"No, thanks. It's only a couple of blocks, and the fresh air will do me good."

As soon as Sam was gone, Rob sent his wife a text: "Be home soon. Keep the doors locked, and I'll come in through the garage."

*****

"Sleep in the car!" shouted Molly angrily as she pointed to the driveway. She had been nervously waiting for Carl, upset with herself that she was terse with him earlier in the office. She was surprised he didn't wait for her in the lobby, but more shocked when he wasn't home when she got there. Had he been in an accident?

When Molly heard the car out front, she hastened to the door to greet him. But as soon as she caught a whiff of wine on his breath, she was over the edge. Her malaise had turned to vexation!

"Wait a minute," pleaded Carl. "I can explain."

"What's there to explain? You left my office without telling me; then it appears you decided to go bar hopping instead of waiting for me. And just so you know who it was you were rudely grilling, his name is Sam Diggins. He will most likely be the next owner of the Minnesota Vikings! Some impression you left him with, huh?!"

Carl was in a no-win situation. He wasn't prepared to tell Molly he just had dinner with Sam Diggins and offered to be a partner in Sam's quest to purchase the Vikings. Carl knew he had to explain to Molly his anomalous behavior over the past week since he left for Florida. Still, he wasn't quite ready to connect the dots in a way she would believe he wasn't psychotic. Carl knew Molly would soon find out he made an offer to buy the Vikings. When that time came, she would figure out Carl had become entirely delusional.

He decided it was best to sleep in the car!

*****

Carl wondered if a human could die from insomnia. At 3:00 a.m., he gave into another restless night and snuck in the house for a shower and change of clothes. Molly was sound asleep. Carl was jealous.

He wasn't going to wait any longer. The FBI was open 24/7, and Carl decided it was time to finally make the call. Caribou Coffee would be closed, but the BP station on Somerset Road was a place one could purchase a cup of twelve-hour-old muddy java in the middle of the night. He was indifferent to the taste—he just needed an injection of caffeine.

Chapter 26

Carl rolled open the office door at four o'clock on Friday morning. After calling the FBI, he planned to spend a few hours strategizing how he would explain everything to his wife. Then he would spend a few minutes booking a nice resort for a weekend getaway. And when they returned to New Richmond, he and Molly would live happily ever after, just like Beauty and the Beast. That was the plan. Carl smiled at the thought.

Carl decided he would call Sam Diggins sometime before noon and tell him the deal was off. He would say he had second thoughts, then apologize for wasting his time last night. He hoped Sam would simply understand and move on, but Carl wanted to ensure Molly was safe. She had no idea the man she interviewed yesterday was deeply involved with a crime syndicate.

Carl was about to Google the FBI's phone number when he noticed an email waiting for him on his Rankins's account. He guessed the FBI would require several hours of his time, so he decided to first take care of whatever obit needed to be published. No use facing the wrath of George Markins again today.

Carl noticed the email had arrived thirty-five minutes ago. He looked at his watch, and it was only 4:20 a.m. Who was writing an obituary in the middle of the night? It must be a grieving family member who couldn't sleep.

Just like all of the obits on the Rankins's account, it was short and sweet. Carl was disgusted so many people couldn't take the time to write a heartfelt eulogy for their loved one. Oh well! Copy, paste, and forward it on to the Gazette. Mindless job!

Pete Callen, age 50 of San Francisco, California, died peacefully in his home on September 17th. He is survived by his wife Doris, two young sons, John and Jim, and many aunts, uncles, nieces, and nephews. His entire extended family resides in Underbrush, Arizona.

Pete will be remembered for his great sense of humor, good sportsmanship, and loving ways.

A memorial service will be held at 7:00 p.m. on Sunday, September 20th, at Morley's Funeral Home in San Francisco. It is advised friends arrive early as a large crowd is expected.

Carl copied the email onto Gazette letterhead and was about to hit send but stopped abruptly. He reread Pete Callen's obituary, and something piqued his interest. It was the last sentence—he had read that exact statement on a previous obituary, but he couldn't place it.

It is advised that friends arrive early as a large crowd is expected.

Could it be merely a coincidence? Carl's paranoia had been inflicting wounds on his emotional well-being since he started this job, but this time he felt sure it was more than just happenstance. He browsed through the previous obits sent to him on his Rankins's account.

It didn't take long to find it. How could he have forgotten about his best friend?

Wally Roseberg, age 23 of Jacksonville, Florida, went home to see his maker on August 2nd. He is survived by his half-brother Keith, a musician in Overland River, Tennessee.

> *Wally will be remembered for his great sense of humor and loving ways.*
>
> *A celebration of life will be held at 4:30 p.m. on Sunday, September 13th, at the Kramer Funeral Home in Jacksonville. It is advised that friends arrive early as a large crowd is expected.*

Carl leaned back in his chair, and his mouth dropped wide open. There it was, sure as sugar draws ants and bees make honey! It's the damn obituaries! The obits sent via the Rankins's email account are using some kind of codes to tip off bettors, just like the recipe card mailed to Jim Bowman. Were all the eulogies sent via the Rankins's email account fake?

Carl printed out Wally Roseberg's and Pete Callen's obituaries and laid them side by side. Both consisted of three simple paragraphs, written without compassion, solicitude, or endearment. Then, like a wrecking ball crashing into his skull, it hit him. Carl thought he had solved the puzzle, but he needed to check something for verification. The FBI would no doubt want to see it. Carl pulled up ESPN on his web browser and searched ***Jaguars vs. Titans***. When the game summary appeared, he clicked on ***Print Screen*** and then laid the printout between the two obituaries.

Sure enough, the answer was right in front of him. Wally's age was correct, but that was only to throw off the reader if someone Googled his name. Twenty-three had been the over/under for the game. Carl remembered broadcasters saying it would be a low-scoring contest because both starting quarterbacks were sidelined with injuries, and both teams had staunch defenses. He also recalled that Wally didn't have a half-brother, and there was no such town as Overland River, Tennessee. Overland must be the code for gamblers to take the "**Over** twenty-three" total points bet, and Tennessee indicated the opposing team. Finally, the starting time of the celebration of life was supposed to be at 4:30, but in reality, the time represented the number four and a half, which must be the code for the point spread. The last sentence was used to pick the team based on where the funeral was held—in Wally's case, Jacksonville. The word "**early**" meant the Jags wouldn't beat the point spread, which they didn't. The final score was twenty-four to twenty-one but would have ended thirty-one to twenty-one had an official not called a false start penalty in the last two minutes of the game. Carl couldn't find the official's name on ESPN's summary, but he was confident the man was as crooked as the officials in the Atlanta-Carolina game.

The dots were beginning to connect at warp speed, and the proof was materializing quickly. Sam Diggins most likely selected which games to target each week, then emailed a coded, fake obituary to the Gazette so readers would know who to bet on. Under Rob Fornasiere's direction, SOTO trained and placed corrupt referees for those NFL games. But Sam may have made a stupid, crucial mistake by using his own name as the assistant funeral director handling Joy Smith's arrangements! Carl wondered who read the obits. In other words, who else was Sam Diggins working with?

Carl looked closely at Pete Callen's obituary, which he still had not forwarded for publishing. He checked the upcoming NFL schedule for Sunday on ESPN. Carl shook his head and rubbed his eyes. He couldn't believe it! His theory was right—the San Francisco 49ers were going to play the Cardinals in Glendale, Arizona. Now knowing the code, the over/under for the game must be fifty points, and gamblers should take the under, seeing the city in Arizona was named "Underbrush." Based on the memorial service's start time and location, the bettors should take San Francisco, but "early" meant they wouldn't clear the spread.

To double-check, Carl Googled "Underbrush, Arizona," and, as expected, found that there was no such town. According to the Whitepages, there was a Pete Callen who was fifty years old and lived in San Francisco. There was also a Morley's Funeral Home. Carl made a note to call Pete's residence later when the Pacific Time Zone was out of darkness. Then he would check to see if Morley's Funeral Home was having a memorial service on Sunday night.

To validate his assumption, Carl decided to check three more obituaries saved on the Rankins's email system—Jalmer Peters, Arnie Kilton, and Joy Smith. Using his editing software's multiple page feature, he placed them side by side to see all of them together. Growing up, Carl had been a master at logic puzzles, Sudoku, and brain teasers. He had been a grand champion at cryptograms in middle school and has a cheap trophy to prove it! It didn't take long for Carl to determine the surreptitious pattern of codes built into the obituaries. He had cracked polyalphabetic and homophonic substitution ciphers in school that were much more difficult than this!

Chapter 27

Carl boldfaced, underlined, and highlighted the keywords, letters, and numbers for each obituary so the FBI wouldn't miss any details of the evidence he uncovered.

> *Jalmer Peters, age* ***51*** *of* ***Dallas****, Texas, passed away unexpectedly on September 11th. He is survived by his wife Gail, sons Kevin and Keith, mother Ruth, and father, Clyde Peters. Jalmer was raised and attended school in* ***Les****terville,* ***New York.***
>
> *Jalmer will be remembered for being friends with everyone he knew. His kindness was incomparable. Jalmer always seemed to be high on life.*
>
> *Funeral services will be held at* ***9:30*** *a.m. on Sunday,* ***September 20th****, at the Bramer Funeral Home on Th****under*** *Lane in* ***Dallas****.*

> *Arnie Kilton, age* ***42*** *of* ***Los Angeles****, California, died following a lingering illness on September 10th. He is survived by his brother George, and sister Myna of* ***Moor****e Lake, a small community near* ***Seattle****, Washington.*

Arnie was a young man whom heaven claimed much too early. He was bright, articulate, and very creative. Arnie will be deeply missed by friends and family alike.

A memorial service will be held at **1:30** *p.m. on Sunday,* **September 20th**, *at the Odella Funeral Home in Seattle. Odella is located on the east end of T***over** *Road.*

Joy Smith, age **86**, *a resident of the Woodlawn Cliffs Rest Home in Hudson, Wisconsin, passed away unexpectedly on July 2nd. She is survived by her sister Wilma, a retired magazine c***over** *editor in* **Denver,** *Colorado.*

Joy will be remembered for her adventurous ways and love of nature.

*Joy graduated from the University of Wisconsin-***Green Bay** *in 1956 with* **17** *other students. She enjoyed traveling to the west coast to visit her sister at her residence on* **Mortland** *Drive, near the* **Colorado State University** *campus.*

A celebration of Joy's life will be held on Saturday, **August 29th**, *at Holmes Mortuary in Hudson. The* **time will be announced at a later date.**

He then turned on his iPhone's voice recorder so he could dictate what he had discovered. It would help him to organize and authenticate how he would approach the FBI, and Molly, with the documentation. It would also serve as an oral record of his discovery should something unfortunate happen to him.

"Today is Friday, September eighteenth, 2020. The time is 7:34 a.m. My position with the Eau Claire Gazette began on July first of this year. I am considered an obituary writing consultant, and my job is to reach out to funeral directors, nursing homes, and families whose loved ones have died. I provide assistance with publishing the deceased's obituary. My predecessor was Jim Bowman, who died under suspicious circumstances. Proof of this is documented in medical records held by Dr. Mike Kohlrusch at his General Hospital office in New Richmond. I believe Jim Bowman was actively involved in an illegal gaming operation run by an unknown crime syndicate, and he is connected with the business through his brother, John. The latter is serving a sentence in an Oregon federal prison for racketeering charges."

Carl paused the recording to listen to his opening statement. That part was straightforward. What came next would be a difficult pill to swallow for FBI agents, who most likely were avid fans of at least one National Football League team. Could Carl convince them that corruption was infiltrating the inner circle of America's favorite fall pastime? His only chance was to delineate the evidence in a manner that would be easily understood. He checked his notes and turned the recorder back on.

"The Gazette has provided me with two business email systems. One is associated with Rankins, which is our holding company. I periodically receive emails on that account containing obituaries that need to be published in the Gazette; however, I'm told never to edit them. I can change spelling and grammar, but nothing else.

"I believe the obituaries transmitted to me via the Rankins's email system are fraudulent. I suspect a man named Sam Diggins, who poses as an assistant funeral director for a Holmes Mortuary in Hudson, is the author of the phony eulogies. My basis for that opinion is that there is no Holmes Mortuary located in western Wisconsin, nor is there a Sam Diggins listed anywhere in any mortuary personnel publications. I will later attempt to verify that the Rankins's emails are false prior to contacting the FBI.

"Looking at the obituaries of Jalmer Peters, Arnie Kilton, and Joy Smith, I see patterns developing that I believe are being used to communicate wagers for illegal gaming. I will attempt to prove the NFL officiating has been compromised. The Sports Officials Training Organization, better known as SOTO, is criminally involved in the gambling scheme. SOTO trains and places the malefactors into the targeted games. The owner and CEO of SOTO is Rob Fornasiere.

"You will notice the obituaries in question are only three or four paragraphs long, which would be an embarrassment to the person who has died if only he or she were alive to read it! Also, except for Joy Smith, the deceased individuals are relatively young, and more importantly, they reside in locations outside of the Eau Claire Gazette's subscription area. I have Googled their names and found that their obituaries have only appeared in the Gazette. If the Gazette is involved, I would need to request whistleblower protection.

"As troubling as it is to say, I believe my high school best friend, Wally Roseberg, and his employer, Randy Hansen, may be involved in this illegal gaming. However, I have no concrete evidence to support that statement. I sincerely hope that's not the case, but I feel the FBI should investigate nonetheless.

"Okay, now to the cryptic evidence and patterns hidden in the obituaries. First, I believe the pro football teams are identified in the obituary's initial paragraph, and the date of the game is in the last paragraph. The deceased's age is the over/under mark for total points scored in the game, and the time of the funeral or memorial service is actually the point spread. I have verified this to be true on the Vegas Insider website.

"For example, according to his obit, Jalmer Peters lived in Dallas, Texas, but was raised in New York. His funeral is on September twentieth. His age is fifty-one, and the time of his funeral is 9:30. Now, look at the screenshot on Vegas Insider of upcoming games and possible wagers for September twentieth. You'll see that the Dallas Cowboys are playing the New York Giants in the Meadowlands, the over/under is fifty-one, and the point spread is nine and a half. Let's move on to Arnie Kilton's obituary.

"His memorial service is also on Sunday, September twentieth, at 1:30. The simple eulogy claims he was forty-two years old when he passed, hailed from Los Angeles, and his surviving relatives are from Seattle. Looking at Vegas Insider, you'll see the Los Angeles Rams are playing the Seahawks in Seattle, the over/under is forty-two, and the point spread is one and a half. Coincidence? I doubt it! My friend Wally Roseberg's obituary was detailed the same way for Sunday, September thirteenth.

"I believe Sam Diggins made a critical mistake when he submitted Joy Smith's eulogy. After checking, I found all the other obituaries sent via the Rankins's email account used real funeral homes; however, the person who submitted it was fake. But not in Ms. Smith's case. Opposite of what I just said, Sam Diggins used his real name and a faux funeral home! I can only assume the error was due to a momentary lapse of judgment. Regardless, if you look at the contest results, I believe there is concrete evidence of tampering. Joy is listed as eighty-six years old, graduated from the University of Wisconsin-Green Bay with seventeen other students, and has a sister who lives near Colorado State University. And by the way, when reading a death notice, who really cares if a person has a relative who lives near somewhere?! Anyway, her celebration of life was on August twenty-ninth, but the time was not identified.

"A couple of things that were confusing to me about Joy's obit made me rethink my hypothesis. First, there was no time published for the celebration of life. It dawned on me that by using a twelve-hour clock for identification, the highest a point spread could be was twelve and a half. So something needed to be changed for spreads of thirteen and above. And there it was, right under my nose! I'm sure that *'seventeen other students'* indicated the spread. Second, the over/under seemed extremely high. Yes, it was an early preseason contest, and teams rarely tipped off defensive strategies in games that didn't matter. The Packers and Broncos were both loaded with offensive juggernauts, so scoring a ton of points was a possibility. Still, it would take quite an effort for two teams to score eighty-six points. To cover both the spread and the over/under, Green Bay or Denver would need to win by a fifty-three to thirty-five margin, or something close to that. I didn't think that was possible, seeing both teams have stout defenses. But then I read a post on the ESPN website back in June claiming most NFL teams planned to rest their defensive starters during the preseason to prevent injuries. Evidently, defensive players are more prone to injuries during preseason than offensive players.

"On an important side note, Joy is very much a real person, and just like Wally Roseberg, she is very much alive! I'm guessing Jalmer and Arnie are also real people, and they, too, are living and breathing! It's my thought that real names were chosen at random from the local White Pages of the cities playing in the NFL. I don't believe Joy, Jalmer, or Arnie were involved in illegal gaming. However, as I mentioned before, I'm not so sure about my high school friend Wally Roseberg.

"So now, here is the tricky part—the coding. The over/under and point spreads are meaningless without codes to tip gamblers on how to bet. But I think I have unraveled the method. According to Jalmer's obit, he was *'raised and attended school in Lesterville, New York.'* There is no such town as Lesterville in New York. My theory is the 'Les' part of Lesterville tips gamblers to bet on the under, seeing that 'less' is somewhat synonymous with the word 'under.'

"In Arnie's eulogy, his siblings live in *'Moore Lake, Washington.'* Once again, there's no such town as Moore Lake. But 'Moore' sounds like 'more,' which tips gamblers to take the 'over.' Needless to say, more and over are somewhat synonymous.

"In Joy's obit, it says she was *'a retired magazine cover editor,'* and 'cover' is the code because it contains the word 'over.' That would suggest bettors take the over. And no, Joy Smith was never a cover editor anywhere!

"Now, skipping to the point spreads, in Jalmer's case, the funeral is at *'9:30'* at *'Bramer Funeral Home on Thunder Lane in Dallas.'* And sure enough, there is a Bramer Funeral Home, but there is no Thunder Lane in Dallas. Because 'thunder' includes the word 'under,' it is my opinion the code tells gamblers to bet the Cowboys won't cover the nine and a half point spread.

"Compare that to Arnie's. The last paragraph of his obit says, *'A memorial service will be held at 1:30 pm on Sunday, September twentieth, at the Odella Funeral Home in Seattle. Odella is located on the east end of Tover Road.'* First, there's no such road as 'Tover,' however, the word 'over' certainly stands out within it. That tells bettors to take Seattle to cover the point spread.

"Finally, look at Joy Smith's obit. It says that Joy's sister lived on *'Mortland Lane'* in Denver. The street is fictitious, but 'Mortland' contains the letters 'mor,' which lets gamblers know to bet on Denver to cover the seventeen point spread."

Carl needed a break. The final proof he was about to decipher for the FBI, and Molly, too, could result in the NFL season being suspended. He turned off the voice recorder and walked briskly through the alley to Caribou Coffee. On the way back to the office, he had a gut feeling he was being watched. Could that be true, or was paranoia reinserting itself into Carl's psyche? To avoid a mental collapse, he had to finish up quickly and call the FBI.

Chapter 28

After studying the three obituaries on the computer screen, Carl replayed his voice recording. It sounded very complicated! Could the FBI comprehend the evidence the way he had presented it, or would they think he was a crackpot?

He pushed record again. "Now, I will explain how a casino makes money or potentially loses money on sports gaming as it relates to football. There are two basic bets—point spreads and moneylines. Let me start with moneyline betting. This is where a gambler picks the winner of the game, and it doesn't matter if his team wins by one point or one hundred points. The gambler has to risk a small additional amount of money to bet on the favored team, usually set at an eleven to ten payout ratio. In other words, if a gambler hopes to win $100, he must wager $110. If his team wins, the sportsbook will pay him $210—the $110 he wagered plus the $100 he won. If the favorite loses, the extra ten dollars is considered the bookie's commission, better known as the vigorish, or vig for short.

"However, if a gambler bets on the underdog, things are different. The payouts are more than the original wager if the underdog wins, and it's usually at a higher rate than eleven to ten. Let's say the payout is listed as 'plus fifteen,' or $150 on a $100 bet. If the underdog is victorious, a gambler who bets $100 will win $250.

"I will use Clemson as an example to try and make things more transparent. Bookies will establish a payout level based on how strongly they feel the favorite is to win. For instance, if Clemson is playing the Citadel, they would be considered a substantial favorite, and the payout level could be forty to ten or even more. However, if they played Alabama, they would be a minimal favorite, and the payout might only be eleven to ten. Let's say a gambler picked Clemson to beat the Citadel with the payout being forty to ten. For him to win $100, he would risk $400. If Clemson won, he would collect $500—the $400 wager plus the $100 win. If a gambler bet on Clemson to beat Alabama with the payout level of eleven to ten, he would risk $110 to win $100. If Clemson lost, he is out the initial $110 wager.

"Sometimes, if the two teams are of equal strength and neither are considered a favorite to win, the odds will be the same, or 'even up,' as they call it in Vegas. If a gambler placed a $100 bet on the winning team, he would collect $200—the $100 wager plus the $100 for winning. Simple and straightforward! But in most games, one team is given an edge, meaning they are considered the favorite, and the other team becomes the underdog.

"The chances of an underdog winning are obviously less than the favorite. Surprisingly, during the 2019 NFL season, the favored teams won eighty-five percent of their games compared to fifteen percent for the underdogs. However, as you can see in my example, if a gambler bets on the underdog, the payout is much greater if an upset does occur. But bookmakers have a sixth sense for picking the correct winner of a game, and trying to guess which ones they're wrong on is certainly risky business for a gambler.

"Every bookmaker's optimum goal is to balance the betting on both sides of a wager. In other words, to have an equal amount of bets placed on each team winning the game. That way, the losing bets would pay for the winning ones, and the sportsbook would pocket the vigorish. A balanced wager spreadsheet would reduce the risk to sportsbooks and guarantee they make money."

Carl paused the recording and listened to it. He still had the same concerns as before. Anyone who gambles on college or pro football will understand what he said, but what if the FBI agents weren't familiar with sports gaming? How could he present his case succinctly? He wasn't sure.

Shaking his head to clear his self-doubt, Carl pressed the red record button again. "Point spread betting is different. Bookmakers predict how many points the favored team will win by, and gamblers must guess if that team will not only win but do so by more points than what the bookies established. Creating the opening point spread has become an exact science based on a multitude of factors such as home-field advantage, injured players, and recent performance.

"As an example, let's look at this Sunday's Bills game against the Jets. Buffalo is a seven-point favorite to win the game. Gamblers win if they take Buffalo, and the Bills are victorious by eight points or more. Or they lose if New York comes within six points or less. It's a push if the game ends with Buffalo winning by exactly seven points. The bettor gets the wager back, and no one wins or loses.

"Sportsbooks make money with point spread betting the same as they do with moneyline—the vigorish. Point spread gamers must wager more than they can win, meaning the casino always gets a cut, usually at or near an eleven to ten payout ratio. Let me use the Bills-Jets game to demonstrate. Ten gamblers each wager $110 on the Bills to win by more than seven points. Conversely, ten gamblers each wager $110 on the Jets to not lose by more than seven points. The casino is now handling a total of $2,200 in bets. There are three possible results when it comes to payouts. If Buffalo wins the game by eight points or more, they have 'covered the spread.' Each of the ten gamblers who picked them would receive $210—their $110 wager plus the win. Thus, the casino pays out a total of $2,100 to customers who took the Bills. If New York wins the game or loses by less than seven points, the casino pays out $2,100 to gamblers who took the Jets. And lastly, if the game ends with the Bills winning the game by exactly seven points, it's a push, and all bets would be returned.

"But let's forget about a push, which neither the gambler nor the casino makes money. The sportsbook owes $2,100 to the ten customers who won the bet. However, they took in $2,200, which means their profit will be $100. As I mentioned earlier, in a perfect world for a casino, their bookmakers would achieve balanced betting on both sides for every game. But, quite frankly, that's impossible to do.

"While bookmakers attempt to adjust the odds to achieve a fifty-fifty split in betting action, it rarely happens. This is where the so-called sharp bettors wreak havoc on sportsbooks. A sharp bettor is a professional gambler who knows a good bet from a bad one by studying statistics and numbers. On the other hand, a square bettor is someone who gambles on sports contests just for fun. And yes, the squares tend to lose frequently! Bookmakers adjust the point spreads up or down when most gamblers are pounding one side or the other. But the sharps know that if the wager receiving the fewest bets appears to fit their numerical formula for being a winner, they gamble much more money than the majority of squares. Their payoff could be phenomenal, and sportsbooks could lose a great deal of money on that bet! However, in the long run, the casinos make money due to the variety of games played each day.

"So, what would happen if the sharp bettors had some help ensuring their teams won games? Especially if the teams with the least amount of bets covered the spread or won the moneyline? Yes, fortunes could be made at the hands of the casinos!"

Carl paused and took a deep breath before continuing. "Now, I will cut to the chase. I believe codes printed in obituaries are used to tip gamblers on wagers to bet on, and I think unethical referees enable unfair outcomes to occur.

"I can prove the code's functionality based on Joy Smith's obituary. That game is over, so let's look at the outcome and compare it to my theory. On August twenty-ninth, Denver beat Green Bay in a preseason game, fifty-six to thirty-one. The Broncos covered the unusually high seventeen point spread. Also, the total points scored was eighty-seven, which was more than the eighty-six points established by the bookmakers. If you think this is just conjecture and not hard evidence, you might be right. But, then again, I doubt it!

"According to Vegas Insider, the majority of gamblers bet on the under, which was logical because eighty-six points was a lofty amount. And, the majority also bet that Denver wouldn't cover the spread because it was too high, especially in a game where the starters wouldn't be playing. Thus, the minority of bettors reaped monetary rewards from the majority who thought the over/under and point spreads were unattainable.

"Connecting the dots, here's what ESPN had to say as part of their Packers vs. Broncos recap:

> *The officiating at the Green Bay versus Denver game was atrocious. Flags were thrown when they should have stayed in the referee's pockets and weren't thrown for obvious penalties. Quite frankly, the stripers didn't have a clue! I hope we don't have to talk about horrendous officiating during the regular season!*

"Now, looking ahead to this Sunday's NFL games reflected in Jalmer and Arnie's obituaries, the majority of gamblers have taken the over fifty-one total points scored and Dallas to cover the nine and a half point spread. That makes sense, seeing five defensive starters for the New York Giants were injured last week and won't be playing. But if the code is correct and the officiating is dishonest, that outcome won't happen, and a minority of gamblers will be rewarded.

"Same with the Rams and Seahawks game. The majority of bets have been placed on the under fifty-two wager and Seattle not covering the one and a half point spread. Why? Because in the last four contests played against each other, the most total points scored has been thirty-four, and Los Angeles has won each game. Also, every NFL expert has picked LA to win the West once again."

Believing he now had enough evidence for the FBI to conduct a thorough investigation, Carl ended the voice recording. He laid the iPhone on his desk and replayed the long narrative twice. He was still worried his description was too complicated for someone who had never bet on a sports game—like, perhaps, Molly. Would the FBI take notes, then joke about his theory?

In elementary school, Carl learned the necessary steps involved in scientific method and experimentation. Had he completed those steps? He thought about it for a moment.

First, he had observed commonalities of each obituary sent to him on the Rankins's email account. That prompted several questions. Then, he formed a hypothesis: If the emails were coded to tip gamblers how to pick the winners, and SOTO produced the officials who would ensure the crooked outcomes, then illegal gaming compromised professional football.

There it was in a nutshell! Time to call the FBI. Carl searched for the closest FBI office on his computer and picked up his phone to make the call. He punched in the number—then abruptly hit cancel. He realized the most crucial step in the scientific method process had not been attempted.

Carl needed to test his theory.

Chapter 29

"What's the worst-case scenario?" muttered Carl to—you guessed it—himself. There was no one he could talk to about what he planned to do—not Molly, not Grandpa Syd, not any of his friends. Carl thought about his predecessor, Jim Bowman. Did he have a guilty conscience and decide to spill the beans? Dr. Kohlrusch had indicated on the autopsy report Jim had died of poisoning—not cancer as everyone believed. If that was true, was it accidental, self-induced, or a homicide?

If Carl's plan failed, he and anyone he told would be at risk of losing their life. He really wanted to tell Wally Roseberg, but Carl wasn't sure what side of the fence his old buddy was on these days. He had second thoughts about letting Molly hear his iPhone recording. Carl didn't want to risk putting her in danger, even though she was still upset with him for the way he was acting. No, if his hypothesis proved correct, he would tell only the FBI. But now that would have to wait until Monday.

Pete Callen was the experiment. Carl hadn't sent the obituary received on his Rankins's email account to his editor. But they needed it by noon to make it on time for tonight's online and Saturday's print edition. Carl glanced at his watch. It was 11:17 a.m. in the Central time zone, which meant it was 9:17 a.m. in San Francisco. People would be at work, and shops, stores, and funeral parlors would be open for business.

First, he wanted to know if Pete Callen was a real person. Carl paid for another Whitepages premium report and got Pete's home, cell, and work numbers. Paydirt! Carl guessed that if Pete was alive, he might not pick up an unknown number displayed on his phone. So he called the work number. The receptionist, Sally Milton, answered.

“Microsoft corporate sales department—may I help you?”

Carl was nervous, and he fumbled the response. “Ah, yes, ah, oh, I’m looking for, or I mean, I need to speak to Pete Callen, please.”

“Mr. Callen is in a meeting with Mr. Gates and Mr. Nadella. May I take a message?”

“Bill Gates?!” responded Carl with an incredulous tone. Could Pete Callen be so high up in the company that he actually meets with the infamous philanthropist and founder of the world-renowned tech organization?

“Yes, of course, Bill Gates and our CEO Satya Nadella.” Sally rolled her eyes and shook her head. Another dingdong who has never heard of Satya Nadella but believes Bill Gates is a Greek God, right up there with Apollo, Ares, and Zeus himself! “May I ask who you are and why you are calling, sir?”

Carl needed to recover his wits before Sally hung up. “Ah, sure, I’m sorry, my name is Rick Smith, and I spoke with Mr. Callen about implementing software for my company here in Salt Lake City.”

“Please hold on for a moment,” said Sally as she punched away at her computer keyboard. Carl was appalled at himself for lying. His dad taught him to be honest and maintain strong moral principles. But he had convinced himself this experiment was worth it. The means would justify the end. “I’m sorry, but I don’t see your name anywhere in our database. When did you last speak to Mr. Callen?”

Carl wasn’t going to continue with this charade. He got the information he needed—Pete Callen was real and still alive! The Whitepages confirmed Pete was 50, as well. “Ah, Sally, I need to go. I’ll call you back later. Thanks!” Carl hung up before Sally could respond. She rolled her eyes once again.

Next, Carl called Morley’s Funeral Home, which he had Googled and found out it was a legit business place. A young female voice answered.

“Morley’s Funeral Home. How may I help you?”

Carl wasn’t going to lie this time. “Yes, I was wondering if you are holding a memorial service on Sunday night?” he asked bluntly.

"No, sir, we don't have funerals on Sunday. It's our day of worship."

"Okay, thanks. That's all I needed to know." Once again, Carl hung up before the sweet gal had a chance to say anything.

It was now or never. Carl decided to change Pete Callen's obituary before submitting it to the Gazette. It was fake anyway, right? Carl guessed Sam Diggins sent it to him on the Rankins's account but didn't know Carl would be the one forwarding it to the newspaper. Or did he? Is it possible Sam was yanking his chain during dinner last night? Did he know what Carl did for a living and was trying to see if he would take the bait?

Sam Diggins probably didn't have enough money himself to purchase the Minnesota Vikings, which meant the crime syndicate he was working for was loaded. And why wouldn't they be? If they could control the outcome of NFL gambling wagers, they would be very well established financially.

Sam Diggins' real job was creating fake obituaries for the syndicate. If they lost a great deal of money due to an inaccurate obituary, they would first go to Sam for answers. Then Sam would eventually come looking for the person who placed obits with the Gazette. It wouldn't take long to track Carl down, and then Sam would think Molly was involved, too. If Carl continued his experiment, his entire family would need FBI protection. Grandpa Syd's sports marketing company could also be in peril.

In the end, Carl thought about what his father would do. And that made the decision easier. Billy West would have said to terminate the corruption and make sure your family is protected. But first, stop the fraud—it's the honorable course of action. And Billy West had been all about honor and integrity!

Carl pulled up Pete Callen's obituary on his computer:

> *Pete Callen, age 50 of San Francisco, California, died peacefully in his home on September 17th. He is survived by his wife Doris, two young sons, John and Jim, and many aunts, uncles, nieces, and*

> *nephews. His entire extended family resides in Underbrush, Arizona.*
>
> *Pete will be remembered for his great sense of humor, good sportsmanship, and loving ways.*
>
> *A memorial service will be held at 7:00 p.m. on Sunday, September 20th, at Morley's Funeral Home in San Francisco. It is advised friends arrive early as a large crowd is expected.*

Then he made the necessary changes and highlighted them only for his own personal file:

> *Pete Callen, age 50 of San Francisco, California, died peacefully in his home on September 17th. He is survived by his wife Doris, two young sons, John and Jim, and many aunts, uncles, nieces, and nephews. His entire extended family resides in* **Oversage**, *Arizona.*
>
> *Pete will be remembered for his great sense of humor, good sportsmanship, and loving ways.*
>
> *A memorial service will be held at 7:00 p.m. on Sunday, September 20th, at Morley's Funeral Home in San Francisco. Due to traffic congestion in the area, visitors should plan ahead so they don't arrive* ***late.***

Carl copied and pasted the corrected obit onto the official Gazette form and reread it three times. Then he took a deep breath and punched the return key.

The hypothesis was now being tested. Sunday night couldn't come soon enough!

Chapter 30

Pete Callen's obituary was posted in the Gazette's digital edition at 6:00 p.m. Central Standard Time. Harvey Jones was waiting in the Caesars Palace sportsbook at 4:00 p.m. Pacific Time Zone when he heard the ping on his iPhone. Harvey had set up his Gazette account to notify him whenever an obituary was published. Who does that?!

An hour earlier, Harvey bet $25,000 on the under fifty-one total point wager in the Dallas versus New York game and another $25,000 on the Cowboys not to cover the nine and a half point spread. Then he placed $25,000 on the over forty-two total points scored in the Rams game against the Seahawks and $25,000 more on Seattle to cover the one and a half point spread. Both wagers were made based on information he extracted from Jalmer Peters' and Arnie Kiltons' obituaries published earlier in the week. Finally, Harvey placed $10,000 on the Miami Dolphins to upset the New England Patriots in Foxborough, Massachusetts. The moneyline was +420 for the lowly Dolphins, which meant if they won, regardless of the point spread, Harvey would rake in $42,000. But even without Tom Brady at the Patriots' helm, there was no way Miami would win on the road. Being considered an underdog was a highly overrated term for that pathetic team!

And now, with the suspiciously watchful eyes of Caesars' security team who were dressed as scantily-clad centurions wandering the streets of ancient Rome, Harvey approached the betting area once again. He asked to take the under fifty total point wager and the 49ers not to cover the seven-point spread against the Cardinals. Then he handed over his last $50,000 voucher he had obtained from the cashier's desk upon his arrival to the Las Vegas

Strip's most famous property. In the sportsbook, Harvey sat down, ordered a Bacardi on the rocks, and then raised his glass in a silent toast to Pete Callen. "May you rest in peace, my friend, whoever you may be," he muttered to himself with a sordid grin.

Harvey Jones was his name this week. Last week it was Gordon Thompson. He wasn't sure about next week because he hadn't spoken to the talented forger who regularly created new driver's licenses and other documents for him. On Tuesday mornings, Harvey or Gordon or whoever he was that week cashed in his winning sportsbook tickets. Because he raked in massive amounts of moola, he needed identification for tax purposes. He never enjoyed the makeup, hairdo, and photo sessions on Tuesday nights, though. It was demeaning for someone as rich and powerful as himself to don a new hairpiece and wear cosmetics every seven days. But to avoid being recognized on the security camera footage shared between casinos, it was the price he had to pay to maintain his luxurious lifestyle. High-rolling winners in Vegas aren't especially welcome in gaming houses. Losers, however, are a whole different story!

Harvey hired sixty men and women to do the same thing he was doing—make professional football wagers and cash in the winnings. Each week, his employees would also change their identities and rotate to different casinos. Besides Las Vegas, Harvey farmed his workers to Reno and Atlantic City. An additional staff of 300 were assigned to online gaming sites, registered everywhere from Canada to the Caribbean Islands. Those gambling operatives would open a new account each week, bet on pro football games, then cash out and close their accounts on Tuesdays.

Harvey was the founder of the syndicate and simply called "the boss" by his employees. None of his workers knew his real name, and none had ever met him or knew what he looked like except for Oliver Harwas, his right-hand man. Oliver was the secret and illegitimate son of a rogue ex-CIA agent from Seminole Bend, Florida, who had created a radar jamming device that caused air disasters in the 1980s. So he wouldn't have to live with the same name as his terrorist father, Oliver changed his surname from Harfield to Harwas but kept his first name out of respect for his dad. Criminal DNA is hard to shake.

Oliver would have gladly placed the bets for his boss, but Harvey enjoyed the thrill of gaming and hanging out in sportsbooks during the football season. Oliver also served as Harvey's pilot and flew his opulent Airbus A380 from one of his fourteen homes located in exotic places worldwide. Early this morning, they had arrived in Sin City from a new residence Harvey was building in the Caymans.

On the flight, Harvey studied this week's new obituaries posted in the Gazette. He identified two obits of interest: Jalmer Peters and Arnie Kilton. While pretending to be a dimwit tycoon who was ready to lose thousands on a wild and crazy gambling vacation, Harvey entered Caesars Palace and handed over $250,000 to the cashier in exchange for vouchers and chips. He strolled through the gaming areas, stopping at the tables to purposely make stupid bets hoping to be noticed for his lack of gambling skills. When he arrived in the sportsbook, Harvey glanced at Caesars' vast scoreboard and saw the two contests representing Jalmer and Arnie's fake death notices.

Then he found the idiotic moneyline upset game coded in a different section of a prominent American newspaper. If the authorities ever caught wind of the Gazette's false obituaries, the syndicate would revert to their other media outlet as a backup. For now, this newspaper only handled the risky moneyline wagers. Risky in the sense that it was much more problematic to control the outcome of those games because a bad team would need to beat a good team to win the bet. Sure, the syndicate could set it up so the favorite won, but those bets' profits would be minimal. To win big on moneyline bets, a gambler needed to pick an underdog that could upset a good opponent. Those wagers were referred to as sucker bets by the casinos.

After Pete Callen's obituary was published, Harvey ambled towards the betting area, then paused to scratch his chin. He wanted security to think he wasn't sure he was making a smart decision.

"Play the gambling imbecile," Harvey told himself. Then he strode confidently to the bookie and placed significant wagers on his targeted game. To anyone in the know, those wagers appeared to be foolish bets.

While Harvey was placing his bets at Caesars Palace, so too were his other 360 operatives either online or at various casinos around the country. They would all place the highest wagers the sportsbook would allow based on Jalmer, Arnie, and Pete's nefariously coded obituary. Because of the uncertainty surrounding the moneyline upset game, only ten of Harvey's employees were selected to make that bet.

Since sports gambling became legal in Las Vegas, a few rich cats wagered six figures on individual games each week in the ritzy casinos such as Wynn, Bellagio, and Caesars Palace. Sometimes they would win, but more often they would lose, much to the establishment's delight. They all had direct debit accounts previously established with those sportsbooks, and they all had thorough background checks designed to weed out cheaters. To avoid being intensely scrutinized by security, unknown gamblers like Harvey-this-week and Gordon-last-week limited their bets to five figures.

Harvey's secret to success was to have his employees arrive at the gambling resort a few hours before the obits were published and exchange a $100,000 cashier's check into casino chips and silver coins. Yes, that would put security on alert—no way to avoid it! Next, act like idiotic spendthrifts and stuff $1,000 into a variety of worthless five-dollar slot machines, then try to lose another grand at the craps or blackjack tables. Have enough alcoholic beverages to appear loud and inebriated. To complete the ruse, the actors were to throw $100 tips to every waitress, dealer, and boxman who came within five feet. The best trick was to toss a $500 chip to a pit boss, knowing, of course, he wouldn't be allowed to keep it, but also knowing the security folks upstairs were now probably laughing. In other words, make it look like they were just foolish wealthy tourists with money to waste in the name of vacation fun! Then, head on down to the sportsbook, place what appeared to be ridiculous bets, and pretend cluelessness and gambling go hand in hand!

In reality, the average wager placed by Harvey's employers in the sportsbook was $20,000. Most of them would make just two bets (the over/under and the point spread) on three games each week, making the amount played by each operative $120,000. Multiplied by sixty-one gamers, which included Harvey, those wagers totaled $7,320,000. The 300 online workers averaged $5,000 per bet or an additional $9,000,000 played. Finally, add the ten operatives who gambled $10,000 each on the moneyline upset game, and the grand total of wagers placed each week was just shy of sixteen and a half million dollars! On average, those weekly bets would generate twenty-million dollars in winnings. Subtract $1.3 million for expenses (employee salaries, airfares, hotels, meals, and throw away money in casinos), and Harvey's syndicate netted nearly $19 million every weekend during the season.

*****

Montreal's Teflon Don, better known as Vito Rizzuto, was the head of the Canadian Cosa Nostra syndicate in 2002 when he decided to test the waters of illegal gaming. His cousin's job was to invest in lavish restaurants throughout North America. Because his cuz was a sports fanatic, Vito assigned him to start up and oversee the illegal gaming operation from an office inside the Capella Tower in Minneapolis.

Vito's cousin initially set up thirty online gambling accounts using fictitious names and bet on pro soccer games worldwide. But to make money, he needed to create an edge to win more times than he lost. So, by offering huge sums of cash, he recruited key players on a handful of teams to help ensure victories by falling, miskicking, or being penalized. If money didn't work, he found that making death threats to the athlete's loved ones did the trick! The Rizzuto family's profits soared, so Vito's cousin decided to try American football next. Once again, he selected just a few teams to make wagers and enlisted star players to do his dirty work. For the first ten years or so, the syndicate won 73.2 percent of their fixed American football games, which was slightly higher than soccer was netting in

Europe and the Middle East. Vito was content with the yield, but his cousin wanted a better win percentage.

When Vito died from cancer in 2013, his cousin decided to make changes that would increase American football profits. That's when he assumed control of SOTO from founder Rob *Fornasiere and expanded his operation to include crooked officiating. Since the infusion of tainted referees, the illegal gaming operation has won 98.7 percent of the time!*

The NFL *playoffs were always a tough nut for the syndicate to crack, though. Because the miscreant athletes who worked for the mob often purposely lost games, their teams rarely made the postseason. But there were a few teams that could still make the playoffs if the syndicate's key player was a superstar.*

Meanwhile, the best referees during the season were selected by votes from coaches and then awarded the officiating rights to the prestigious playoff contests. It was a chance to demonstrate their skills in front of millions of fans. To overcome that obstacle, the syndicate had specialists who could create car accidents or infectious diseases for those elite referees, opening the door for substitute officials assigned by SOTO. And that plan would have worked extraordinarily well during the 2015 Super Bowl had Billy West not screwed everything up!

Chapter 31

"You flew the InterPlan Learjet?!" whinged Harvey. "Are you nuts?! You don't think Randy will know something's up?!"

"I'll fly to the Caymans tonight," replied Wally, with no emotion. "Even with the time changes, I'll touch down on your landing strip before dawn. Randy will still be sleeping."

"The Learjet automatically logs flying hours. His hired pilot will notice you detoured quite a distance from your flight plan out of Palm Beach!"

"I'll take care of that. Will you please just tell me about this job offer of yours?"

"Okay. Let me start by saying I'm Harvey Jones to you. That's my name this week. Don't call me by my real name. Understand?"

Wally had become good friends with Harvey during the designing and construction of his private island home in the Caymans. Harvey loved and worshipped gifted athletes—former, present, and future. He was too involved in purchasing and running restaurants for Vito to think about having a wife and kids. After a one night stand went south and a baby was on the way, he married the gal out of guilt and nothing else. The union lasted a short time, then Harvey ditched what he termed his "biggest mistake," leaving them to fend for themselves.

When he finally found the love of his life, she already had two children from a previous marriage. Harvey's stepdaughter was a brainiac but not much of an athlete. His stepson was ten years older than his stepdaughter and played college sports, but never amounted to much in his stepfather's eyes. If only he could turn back time and start over again. Harvey was sure his gene pool had the potential to procreate the finest competitors ever to grace the earth!

So when he met Wally, he could tell the young man had been a talented jock at some point in his life. He had a never-say-die attitude, and his muscular physique was exceptional—not an ounce of fat on his body. But the clincher was when Wally skunked Harvey in a tennis game: 6-0, 6-0, 6-0. Harvey had a 5.0 rating and could whip most everyone he played, including kids decades younger. Needless to say, he was impressed!

While sipping on mojitos at Harvey's restaurant in Bodden Town, Wally let it slip that he had played high school ball with Carl West, the son of the infamous Billy West. Wally never wanted anyone to be his friend simply by who he knew. The alcohol was playing ventriloquist with his lips again.

That's when Harvey had a great idea. Once InterPlan had completed his island estate, Harvey wanted to offer Wally a full-time position within his organization. But he couldn't explain what the job entailed—he needed to show Wally firsthand.

Now Wally was sitting next to Harvey in Caesars Sportsbook, even though he barely recognized him. Harvey was covered in thick makeup and wearing a Tommy Bahama Fuego Palms camp shirt that hung loosely over his white dress slacks.

"Harvey Jones?" asked Wally, not sure he heard the fake name correctly. "Okay, no problem. So what's this all about?"

"I have a hobby that's quite financially lucrative," said Harvey, stretching the truth with a little white lie. Many people gamble as a hobby. Rarely do they become multimillionaires! "I think you would enjoy helping me succeed—for a generous salary, of course!"

"People I know plant gardens, make model airplanes, or play golf as a hobby. Some even gamble—but they seldom win. Seeing you had me fly to Las Vegas, and we're sitting in a casino, I believe your hobby is pretty much transparent. But how can I help you succeed? That is what you said, right? Succeed."

"Come. Let's have an early dinner in the Forum Shops, and we can chat there before you fly back to paradise."

Harvey tucked the chits for his NFL wagers into his wallet. He was certain that come Tuesday when he cashed them in, Caesars' security cameras would be tracking him everywhere he went inside the casino. He would fly back to the Caymans to see how the mansion was coming along, then make another trek to Vegas on Friday and do it all again at Wynn's sportsbook.

Football season was tough on his marriage. For twenty-one weeks, including the playoffs, Harvey spent only a handful of days with his wife, who thought her husband was busy running the restaurants. She didn't know about the sports bets, and she spent many hours crying when Harvey was gone on Thanksgiving, Christmas, and New Year's. Thank goodness for her grown children.

In between bites of King Crab at Joe's Seafood, Harvey detailed his illegal gaming scheme to Wally. The plan was for Wally to recruit star players on a few targeted teams who would throw interceptions, drop passes, or fumble handoffs when necessary to help the crooked officials cover the point spreads. In return, Wally would receive a ten percent cut of the syndicate's profits. That had to be much better than what Randy Hansen was paying him!

Two hours later, Harvey tried to close the deal. "So, what do you think? Will you join me?"

"What makes you think I will be able to recruit players to break bad? And more importantly, what makes you think I'm willing to break bad?!"

"Oh, come on, son! Get real! Everyone could use a little extra cash! You'll succeed because I see a strong-willed man who knows how to get things done. And, you have nothing to lose. You can still keep your job at InterPlan and recruit on the side. If it doesn't work out, well then, easy come, easy go. You can quit and be an architect full-time."

"I need a few days to think about this, okay?"

"Of course! Take your time. I'm ready when you are."

"One last question—what makes you so sure I won't go straight to the feds when I leave here?"

"Trust, my boy, trust! We've been friends since you started working on my house in the Caymans. Friends don't get friends in trouble!" Harvey winked at Wally, then stood and shook hands. "Have a safe flight, my friend. We'll talk soon."

After Wally was out of sight, Harvey punched a number into his cell phone. Three rings later, Oliver Harwas picked up.

"I'm listening," said Oliver.

"Follow him. If he goes in any direction that is not a beeline to the airport, shoot him."

Chapter 32

"Yes!" exclaimed Curt Anderson as he jumped from the couch in his den and high-fived Carl. The Dallas Cowboys had just finished their game in the Meadowlands and had beaten the Giants twenty-eight to twenty-one. The Cowboys should have won thirty-one to twenty-one. A false start penalty was called on right guard Zack Martin with 1:48 left on the clock as the ball was headed through the uprights for a successful field goal. It was a strangely delayed penalty, as it appeared the official waited to see if the kick was good before tossing his flag. After moving the ball back five yards to the Giants' thirty-eight-yard line, Dallas elected to punt instead of risking a second field goal would be missed, and the Giants would take over on their own forty-five-yard line.

Even though the punt pinned down the Giants on the four-yard line, head coach Mike McCarthy was still jawing with referee Calvin Appleby about the false start penalty. He kept pointing to the Jumbotron and asking Calvin to show him where Zack Martin had moved. It was a head-scratcher, alright. McCarthy was absolutely right—Martin had not moved a muscle!

When he saw Mike McCarthy's red face and spittle being launched at referee Appleby, Carl hopped off the couch and moved toward the TV set to get a close-up view of the argument. "Oh my God," uttered Carl. "It can't be!"

"What can't be, bro-in-law?" asked Curt jubilantly. He appeared ecstatic about the outcome of the game.

"Ah, nothing," replied Carl, tongue in cheek. Carl noticed immediately that Calvin Appleby looked exactly like Miles Milton, the back judge from last week's Atlanta-Carolina game. He was the official who messed up the call in overtime, wrongly claiming Desmond Trufant had been down by contact after intercepting Teddy Bridgewater's pass. The Falcons were forced to kick a field goal to win, but they didn't cover the spread. Carl thought about it a minute, then was sure last week's Miles Milton was the same person as this week's Calvin Appleby. So that's how SOTO does it—they recycle corrupt officials by changing their names every Sunday!

Curt didn't like it when someone knew something he didn't. What did Carl see that shocked him? "Don't give me that 'ah, nothing' crap. What did you see?"

Carl decided one more little white lie wouldn't hurt anyone. "I thought Mike McCarthy was wearing a headset with the Packers' logo instead of his new team, the Cowboys, on it. But when I looked closer, I was wrong. That's all."

Curt laughed. "Yeah, I'm sure Mikey would want nothing to do with the team that axed him in midseason! Hey, are you ready for another beer before the Rams and Seahawks game starts? Or should we toss around the pigskin in my back yard, instead?"

"My my, aren't you the jovial one today," exclaimed Carl. "Why are you so cheerful?"

"Dallas didn't cover the nine and a half point spread, and the total points were less than fifty-one. I won both those bets. So guess what? I'm supplying the cherished Johnsonville beer brats for tonight's game between the 49ers and the Cards! Pretty dang generous of me, wouldn't you say?!" Curt punched his brother-in-law playfully on the arm.

"You shouldn't have won either bet. There was no false start penalty on the field goal attempt. Watch the replays. Had that kick stood, the total points would have been fifty-two, and Dallas would have covered the spread with a ten-point victory!"

"Woulda, coulda, shoulda—that's exactly what the Russians were saying when Neil Armstrong stepped on the moon! Come on, let's throw the football around for a few minutes."

"How would I know what the Russians said? I wasn't around when the Americans won the space race!"

Carl knew he should head back to New Richmond instead of watching two more games. Molly had given him the cold shoulder when he came home on Friday, so when Curt invited him to his place in Eau Claire for the weekend, he gladly took him up on the offer. Instead of fishing or hunting, Curt wanted to play golf on Saturday. Soon the leaves would be changing colors, which meant snow would be falling before long. The courses would be shutting down for the winter.

But Carl also had an ulterior motive for spending the weekend with Curt. He wanted to know what NFL games his brother-in-law had made wagers. If Curt placed six longshot bets, the over/under and point spreads for three teams that were coded in the Jalmer Peters, Arnie Kilton, and Pete Callen obituaries, it would confirm his suspicions that Molly's brother was involved in illegal gambling. Once he had the evidence validated from his experiment of falsifying Pete Callen's eulogy, he would tell the FBI and Molly. That could cause a family conflict—to say the least! Carl wasn't sure he would inform the feds of his brother-in-law's involvement. Curt was probably his best friend in Wisconsin.

Curt was still giddy from a mix of positive emotions following the Dallas win and the six-pack of Miller Lite he downed watching the game. Because he wanted to show off his arm strength, he and Carl moved the football toss to the street out front. The majority of his throws were wobbly ducks that barely made it twenty yards, but Carl's great prowess in the same game that made his father a legend enabled him to catch each one. Delusionally, Curt would assume all the credit, strutting around like Michael Jordan and punching the air with his fist like Muhammed Ali. Once, Carl heard him bellow, "Eat your heart out, Aaron Rodgers!"

Curt and Carl missed the first half of the Rams-Seahawks game when the arm demonstration, or lack thereof, morphed into a two-on-two touch football game with a couple of teenage neighbor boys who were skateboarding in the street. Curt's cockiness dwindled quickly when his high school teammate didn't have the skills to make plays with the QB-wannabe's inaccurate throws. Meanwhile, Carl proved he had the same genes as his daddy when it came to football.

Curt needed another six-pack to quench his thirst while perched on the couch, watching the second half of Seattle's game. When the two-minute warning sounded, Carl could see anxiety in Curt's facial expressions. And he knew why. The Rams were up twenty-one to seventeen and had the ball on their own thirty-six-yard line. It was second down with nine yards to go for a first, but the Seahawks had used up all their timeouts. If Seattle could make two stops and force LA to punt, they would get the ball back with around thirty seconds left in the game. Carl remembered Arnie Kilton's coded obituary said to take the over forty-two total points and Seattle to cover the one and a half point spread. As it stood now, the total was thirty-eight, and the Seahawks needed a touchdown to beat the spread. Curt was worried he was about to lose both bets.

On second down, Jared Goff kept the ball and scrambled in the backfield, trying to eat up precious seconds before taking a knee. He lost four yards but let the clock tick down to 1:06 before calling a timeout to prevent a delay of game penalty. Because the second down play had no chance of moving the ball forward, it was apparent the Rams were content with running down the clock on third, then punting. They would give the pigskin to their sure-handed superstar running back, John Warner. He could eat up more time because linemen and linebackers alike had a tough time bringing him to the ground.

*****

As a rookie last year, Warner was the NFL's leading rusher. Out of the University of Colorado, he was the first player selected in the 2019 draft. The Rams traded away their first-round pick and two second-rounders to move up in the draft and grab the former Buffs sensation. John signed a five-year contract for $75,000,000, not including a $20,000,000 signing bonus. And Warner didn't *disappoint—he ran for 2,102 yards in his rookie season, four yards shy of besting ex-Rams' halfback Eric Dickerson's NFL record.*

But early in the summer of 2020, the news broke that John Warner had accepted a Porsche 911 Carrera as a gift from a Colorado booster during his senior year in college. The NFL disciplined him by taking away both his salary and his signing bonus, reducing the shell-shocked running back's contract to the rookie minimum of $495,000. The Colorado Buffalos' football program was placed on five years probation, as well.

John was adamant he never received a car, nor was he ever approached by a booster club member. Unfortunately, the Colorado Department of Transportation couldn't corroborate John's statement. They had both a title and registration for the vehicle in their databanks. Federal agents found the luxury sports car parked at the Warner family's winter ski condominium in Aspen. John's mom and pop were both dumbfounded about how the vehicle got there!

Warner's parents hired a private investigator to find out who had set up their son. The PI was paid a $50,000 retainer in July but hadn't been heard from since. John became overly depressed. He was about to retire from football after one season but was talked into continuing by Syd West. Syd's sports marketing company thought they could still make a lot of money by representing John—as long as he performed up to everyone's expectations. And John was thrilled Billy West's dad had faith in him.

*****

Jared Goff couldn't believe it! He was at the scrimmage line, ready for the snap, when he noticed the Seahawks in complete disarray. Their five-two defensive alignment to stop the run was missing a linebacker! They had only ten men on the field and were frantically waving to the sideline to send in a player. The number three gap on the right side was wide open. Goff audibled away from the original plan to run left. If Warner could beat the free safety, he would be off to the races—an easy first down, and perhaps a touchdown to boot!

Goff put up three fingers behind his back to make sure John knew which hole to run through. The Seahawks had no way to stop the clock to get their linebacker in the game. This was going to be a piece of cake! Before calling for the snap, Goff sarcastically yelled loud enough for both teams to hear, "Game over, boys. Time to get on the bus to Sea-Tac!"

The hike was clean, and so was the handoff. Warner could have exploded through the three-gap but stopped at the line and shuffled left for some inexplicable reason. Defensive tackle, Poona Ford, couldn't believe his luck. The 311-pound lineman crunched John head-on and jarred the ball loose. Ford grabbed the ball and tucked it away. Strangely, Warner didn't even make an effort to regain control of the pigskin!

Now things were getting interesting. Seattle had the ball on the Rams thirty-one-yard line with no time outs but fifty-five seconds to play. Warner dropped his head in embarrassment and frustration as he walked sheepishly to the sideline. The entire Seahawks' defense surrounded Jared Goff and harassed the distressed quarterback, mimicking his bus ride announcement to the airport. The jubilant CenturyLink Field crowd was blaring decibels louder than the Boeing jumbojet test facility down I-5 in Everett! Curt Anderson perked up and slid to the edge of his seat.

The Seahawks still needed a touchdown, and that wasn't an easy task against the stout Rams' defense, especially with no timeouts. Russell Wilson had been in this position before, and he jogged out to the huddle as calm as a cucumber. For the All-Pro quarterback, fifty-five seconds was an eternity.

Chapter 33

The dark, bluish-gray cumulonimbus clouds moving slowly eastward from the Olympic range finally passed directly over CenturyLink Field during the change-of-possession commercial break. Starbucks' chance of running out of coffee in Seattle is greater than a rainstorm missing the Emerald City. By the time Russell Wilson received the ball from the center, a downpour was wreaking havoc on the FieldTurf artificial surface.

After calling for a play-action pass, Wilson bobbled the snap, regained a tenuous grip on the slick football, rolled out to his left, then slipped on the wet turf at the thirty-eight-yard line. A split-second later, defensive tackle Aaron Donald pounced on him, then pinned him down so the irate quarterback couldn't move. The clock was ticking ominously as Wilson's teammates were scrambling to pull Donald off their MVP. The crowd was booing vociferously!

Back home in Wisconsin, Curt Anderson was beside himself. "Get up, Russell, damn it! Get up! Come on, ref, that should be a personal foul on Donald! Get him off him! Hurry up!"

Carl knew Curt had made large wagers on the over forty-two total points and Seattle to cover the spread. He bit his lip with a slight grin as he watched his brother-in-law lose all control and start cussing at the TV. It looked like Mother Nature was going to trump the crime syndicate on this game! That was until back judge Kevin Yustis offered some help to the home team.

When Aaron Donald finally removed his 284 pounds of solid muscle off Wilson, the Hawk's quarterback jogged slowly with a noticeable limp back to the line. The play clock was down to twenty-six seconds when Yustis started waving his arms. The clock stopped, and the referees huddled. Then the head linesman walked to the center of the field and announced to the fans, "Seattle is charged with an injury-related timeout. Because they have none remaining, this will be an excessive fourth timeout and result in a ten-second runoff. Play clock operator, please set the time to sixteen seconds and start the twenty-five-second clock on my signal."

The crowd was eerily silent. Most were having a difficult time comprehending what just happened and the rule that was invoked. However, in the end, the raucous Seahawk fans were thrilled the clock had stopped. Russell once again limped to the line and stood behind center. But because he didn't have to spike the ball to stop the clock, he could look over the defensive alignment before calling the audible. Wilson stepped back three steps into a shotgun formation. The snap was good, and Wilson tried to hit DK Metcalf on a quick down and out, hoping he would gain fifteen yards and stop the clock by stepping out of bounds. But the ball slipped through Metcalf's fingers for an incomplete pass. It was third down with eight seconds left in the game, and the football rested on the thirty-eight-yard line. Wilson had no choice—it was time for a Hail Mary.

When Metcalf didn't make the catch, Curt put his hands over his face and shook his head. Two more cuss words slipped out.

Wilson took the snap and rolled left, giving his five wide receivers time to get into the end zone. Aaron Donald had once again sidestepped his blocker, and he could sense a game-ending sack was about to make him today's hero back home in Southern California. But as Donald dove for Wilson's thighs, Russell side-stepped, avoiding the tackle. He scrambled right as the time clock expired. When his receivers were in place, he launched the ball with a high arc and watched the melee ensue near the goalposts. Free safety Taylor Rapp jumped up with two hands and knocked the ball to the ground, and the Rams' frenzied celebratory dance had begun. The dejected Seahawks lowered their heads and walked off the field. Curt Anderson threw an empty beer bottle at the wall putting a rather large dent in the sheetrock!

But then the unbelievable happened. Twelve seconds after the play had ended, a flag was thrown high in the air by none other than back judge Keven Yustis. The Seattle fans saw it and let out a roar. Would they get another chance?

The call came in that the Hawk's Tyler Lockett had been interfered with by John Johnson. Terry Bradshaw was beside himself in the Fox Sports booth. "What the hell kind of penalty was that?!" he screeched into the mike, too fast for the editing crew to bleep out the underworld synonym.

Both teams had to regroup as players were beginning to shake hands, and some were heading to midfield for the postgame prayer. The Rams' coaching staff were accosting the referees with words Curt Anderson had never heard! Kevin Yustis walked away, shrugging his shoulders and smiling in contempt.

So, the Seahawks had one last chance. And as luck would have it, they had the ball on the one-yard line. The play was untimed, and barring a defensive penalty, it would be the final play.

After busting up his wall, Curt had stormed out to the porch to sulk. Carl hustled to him and yelled, "Get back in here. There was a horrific penalty called on LA, and Seattle has one last chance!"

"What?!" exclaimed Curt. "No crap, really?!" He slammed the door and took a seat back on the couch.

Russell Wilson called for a quarterback sneak. The Rams were waiting for it and flattened Wilson at the line of scrimmage. But this time, the celebration had no time to take root. Yustis had tossed the flag immediately but didn't blow his whistle to stop the play. According to the most hated man in LA, the Rams were offside. Head Coach Sean McVay sprinted onto the field and went nose-to-nose with Yustis. Five minutes later, he was escorted off the grounds by three security guards and would face a rather substantial fine for being expelled from the game.

Meanwhile, Fox Sports showed the play from every imaginable angle and could not see any Rams' player lined up offside or jump the snap. Howie Long was pleading on the air to NFL commissioner, Roger Goodell, to have Yustis fired. Even the Seattle fans' cheers had turned to laughter. They couldn't believe their good fortune. Either could Curt Anderson. Carl West knew it had nothing to do with luck.

After two half-the-distance-to-the-goal flags were assessed, one for the offsides and the other for Coach McVay's unsportsmanlike conduct penalty, the football was placed nine inches from the goal line. This time, Wilson faked a fullback plunge and ran the ball untouched on a bootleg. Seattle fans were hysterical with joy. As a safety precaution, the Seahawks declined to kick the extra point. The officials made haste to get off the field before the Rams' players could confront them. Kevin Yustis led the way.

"Wowser, wowser, wowser! That was a close call!" bellowed Curt. "Thank the Lord for great officials!"

Carl shook his head in disgust. "How on God's green earth do you think that was a fairly reffed game?"

"Oh, come on, you spoilsport. You should be happy for me. I just made several thousand more dollars. Final score was twenty-three to twenty-one, so the over forty-two bet was good. And Seattle covered the one and a half point spread. It just don't get no better than that, my friend!"

Curt didn't tell Carl that he also raked in $4,200 when the Dolphins implausibly upset the Patriots on the road. He didn't want to brag!

Chapter 34

Curt threw some burgers and brats on the grill after the miraculous and undeserved Seattle victory over LA was in the history books. Carl wondered if he was the only person, other than the crime syndicate themselves, who could see something fishy taking place inside the NFL. Last week's terrible officiating probably didn't alter which team won the game in Jacksonville and Carolina, but it did affect those who bet on the point spread and over/under. This week was a whole different story—the corrupt officiating did much more than disappoint a majority of legit gamblers—it changed the outcome of a crucial division football game. Making the playoffs would be one step harder for the Rams.

Carl shuddered at the thought of what he had just done. Was he right to interfere with the upcoming Sunday night game under the guise of a hypothetical criminal experiment?! Had he demolished professional sports integrity in an attempt to trap a crime syndicate's illegal gambling scheme? Was that not hypocrisy? By possibly adjusting the outcome of the 49ers vs. Cardinals game, he was just as bad as the crooks he was trying to stop! If he got caught in the middle, not only would Carl be facing prison time, his father's honor would be at stake. The newspapers would link Carl's failures as a fault of his upbringing. It could mar Billy West's squeaky clean reputation.

Thinking about the experiment, Carl panicked. Yes, the syndicate would suffer from the revision of Pete Callen's obituary, but so would either the 49ers or the Cardinals. Now he wondered if he should call the FBI or not. Once Carl reported what he had done, he, too, would be a felon. The FBI might appreciate his research into the illegal gaming operation, but they would disapprove of Carl's handling the matter independently. Molly would certainly divorce him, Grandpa Syd would eschew him, and his dad would be embittered somewhere in heaven.

As his anxious mind was about to explode with considerable trepidation, Carl took two bites of the bratwurst and placed it back on his paper plate. Curt didn't even notice his brother-in-law's discomposure—he was too euphoric about Seattle's win to perceive how thick the air had become. The men watched *Football Night in America*, NBC's pregame wrap-up of the day's games, and a preview of tonight's showcase event—the San Francisco 49ers at the Arizona Cardinals. For a good ten minutes, all Al Michaels and Cris Collingsworth could talk about was the Rams' shafting at the hands of referee Kevin Yustis. Carl was sick to his stomach.

The topper was when NBC replayed clips from last week's Carolina-Atlanta game, specifically the three nullified touchdowns called back by head linesman Jake Shrum. Collingsworth was risking his job by crucifying the NFL officials, but he didn't seem to care. "Referees need to be held accountable for the integrity of the game!"

Al Michaels then pointed out that Jake Shrum would be the head linesman for tonight's contest from Glendale, Arizona. Rules analyst Terry McAuley was asked to comment on why Shrum hadn't been suspended following a review of his mistaken calls in Charlotte last Sunday. Carl became nauseous listening to McAuley's response.

"Minneapolis-based Sports Officials Training Organization, better known as SOTO, has a contract with the NFL to train and place officials each week. I know this to be true because, during my last couple of years officiating, SOTO assigned my games, printed my paychecks, and gave me two performance reviews. In other words, the NFL has outsourced this important function to them.

"I spoke to SOTO's director, Rob Fornasiere, this week about Jake Shrum's performance on the field in Carolina. Citing a privacy agreement he has in place to protect his employees and their families from harassment, Rob indicated he couldn't get into specific details. However, he said Shrum received a formal reprimand and ten hours of mandatory retraining at their headquarters. Rob assured me that Shrum is an excellent referee and shouldn't be judged by just one game. So, I guess we'll see how he does tonight, right?"

Cris Collinsworth rolled his eyes, very much visible to the viewing audience. "Yeah, sure. I can't wait. Well then, let's move on to the game. Normally a player who says little beforehand, the Cardinals' Larry Fitzgerald made a bold prediction this week."

"Really?" asked Michaels in astonishment. "What did he have to say?"

Collinsworth grinned as he replied, "Larry predicted the team who played better would probably win. But if that didn't prove true, he claimed whoever scored the most points might be victorious."

Al Michaels laughed out loud. "***Probably*** win and ***might*** be victorious—well, Larry, don't quit your day job and become a bookie in Las Vegas!"

Carl stood and muttered at the television, "If they only knew."

"If who knew what?" asked Curt just to make small talk.

"Forget about it," responded Carl somberly. He then staggered to the porch and grabbed another beer from the cooler. He was dizzy, but it had nothing to do with alcohol.

Carl wasn't sure he could bear to watch the game.

Chapter 35

Sam Diggins rigged his Beneteau Oceanis luxury yacht with all the bells and whistles necessary for sailing alone: hi-tech electronics, automatic pilot, advanced radar system, and, of course, a windlass. But parking the sloop solo had always been a challenge. Through the wisdom that can only beget by years of practice, Sam had been able to adapt to the physical stress of launching and docking the sailboat by himself.

The yacht's name was Lucky, apropos for a boat owned by a lifelong gambler. Sam was looking forward to the day he could sail Lucky down its home on the St. Croix River to the Mississippi, then to the Gulf of Mexico and eventually around the world. If this year were profitable for him, he would take next year off and complete his bucket-list journey.

Sam had only a few more weekends to cruise on the St. Croix before the cold weather arrived, and the ice would force him to dry dock at the marina in Hudson for the winter. He had never married, nor did he ever want to be tied down with a wife and kids. Max, a purebred golden retriever, was his only family, and perhaps his only friend. Sam was an avid hunter who trained Max as a puppy, and the dog never lost a dead or wounded duck to a lake, river, or swamp in his three short years of life.

Sam's private dock could barely be seen by sailors navigating the river, and his mansion was hidden by prodigious red oaks, sugar maples, and dogwood trees. In autumn, the natural beauty when the leaves painted the bluffs in brilliant colors was more spectacular than a Monet masterpiece. His property sat on 325 acres of Wisconsin woodland and open prairie with 1,500 feet of frontage on the St. Croix. The residence was perched high on the bluffs and faced west towards Minnesota. The views through the massive walls of glass were extraordinary!

Sam acquired the property from the Wisconsin Department of Natural Resources during an auction held in 2018. A few folks raised an eyebrow when they heard he needed no loan to secure the land or house he was planning to build. On the auction qualification form, Sam wrote that he was an assistant funeral director. Could burying the dead be that profitable?

Through the grapevine, he heard that an architect from Florida was the best of the best when transforming a dream house into a reality. Randy Hansen was skeptical the assistant funeral director from Holmes Mortuary could afford his services. But when a $1,000,000 retainer was wired to InterPlan Architects, Randy was on his LearJet the next day heading for Wisconsin.

After bouncing around the beautiful wooded property on an ATV, Randy had an idea for constructing a stately country manor that blended with the environment. He meticulously designed Sam's home so it combined old-world elegance with modern perpetuity. Skylights provided extensive natural light throughout the charming and serene formal and informal areas. Stylish outdoor spaces and a magnificent private courtyard enhanced the panoramic riverscape named Rivière Tombeaux by Father Louis Hennepin in 1683. Randy incorporated a sports court and exercise room into the blueprint, then added a gambling parlor and small theater with a thirty-four-foot-wide screen to entertain guests, who were actually Sam's business associates.

Sam was so delighted with the finished product that he passed Randy Hansen's name on to his boss. The head honcho of Holmes Mortuary owned several homes throughout the world and planned to build a new villa on a private island in the Caymans. Randy had no idea what his clients did for a living, but he was sure that providing the deceased with a final resting place here on earth wasn't it.

*****

Sam opened a bottle of Dos Equis, then plopped down on the massive leather couch in the den and turned on the seventy-two-inch Sony OLED television. Max vehemently wagged his tail, then laid down on a Persian carpet at Sam's feet. Both had dined on grilled ribeyes as they watched the reddish-orange sunset light up the sky on a perfect fall evening in the midwest.

Sam turned on ESPN to check the scores, but more specifically, the scores that supported his lavish lifestyle. Dallas won twenty-eight to twenty-one over New York but didn't cover the nine and a half point spread. Check. The total points scored was less than fifty-one. Check. The Seahawks nipped the Rams twenty-three to twenty-one, covering the one and a half point spread. And, the total points scored was over forty-two. Check check. The announcers were squawking about poor officiating, causing Sam to chuckle. He petted Max and declared, "Ah, referees, you can't live with them—and you can't live without them!" Max wagged his tail once again.

Last on his checklist was the Miami Dolphins contest with the New England Patriots in Foxborough. Each week, the crime syndicate wagered on one team that had little chance to win. Sam's biggest challenge was to rig a moneyline upset game. The payouts were much higher than either the spreads or total points bets—as long as the underdog won. But a moneyline wager was a higher risk for the organization. The syndicate would need both corrupt officials and players to ensure a win. And that could be tricky because some teams were so bad even the devious manipulations didn't help!

Sam didn't use the Rankins's email account or obituaries for the weekly moneyline game. Instead, he texted a disreputable employee of a major newspaper—not the Gazette—to publish a code illegal gamers could use to pick the NFL upset winner that week. This moneyline cipher was printed in a different section of the newspaper than the death notices.

Since the beginning of sports gambling, major upsets in football were prone to suspicion. At the college level, how could Troy State defeat Alabama? How could Appalachian State beat Michigan in the Big House? Last week, tiny Ohio Dominican University almost blew their golden opportunity several times but held on to edge mighty Ohio State twenty-two to twenty-one.

The syndicate thought about fixing college football games but had no in with the selection of officials. So they focused solely on the NFL and relied on SOTO to do their dirty work. This week, the Miami Dolphins nipped the New England Patriots seventeen to fourteen on a last-second field goal. Like magic, Sam and Rob Fornasiere perfectly planned and placed key players and officials on the field, and voilà, the upset game of the week was a success!

During the first half of the 49ers versus Cardinals game, Sam fell asleep on the couch. Max did the same on the rug next to him. It had been a terrific weekend for sailing, and Sam spent Saturday night anchored underneath the full moon listening to the Yacht Rock classics on Sirius Satellite Radio. But his mind wandered to thoughts of the syndicate's future purchase of the Minnesota Vikings, and he worried things might not go as planned. Would taking on Carl West be a good thing or a bad thing? Sam finally dozed off just before daybreak.

Three minutes were remaining in the game when Sam woke up with a stiff neck from lying awkwardly on the couch. Max was licking Sam's face, wagging his tail, and ready for a Sojo's Peanut Butter and Jelly Flavor dog treat. He also thought it was time for some serious petting and belly itching.

Sam glanced at the game, then sat up and smiled. Another clean sweep for the syndicate! San Francisco was holding on to a four-point lead, twenty-four to twenty, against the hometown Cardinals. The 49ers had the ball and were running out the clock. Arizona was out of time outs.

"Well, Max, we can put this game to bed and start planning out next week." He tickled Max under the ears, and his best friend started barking with joy. A Soji dog treat would be the pièce de résistance!

Chapter 36

Without saying a word, Curt Anderson flounced angrily out of the den to the backyard. He then grabbed two cold, leftover bratwursts from the grill and tossed them over the fence. Carl could hear him kicking the patio furniture and cussing up a storm.

Carl gulped the last sips of his Miller Lite, then sauntered carefully to the sliding glass door that Curt left open. He was trying to think of something to say that would calm down his brother-in-law. "Hey, got to go, bro. Thanks for a great time! Maybe let's do some duck hunting next time, huh?" Curt didn't respond—he was pacing the patio like a madman!

Carl smiled as he shut the Tesla's door and drove off. By God, the experiment worked! But unfortunately, he was now sure Curt had connections with the syndicate, or worse yet, was part of their organization. Carl had no doubt Pete Callen's obituary prompted Curt to wager on the over fifty total points scored in the Sunday night game, as well as betting on the 49ers to cover the seven-point spread. And Curt wouldn't be the only loser—the syndicate probably took a considerable hit to their cash flow.

What if this so-called crime syndicate was actually the Mafia? People in the know always suspected they controlled various casinos in Las Vegas. How was he ever going to explain to Molly that her brother was associated with the mob?

Carl slammed on the brakes and pulled over to the side of the road. His feet were now firmly planted in a catch-twenty-two situation. If he turned over his evidence to the FBI, he could be charged with fraud because Pete Callen is a real, living person who Carl knowingly misrepresented as being deceased. If Pete caught wind of his fake death notice, he could sue both Carl and the Gazette for libel. But if Carl didn't turn over the evidence, the syndicate or mob or whoever they are would continue their racketeering ways, albeit with something other than a coded obituary. They would not be stung twice by a troublemaking journalist.

Carl's thoughts turned to Jim Bowman, his predecessor at the Gazette. The documents he found in Dr. Kohlrusch's desk indicated Jim didn't die from cancer. Instead, he was poisoned. Had Jim tried to cross up the mob, too?

Carl still wasn't sure that Sam Diggins knew he had replaced Jim. However, if he didn't know now, he soon would. Carl had a gut feeling that Curt would totally disregard family ties and tell Sam the truth. The syndicate would then realize he was the instigator of their gambling losses from the Sunday Night Game of the Week. Sooner or later, they would track him down and kill him. Carl would place his bet on sooner rather than later—no pun intended!

He pounded the steering wheel with his fists. Carl reflected on why he chose this experiment in the first place. He wanted to stop the syndicate from compromising the NFL. His dad, the great Billy West, would have called it the honorable thing to do! What a mess he had created! It just now occurred to Carl that his boss, George Markins, was most likely involved, as well. He and Curt were close friends, and it was Curt's recommendation to George that got him the job. If the feds investigated, George would deny any complicity related to racketeering. He would say Carl sent the eulogies directly to the editor, and he had no idea the obituaries were fakes. George always phoned Carl when he wanted him to submit obits from the Rankins's account. He never emailed Carl or left a paper trail. And regrettably, Carl had deleted George's voicemails out of frustration with his boss's demands. How stupid! He pounded his fists on the dash, then once more on the steering wheel.

Carl had only one logical option at this point. He needed to pick up Molly and hightail it out of New Richmond. After arriving at a place to hide, he would tell her everything and show her the evidence. Molly needed to abandon her columnist position immediately at the Dispatch. Sam Diggins knew precisely where her office was located. Once he found out that Carl betrayed the syndicate, they would come looking for her, too.

*****

Max's excessive barking from the kitchen woke Sam up a few minutes before the light of dawn. He glanced at the clock and noticed it was 6:13 a.m. Usually, Max could hold his need to relieve himself until Sam let him outside around 7:30. Sam guessed Max had too much to drink last night—just like himself. He rolled groggily off the mattress and lumbered to the kitchen. There he was greeted by a Glock Twenty-Two pointed at his face.

Instinctively, Sam stopped on a dime and raised his hands in the air. "Whoa, whoa, whoa!" he exclaimed. "What's this all about?!"

Sitting in a chair was Oliver Harwas, the syndicate boss's right-hand man. He had his finger on the trigger and was itching to pull it. He was tired from flying the Airbus A380 all night from the Caymans to Minneapolis-St. Paul International airport, and despite FAA regulations to the contrary, he would be logging another five hours on the return trip shortly.

"I'm holding you accountable, Sam," said Oliver calmly. "Rob Fornasiere is your puppet, and you are supposed to pull his strings to make sure we win our bets."

Sam was deeply perplexed. "What are you talking about? Everything went as planned. We won all our wagers!"

Oliver stared at Sam and didn't say a word for what seemed like an eternity. "Are you messing with me, Sam?! Trust me, you don't want to mess with me." Oliver stood up and took a step toward Sam with the gun aimed at his nose.

"I honestly don't know what you're talking about!" Sam's face turned several shades of pale, and beads of sweat dripped off his forehead. "Please, explain why you are upset!" He inched backward a few steps, and Max started barking incessantly.

Oliver changed his aim from Sam to Max. "Shut the dog up, or I'll put both you and him out of your misery." Sam grabbed Max's collar, slowly moved him to the patio door, and let him outside. Max sensed danger. He continued yapping and jumping back and forth on the glass, trying to help his best friend. Sam ambled back to the kitchen.

"Were you sleeping through the Cardinals-49ers game?" asked Oliver sarcastically. "We lost both bets—the over/under and the point spread, you idiot!"

Sam shook his head. "No way! We won them both! I swear! The final score was twenty-four to twenty, which meant we won the under fifty. And the 49ers didn't cover the seven-point spread!"

Oliver scrunched his nose and squinted his eyes. "Are you loco, son?! We took the over fifty, not the under, and the 49ers were supposed to cover the spread. I have Pete Callen's obituary right here to prove it!" Oliver handed Sam his iPhone with Pete's obit opened from the Gazette website:

> *Pete Callen, age 50 of San Francisco, California, died peacefully in his home on September 17th. He is survived by his wife Doris, two young sons, John and Jim, and many aunts, uncles, nieces, and nephews. His entire extended family resides in Oversage, Arizona.*
>
> *Pete will be remembered for his great sense of humor, good sportsmanship, and loving ways.*
>
> *A memorial service will be held at 7:00 p.m on Sunday, September 20th, at Morley's Funeral Home in San Francisco. Due to traffic congestion in the area, visitors should plan ahead so they don't arrive late.*

Sam scanned it, then frantically pleaded, "No, no, no! This isn't what I sent to the Gazette! It's totally the damn opposite! Let me show you what I sent to our agent on the Rankins's account!"

Panic-stricken, Sam pulled up the Rankins's email he had sent:

> *Pete Callen, age 50 of San Francisco, California, died peacefully in his home on September 17th. He is survived by his wife Doris, two young sons, John and Jim, and many aunts, uncles, nieces, and nephews. His entire extended family resides in Underbrush, Arizona.*
>
> *Pete will be remembered for his great sense of humor, good sportsmanship, and loving ways.*
>
> *A memorial service will be held at 7:00 p.m on Sunday, September 20th, at Morley's Funeral Home in San Francisco. It is advised friends arrive early as a large crowd is expected.*

Sam pointed frenetically at the keywords. "There! I specifically stated ***Underbrush***, but the obit now says ***Oversage***! And I said ***early*** in the last sentence, but it was published as ***late***! There's only one possible explanation—our obit writer is screwing us! Just like that damn Jim Bowman did!"

Remaining composed, Oliver reread Pete Callen's obituary. Then he slipped the Glock back into his belt and sat down. "Who is this new guy who works for the Gazette?"

Sam was confused by the question. Why wasn't Oliver Harwas, his boss's confidant, aware Carl West had replaced Jim Bowman? Oliver must not have been told that Molly was married to the obit writer. Maybe the boss didn't want Oliver to know! If that was the case, Sam wasn't about to tell him. In this organization, it's best to keep your mouth shut! Sam took a deep breath to gather himself. "A man Markins hired back in July. I trusted George to find someone dependable."

"What about Rob Fornasiere? Why didn't he notice the obituary that was published was different than the one you sent to him?"

"Rob doesn't read the obits, and neither do the officials or the players we have recruited. I call or text him, and he sets everything up. Our gambling operatives in the casinos and online are the only ones who read the obits, and they make the wagers based upon the codes!"

"Why the hell don't you have him check the obituaries as a failsafe measure?!" Oliver's composure was beginning to fade.

"Because he needs extra time to arrange the officials and coordinate with the players. Most times, the obituary isn't published until Friday afternoon. That's barely enough time for Rob to get everyone in place. That's why I just call or text him with the info."

Oliver stood up and slowly paced the kitchen while rubbing his chin. He debated placing a call to the Caymans and asking the boss what he should do, but the boss trusted him to make the right decisions on his behalf. Sam said nothing as he watched and waited for Oliver to say something. Sam's thoughts were moving in a thousand different directions. How could this happen?!

Oliver shot a stern glance at Sam. Then he issued an ominous order. "This new obit writer, whoever he is, I trust you will find him and take care of the situation. Do you get my drift?"

Sam nodded and followed Oliver out the door. Max barked and growled as Sam hurried to restrain his pet.

Oliver flew the Airbus back to the boss's private island in the Caymans. Little did he know that he would be returning to the Midwest before the day had ended.

Chapter 37

"We need to leave now, Molly!" pleaded Carl frantically.

"You haven't told me why, Carl. Unless you do, I need to go to work. And so do you! You can't be skipping out like last week!" Molly was applying makeup as rapidly as was humanly possible. Monday mornings were horrible, and she hadn't slept well since Carl stormed into the house at 1:30 a.m and demanded they pack up and head out to Lake Tahoe immediately. She blew him off and told him they would talk before she drove into Minneapolis, but for now, she needed to sleep. Carl had loaded his hunting rifle and guarded the front door until she awoke. Another night of insomnia—this time by choice.

On the way back to New Richmond from Eau Claire, Carl had decided to act on the lesser of two evils—he would meet with the FBI after showing Molly the evidence. Yes, he would most likely be charged with fraud, but if he were instrumental in shutting down the crime syndicate's illegal gaming operation, perhaps he would be given leniency. The do-nothing option no longer existed. Once the syndicate knew he was their culprit, his entire family would be in peril.

Carl didn't want to go into detail with Molly at the house, so he decided they would drive to the safest place he could think of—Grandpa Syd's home in Nevada. His grandfather had a hunting cabin tucked neatly away in the Sierras that could only be accessed by an all-terrain vehicle. Carl would phone his grandfather and try to convince him that he had uncovered something that put his life in danger and suggest the three of them move temporarily into the tiny mountain cottage. There, Carl would interpret the evidence and untangle the gambling scheme, then have them hunker down while he drove to the FBI's field office in Sacramento.

But now he had an obstacle to overcome. Molly wasn't about to accompany him anywhere until he explained his reasoning. "I promise you will know everything as soon as we get to Grandpa's place! Please, Molly, just trust me!"

"Now that I think about it, you should stay home from work today and talk to a psychiatrist about your paranoia! You're scaring me, Carl!" Molly gave him a peck on the cheek. "Okay, I've got to go. Please move your car so I can get mine out of the garage."

Carl stood with his hands on his hips and refused to budge. Molly shook her head in disgust and shuffled around him. She moved the Tesla herself with the extra set of keys she had in her purse. Furious with her husband, she squealed the tires as she sped out of the neighborhood.

Carl had no other alternative than to tell Molly everything when she got home from work. She would never agree to a twenty-seven-hour road trip to Nevada without knowing. But the more Carl thought about it, maybe waiting until tomorrow would be better anyway. Today, he would remove everything from his office that the FBI might want to see—computers, phone systems, and files. His handwritten notes would demonstrate he was trying to expose the problem, not become part of it.

Carl showered and hustled to Caribou Coffee for his morning fix. He ordered two large mocha lattes to go, each with a triple shot of espresso. If the caffeine didn't wake him up, perhaps the sugar rush would do the trick. After paying for the coffee, he turned from the counter and was startled to see the man waiting in line behind him.

"Well, if it isn't my good friend Carl West!" exclaimed Dr. Mike Kohlrusch. "Hey, I've got a few minutes to kill before I need to go to the hospital. Wanna chat about yesterday's games? I'd love to get an expert's opinion!"

Carl really didn't have the time to talk about NFL strategies and blunders, but after breaking into Mike's office a few nights ago, Carl was on a guilt trip. He wanted to know if anyone at the hospital had mentioned seeing a Dr. Kildare—like, perhaps, Jalen, the custodian who had given Carl the master keys. Or did Mike know his office has been entered? Even though he was masked and covered up well, Carl knew the security cameras were running. If Mike said something about the incident, was Carl bold enough to tell him the truth? Could he then ask about Jim Bowman's poisoning?

Carl was overly fatigued and extremely exhausted. His mind was focused on emptying his office and then getting the hell out of Dodge with his wife. But Jim's death was a crucial part of the evidence he was about to present to the FBI. Could he get Mike Kohlrusch to spill the beans? It was worth a few minutes of coffee conversation to find out.

"Yeah, sure, Mike! What could be better than a chat with my esteemed doctor friend?!"

*****

Mike talked about nothing other than football—the New Richmond Tigers high school team, the Wisconsin Badgers, and yesterday's NFL games. He commented on the lack of good officiating and even mentioned retiring and becoming an NFL referee himself. When Carl asked him about news from the hospital, Mike smiled and said, "Same ol', same ol'!" A break in to his office was never mentioned.

At nine o'clock, Mike said he needed to go. Carl had downed both lattes and was wired. As he was opening the Tesla door, Carl saw a black Chevy Tahoe out of the corner of his eye. It was parked near the liquor store entrance. He turned and stared, then saw the same bald man who had been following him weeks ago sitting in the driver's seat. This time, the man was staring back.

Carl thought about approaching the bald man, but time wasn't on his side. He needed to wrap things up at the office quickly. Soon he would be long gone from New Richmond—and long gone from the stranger in the Chevy Tahoe. He fired up the Tesla and drove to work.

Carl rolled up the office door and froze. There was nothing there! Not even his Ikea desk and chair! The computer and phone systems were gone, as were his files and bulletin board. The notes he had planned to show the FBI had disappeared! Carl dropped down on his haunches and pounded the floor with both fists.

"Stand up and turn around!" shouted a voice a few feet away. Stunned, Carl quickly stood, then instinctively raised his hands in the air. The barrel of a .38 Smith and Wesson Special was placed on his forehead. The man holding the revolver had his finger firmly set on the trigger. Carl knew him well. It was his boss.

"You double-crossed me, Carl," stated George Markins. "That's very unfortunate for you."

Carl didn't even try to play dumb. He knew exactly why George was here. But still, the gun surprised him. "George, what the hell, man! Put the gun down—please!"

"I don't think so, Carl. Even though you're my best friend's brother-in-law, I can't let you live. I saw your notes—you know too much."

"Look. Obviously, I know about the gambling scheme. But I promise that it ends right here and now. I won't say a word to anyone—even Molly. Just fire me, and I'll start a new life a long way away from here. You'll never hear from me again! Please, George!"

"Sorry, no can do. I have my orders from up above. You messed with the wrong people, Carl. But I'll give you a choice on how you want to die." George held the gun in his right hand while he reached into his shirt pocket with his left hand. He pulled out a syringe with a long needle attached. George lifted it to eye level, so it was displayed next to his revolver. "One quick jab to your carotid, and you'll doze off peacefully with minimal pain. It will look like you passed away from food poisoning. Maybe the authorities will blame Caribou Coffee!" George's attempt at humor angered Carl.

"You were the person who poisoned Jim Bowman, weren't you?" asked Carl, clearly stalling for time.

"Yes, that was me. You're a smart man, Carl! Jimmy tried to run and tell, too. The difference between you and him was that he knew he would be working for the syndicate when he was hired. You were clueless. You should have stayed clueless, my friend!"

"I ain't your friend—and I never was, you SOB." Carl was trying to keep George talking. If the gun dropped even an inch, Carl would make his move and grab George's arm.

George laughed. "So, what's it going to be, Carl, needle or bullet?"

"This place is rented by the Gazette. If you shoot me here, it will trace back to you. You'll rot in the Supermax prison in Boscobel dreaming about your glory days."

"Well, then, I guess we'll find out." George lowered the gun slightly to the bridge of Carl's nose and started to pull the trigger. Suddenly, a blast sounded from the alley. Blood and brain matter exploded from the back of George's skull, and he hit the ground hard.

Dumbfounded, Carl's mouth was wide open in disbelief. He was now staring directly at George's assassin, who had lowered his weapon and was staring back with a grim expression on his face.

"Time to go! We'll take your car!" demanded the old bald man as he waved frantically at Carl. They rolled down the office door with George Markins tucked away inside, his corpse lying face down in a pool of his own blood. Carl and the bald man dashed to the Tesla and gunned the sportscar down the alley.

"Where to?" asked a distraught Carl.

"Park your car in front of the library. Then we'll switch vehicles. My Chevy Tahoe is across the street by the Civic Center."

Carl slipped the Tesla into an open slot, and the two men scampered across First Street. After they slammed the doors of the bald man's SUV, Carl shot a glance at him. He was both grateful and perplexed that this mystery man had just saved his life.

"You have a lot of explaining to do," Carl declared.

Chapter 38

The bald man wove his black Chevy Tahoe through New Richmond's residential streets as if he were on the final lap at Monaco. He headed east out of town on County Road K for four miles, then exploded south on T, running stop signs with barely a tap on his brakes. Carl could see the Tahoe's speedometer—it was buried at 140 mph! He could also see the .45 caliber Winchester Magnum semiautomatic pistol resting loosely on the man's lap—the same gun that ended George Markins's life. The two men drove in silence, mainly because the passenger didn't want to distract the driver. A loss of control now and this ride could end upside-down in the rubble of a collapsed silo.

The Tahoe finally slowed a half-mile from the Hammond Golf Course, and the bald man turned sharply onto a tractor road that led into the woods. Carl knew precisely where he was because he had been down this path during his first week on the job. This led to Jim Bowman's gorgeous cottage home.

"Wait here!" ordered the bald man after slamming the brakes just short of Jim's wraparound deck. Carl shot a baffled look at him but didn't say a word. The man exited the car slowly, unlocked the safety of his gun, and ambled carefully up the steps to the front door. Carl watched him walk methodically around the perimeter of the cottage, checking windows and doors. Who did he think was in there?!

When it appeared the property was secure, the bald man pulled a key out of his pocket, unlocked the front door, and entered slowly with his gun pointed forward. A few anxious moments later, he reappeared at the door and motioned for Carl to come in. Carl was a bundle of nerves. He opened the passenger door and surveyed his surroundings, unsure what he was looking for but agitated nonetheless. He cautiously entered the house as if he were afraid of stepping on a land mine.

The bald man pointed to a leather chair in the den, and Carl sat down guardedly. The man left the room momentarily, then returned with a Crown Royal bottle, two glasses, and an ice bucket. "Want one?" he asked.

"Yes, please," replied Carl faintly. "Straight up, no ice. Fill it to the top if you don't mind."

The bald man sat in a recliner on the other side of an end table from Carl. Deep in thought, he slowly took a sip of the Canadian whiskey, then another. Finally, without looking at Carl, the man muttered, "Okay, so where do I begin?"

*****

"My name is Jack Bowman," stated the bald man impassively. Carl stared at him in circumspect silence. "My son is Jim Bowman. I'm an ex-CIA agent."

Carl nodded. "Go on."

"Jim and I had a falling out a few years ago when he up and left his advertising job with the *Norfolk Virginia-Pilot* newspaper to move to Wisconsin. No offense to you, but I couldn't understand why he would want to write obituaries for a living. I hadn't spoken to him for months, so last June I called his cell phone and found out it was no longer in service. Then I phoned the Gazette, and they told me he had recently passed away. I was overcome with grief and felt an enormous amount of guilt for not communicating with him for such a long time. He was buried up in some small town named Siren instead of near me, for God's sake! I couldn't believe it!

"My days with the CIA taught me to be cynical of most everyone and everything. Jim was a healthy young man, and I couldn't envision him getting cancer in his thirties. Being retired, I decided to ease my mind and make sure everything surrounding his career and death was on the up-and-up. When I read the obituaries he had written, I knew something was very wrong. They were not beautiful eulogies or biographies family members of a deceased love one would have expected. Simply put, they were terribly short and horribly written!

Mary Reppe, an ex-colleague of mine in the CIA, deciphered codes for a living. I emailed Jim's obits to her, and she immediately suspected foul play. She guessed Jim was involved in illegal activities and was using his position to tip off criminals somehow. Mary suggested it might deal with professional sports and point shaving. She checked with a friend in the FBI, and sure enough, the bureau was investigating an online gambling ring that was using a variety of offshore accounts to funnel their winnings.

"I started following you because I wasn't sure if you had something to do with my son's death. You assumed his position with the Gazette shortly after he died, and the obituaries you wrote were very similar to his. I now believe you are an innocent victim of a massive illegal gaming scheme."

"And what makes you believe that?" asked Carl tepidly.

"I broke into your office one night and hacked your computer. I forwarded all your emails to my personal account. Then, I perused your makeshift bulletin board and the Post-Its you made. After studying your notes, I knew you were on to something. I was beginning to understand the codes printed in the Gazette, so I carefully read every obituary you wrote since you were hired. I verified the obits sent to you contained information to tip off gamblers.

"Yesterday, I watched the Cowboys-Giants game and the Seahawks-Rams contest, and I noticed everything went as planned according to your notes. I checked the emails and correlated them to the published obits on the Gazette website. Then, I read your email that contained Pete Callen's eulogy. I assumed the Cardinals-49ers game would end with less than fifty points scored, and the 49ers wouldn't cover the spread. When that didn't happen, I was confused. So I checked Pete Callen's obit on the website, and I noticed it wasn't the same as the email. I put two and two together and realized you must have changed the wording to trap the syndicate. I knew right then your life would be in danger. That's why I showed up at your office this morning—to warn you. I had no plan to kill anyone. I didn't think the mob would act so rapidly."

Carl relaxed a bit but needed to know more. Jack had used the word mob in place of the syndicate, but Carl thought he was just talking loosely. "Thank you, Mr. Bowman. I owe you my life."

"No, son, you don't owe me anything. And please call me Jack. Even my kids called me by my first name. Evidently, they had a problem with the word dad."

"And you may call me Carl. How did you find out about Jim's involvement with the syndicate?"

"First of all, Carl, refer to them what they are—the mob. They have connections to the Sicilian Mafia, and they use multiple offshore accounts. Their operatives wager online, and thanks to your notes, I now know how the bets are made. Mary gave me a list of some names the FBI suspects work for them."

Carl was dazed! He should have known! A wave of fear blasted over him like hurricane-force winds. Yes, the Mafia would kill his wife and grandfather at the drop of a hat to keep their activities a secret. He needed to get Molly now! But he required confirmation of one other concern, and maybe Jack would know. "You said Mary had the names of some of the operatives who are gaming illegally online."

"Yes," replied Jack. He opened his wallet and pulled out a folded piece of paper with twenty-eight names on it. "I have the list right here. But Mary said there might be many more people involved."

"Would you check your list for a name? Curt Anderson, my brother-in-law. Is he part of the—?"

Jack finished the sentence for Carl. "The mob? I'm sorry to tell you this, but yes, Carl, your brother-in-law is an operative."

"What do you mean by that? You didn't even glance at your list! How do you even know my brother-in-law?!"

Ignoring the question, Jack added, "I also know the man I killed was George Markins, your boss."

Puzzled, Carl leaned toward Jack and asked, "You knew George and Curt?! How?!"

"They were old friends of Jim's from his college days. I'll explain more about that later. Anyway, knowing George worked with my son Jim at the Gazette, I asked Mary Reppe to put a tracer on George's cell phone to see who he called. To make a long story short, George was in contact with Curt Anderson at all hours of the day and night. Thanks to new CIA technologies, Mary could remotely tap into Curt's emails and IP address. In other words, she knows the websites he visits and the frequency. Carl, we're certain your brother-in-law gambles online for the mob. What you may not know is that he double dips, which is a very dangerous activity!"

"What do you mean by 'double dips'?" asked Carl hesitantly. He thought he knew the answer but wanted to hear it from Jack.

"We're pretty sure the mob has no idea Curt uses his own money to place the same wagers for himself. Doing so would put their entire scheme at high risk. Online casinos track IP addresses and keep a careful watch on their bettors. Most gamblers don't know they're being monitored. When one person makes two bets on the same wager instead of one bigger bet, it raises a red flag. Sportsbooks would think the gambler was circumventing the maximum bet threshold, which violates casino rules. To minimize suspicions, the syndicate would explicitly nix double-dipping for its operatives. Obviously, Curt hasn't been caught. If he had, he would be your next obituary. You don't mess with the mob's rules!"

"Since you and Mary were able to figure out the illegal gaming scheme, why haven't you turned it over to the FBI?"

"We're waiting until we can produce more evidence. We're sure of the Mafia's involvement, but not sure which division within the organization controls the operation. In other words, we don't know who's running the show. Until I broke into your office and read your notes, I thought you were one of them. That's why I hung around New Richmond off and on for the past three months. Seeing you were there, I decided to centralize my investigation in your community. I've rented a house a couple of homes down from you on Lincoln Road."

Astonished, Carl asked rhetorically, "You're one of our neighbors?!"

"Yes, and I've tracked when you and Molly leave the house and who has visited you."

"How do you know who visits us?"

"License plates, Carl. I'm ex-CIA, remember? But that's not important. There's one other reason I have for not turning the investigation over to the FBI. I need to find a way to help my other son, John."

"John's in prison for racketeering," stated Carl. He observed Jack's face, looking for a reaction.

Surprised, Jack raised an eyebrow. "So, you know about John. I'm impressed with your inquiry skills! But there's something you may not know."

"What's that?"

"John is one hundred percent innocent. He pled guilty to save his brother." Carl peered at Jack skeptically, and Jack could feel his doubt. "Okay, let's go back a few months and begin when I arrived in New Richmond and started following you. I knew you saw me and were suspicious right from the get-go. As you were pulling out of the Hammond Golf Course, you stopped and looked in the rearview mirror. I've been trained to notice little things like that, Carl. But I was just as apprehensive of you. Remember, I didn't know Jim was involved in illegal gaming until I got here and began investigating his death. Once I discovered what he was doing, I thought about my other son John."

"What do you mean? I'm not sure I understand."

"I hadn't heard from John for a couple of years, which was strange because he and I got along great. He had phoned or emailed me at least once a week after his mother passed. But I knew he was working in a remote location on the Arctic Ocean, so I assumed he had limited Internet and wireless, which was why we had lost touch.

I tried to call his cell but got a recording that it was no longer in service. Then, two years later, I received a shocking letter from John. He wrote to me from a federal prison in Oregon and told me he had been sentenced to thirty years for racketeering. He didn't say what or why or how or anything! The only thing John did say was 'for the sake of the family, don't ever come to visit me!' I couldn't believe it! Not my son, no way! He had been an exemplary kid growing up—excellent student, great athlete, and tons of friends!"

Jack's voice was beginning to crack. He paused a moment to regain his composure. Another sip of Crown Royal seemed to help.

Jack continued. "Think back to July or August when you didn't see me for a month or so." Carl nodded. "Well, I drove up to Alaska to check out John's story, and to see if his racketeering charges could be linked to Jim's illegal gambling operation. I feared both my sons had broke bad after their mother died, and I had failed in my parental duties."

"What did you find out?"

"The syndicate's gaming operation is headquartered in Prudhoe Bay, Alaska. I'm sure they built it there to be as far from the FBI and IRS as possible. The building has a sign out front that says Holmes Mortuary, and the paperwork filed in the North Slope borough indicates they are a subsidiary of Rankins Corporation. As I'm sure you know by now, Rankins is the holding company for several newspapers, including the Eau Claire Gazette. They always file their taxes on time and have never received disciplinary action from an audit. The Mafia profits from illegal activities, but they know better than to screw with the US government's revenue stream!

"Anyway, Holmes Mortuary is a false front for a nonexistent business. And, it's the only funeral home listed in Prudhoe Bay. I talked to several local folks who knew of the place, but they had no idea who owned it. They all said Prudhoe Bay existed for the petroleum industry, and the workers considered themselves temporary residents. So, when someone died, the body was flown back to their permanent homes, usually somewhere in the lower forty-eight. They all wondered how Holmes stayed in business because they never had any customers!"

"So, how did John become involved in all this," asked Carl. "And what makes you sure he was innocent?"

"As I mentioned, it all started with our probe into Jim's job. Let me explain. Mary Reppe tapped into the Gazette personnel files. Remarkably, they have a cloud-based backup system in the event of fire or theft. Except for people who work in a high-tech industry, most US citizens have no idea the CIA can access any cloud account. Anyway, Jim was hired by George Markins, but we first wanted to find out how the Gazette employed Markins.

"It seems George came on board due to a glowing reference from Giuseppe Benotti."

"Are you talking about Giuseppe Benotti, the soccer star from Italy?"

"Yes, one and the same. We believe Giuseppe had connections to the Mafia, and someone inside the mob asked him to write a letter of recommendation for George. Knowing that George played soccer for UW-Eau Claire, Guiseppe spiced up the letter with a jaw-dropping athletic overtone. Add in the fact that George was a local boy, and a few days later, he was brought on as the assistant human resources director. Remember when I said George and Curt were friends with my son Jim during his college years?"

Carl's curiosity was peaking. "Yes."

"Well, George hired my son Jim at the Gazette, no doubt because of their friendship. Jim was a great kid but just average in school. Whereas John graduated with honors from MIT, Jim barely finished with a C average in journalism from Old Dominion."

"If George and Curt both went to UW-Eau Claire, how did they ever meet Jim?"

"Okay, here's the kicker—no pun intended. Jim was the goalie on the Monarch's soccer team. He met George and Curt during his freshman year at a week-long tournament in Madison, and they became good friends. The following summer, Jim vacationed in Wisconsin for a month before landing a job as a blackjack dealer in

Atlantic City. Curt and George loved to gamble, so they flew to New Jersey and hung out with him for a few weeks. Jim told me the threesome were best buddies."

"Let me see if I'm catching your drift," stated Carl. "You think Jim got involved in the illegal gaming operation because he was friends with George and Curt? That would make sense. But how does this all relate to John's innocence on racketeering charges? You told me you think he was protecting Jim. Why?"

"While I was up in Prudhoe Bay, I broke into Holmes Mortuary one evening. I had scouted the place for a week and noticed they have four security guards on the nightshift that follow a specific routine. They arrive at 10:00 p.m. to replace the afternoon shift, walk the premises, then check doors until precisely 2:00 a.m. Now get this—all four take a forty-five-minute break at the same time and play poker in the lounge. Unbelievably stupid!

"Anyway, I had to act quickly. They don't even attempt to look like a mortuary! No false lobby with caskets for sale or anything like that. But, they have a receptionist's desk where you enter from the parking lot. There's a total of five rooms—four offices and the lounge. Each office has a Rankins's computer—no, not an IBM, Dell, or Apple—a Rankins's homemade contraption!"

Carl nodded. "I think I know exactly what it looks like. I had one in my office that was basically off-limits to me."

"I only had time to enter one room. I think I hit the jackpot with the one I picked. According to a paystub left on the desk, the office belonged to Enzo Esposito. I tried to turn on the computer, but the security system was something I've never seen before. I worked at it a few minutes, then gave up. However, the phone had a digital voice recorder that was full of messages. I downloaded the messages onto my iPhone and got out of there."

"What do you mean you downloaded the messages? How?"

"I have a device. It's a CIA toy. Please just leave it at that."

"What was on the messages?"

"Several things of interest. But a rather long message was from George Markins. He was telling Enzo about a party he had attended with my son Jim in Eau Claire. It seems George and Jim were talking informally about their families, and Jim happened to mention he had a brother who worked on the North Slope of Alaska. Being a good company man, George thought Rankins could use the family connection to their advantage."

Jack pulled a notepad from his shirt pocket and flipped it open. "Let me read George's exact words: *Enzo, find a guy named John Bowman who is a petro engineer for ConocoPhillips and recruit him. I've just hired his brother, Jim, to submit the coded obituaries for Rankins. What a coincidence, right?! Dude, what are the chances Jim has a brother who lives in your tiny isolated village on the Arctic Circle?! A billion to one might be lowballing the odds!*

Jim's a friend, but I don't completely trust him to do our dirty work. He's somewhat of a goody-two-shoes! We might be able to use some blackmail down the road. Try to lure his brother John into the organization with something innocent. If he knows we are involved in illegal gaming, he'll never play along. Once he unknowingly commits a crime, we've got him! Then, if Jim ever decides to turn on us, we'll use John as bait to shut him up!"

"That's an open and shut case of extortion if I ever heard one!" exclaimed Carl. "Won't that be enough evidence to get your son out of prison and shut Rankins down for good?"

"Well, it would be if the voicemail could be used in court. But I stole it from Esposito's office without a judge's order. It would be inadmissible."

"But the original voicemail is still in Enzo's office, right? Can you get a court order after the fact?"

"As long as I, or the FBI, can explain to a judge how they know a voicemail exists if we haven't heard it. That would be a tough nut to crack. It's difficult to lie and get away with it, Carl, even for CIA agents. However, if we can find a way to point criminal evidence at the fake Holmes Mortuary, we should be able to confiscate everything in the building, including the voicemail."

"What happened after George made the call to Enzo?"

"Good question! I can only speculate based on court documents from his trial at the US district court in Fairbanks and one other voicemail. John believed he was completely innocent. Against the advice of his attorney, he demanded to take the stand early on in the trial. The federal prosecutors obliged by calling him to testify first. John claimed he met Enzo at Stallion's Gitty-Up Espresso coffee shop one morning. Esposito pretended he didn't know John and introduced himself as the owner of Holmes Mortuary. That's when Enzo mentioned that his staff participates in this friendly football lottery every fall. He explained to John how it worked and convinced him to recruit his buddies at ConocoPhillips to join in. John thought it would be fun—a form of entertainment in a tiny town that had little to offer in that arena. Nothing more. In the end, 138 oil workers participated with the knowledge it was just for fun!"

"How did the lottery work," asked Carl.

"Unlike Powerball or Mega Millions, this was based on a monthlong football parlay. One NFL team would be generated randomly by a computer, and if that team won four games in a row during September of 2019, the group would win $50 million. But here's what made it so appealing: it only cost $10 to get in on the deal. If your team won the first week, you needed to put in $20 more to stay with the group. If the team won the second week, it cost you $100 to stay in the group for the third week. And if they won that week, players had to dish out $500 for the final game. So, in theory, the amount wagered for four weeks was $630, but the payout per person would be $362,319 each if their team could win four in a row. The buy-in of $630 was a drop in the bucket for an oil worker on the North Slope."

"What team did the computer pick for them?"

"A team with a decent chance to win four in a row—the Green Bay Packers, which made most of them happy. In fact, none of them dropped out. They all stuck it out until the end. Had the computer picked the Cleveland Browns, most, if not all, would have quit after the first week even if they had won!"

"So, the Packers won all their games last September?"

"No, Carl, had that happened, I doubt anyone would have come forward and complained to the feds. Green Bay won their opener with a stunning defeat of the Bears in Chicago. The group perked up because the next three games were going to be held at Lambeau Field. The Pack defeated the Vikings in the second week and the Broncos in the third week. The Eagles came to town for the final game and were blessed by favorable calls the entire sixty minutes. Flags for nonexistent penalties against the Packers were thrown at critical moments, and clear pass interference calls were totally ignored. Aaron Rodgers was furious, as was the sellout crowd. In fact, with twenty-eight seconds left in the game and Green Bay having a shot at overtime, Rodgers' pass in the end zone to Marquez Valdes-Scantling was tipped and picked off. But replays show Marquez was pushed, giving him no chance to make the play. Obvious pass interference. The next day, even the Philadelphia media claimed the Eagles might have stolen one in Lambeau."

Carl finished his Crown Royal and walked in silence to the liquor cabinet to pour himself a second drink. Jack wanted to give him a few minutes to process what he had heard. Carl paced the room nervously, sipping the whiskey slowly. With Jack Bowman's help, he was about to shock the entire football world with what he knew. That is if he could survive long enough to tell the FBI.

Carl wondered about the depth of Jack's knowledge. Jack knew Rankins fixed games and that his son Jim had been tipping off gamblers by using coded obituaries. But Carl guessed Jack had no idea how Rankins actually did it. Did he know about SOTO and Rob Fornasiere and Sam Diggins? He needed to find out.

Carl gulped the remaining Crown, sat back down, and turned to Jack. "What happened after the game? The oil workers couldn't have blamed John! How could he have anything to do with the outcome of the game?"

"Rankins, aka Holmes Mortuary, somehow hired corrupt officials for the Eagles versus Packers game. I'm sure they were involved in placing bad guy referees in all the games Jim, and later, you, coded. I just haven't figured out how yet." Jack paused a moment and leaned forward to make sure Carl understood the gravity of what he was about to say next. "But I'm guessing you know how they did it, don't you, Carl?"

There was no use keeping it from Jack. Shoot, the man was ex-CIA—he would find out sooner or later! But more importantly, Carl needed Jack's skills to get to the bottom of this mess. "Yeah, I think I have a pretty good idea how Rankins does it. It's complicated, to say the least. I'm curious—how did you know about the dishonest officiating?"

"What else could it be? Realistically, only three people can alter a game's outcome: players, coaches purposely calling bad plays, or miscreant officials. After watching the games coded in the obituaries, it was easy to tell the referees were the problem. Then, unbeknownst to the media, fans, players, or teams, the NFL fired two officials—the head linesman and a back judge who reffed the Packers-Eagles game."

Surprised, Carl asked, "If no one knew they had been fired, how did you?"

"Remember I mentioned there was a second voicemail on the Rankins's recorder that was of interest?" Carl nodded, and Jack flipped his notebook to the next page. "The caller said this: *The damn NFL ordered Rob to terminate two officials from the Packers' game! They don't want it to leak to the press, players, or teams because they suspect foul play. Things are getting too close for comfort. We need to cool it for a while, so no obits for two weeks. Understand?*"

"Holy crap!" exclaimed Carl. "That voice recording is a gold mine if we could find a way to use it legally!"

Jack ignored Carl's comment. "Do you know who the 'Rob' is that's mentioned on the recording?"

"Yes, I'm afraid I do."

"Would you be so kind as to bring me up to speed?"

"I'm not sure where to start."

"How about at the beginning? How did you get involved working for George Markins and the Gazette?"

Chapter 39

It was noon when Carl wrapped up his story. Jack took notes and asked a few pointed questions. But Carl could tell Jack's CIA thinking skills were sharp. Yes, he was happy to have him on his side, moving forward.

Carl told him everything he could remember, beginning with meeting Curt Anderson when he was dating Molly. They quickly became good friends, and at first, Carl thought Curt was a gambling addict. Only later did he suspect Curt was involved in an illegal gaming scheme.

Jim Bowman had been using coded obituaries to tip off gamblers, and Carl had been doing the same thing unknowingly. He told Jack about going to his friend Wally Roseberg's funeral in Florida and finding out it was all a hoax. Carl mentioned he wasn't sure if Wally was part of the crime syndicate or not. Wally had the ability to play major college football virtually at any school in the nation, but he chose the University of Nevada at Las Vegas. Carl thought perhaps it was the mob that influenced Wally to play ball in Sin City.

During his visit to Prudhoe Bay, Jack learned about Rankins Corporation. He discovered they were a holding company for Holmes Mortuary and the Gazette. Jack was intrigued when Carl explained how he would receive obituaries from a man named Sam Diggins, who posed as a fake assistant funeral director for Holmes. Carl was dumbfounded as to why he was not allowed to make changes to any of his death notices, seeing the eulogies were only three short paragraphs of nothingness! That's when Carl first became suspicious of possible wrongdoing. By putting the pieces together, he assumed that NFL games were being compromised.

Jack had been scrutinizing Carl's obituaries; thus, he knew about the rigged games. Mary Reppe had guessed the code, so she and Jack read all of Jim's past obits and found that pro football contests had been tainted for the last three seasons. But until Carl told him, Jack had never heard of Sam Diggins or the Sports Officials Training Organization, nor did he know SOTO assigned the referees for NFL games.

More importantly, Jack now knew who "Rob" was on the voicemail. Rob Fornasiere, the person responsible for training officials how to cheat—then assigning them to NFL games so the mob could win millions!

*****

When Carl finished talking, he had questions of his own. "You said two officials were fired after the Packers' game with the Eagles, and everything was hush-hush. Now that you know about SOTO and Rob Fornasiere, why do you think they weren't exposed at that time? I mean, wouldn't you assume Fornasiere's contract would have been dissolved? To keep fans from the truth, I understand why the NFL may not have wanted to turn him over to the feds. But surely they would have disbanded their partnership with SOTO, right?!"

"I can't answer that, Carl. I can only guess Rob played dumb and claimed he knew nothing about the corruption. He probably convinced the NFL that some of his trainees had gone bad on their own. And he probably assured them he would work hard to clean up the organization and filter out the malefactors."

"But back to your son, John. How could he be falsely charged with racketeering, yet, Holmes Mortuary continues to exist to this day?"

"Well, going back to the transcripts from John's trial, I can only make an assumption. Right now, the court documents are my only lead. Here's what happened. A disgruntled oil worker who watched the Packers' game and was upset with the officiating caused a scene at the company the next day. Evidently, he slammed his fist through the lounge wall during lunch break, then punched a coworker in the nose when he asked him to calm down. The boss was called down to the lounge, and that was the first he had heard about his employees taking part in the football parlay. He wanted to know who got them involved, and John admitted it was him. He told the boss about having coffee with Enzo Esposito, the owner of Holmes Mortuary, who participated in the lottery every fall. It was all just for fun.

"But the boss was mad that his pipeline workers were all up in arms about losing, and it had led to a damaged wall and a fistfight. He told John the lottery was illegal, which surprised him. How could an innocent little football parlay be unlawful?

"Just to scare John, the boss called the FBI in Fairbanks, and they assigned Agent Nanouk Brown to check it out. Agent Brown didn't believe a major crime had been committed, so he simply made phone calls and never visited Prudhoe Bay. Had he flown up to the North Slope, he would have seen what I saw—that Holmes Mortuary is a fake and doesn't even have a casket anywhere in the place! Anyway, Enzo Esposito denied ever knowing John and said there was no way anyone working for his company was involved in a lottery.

"Now, get this. Agent Brown phones John and asks him to fly to Fairbanks for a meeting regarding the football lottery. The agent was amiable and said he needed to talk to John to wrap up the case and file the paperwork. Brown said John would need to sign some forms. John asked Brown if he was in trouble and if he needed a lawyer. The agent laughed and said, 'Just come on down.' All of this was presented at the trial, and interestingly, Agent Brown never denied saying any of it!"

"I still don't understand what John did wrong. Why is a football lottery against the law? I mean, almost every business I know runs a weekly NFL pool!"

"Well, let me finish the story first. So John flys to Fairbanks in one of ConocoPhillips company planes. Agent Brown meets him at the airport and takes him to lunch. They talk about salmon fishing on the Kenai Peninsula, climbing Denali, and rafting on the Tanana River. The owner of the restaurant testified both John and Nanouk were having a good time. John hadn't slept, worrying about the trip to Fairbanks. But after lunch, he relaxed, thinking he was happy about having a day off from work. He even planned to go moose hunting with Agent Brown someday. But that would never happen.

"At FBI headquarters, John was given a stack of papers to initial and sign. He and Brown were laughing and joking about a Netflix series they had both watched while he was autographing the forms. John was so comfortable with his new friend Nanouk that he didn't read a written word on the documents or even ask what he was inscribing. A few seconds after he was done signing, another agent entered the room. The agent and Brown handcuffed John, told him he was in violation of the Racketeer Influenced and Corrupt Organizations Act, then read him his rights!"

"What?! Your kidding, Jack! How can that be?"

"Federal law regulates the businesses and casinos that are allowed to accept bets and promote gambling. Illegal gaming falls within those regulations. Unless certified by the US government and Alaska gaming commissions, it is unlawful for an individual or business to involve five or more people in a gambling operation. That includes people taking bets, making bets, or running the show. As you know, John recruited 138 coworkers to participate in the parlay.

"The law also states that it's illegal to operate an unregulated gaming business if the gross revenue is over $2,000 in a single day. The first week of the lottery, the buy-in was only $10, so that was okay. But the second week, it was $20, and that put John over the $2,000 threshold."

"Come on, Jack. This is crazy! How could John end up with a thirty-year prison sentence over this? It just doesn't make sense!"

"You're right, Carl. It doesn't make sense, and if running the lottery was the only thing John was found guilty of, he most likely would have received some jail time or just a slap on the wrist. But because he didn't have a lawyer present and didn't bother reading what he was signing, he screwed himself."

"What do you mean by that?"

"The FBI claimed John invented the football lottery and that it never really existed. No such parlay could be found on the Internet—either legal or illegal. They said John kept his coworker's money and had no plans to pay out had the Packers won the fourth and final game. The FBI thought he would have skipped town!"

"And John signed a form admitting to that without ever reading it! Wow!"

"Yeah, wow. But he still shouldn't have gone to prison. His defense attorney was making headway in the trial. Under oath, Agent Brown acknowledged he might have tricked John by pretending to be his friend. Brown told the jury that had he not done so, John most likely would have scrutinized what he was signing. He also would have asked for a lawyer to be present.

"The defense attorney also argued it was incomprehensible the FBI didn't travel to Prudhoe Bay and investigate John's claims that Holmes Mortuary initiated the football parlay and handled the wagers. He asked for a mistrial and demanded a thorough probe of the funeral parlor and its employees. The judge called a recess for the rest of the day to think about the motion. That's when things came unhinged.

"The next morning, a bomb threat was called in to the courtroom a few minutes after everyone had been seated. The judge calmly announced to all present that they should follow him through the back doors leading to his chambers. From there, they would be escorted to a bomb shelter located in the basement of the building. Then the whole ordeal morphed into something resembling a scene from *The Godfather*! Gunshots ravaged the entrance door. Everyone scrambled to find safety. The bailiff hustled the judge out the back door, and the attorneys, jurors, and most of the onlookers were close behind. A reporter for the *Fairbanks Daily News-Miner* ducked down and started snapping pictures left and right.

"Meanwhile, John hit the floor and covered his head with his hands, as did a few other people in the crowd. Then the entrance doors burst open, and three gunmen charged in. The reporter said they appeared stunned that the courtroom had cleared so quickly. But he also said they grabbed John and forced him out of the courtroom the same way they had gotten in.

"An hour later, an all-points bulletin was issued for the state of Alaska to locate and apprehend John. The Canadian authorities were also notified. The FBI believed he had planned and initiated the bomb threat to escape justice, but they had no clue who helped him. Agents from all over the west coast were flown to Fairbanks to assist in the massive manhunt. But that was all unnecessary."

"Unnecessary?!" asked Carl from the edge of his seat. This was all sounding like a scene from a thriller novel. "Why was it unnecessary?"

"John walked into FBI headquarters the next morning and turned himself in. His lawyer made a deal with the prosecution. John would plead guilty to racketeering, and the charges for endangering a federal court and escaping justice would be dropped. When court resumed the following week, the judge threw the book at John—thirty years in a high-security federal prison in Oregon. No parole for twenty years."

"What do you think happened, Jack? It sounded like John was on the verge of a mistrial, and the next thing you know, he admits to racketeering. That's ridiculous!"

"I think the people at Holmes Mortuary, or Rankins, or the mob, got to him. They kidnapped John from the courtroom, knowing all hell would break loose once they called in a bomb threat and blasted the door to pieces. Then they threatened him by threatening his little brother."

"What do you mean?"

"If a mistrial had been granted, the judge would have ordered the FBI to investigate Holmes Mortuary. That could have spelled doom for Rankins and the entire illegal gaming operation. I believe the mobsters told John that Jim was deeply involved with their crime syndicate, and if John didn't plead guilty and end the investigation, they would kill his brother."

"Wow! Is there any way you can prove the extortion, Jack?"

"I have one phone record that could be valuable. The night John was taken from the courtroom, he called Jim, and they talked for nearly three hours. The next morning, John turned himself in. I wish I knew what they chatted about for that length of time."

Carl looked at his watch. It was one o'clock, and dark storm clouds were forming to the west. Carl began to pace nervously around the room. Jack sat and watched silently. A few minutes later, Carl stopped and faced his new friend. "We need to tell the FBI everything we know. And we should do so before someone stumbles upon George Markins's body."

"I'm not so sure," opposed Jack.

"What?! Why not?! We've got enough evidence to shut down Rankins for good! I'm not thrilled to be turning in my brother-in-law, but Curt made his own bed!"

"Ramifications. That's why Carl. The ramifications."

"What the hell does that mean?! We need to end this crazy subversion and put these people away for good!"

"Yes, we do. But at what expense? As soon as the FBI starts investigating, the media will know the NFL has been tampered with for at least three years. Fans will have a snit, and the consequences would be severe. They would be hard-pressed ever to accept the outcome of games again, and viewership could dwindle. Football drives our economy almost as much as Wall Street. Billions of dollars are spent on marketing and sponsorships. If we turn them in, Carl, it could spell the end of a great American pastime and our nation's most illustrious form of entertainment."

"But what are our options? George Markins is dead; your son is serving a lengthy prison sentence for something he didn't do, and my family is in danger!"

"You realize if we expose the illegal gambling operation, we will ultimately affect the reputation of the game. That includes the legacies of everyone who has ever been a part of the NFL, including guys like Vince Lombardi, Mean Joe Greene, and, yes, even your father, Billy West.

"Are you really ready to destroy their accomplishments, or worse yet, to bend their honor?"

Chapter 40

"Tell me you have a plan, Jack, because I don't have much experience taking down the Mafia!"

"Sarcasm is a waste of energy, Carl. We need to brainstorm. But the first order of business is to dispose of George Markins's corpse and clean up your office."

The two men were in the Chevy Tahoe racing back to New Richmond on County Road T. The revolver was resting once again on Jack's lap. The idea of calling the FBI had been scrapped until they devised a strategy that would protect the game's integrity. In the meantime, there were two items of immediate importance—keep Markins's body from being discovered, and move Molly to a safe place.

They stopped at Carl's house to get cleaning supplies and a bedspread to wrap up the corpse. Molly left a note on the kitchen table that appeared to be a half-hearted attempt at an apology. She said they should have a date night similar to the kind they had in college—beer and wings at Champs while watching Monday Night Football. Carl smiled at the thought until reality slapped him in the face. He had a critical task to do, and there was no room for error. But Carl was bothered by the fact that he would soon be a full-fledged criminal. Sure, he had broken into Mike Kohlrusch's office and taken some pictures of documents, but that was minor compared to what he was about to do. Up to this point, being an accessory to George's killing was merely self-defense. But by disposing of his body without reporting his actions to the authorities, he was now committing a felony. Carl regained his focus, and the two men loaded up the SUV and hurried to the office.

After checking that no one was watching from the alley, Jack backed the Tahoe as close to the rollup door as possible and lifted the tailgate. He and Carl wrapped George in the bedspread and lifted him carefully into the SUV. Rigor mortis had stiffened George's body, and most of his blood had dried. That helped keep the comforter from becoming stained, which would leave DNA evidence in the Chevy.

Carl scrubbed down the office floors, walls, and ceiling while Jack drove to Warner's Dock with George's foul-smelling corpse permeating the air throughout the interior of the vehicle. At Warner's, he purchased a heavy anchor, then transported the body to the end of Mary Park. There was no one to be seen anywhere on the recreational grounds with kids in school and adults working. Jack wrapped the anchor line around George's chest, then dumped him in the shallow lake. He hoped algae would cling to the body cavity, and the catfish and suckers would devour the decaying flesh before anyone found him.

Parked in the alley next to Carl's office was a small cargo truck with ***Eau Claire Gazette*** printed on the side. George had loaded it with Carl's furniture, files, and computers. Jack convinced Carl to move his things back into the office to appear as if nothing happened. Before leaving, they downloaded the computer files onto a flash drive and tucked the important folders into a document box. When they were finished, Jack drove Carl to where his Tesla was parked. The plan was for Carl to hustle to the Dispatch building and pick up Molly, and the three of them would rendezvous at the Minneapolis-St. Paul airport. Carl and Jack would leave their cars in the long-term lot, and they would all fly to Reno. Once Grandpa Syd was safe and secure, they would create a scheme to end this nightmare.

But, as Robert Burns so aptly put it, "The best-laid plans often go awry."

*****

Sun Country had a flight to Reno leaving at 8:00 p.m, and Jack texted Carl stating he had booked three seats. He was happy the plane departed from Terminal Two, which was much smaller and less crowded than the Lindbergh Terminal. Terminal Two was also known as the Humphrey Terminal, named for Minnesota's favorite son, Hubert Horatio Humphrey, a long-time senator and the thirty-eighth vice president of the United States. Humphrey was a diehard Twins and Vikings fan, and the first domed stadium in Minnesota was named after him. Jack guessed the late vice president would be turning over in his grave if he knew about the corruption taking place in the NFL.

Carl had arrived at the Dispatch at 3:00 p.m., but, as usual, Molly was in a meeting. Jan Willows, her secretary, informed him that she was with her boss, and it might be a while before she was available. Carl was glad Molly wasn't with Sam Diggins again! He settled down in a comfortable leather chair in the lobby and reached for a newspaper on the oversized coffee table.

There were at least ten back issues of the Dispatch to pick from, and Carl didn't care which one he chose. He just needed something to pass the time as he anxiously waited for his wife to finish. He happened to pick up last Wednesday's paper and turned to the sports section to read Molly's column. Strangely, the second to last paragraph was dedicated to the Miami versus New England game that would be played in Foxborough on Sunday—which was yesterday. Who in Minnesota gave two hoots about the Dolphins or the Patriots?! The only teams anyone cared about in Nordic country were fellow NFC Central foes—the Packers, Bears, and Lions. And all they hoped for were their rival's demise!

Something caught Carl's eye as he perused Molly's column. It was like déjà vu. He'd seen some of those same words before. Carl reread the paragraph about the Dolphins-Patriots match:

> *Keep a close eye on the Miami contest*
> *against New England in Massachusetts.*
> *Without Tom Brady at the helm, the*

Dolphins could surprise the heavily favored Patriots in Gillette Stadium. What an upset that would be!

In her last paragraph, Molly concluded with a brief narrative praising a high school athlete from Minnesota, which is how she wrapped up her column every Wednesday. That was Molly's strategy to maintain her readership. Everyone loved reading about potential future NCAA stars, and perhaps, professional players from the land of 10,000 lakes who made it big. Just thinking about Kevin McHale, Dave Winfield, Kent Hrbek, and Paul Molitor brought terrific memories to every Minnesota sports fan. So why would Molly even bother writing about a horrible team from a city almost 2,000 miles away? Who cared?!

Carl thought about his feeling of déjà vu, and then he remembered Molly's column from two weeks ago. He politely asked Jan Willows if he could see the Wednesday, September ninth issue of the Dispatch. She smiled and went into a storage room to fetch one.

Carl found what he was looking for in the second to last paragraph, which, ironically, was the same location Molly wrote about the Dolphins-Patriots game. A chill ran down Carl's spine when he read it. The wording of the first and last sentence was identical.

Keep a close eye on the Chicago contest against our own Minnesota Vikings in Minneapolis this week. Yes, the Bears are without quarterbacks Mitch Trubisky and Nick Foles due to injuries, but third-stringer Tyler Bray could surprise everyone at US Bank Stadium. Chicago has more players bruised up than any other team in the NFL; however, be careful! The Bears could surprise our heavily favored

Vikings on Sunday. What an upset that would be!

It was as if a Bowie knife had sliced Carl's chest open and ripped his heart to shreds! Yes, the wording was virtually the same, and the reference was unmistakable! Two weeks ago, Molly placed a quick blurb in the second to last paragraph about a possible upset brewing that involved her own team, the Vikings. Why hadn't she mentioned it earlier in any of her previous columns? She was the Vikings' correspondent, after all! Then last week, Molly had chosen to insert a brief comment about a meaningless game taking place in a location that no one in her readership area cared about. And, it just so happened both games ended with the underdog winning!

Moneyline! It had to be! Carl now knew more about gambling, more so the illegal variety, than he ever cared to know! Point spreads and total scores were being coded in the Gazette obituaries. The Dispatch must be coding moneyline games in their sports columns! It couldn't be more obvious: Wednesday's columns, second to last paragraph, begin with ***Keep a close eye on***, and end with ***What an upset that would be!***

So, the crime syndicate was also rigging games to win moneyline bets, and Carl's newlywed wife seemed to be communicating the upset-game-of-the-week for her readers! Was she working for the Mafia? Is that why Sam Diggins was meeting with her last week?!

"Please, God, don't let it be!" uttered Carl out loud, forgetting he was in a public lobby. The secretary glanced up from the paperwork on her desk. Carl's faced turned red, and he looked at Jan. "Sorry!"

Carl's mind was scrambling in every possible direction. Did Molly's brother, Curt, recruit her into the business? That would make sense, but when did it happen? Certainly not before they were married, right? Did someone get to Molly after she was hired at the Dispatch? Or was she hired to write her column for the mob's illegal gaming operation? After all, she was given the job without much effort!

Then it hit him. Rankins was the holding company for the Gazette. Was it possible they were also financially involved with the Dispatch? If so, perhaps Molly didn't know she's coding moneyline games. Maybe she has a Rankins's computer like he has, and she's required to place a coded blurb each week even if she disagrees with the material—just like Carl did with the obituaries!

There was no one else in the lobby, so Carl cleared his throat to get Ms. Willow's attention. "Excuse me. Sorry to bother you, Jan, but I was wondering if a company by the name of Rankins is part owner of the Dispatch?"

"Why, yes, Carl, they are our main financial holding company. Why do you ask?"

"Oh, I don't know. I think I'd read that somewhere. Do they have any say in the day-to-day operations of the newspaper?"

"Not much. But one of the Rankins's executives—I can't recall his name—did recommend your wife for her job back in July. That I do remember."

"Was his recommendation written in a letter? Could you have human resources check his name?"

"I'd sure like to help, Carl, but Molly's personnel file is private. Only if she dies is it available to the next of kin. And you don't want that to happen, do you?!" Jan laughed at her sarcastic joke.

Despairingly, Carl was suddenly not so sure.

*****

"Please don't tell Molly that I was here," said Carl nervously. "I need to go, and she would be upset if she knew I couldn't wait for her."

"Well, okay, I won't say a word to Molly," replied Jan as she looked at him inquisitively. "But you don't sound too good, Carl. Are you okay?"

"I'm fine, but I must leave now. May I take these two newspapers with me?" He lifted up the past two Wednesday issues of the Dispatch he had been reading.

"Of course! Trust me. We have plenty of those!"

Carl thanked Jan and hustled back to his Tesla in the parking lot. He sat in the driver's seat, thinking about what to do next.

"Molly may be completely innocent, right?" muttered Carl to himself. "I didn't know I was coding obituaries, so she probably doesn't know what she's doing either!"

The other voice inside his brain replied, "Wishful thinking." Carl pounded the palm of his hand onto his forehead several times as he sped away to the airport. He wanted to stay positive, but he was suffering from auditory hallucinations. Carl was on the verge of a schizophrenic meltdown!

Chapter 41

Wally Roseberg observed as the tech crew finished wiring the mansion, guest house, and private airport. It was Monday night, a few minutes before sundown in the Caymans. As soon as the specialists were airborne and heading back to the United States, Wally phoned Randy Hansen.

"The technicians are gone, and there are cameras all over the property. I believe we're ready to finalize the project."

"Are the aesthetics completed to his liking? I don't give two hoots about the security crap. All I care about is billing the jerk!"

Wally laughed. "Be cautious what you say, Randy. He'll probably pass your name along to his spoiled-rich friends!"

"As long as his friends aren't in the mortuary business. After designing Sam Diggins' place on the St. Croix in Wisconsin, and now this monstrosity in the Caymans, I've had it with living people making millions off of burying dead people! When I die, please make sure someone other than Holmes Mortuary shoots preservatives into my arteries!"

Wally laughed even louder. "I doubt I'll be the one to make that decision, my friend."

"Well, then, get my Learjet back to Palm Beach where it belongs. I'm thinking about flying up to Bar Harbor to watch the leaves change colors in Maine. Fresh lobsters and a few bottles of Sam Adams—life don't get much better than that!"

"I hear ya! I'll wrap up and be home by midnight."

Randy Hansen slipped the iPhone into his pocket, locked the doors to InterPlan Architecture, and headed home to pack some warm clothes. It would be getting chilly in New England.

*****

"I've decided to accept your offer," said Wally to his wealthiest client as they shook hands. He was on the private runway with his briefcase and an overnight bag filled to the brim with dirty laundry. Every item was sparkling clean when he departed on the Learjet from Palm Beach last Thursday. But after wearing those clothes in Las Vegas and the Caymans, they had become stained with coffee, sweat, and rum.

Last week his client called himself Harvey Jones. This week—who knew? Harvey, or whoever, was ready to board his jet for another trip to Sin City, while Wally was headed home to Florida. The filthy-rich mogul had approached him to recruit miscreant football players who would fumble balls or miss tackles in exchange for loads of cash. Wally's now ex-architectural client was about to become his new boss.

"Good, good, good, my boy! You won't regret it—especially when you're living out your life on easy street! Do you have any athletes in mind?"

"I have some ideas. I'll get to work on it tomorrow. Randy is taking a vacation to Maine, so I'll have time on my hands."

"That's my boy, Wally! A man named Enzo Esposito will be contacting you soon. He's my associate up in Prudhoe Bay, Alaska."

"Prudhoe Bay? Isn't that on the Arctic Ocean? Is this guy an oil worker?" Wally knew from his meeting with Harvey in Las Vegas that the tycoon was running an illegal gaming operation. But he had no idea the organization had connections in Alaska.

"No, son, he manages the Holmes Mortuary up there. But that doesn't pertain to you, so just leave it at that."

Wally nodded, and the two men shook hands again. Wally boarded the InterPlan Learjet that he would pilot back to Palm Beach, while his new boss climbed the ramp into the cabin of the Rankins's aircraft that was fueled and ready for takeoff. But he wouldn't be headed to Las Vegas this time.

After Oliver Harwas had briefed him on his meeting with Sam Diggins, Harvey decided to deal with a serious situation in Minneapolis first.

*****

Carl showed Jack the column Molly had written the past two Wednesdays, and Jack agreed it looked very suspicious. They were tucked back in the corner of Starbucks in the Humphrey Terminal, waiting for their flight to Reno.

"I'm still hoping against all odds that Molly is innocent." Carl sounded like he was pleading for Jack to believe him, yet, he wasn't sure he felt it himself. "She may have been forced to incorporate those upset blurbs into her column, just like I was forced to code point spreads and over/unders in my obituaries."

"You could be right, Carl." Jack was trying to console his agitated new friend. "Try and stay positive while we think this through."

"I know Rankins used Jim and me to code with obituaries. What I don't understand is why hire us to review them when all George Markins had to do was forward the made-up obits to his editor?"

"My theory is he was trying to create a diversion," responded Jack. "If the Gazette were ever investigated, George would play dumb. He would blame you and Jim and claim he knew nothing about it. You guys were the middlemen—hired only to take the blame if things got out of control. The Rankins's emails were routed to your office to provide a shield from the feds directly pointing the finger at George."

"And the same could be true with Molly's job—she's just an unsuspecting rookie writer caught in the middle. It would make sense. I found out a few hours ago that Rankins is also a holding company for the Dispatch."

"Carl, we need to make a decision. The flight will be leaving soon."

"I can't get on the plane. I can't leave Minneapolis without Molly. The mob knows I screwed them, and they'll be looking for my family and me!"

"I understand, Carl. But what about your grandfather? He knows nothing about the illegal gaming operation or your involvement with the mob. They may come looking for him, too. Perhaps I should go to Nevada and move your grandfather to a safe location."

"That might work. But all I know right now is that I must go to New Richmond and protect Molly. She's probably just getting home and will be expecting me to be there. That's what I told her secretary."

"Okay. In that case, I'll call you when I get to your grandfather's place. He made need some coaxing from you."

"Fine, but there's—" Carl hesitated because he wasn't sure now was the best time. A moment later, he continued. "There's something I need to ask you about your son Jim."

Chapter 42

"You said you came to Wisconsin after you heard Jim died," said Carl soberly. "And that's when you began to suspect something fishy going on."

Jack gave Carl a puzzled look. "Is there a question?"

"What did you find out about Jim's death?" Yes, Carl knew that Jim had died from poisoning. But he found it strange that Jack hadn't mentioned it. Did he know the truth?

"Well, according to his death certificate, he died from leukemia. That's also what was published in his obituary. But you already know this, so why are you asking?"

The certificate stated the cause of death as leukemia?! Carl was perplexed. That's impossible—it had to have said poisoning! He had read the handwritten medical examiner's report after he broke into Mike Kohlrusch's office. In fact, he took a picture of it with his iPhone. "Did you actually see the death certificate?"

"Yes, I went to the courthouse in Hudson and made copies to have on file. I'm very curious to know why you're asking."

"Did you do any further investigation?"

"Not much. I didn't feel the need. After leaving Hudson, I met with Dr. Mike Kohlrusch, the medical examiner who signed the certificate. Nice guy! I found out that not only was he an assistant coroner for St. Croix County, but he was also Jim's personnel physician. He treated my son's cancer. I had no reason to doubt Mike. I can't remember ever meeting a nicer and more competent doctor in my life!"

"What you just said doesn't jive with what I know, Jack."

"What did I say wrong?"

"You said Dr. Kohlrusch signed the certificate and indicated the cause of death was leukemia. But according to Mike's draft copy, Jim died from arsenic poisoning."

"Huh?! What draft copy? You must be mistaken!"

"It's a long story, Jack, but I can tell you this. I had doubts Jim died from cancer. So, I broke into Dr. Kohlrusch's office one night and took pictures of his notes." Jack's jaw dropped open in confusion.

Carl punched the photo app on his iPhone and found the handwritten medical examiner's report. Jack pulled a pair of reading glasses from his pocket and examined the death summary carefully:

> DETERMINATION: *Acute arsenic poisoning by self-induced ingestion.*
> SUMMARY: *James William Bowman was transferred by an unidentified male and admitted to General Emergency Room on June 13, 2020, at 5:37 p.m. He was unconscious, unresponsive, and appeared to suffer from severe gastroenteritis and hypersalivation. George Cowan, MD, ordered bowel irrigation, and at 6:03 p.m., the rectal catheter was in place, and the procedure began. At the request of Dr. Cowan, Michael Kohlrusch, MD, arrived at 6:58 p.m. to assist with diagnosis and treatment. Dr. Kohlrusch ordered a group-specific blood transfusion (Type O-Rh Negative) to remove suspected arsenic from the circulatory system. Transfusion commenced at 7:46 p.m. and was completed at 9:38 p.m. Mr. Bowman suffered a sequence of multi-organ failures: Hypoxemia (10:14 p.m.); Acute Respiratory Distress Syndrome (11:24 p.m.); acute renal dysfunction (12:16 a.m.); and cardiac arrest (12:38 a.m.).*
> TIME OF DEATH: *12:46 a.m., June 14, 2020.*

"Acute arsenic poisoning?! Self-induced?! What does all that mean?!" Carl gave Jack a solemn look but didn't reply. Stunned, Jack stood dizzily and excused himself. "I'll be right back. I need to cancel my flight to Reno."

"What are your plans now, Jack?" asked Carl softly.

"I'm going to find out which one of those Rankins's bastards killed my son!"

*****

Ten minutes later, Jack returned to find Carl pacing in front of Starbucks, a visible bundle of nerves.

"Whoa, slow down, my friend," heartened Jack as he gently grabbed Carl by the shoulder. "We'll get to the bottom of this. I assure you."

Carl turned to face Jack. "There's one more thing I forgot to mention."

"What's that?"

"The day I first met Sam Diggins in Molly's office, I watched him as he headed to his car in the parking lot. He was talking to someone on his cell, and he wasn't happy."

"Okay, so he was mad at someone. Go on."

"Well, in his anger, he tossed the phone, and it busted on the pavement. To make a long story short, I have it. The cell was a burner—one and done. Literally! It broke into pieces and won't turn on. I have it in my glove compartment."

"Carl, let me have the phone. I want to find out who Sam called. It could be a start. Also, it could be evidence to use in court."

"Wouldn't it be inadmissible, just like the voice recording you snatched at Holmes in Prudhoe Bay?"

"Sam disposed of the property with no intention of wanting it back. That makes it fair game in the evidence world!"

"How can you trace the calls? The cell won't even turn on."

Jack smirked at Carl, and Carl got the hint. He was ex-CIA. They had to have a way to power up a burned-out burner phone!

"I've decided to drive to Washington tonight. There is someone I need to speak to, and I need some things from my house. I'll hand carry the burner to Mary Reppe tomorrow afternoon. We'll know in a couple of days who Sam was talking to."

"Are you crazy?! You're planning to drive all night? At your age?!" Carl wished he could take that back. "Sorry, Jack, I'm just concerned about your health, that's all!"

"Don't be, Carl. I'm used to long drives. And I've never gotten more than four hours of sleep since I signed up with the CIA. I will pull over at a rest stop for a twenty-minute nap, and I'll be as good as new. Now, give me that cell phone so I can get on the road."

The two men hustled to the parking lot. Carl retrieved the shattered burner from the Tesla's glove compartment. He and Jack shook hands to bid farewell, and then Jack dropped a bomb.

"Carl, I've been thinking. Say nothing to Molly about any of this!" he ordered. "Lay low until I hear from Mary, probably on Wednesday."

"What am I supposed to do?! When George Markins doesn't report to work, the Gazette will eventually report him as missing, and the police will be knocking on my door. In the meantime, you know the mob will be after me! I just screwed them out of millions of dollars! And, if Molly is a willing employee of theirs, my chances of survival seem minimal, wouldn't you say?!"

"First, you need to calm down. I understand your fear, but you need a clear head if we're going to proceed."

"Proceed with what, damn it! You don't have a plan, and neither do I!"

"I have another friend at FBI headquarters in Washington, DC. He supervises all the agents assigned to the southern states—Louisiana to Florida, and even the Caribbean Islands. We are golf buddies, or I should say 'were' golf buddies. I haven't seen him since I left Virginia. He owes me a favor. I provided some CIA intel several years back that helped him solve a significant case, which, in all honesty, got him promoted to supervisor. If I ask, he will assist me on the QT. No one will know what we're investigating, nor will it spill out to the press. Guaranteed. What I'm trying to say, Carl, is please trust me. Yes, I believe I do have a plan."

"But I can't go home!"

"I know. Call Molly and tell her you felt like seeing Grandpa Syd, and you had a few days off from work, so you decided to travel to Nevada."

"She'll be ticked off! I don't think I can lie to her like that!"

"Better her ticked off than you dead! Remember George Markins! Do it, Carl. I'll be in touch."

Jack jogged to his Chevy Tahoe and flipped the switch on his radar detector. He didn't have time to mess with speed traps on the road to Virginia.

Chapter 43

"So you think Molly told him?" asked the syndicate boss as he stared up through the office window of the IDS building's forty-first floor into the pitch-black sky. Clouds were blocking the stars and the moon on this early autumn night. Below, the lights of downtown Minneapolis glistened. Sam Diggins had picked his boss up at the airport and brought him to SOTO's headquarters an hour earlier. The boss's protector and pilot, Oliver Harwas, stayed on the plane to catch a few winks. This was his second trip from the Caymans in the past twenty-four hours, and he needed some rest. Dawn would be breaking in three hours, and the boss wanted to be in Las Vegas before the sun rose. Tuesday's forecast for the Twin Cities was less than perfect as a cold front was moving in from Canada. Soon Minnesota would be the land of 10,000 frozen lakes!

"It stands to reason," replied Sam. "Markins assured me that Carl would never know he was coding subliminally, and Molly would make sure he never did. I was suspicious of Carl right from the time I first met him. In Molly's office, no less! But there's something I didn't tell you that you now need to know."

The boss turned abruptly from the window to face Sam who sat nervously on Rob Fornasiere's office couch. Rob leaned back in his leather desk chair, listening with apprehension.

"You held something back from me?!" roared the boss with a threatening glare. "That could end your career, I hope you know! What do you need to tell me?"

"Carl met with Rob and me last week. He bought us dinner in a swanky restaurant." Sam paused as trepidation silenced him momentarily. He needed to be careful how he worded what he had to say. The boss wasn't going to be happy!

"You needed to tell me you ate in a nice restaurant?! Well, I'm so very delighted for you two! Now, come on, Sam, get to the point, damn it!"

"I ordered a hit on Carl yesterday morning after he purposely altered Pete Callen's obituary. George Markins was sent to kill him."

"You what?! Are you kidding me?!"

His boss's reaction flustered Sam. "Sorry, Oliver told me to take care of the situation. I guess I just assumed that's what you wanted me to do."

"What the hell, Sam! You assumed?! You were supposed to scare Carl into becoming a willful part of the syndicate, just like we did with Jim Bowman! How do you think Molly will react when she hears you executed her husband?! You idiot! And what did you do with his body? I hope you didn't just leave it somewhere for the cops to find!"

"George was going to make it look like food poisoning or a hunting accident, that's all I know. I haven't spoken to him yet. But there's another reason I put out a hit. The night at the restaurant, Carl wanted to invest in our offer to purchase the Vikings from Zygi Wilf. Molly must have told him what we were planning. But then he backed out the next day. I'm sure he was playing us." Sam glanced at Rob who nodded in affirmation.

The boss's face was deep red with anger. He walked to the desk and swept everything to the floor with his right arm. Then, with both hands perched on the desktop to support his body, he leaned toward Sam with a look that could kill. "Are you finished?!"

Sam paused to gather his thoughts, then said the words his boss wouldn't want to hear. "I think Molly has turned on us. She's been coding what we wanted in her column so far, but I'm losing trust. She could screw us like Carl just did if we're not careful. Sorry, I know that's not what you wanted to hear."

"Who would want to hear that his stepdaughter was plotting to extort from her own stepfather?!"

*****

Burt Merriman pounded the wall with his fist, putting a rather large dent in the sheetrock. The flight to Vegas was now on hold. There was nothing he could do about the past. Carl was dead, and he needed to put it behind him quickly. Now was time to implement Plan B, one he hoped he never had to initiate because Plan A had worked so well.

"Okay, we need to move forward. The obituary strategy has been compromised and is beyond repair. Jim Bowman turned on us, and so did my son-in-law. As of today, we're done with point spreads and over/unders. From here on out, we only gamble on moneyline. Yes, bigger risks, but much better rewards. Sam, email George Markins with our final obituary. He'll have to submit it himself. I know that threatens his cover, but the operatives will be waiting for their assigned wagers today."

"You want me to send over the emergency shut down code? Remember, once they read that, our guys have been trained to immediately stop betting, disregard any further obits from the Gazette, destroy their business cell phones, and wait for new directions. They won't be able to make wagers until we hand-deliver new phones, along with new gaming instructions, to their homes. That could take a few weeks, sir. We stand to lose millions of dollars in revenue, not including the cost of replacement cell phones."

"I wrote the damn Plan B, Sam, so you don't need to tell me how costly this is to our organization! But until I see what side of the fence Molly is on, we have no choice. If she has compromised the newspaper, Rankins will need to invest in another media company and wash their hands of the Gazette and the Dispatch."

"If we're worried about Molly, why are we betting on moneylines? It's her column that codes those games."

"Because you're going to tell her that you had her husband murdered for screwing us, that's why! She won't want to take the chance of messing with us after that! And you will assume all the blame and let her know that I had nothing to do with Carl's death. Do you understand?!"

"Molly is going to be angry, you know."

"You made your own bed when you ordered him killed! Now sleep in it, damn it! And when you're done talking to Molly, I want you to call Zygi and tell him you are no longer interested in purchasing the Vikings."

"But why not? Our idea was to have an NFL team in our pocket, one we could manipulate to win or lose with the help of Rob and SOTO."

"Think about it, you idiot! You told me Carl wanted to go in with us as an investment. You said he turned up at the SOTO headquarters. You even told me that Molly must have tipped him off. Buying the Vikings would need to be approved by the league; thus, there would be an investigation into Rankins. We would have handled that easily, but Molly now poses a problem."

"What about the Super Bowl? How do we set that up without Molly on board? That was to be our biggest rake of the year."

"Molly better be on board! If not, she can be replaced and silenced. You know all about that, don't you, Sam?! Now, shut down point spreads and over/unders for good with an email to George telling him to post our final obituary. Then, purchase replacement cell phones and get them delivered ASAP with new instructions. Let the ops know that from here on out, we are only betting on moneylines via Molly's column. Because those payouts are much higher, we should be able to recoup our losses in a matter of a few weeks."

"After I tell Molly about Carl, how do I handle her? Should I threaten and coerce, or handle it with kid gloves?"

"Do whatever it takes!"

Sam drove Burt back to the airport while Rob sat dazed in his office, staring at the wall. He hadn't said a word during the meeting, which was his style. Don't speak unless spoken to. But now, the killing of Jim Bowman and Carl West was eating at him. This wasn't what he bargained for, but now he was too deeply involved to save face and get out alive.

Unfortunately for Rob and his family, moneyline games were difficult to fix. Bad teams would have to beat good teams consistently for the syndicate to be happy, and if that happened too many times, red flags would be flying all over the gambling world.

Then what?

*****

Trying to think where he could go, Carl reclined the driver's seat of the Tesla and was nervously twiddling his thumbs. He was still parked in the lot at the Humphrey Terminal. Carl had received one text since Jack departed for Washington. It was from Molly, and although it was only three words long, he pondered for quite some time on how to respond: "Where are you?"

Carl's paranoia overwhelmed him, and his mishmash of brain neurons was freaking him out. What if Molly was working with the mob and knew exactly what she was doing when she coded her sports column? Did she know that George Markins tried to kill him? Or worse yet, was that her call? If he answered her text, would she send someone else out to murder him?!

Carl raised the seat and stared out through the windshield in a daze. Until he could confirm Molly's innocence, he needed to avoid her at all costs. If she was blameless, Carl was acutely aware his ignorance could trigger a divorce. But for right now, that was a chance he needed to take.

Carl texted Jack: "Don't know where I'm going, but I need to get rid of my cell phone. I fear the mob could track me using Molly's *Find My iPhone* app since our accounts are linked. I'll buy a burner and let you know my number, but I'm off the grid until then. CW."

After Carl sent the message, he used a tire iron to smash his iPhone into hundreds of tiny pieces on the parking lot's cement floor. Then he fired up the Tesla and sped to downtown Minneapolis. Carl still had a few hours of darkness to work with before SOTO's employees would be heading to the office. Breaking and entering was a new skill he acquired the night he raided Mike Kohlrusch's office. Tonight he would look through Rob Fornasiere's documents for evidence of Molly's involvement with the crime syndicate.

Carl stopped briefly at an all-night Walmart next to the Mall of America to purchase an iPad. Seeing he had no phone, he could use it to scan Fornasiere's files. It took forty-five minutes to run the initial boot up and download a scanner app from the Apple Store. He arrived at the IDS underground parking facility at 3:00 a.m. and pulled into an empty spot twenty yards from a vehicle that had just entered before him. Carl recognized the car—it was the same black Toyota Land Cruiser he saw parked at the Dispatch last week. Sam Diggins owned it.

Carl ducked down in his seat and watched Sam exit and hustle to the opposite door to help his passenger get out. Could the passenger be elderly and need assistance? Carl thought that might be strange. Why would Sam bring an old relative or friend to the IDS Tower in the middle of the night? Could it be that the person was some sort of VIP—Sam's boss or something?

When the passenger emerged from the Land Cruiser, Carl's heart skipped several beats. He couldn't believe who he saw.

The man who Sam seemed to be idolizing was none other than his father-in-law, Burt Merriman.

*****

Neither Sam nor Burt saw Carl's Tesla parked a few yards down from the Land Cruiser. As the two men walked briskly to the building's entry doors, Carl lifted the new iPad to the window and began snapping pictures with the camera app. Most of the photos were side views; however, when Burt turned to say something to Sam, Carl caught a perfect front-on image of Burt's face.

Breaking into SOTO would now be impossible. Carl guessed that Sam and Burt would be meeting with Rob Fornasiere in Rob's office. Then an idea popped into Carl's head. He cranked the ignition of the Tesla, and a few minutes later, he was on I-94 cruising east towards Wisconsin.

With very little traffic on the roads at this time of the night, Carl knew he could be in Boardman in less than an hour.

Chapter 44

The St. Croix County sheriff's squad car was camouflaged by an elm tree in the back of Meister's Bar and Grill, the same location where it was hidden a couple of weeks earlier when Carl was stopped for doing 102 mph in a thirty-five zone. As he approached the rural tavern, he could only hope to find the same officer working the night shift. Carl pulled the Tesla next to the Ford Police Interceptor Utility Vehicle and shut off the engine. The officer recognized the Tesla and exited his car with a sweeping grin from cheek to cheek.

"Carl West!" shouted sheriff's deputy Bruce Merriman, loud enough to cause a dog to bark in a house a block away. He reached into the Tesla's window and gripped Carl's hand, shaking it much longer than necessary. "What are you doing back in Boardman in the middle of the night?!"

"I gambled you might still be running radar in the wee hours from your nest here in Boardman," chuckled Carl in response. A profound relief came over him when he saw the man who once held a loaded gun to his head! "I need to talk to you."

"Don't tell me you've got the Packer-Viking tickets with you!" The deputy's eyes opened wide, like a young child on Christmas day when he finds Santa's gift under the tree.

"No, sorry, Bruce, not yet. But I surely will be getting a pair for you. I wanted to ask you a question."

"Go ahead—shoot!" Bruce tapped his holster and smiled. "No pun intended, my friend. I'll keep this baby strapped to my waist this time!" He snickered, remembering how he had pointed it at Carl the first time they met.

"Bruce, you mentioned to me that you were an only child growing up, right?"

"Yep, that's correct. Why do you ask?"

"You said your father left you and your mom when you were six. He was a wealthy restaurateur but gave you nothing when he left. Do I remember that correctly?"

"True! He was one effing SOB if you ask me!"

"You mentioned that you hadn't seen or heard from him since he moved out. Do you have any idea what he looks like?"

"Kind of, from old pictures of him with us. I can't figure out why mom kept them, but she did. They're from quite a while back—sixteen or seventeen years, I'd say."

"Let me show you a photo I took just an hour ago." Carl opened the Gallery app on his iPad and pointed to Burt Merriman. "Could this be your father?"

Bruce held the tablet and zoomed in. A moment later, he replied with an unsettled tone, "Yes, that's definitely him! Where did you take this picture?"

"Long story. Is there somewhere we can go to talk privately—and off the record?"

*****

The TA Truck Stop on the corner of Highway 12 and I-94 is an all-night café catering to long-haul drivers, college kids from UW-River Falls who have just closed down the bars, and anyone who enjoys the ultimate in greasy spoon cuisine. But their turkey burgers are delightful, made from the breasts of the noisy gobblers that had lived a jam-packed existence in the old Doboy research farms down on Mackin Road outside of New Richmond. And you couldn't find a fresher pot of coffee anywhere at this time of the night, which made the restaurant the go-to place for law enforcement officers to chat during their breaks. Bruce Merriman was a regular customer.

Carl and Bruce sat in a corner booth in the back of the surprisingly crowded café and ordered double-shot mocha lattes.

Since his trip to Florida, Carl was becoming used to sleeping only two hours at night, but fatigue plagued him 24/7, and caffeine was his drug of choice. On the other hand, Bruce had a sweet tooth that needed mollycoddling before, after, and between meals.

"Bruce, I need your help—not because you are a police officer, but because I need information about your father. What I'm about to tell you stays right here between you and me, okay? It's a matter of life and death."

As a force of habit, Bruce put a hand on his holster. It's what he was trained to do when threatened or when someone needed protection. Carl's voice sounded desperate.

"You're worrying me, Carl. But yeah, I'll keep this off the record. What do you need to say?"

"I need to start by telling you that we're somewhat related. You're my stepbrother-in-law."

"Huh?! Say what?"

*****

Carl tried to succinctly explain to Bruce everything that had happened to him since he graduated from Oklahoma. Going far back in time was critical for Bruce to understand the situation. He needed to see the whole picture, including how Carl met Bruce's stepsister, Molly, and his stepbrother, Curt.

Only Carl and Jack Bowman were privy to the mob's inner workings that controlled the gambling syndicate. But for some unknown reason, he trusted Bruce Merriman enough to lay out everything for him. As dawn approached, Carl detailed the entire illegal gaming operation from the time he started working for the Gazette until he snapped the photo of Burt Merriman a few hours earlier. The police walkie talkie spattered out staticky orders for deputies to report here or there, but fortunately, Bruce was never requested as a backup anywhere. He listened carefully with awe but never said a word.

When Carl was finished telling his story, Bruce leaned back in his chair to ponder everything he had heard. Carl let him think about it a few minutes, then asked, "Do you have any questions, Bruce?"

"Yes, but let's start with this one. Why don't you want me to open up an official investigation through the St. Croix County Sheriff's Department? We can offer you protection, you know."

"Jack and I want to keep this from reaching the press. An official investigation is public knowledge, and the media outlets around the world would have a field day with it. It could mean the end of the NFL as we know it. We want to stop the corruption in football first and foremost. But we want to maintain the honor of the game and its players—past and present."

"I can appreciate that Carl, I really can. But I'm sworn to uphold the law in this county. Illegal gaming falls under the jurisdiction of the FBI, so I can keep that part quiet. But I can't honorably ignore a possible crime that is clearly within our authority to investigate and solve. You said your friend Jack shot and killed your boss, then disposed of his body. I have to check that out. If it is as you say, then you have an open and shut case of self-defense."

"If you do that, Bruce, I'm worried it will eventually lead to discovering the mob's corruption of the NFL. A sharp detective will be able to put two and two together sooner or later. Look, you agreed that if I told you everything, you would keep it private. My boss, George Markins, was nothing more than a thug. A bad guy! I brought you into the loop so you could help Jack and me. I trusted you, brother-in-law!"

A guilt complex suddenly overwhelmed Bruce. He could see Carl's point. The Gazette would report George Markins missing anyway, and when they did, an investigation would soon commence. There was no need to tell anyone.

"Okay, Carl, you're right. No one will know about this conversation. But do you want me to give you my thoughts based on what you told me?"

"Yes, of course!"

"First, I think my father is not only part of the crime syndicate; I think he may be running the whole show."

Startled, Carl blurted, "What?! Why?!"

"My mom had to sell our house after he abandoned us. Our realtor needed my father to sign some documents, but no one knew where he went. The real estate agent was married to a private investigator, so he tried to track Burt down during some off time. He found him at one of his restaurants—I can't think of the name, but it was in Chicago. To get his signature, the investigator had to interrupt dad's dinner he was having with a VIP."

"What do you mean by VIP? Who was it?"

"Ever heard of Vito Rizzuto?"

"You mean Teflon Don, the Mafia's main man in Montreal?"

"Yep, one and the same. Anyway, he and Burt were pretty chummy. I overheard the PI tell mom he couldn't figure out which one was the boss. He said Burt appeared to be on the same level as Vito!"

"What did your mom say?"

"She wouldn't tell me much. I was only ten years old at the time. I asked what the Mafia was, and she told me it was none of my business. Mom was never rude to me, so I was upset and went to my room. The next day at school, I asked my teacher, and she explained to me that the Mafia was a dangerous organization. Then I wondered who Vito Rizzuto was, and she looked it up online. My teacher wanted to know why I was interested in the mob. I lied and said I had watched a crime show on TV and didn't understand a bunch of things. She believed me, and luckily, never mentioned it to mom. And I never asked mom about it again."

"Wow! You may be right. Burt Merriman might be the top dog in all of this! That never even dawned on me before now!"

"But that's not all, Carl. You said Burt and your grandfather appeared to be good friends at your wedding. I wouldn't be so sure that Grandpa Syd is not involved, too."

Carl slumped in his chair in shock. He hadn't thought about that possible connection. Another blitzkrieg of warring neurons had swarmed around in his brain. If his grandfather was part of the mob, how had he missed it? He lived with him after his parents died, and Syd helped him get into Oklahoma. There's no way his grandpa was part of a crime syndicate. No way! But deep down, Carl wasn't so sure.

In a defeated tone, Carl asked, "Anything else, Bruce? I'm not sure how much more I can handle."

"Yes, this friend of yours, Wally Roseberg, be cautious about trusting him. And one last thing. I'm sorry to say this, Carl, but until you hear back from Jack, I'd stay away from Molly. This is just my professional opinion as a law enforcement officer."

"She's my wife, Bruce! I'm not sure I can do that!"

"I've got to get back to work now, but I will put in for a vacation as soon as my shift is over. I've got two weeks coming to me, and the county will grant me a leave beginning tomorrow if they can juggle everyone's schedule around. They're pretty good about doing that for us, so plan on me being at your disposal. I want you to know I am more than glad to help you solve this problem!"

"Thanks, Bruce. But you realize this could turn bad, right? What we want to accomplish is extremely dangerous. Not too many people mess with the mob and get out alive!"

"I'll take that chance. To see my father rot in prison for the rest of his life is well worth it! So, call me as soon as you get your burner phone, and we'll meet up. Take care, Carl!" The men shook hands, and Bruce headed back to the squad car.

Carl sat back down, ordered another coffee, and thought about his best friend, grandfather, and wife. How had his life gone so wrong?

Chapter 45

After dropping Burt off at the airport, Sam drove to his mansion on the St. Croix River. At 11:17 a.m. on Tuesday, Sam emailed George Markins with the emergency shutdown obituary.

> *Allen Betsmer Offhauser, age 21 of Eau Claire, Wisconsin, died from injuries sustained in a car accident on September 24th. He is survived by his father, Keith, his mother, Karen, his brother, Bill, and many aunts, uncles, and cousins.*
>
> *Allen will be remembered for his kind heart, outgoing personality, love of nature, and great sense of humor.*
>
> *The family will be holding a private memorial service at their home in the near future.*

All of Burt Merriman's operatives knew that an Allen Offhauser obituary was similar to a flashing yellow light—read with caution. The first few letters of his name indicated their directive: All Bets Off. September twenty-fourth was the effective date, and the last paragraph told the operatives that further instructions would be hand-delivered to their homes soon. They all knew to destroy their cell phone immediately.

Two hours later, Sam still hadn't received an acknowledgment from George Markins. He pounded the table with his fist and grumbled, "Why hasn't he read my damn email?!" Max barked and wagged his tail—obviously in agreement.

At two o'clock, Sam tried George's cell phone. Nothing. One ring and click. He tried again. One ring and click. No voicemail, no out-of-service recording, nothing! It was as if the cell phone was drowning in the water somewhere!

At three o'clock, Sam couldn't wait any longer. The operatives would be anxiously waiting to place this week's wagers. He called the Gazette and asked for George.

"Mr. Markins is not here today," stated the receptionist. "May I leave a message for him?"

"Where is he?!" said Sam with frustration.

The receptionist was taken aback. "I'm sorry, sir, but I'm not at liberty to give out that information."

"Okay, please forgive me for my tone. I just need to place an obituary immediately."

"Let me give you the email address for our obituary consultant, Carl West. He handles our death notices and can even provide you some guidance while writing it."

Sam rolled his eyes and took a deep breath. The Gazette didn't know Carl was dead! "Oh, yes, I did see his name on your website as the contact person, but he was unavailable, and I need to have the obit posted as soon as possible."

"Well, then, let me have you speak to our editor. Sorry for the hassle, sir. And I'm very sorry for your loss!"

"Yes, thank you!" An hour later, Allen Betsmer Offhauser's short and sweet eulogy was posted online.

But Sam was nervous. Where was George?!

*****

"I'm worried, Curt. I was mad at Carl when he got home late from your place last weekend. He was acting crazy! He pleaded for me to pack up and go with him to Syd's house on Lake Tahoe, but he wouldn't tell me why. I went back to bed, but when I got up to get ready for work on Monday, he tried to keep me from leaving. I brushed him off and went to the office and haven't seen him since!"

Molly was standing by the picture window of her office watching the rush hour traffic grip the city of Minneapolis with its daily gridlock of afternoon commuters. She was having a difficult time holding back the tears.

"Do you think he knows?" asked Curt. "I certainly didn't see any odd behavior at my place. He asked questions about my gambling, but just to make conversation. I'm pretty sure he doesn't know he's a whipping boy for the Mafia."

"He definitely knows something isn't kosher. I've been dealing with his paranoia since he started the job with the Gazette. But we haven't spoken much lately. When Sam unwittingly chose Wally Roseberg from the White Pages as his victim, well, that was a huge mistake! Carl hasn't been the same since he got back from Florida, knowing Wally is still alive."

"That wasn't Sam's fault. It was merely a coincidence. You said it yourself, Molly. He picked a name randomly out of the Jacksonville White Pages to use for the obituary, seeing the game was in Jacksonville. He had no idea that Wally Roseberg was someone Carl grew up with."

"That was a coincidence with astronomical odds, Curt! What were the chances Sam would pick the name of Carl's best friend to code a eulogy?! Winning the Powerball would be easier! Why doesn't Sam just make up a fake name?! I don't get it?!"

"To avoid suspicion. If Carl ever questioned what he was doing and decided to Google the deceased, it would be a real person."

Suddenly, a traumatic thought occurred to Molly. "Jim Bowman, the man Carl replaced, was a friend of yours, right?"

"Yep, right. We played soccer against each other. Why?"

"You said he died from cancer. Are you sure of that?"

"That's what George Markins told me. Why?"

"Is it possible Jim was caught by the syndicate doing something wrong, and they simply got rid of him? I'm talking about having him killed."

"Calm down, Sis! Now, who's paranoid? The people we work for are a minacious group, but I don't think they are murderers."

"You don't think?! That's not very assuring!"

"Okay, sorry, you're right. But I need to end this call. I'm using my business cell and need to permanently disable it by six o'clock."

"What do you mean by that? What's going on?"

"You haven't heard? The operatives are shutting down until further notice. The syndicate will be hand-delivering new phones with new instructions on how to proceed."

"Shutting down?! Why?! And why hasn't anyone told me?" Molly was both angry and worried. She began pacing the office.

"We suffered big losses on the 49ers game against Arizona. The 49ers didn't cover the spread, and the total points came up short of the over/under. The ops don't know what went wrong, but I'm guessing the officials blew it. I assume the syndicate is just taking safety precautions, not knowing if the officials purposely tried to screw us."

"Could they blame Carl? I mean, he's the one who submitted the obituary."

"Oh, come on, Molly! All Carl does is forward the Rankins's emails to his editor. Surely, he couldn't have done anything wrong!"

"But what if he accidentally made a mistake and miscoded the obit? What would they do to him? Would he be fired or something?"

"The answer to that is beyond my grade code, Sis! Hey, sorry, but I really need to go. I'll call you with my new business cell number after it's been delivered."

Curt hung up, and Molly eased into her chair, trying to make sense of everything she just heard. If the operatives had shut down, why weren't they shutting her down, too? She hadn't been informed of her moneyline game for the upcoming weekend, which was strange because Sam typically emailed her on Tuesday. However, she also hadn't been told that it wouldn't happen. Why wasn't Rankins keeping her in the loop?

Molly didn't have to wait long for the answer. Sam Diggins was waiting in the lobby to see her.

*****

Sam plopped down in the leather chair without an invitation to do so, and Molly could see he was upset. He motioned with his finger for Molly to sit down in her desk chair opposite him. She did so reluctantly.

"What's up, Sam? You look agitated." Molly wondered how much he would tell her. She was determined to stay calm.

"Okay, where do I start?" Sam was gathering his thoughts like a lawyer preparing for his closing argument. "First things first. Rankins is no longer interested in purchasing the Vikings. It's a long story."

Molly was stunned, and she struggled to keep a straight face. Was Sam going to explain why?

Sam continued. "You probably know by now that we took a major loss on the San Francisco-Arizona game." He waited for a response, and Molly felt pressured to give one.

"Yes, I just heard from Curt. I understand the referees didn't do what they were asked."

"No, Molly. Sorry, but Curt and the operatives are creating false rumors. That's not what happened. The officials followed the code to the tee."

"But, then, . . . huh? I don't get it. What are you saying?"

"I'm saying Pete Callen's eulogy was published the exact opposite of what I submitted to Carl. Your husband screwed us, Molly. And now we've decided to end the point spreads and over/unders and, quite frankly, obituaries. From now on, we gamble only on moneyline games with high payouts for the underdogs, which, of course, is who we will bet on. Your column will be the key to our success."

Molly could no longer hide her emotions. She stood up and walked to the window, keeping her back to Sam so he wouldn't see the panic and fear painted all over her face. She stared back down at the busy streets of Minneapolis but registered nothing in her brain.

She was afraid to speak, worried her voice would crack. But Sam knew what she was thinking and spoke for her.

"You're wondering about Carl, aren't you?"

Molly hesitated, then turned slowly around to look at Sam. "Yes, I haven't seen him since Monday morning. Do you know where he is?" Molly wasn't sure she wanted to hear the answer.

"Let's just say we terminated his employment."

"Terminated his employment! What do you mean by that?! Damn it, where is my husband?!"

"I'm not at liberty to say, Molly. I'm not sure I can trust you. Were you and Carl working together?"

Molly ignored the question. "Did you kill him?! Is that what you're saying?!" Molly's fear turned to anger as she approached Sam and shouted, "Where is he?! Answer me, you son-of-a-bitch!"

Molly's secretary, Jan Willows, overheard the commotion through the closed door but could only make out one word: *kill*. She buzzed security, and within a minute, two tall, muscular officers arrived and waited for an explanation from Jan.

"You answer to me, Molly," replied Sam calmly. "I don't answer to you. So this is how it's going to shake out: The operatives will be receiving new phones and instructions by early next week. There will be no betting on the upcoming games this weekend—including your moneyline wager. Once we are back in action, you will code one NFL game each Sunday, pointing to the underdog to bet on. Any questions?"

Molly could only think about Carl. Where was he? Did Sam kill him or have him killed? They wouldn't do that, right? No way! Carl probably went to see Grandpa Syd, that's all! He was upset Molly didn't go with him, so he left in anger without saying a word. She was sure that's what happened!

Molly tried to regain her composure. She was in this for the long haul and needed to focus on the new task at hand. "Just one question, Sam, then I'll let you go. Why me? Why do I need to tip off our operatives using my sports column? Why don't you just text or email them yourself?"

Sam laughed. "That's three questions, Molly. But I will answer them for you. Your father is the head honcho of this organization, and he has selected you for this job. But make no mistake—if you turn on us as Carl did, your stepdaddy will be unforgiving. Second, the FBI can intercept texts and emails, especially when I send out over 360 of them each week. That's obviously an enormous risk for our endeavor, wouldn't you say?"

Sam paused momentarily to give Molly a chance to respond, but she said nothing. Sam continued. "As we have been doing, I will call you with the moneyline games on Tuesdays using a burner phone; then I will destroy the cell so the call can't be traced back to me."

"So, if we ever get caught, I'm guessing you will leave me hanging out to dry. You'll hide behind the shield of Holmes Mortuary and pretend you are an assistant funeral director!" Molly knew she shouldn't have said it, but at this point, she couldn't resist.

Sam laughed again. Yes, she was right—no use trying to deny it. "There's one more thing we need to discuss. We can do it now, or I'll come back when you've calmed down."

Molly's face turned a deep shade of red. "Tell me now, Sam. Let's get everything on the table."

"As I told you, we are no longer making point spread and over/under bets, which is why we backed out of the offer to purchase the Vikings. Our plan was to own the Vikes so we could influence key players with cash incentives for years to come. It would be easy to shave points by having them fumble, throw interceptions, whatever, when told to do so. However, we are now pursuing a different goal, and we need to use the Vikings for our final money-making haul—the Super Bowl. Your dad has found a new man who will be recruiting unscrupulous players on all the NFL teams to help us with that mission! He didn't tell me his name, but I assume the guy must know people inside the game.

"Anyway, the Vikings are currently at 175 to one odds to win the Super Bowl after starting the season zero and two. We will make sure they lose their next game, too. Rob Fornasiere will assign all our referees to that game, seeing there are no other contests to fix this week. No team has ever even played in the Super Bowl after starting the season zero and three. The odds will probably be in the neighborhood of 400 to one come Monday. Assuming the operatives have their new phones hand-delivered by then, they will also be given instructions to immediately wager $10,000 on Minnesota to win the Super Bowl. Rob will make sure the Vikes win enough games to make the playoffs, and of course, the Super Bowl."

Molly shook her head in disagreement. "That will be a risky bet! The Vegas bookies and our online gaming site administrators will certainly perk up! That amount of money gambled during one week for a team with virtually no chance of winning is unconscionable. It will send up red flags all over the place!"

"You need not worry about that, Molly. The Super Bowl is out of your hands. The operatives will be told at the same time their phones are delivered to make the wager. You won't need to code anything in your sports column relative to the Super Bowl."

"What's at stake if the Vikings don't win the Super Bowl?"

"You don't want to know, my dear!"

*****

After Sam departed and Jan Willows left for home, Molly sat alone in her office with her head on the desk. She attempted three phone calls, desperately trying to get answers to questions she was hesitant to ask. But all three went to voicemail.

The first was to Carl. Where was he?! The second to her grandfather-in-law, Syd West. Was Carl with him? And the last one to her stepfather, Burt Merriman. Was he responsible for Carl's disappearance?! Please, God, don't let my husband be dead!

Molly waited until midnight, but none of the three returned her call.

Chapter 46

On Wednesday morning, Carl walked unassumingly into First National Bank in New Richmond and cashed in a $100,000 certificate of deposit that he had opened in July. The money was part of his father's life insurance payout NFL teams establish for all of their employees—players, coaches, office staff, marketers, ground maintenance crew, and even ushers. Molly wasn't aware that Carl opened the CD because it was a secret. He was saving to take her on a seven-day cruise around the Galapagos Islands to celebrate their first anniversary next year. After scuba diving in the crystal clear Pacific waters, they would hike Macchu Picchu, then spend a couple of days at the Mayan Palace in Acapulco on the return trip. Luxury accommodations all the way—first-class flights and opulent suites. And, of course, a South Sea golden pearl necklace from Tiffany's to surprise her at dinner on their celebratory night.

That dream was now history. Carl received half in $100 bills, and the rest in a cashier's check. He drove to the Walmart south of town to purchase and activate a burner phone, then moved his Tesla to a parking spot near a lamppost. The store was open 24 hours, so leaving the car there for several days might not raise anyone's suspicions. Might is a powerful word that instills confidence in optimists and dread in pessimists. Carl wasn't sure which side of the mental attitude teeter-totter he weighed on most heavily.

Carl phoned an Uber driver to take him to a country home outside of Somerset, a typical rural American community seven miles from New Richmond. Somerset was known for tubing on the Apple River, pea soup, and corn hole tournaments at the local bars. For several months, Carl had seen a 1976 Winnebago motorhome with 425,000 miles parked in the front yard of the farmhouse with a *For Sale* sign on the windshield. Twenty minutes after being dropped off, Carl made a deal with the ecstatic owner who was ready to donate the RV to the Goodwill. Carl handed him $500 in cash, and after struggling to get the flooded engine started, he was on his way to Hudson to register it with the Department of Motor Vehicles.

The Winnebago overheated ten miles down the road, and Carl had to call AAA to tow it to the nearest repair facility, which happened to be Moe's RV. He offered Doug Moe, the owner, a $1,000 bonus if his service staff could fix the motorhome that same day. Doug happily assigned all six of his mechanics to get the Winnebago up and running. Instead of waiting, Carl hiked three miles to the courthouse to get a new vehicle license plate. Because the previous owner had the RV officially examined before he listed it for sale, an inspection wasn't necessary, which meant the Wisconsin DMV didn't have to see the Winnebago. Obviously, a radiator check was not included in their assessment!

Ten hours and $9,375 later, Carl was back on the road. Not sure where he was headed in the dilapidated camper, Carl drove south on County Road F, searching in the darkness for a place to hide until he could figure things out. Doug Moe told him about a remote camping area on the Kinnickinnic River that was easy to find but risky to enter. The state-owned land would someday be developed into a trout farm if Madison's tightwad legislators ever approved the funding. The dirt service road was precisely where Doug said it would be—exactly 7.6 miles from the corner of F and FF, opposite Kinnickinnic State Park. The muddy entrance was clearly marked with an ominous sign posted on a swinging barrier gate: ***DNR Vehicles Only!***

Carl hadn't seen a car since he was out of the Hudson city limits, and he doubted that many people were camping at the state park on a school night in September. He pulled into the service road and shined his lights on the small chain and lock that kept the gate closed. Using a bolt cutter Doug Moe had given him, Carl quickly sliced through the chain. He pushed the barrier open, drove through the gate, then replaced the chain the best he could to make it look like it was secure. He followed the dirt path for a mile until it stopped. At the end was a cozy cleared space alongside the rapidly flowing Kinnickinnic River. Carl exited the motorhome and took a deep breath of the crisp night air, smiling as he listened to the water ripple across the rocks. It was midnight, and he couldn't think of a more peaceful and serene location to escape from his worries.

Tomorrow he would call Jack Bowman and find out the status of his investigation. But for tonight, Carl would slumber under the stars on the banks of the roaring Kinnickinnic and slip away into glorious oblivion.

Ah, sleep! Finally!

*****

The sun was high in the sky when Carl awoke from a dream that seemed to have lasted all night. In it, he had escaped to Mars in a converted Winnebago Chieftain rocket ship, and he was now exploring the red planet with none other than Sam Diggins. Sam was dressed as a Viking warrior, complete with a cloak made of heavy fabric, decorated textile embroidery, studded leather, and thick fur. Carl's dream fizzled into reality just as Sam was about to use his shield and sword to defend himself from a furry Martian animal wearing a Chicago Bears' jersey.

Carl looked at his watch. In five minutes, it would be noon. He had slept almost twelve hours, a feat he had never remembered doing in his twenty-three years on Earth. He felt groggy but well-rested nonetheless.

The burner he had purchased at Walmart was a simple Tracfone. No Internet, camera, or apps. He could make voice calls or text, but he couldn't check the weather. This would be a pretty worthless gift for a teenager!

Carl had written Jack Bowman's phone number on a Post-It and stuck it in his wallet. He dialed, and Jack immediately picked up.

"What took you so long?!" Jack sounded panicked. It was 3:00 p.m. in Washington, DC, and he had been impatiently waiting for Carl to call. He didn't wait for a response. "I have interesting news from Mary Reppe. She was able to decipher the calls Sam had made on his burner phone."

"And hello to you, too, Jack!" said Carl sarcastically. "Okay, that's great news. Who did he call?"

"Several calls were made to Holmes Mortuary in Prudhoe Bay and six to Rob Fornasiere at SOTO. Sam also called your wife four times. Sorry!"

"No apologies necessary. Go on."

"He only phoned one more number but did so eight times. I doubt that person is of any interest to you, Carl. But, Mary did some research on those calls."

"Tell me who Sam called. I need to know, Jack!"

"As I said, you won't know him. But he has a connection to the Mafia, so I'm trying to tell you to be careful. If Sam has phoned a bigshot in the mob, chances are Rankins, aka Holmes Mortuary, are partners."

"Jack, I need to tell you something, too. But you must first tell me who Sam called! I will explain—I promise!"

"Okay. The man's name is Burt Merriman. Documents show he is the CEO and primary shareholder of Rankins Corporation, even though they are not a publicly-traded company. Mary believes he was an associate of Vito Rizzuto, better known as Teflon Don. This Burt fellow owns fine restaurants all over the world and has several places he calls home. He has no criminal record. Contrarily, he has hosted parties for several presidents. Today, Mary will try to track down Burt's friends and relatives, but I doubt that information will lead to anything substantial. However, it could lead to the proof I need to exonerate my son and get him out of prison. Now, what was it you promised to tell me?"

"Burt Merriman is Molly's stepfather."

Chapter 47

"You're staying in a Winnebago on what river?!" asked Jack. "Are you one hundred percent positive no one can find you?! What about this deputy sheriff? Are you sure he can be trusted?"

Carl spent the last hour telling Jack everything that had happened since Jack left for the east coast, including seeing Burt and Sam go into SOTO headquarters in Minneapolis. Jack was most curious about Carl's meeting with Burt's son Bruce at the TA truck stop.

"Relax a bit, okay, Jack? First, it's called the Kinnickinnic River, and I doubt anyone will travel down this gravel path again until next summer. It's next to a state park with *No Hunting* signs posted everywhere, and with the crazy weather in the Midwest, the area could be covered in snow in a couple of weeks.

"As for Bruce Merriman, yes, I believe him and trust him. He's taking a two-week vacation and has offered to help us investigate Burt without involving the police. Burt abandoned his mother and him as a child, so he's motivated to put him away for life."

Jack waited a few seconds to respond, and Carl could hear him take a few deep breaths. "Okay, Carl, we'll let Bruce help us. But there is something I'm going to demand of you that you won't like. You must not visit, call, or text Molly, Curt, or your grandfather Syd until I give the green light. Do you understand?"

"You realize they will think I'm dead, don't you? And when Molly finds out that I screwed Rankins, she'll think her stepfather ordered me killed. Would Burt Merriman try to have her silenced? Would he try to kill her, too? I can't live thinking about that, Jack!"

"I'm sorry to say this, Carl, but I believe Molly is a key player in their organization. So too are Curt and Grandpa Syd. I really don't think you need to worry about their safety."

Anger was boiling up inside Carl. But deep down, he knew Jack was right. Burt and his syndicate needed Molly, especially now that they couldn't use him anymore for coding at the Gazette. But where did his grandfather come into play?

"You may be right about Molly and Curt being safe. Not only are they employees—they are family. But what evidence do we have that Grandpa Syd did anything wrong? All we know is that Grandpa is a friend of Burt Merriman because he was chummy with him at our wedding. Who knows why Sam Diggins tried to call him on a burner phone? Syd is the CEO of a huge sports marketing company, and Sam may have needed some assistance with sponsorships, that's all! That doesn't make him a business partner. You said yourself Burt was associated with past American presidents, but that didn't mean they knew the man was part of the mob."

"Carl, listen to what you're saying. Why would an assistant funeral director of a fake funeral parlor need anything from a sports marketing company? It's very doubtful he would spend any money advertising for a mortuary that doesn't exist. However, you're right. We don't know that Syd is affiliated with the Mafia. But we don't know that he isn't either. All I'm saying is we need to take every precaution if we're going to find a way to crush the syndicate without telling the FBI. And there's one other thing I hesitate to tell you. It's about your friend, Wally Roseberg. There's something fishy going on."

Carl sighed loudly. Thoughts of his family's corruption were tearing him apart. Now, what was Jack going to say about his best friend? He couldn't take much more! "What about Wally?"

"I called the cell number you gave me for Wally. It's been disconnected. Then I called InterPlan Architects in Palm Beach and pretended to be a potential client from Wisconsin. I asked for Wally, and the receptionist said all new business had to go through the owner, Randy Hansen. After I gave her my cell number for a return call, she said something that caught me off guard. Believing I was from Wisconsin, she wondered if I had been referred to InterPlan by Sam Diggins. Seems they built a mansion for him on the St. Croix River! Anyway, I lied and said yes. I noted that Sam gave me Wally's name as the contact person instead of Randy's. So the receptionist said she would have him phone me when he returned to the office. As of yet, he hasn't returned the call."

Carl was utterly stunned! "You're telling me that Wally designed a home for Sam Diggins?! Oh my God, Jack, I can't believe it!"

"And there's more. Wally doesn't have a bank account anywhere that I could locate, and he hasn't filed a tax return for years. He doesn't have a wife or kids, but there's one thing he does have."

"What's that, Jack?!"

"A death certificate. Seems he died long before you saw his fake obituary published in the Gazette. Like a few years before!"

"Huh?!"

"I assume the death certificate is a fake—perhaps Wally's way of avoiding taxes, or hiding the fact he works for the mob, or both! I'm also guessing that outside of his parents, whom you talked to, and the folks at InterPlan, the only one who knows of his existence is Sam Diggins."

"Are you kidding me?! So when will this nightmare end?!" Carl stood by the riverbank and stared up at the smattering of clouds in the sky, perhaps searching heaven for an answer. "Where do we go from here, Jack? What's next? I need to see a light at the end of the tunnel."

"Can your Winnebago survive a trip to Florida? We need to find Wally Roseberg."

*****

Carl thought about abandoning his motorhome and taking the Tesla to Florida. But it made sense to drive the boxy rustbucket if it could get there without breaking down. There would be no record of him checking into hotels, nor would anyone be able to identify him at a restaurant. He pulled out of his camping spot, filled up with gas in Hudson, and picked up Bruce Merriman at his studio apartment on Laurel Avenue. There, Carl told Bruce about Wally Roseberg and what Jack had discovered, which was why they were heading to Florida.

"Florida?! Well, let me get packing! This two-week vacation with you is sounding a whole lot better, my friend!"

A few minutes later, Carl maneuvered the Winnebago onto I-94 and floored the accelerator. The camper maxed out at sixty-two miles per hour and would get five miles to a gallon—if a strong wind pushed it from behind! It was 3:00 p.m. on Wednesday in Wisconsin, and at this point, the Sunshine State seemed like a pipe dream. Bruce wore a faded and ripped Packer t-shirt, blue denim shorts, and flip-flops—he was ready for the beach!

"The Gazette filed a missing person report today," Bruce announced while bouncing around in the passenger seat. The Winnebago needed new shock absorbers, something Doug Moe must have missed during his $9,375 repair job. "Well, two, actually."

"What do you mean by two?" asked Carl. The motorhome didn't have cruise control, and he wasn't totally focused on Bruce's conversation. He thought his right foot would be fatigued about the time they crossed the Mason-Dixon line.

"George Markins, of course. And you."

"Me?!" Carl hadn't thought about that! He just assumed the Gazette wouldn't even know their obituary consultant was gone. He was a part-timer who worked whenever he wanted, not a full-time employee like George, who was expected to show up every day. "That's not good! Has my picture been distributed?"

"From here to Timbuktu and everywhere in between! But only on the police wires for now. It's a photo of you posing with your dad before the Super Bowl. The Eau Claire County Sheriff's Department must have done a Google search to find the picture. You were a few years younger then. Maybe that will help keep you incognito."

"Why did you say 'for now?'"

"If you're not found in two weeks, your photograph will be posted in public places around the country. However, don't sweat it. Most people don't bother to look at the posters, and you're too old to end up on a milk carton!" Bruce chuckled, but Carl failed to see the humor. His life was at stake.

It was past midnight when the Winnebago entered Indiana and the eastern time zone. He pulled into a truck stop in Lafayette for a few hours of rest. Carl was fed up with the confounded Illinois Turnpike and its endless lineup of toll booths, but he was glad to have avoided an accident with distracted Chicago drivers who text at all times of the day and night.

Carl decided right then and there that a Florida junkyard would be a perfect final resting place for the Winnebago.

*****

Carl and Bruce loaded up the camper with food from a nearby Kroger store and began the long haul south on I-65. Taking turns driving, they only stopped for gas and an occasional jog around a rest area. Bruce would struggle to keep pace, but thrilled to death to be exercising with the son of the great quarterback, Billy West!

They arrived at Palm Beach International Airport at noon on Friday, September twenty-fifth. Jack Bowman's United Express flight from Washington Dulles was due to touchdown at 1:16 p.m. Bruce and Carl decided to wait for Jack inside the terminal at Rooney's Public House. The Gold Coast's heat and humidity were stifling, and the Winnebago's air conditioner had seen better days. An ice-cold draft was just what the doctor ordered for two thirsty snowbirds from the Upper Midwest. They sat at a table outside the pub and watched as travelers hurried to and from their flights.

Carl was wiping Guinness stout foam off his chin when an older man strode briskly by him carrying a Maxwell Scott brown leather attache case. Doing a double-take, Carl accidentally knocked the empty beer glass on the floor, shattering it into hundreds of tiny shards. Bruce instinctively jumped at the sound, then saw Carl staring at the man who was hustling down the walkway.

"Is that somebody you know?" asked Bruce.

"Most definitely! That's my grandfather, Syd."

Chapter 48

Carl tossed a twenty-dollar bill on the table, and he and Bruce hustled to catch up with Syd. From ten yards behind, they followed him to the exit. A man in a red 1965 Mustang convertible pulled up, and Syd got in the passenger seat. A cab was sitting in the taxi stand, and no customers were waiting to be picked up, so Bruce and Carl quickly jumped in the back and slammed the doors. Carl pulled a one hundred dollar bill from his wallet and waved it at the driver.

"Stay with that Mustang, and this will be your tip! Don't let the driver see you!"

"Yessiree, sir! I can do that! No problem, dude!"

Surprisingly, the Mustang stayed under the speed limit from the airport all the way to Tequesta. The cab driver was getting antsy. He was hoping for some James Bond action but instead was following a law-abiding goody two shoe who happened to own the hottest antique car on the road! The cabbie shouted at his windshield, "Come on, man! Show me a little Mario Andretti racing savvy, would you please!"

The Mustang crossed the bridge over the Loxahatchee River, and Carl recognized several roads and buildings. "I've been here before," he stated to Bruce. The Mustang pulled into a small parking lot. "That's InterPlan Architecture, where Wally Roseberg works! Pull over here!" The cab driver darted for the curb, and two cars slammed on their brakes to avoid crunching the taxi. They immediately blasted their horns and raised their fists at the cabbie, like any good New York City transplant had been trained to do!

Carl tossed two one-hundred-dollar bills at the driver and told him to keep the change. Then he and Bruce watched from a distance as Grandpa Syd walked to the front entrance with the man who had been driving the Mustang. The man pulled the door open for Syd, then turned his head slightly, just enough for Carl to do another double-take.

Bruce saw Carl flinch. "Let me guess—that's your friend Wally."

Carl nodded but was too surprised and upset to say anything. His abysmal nightmare was playing out in front of his eyes. How could his grandfather be part of an illegal gaming crime syndicate?! Worse yet, how did Carl not know?! Grandpa Syd raised his son Billy to be an NFL superstar—a good and honorable athlete and human being beyond reproach! And he did the same for his grandson Carl! This can't be happening!

Bruce, being a cop who knows better than to make hasty decisions, took a step forward and turned so Carl was blocked from staring at the InterPlan building. "Yes, this looks bad, my friend. But you don't have any evidence of your grandfather's wrongdoing. Perhaps Wally is designing a new building for Syd's sports marketing firm. They would know each other because of you, right?"

"You're the one who told me to be wary of both Grandpa Syd and Wally! You're only changing your tune to make me feel better! I get that, but Wally designed Sam Diggins' mansion, Bruce. He doesn't exactly associate himself with exemplary clients! I'm going to get to the bottom of this right now!" He lightly pushed Bruce out of his way and started walking to the InterPlan building. Bruce tagged alongside but had a difficult time keeping up.

They were thirty feet from the door when a limousine pulled into the InterPlan parking lot. Carl and Bruce stopped on a dime and watched as a young, well-built man emerged from the back seat and hastened to the entry. Bruce glanced at Carl and asked, "Do you recognize him?"

"Recognize him? Are you kidding me? Have you ever seen the cover of Sports Illustrated? That man's been on three of them!"

Bruce stared at the man and replied anxiously, "Who is it?!"

"John Warner, the LA Rams' phenom running back, that's who."

"Holy crap! What's he doing here?!"

"Your guess is as good as mine, but I know Grandpa Syd's marketing company represents him. Warner was the first pick in the 2019 draft and almost quit football after his sensational rookie season."

"I remember that. Warner lost millions on his contract after the news broke he received a Porsche in college from a booster club supporter. He was forced to give back the money and play for the minimum salary. That's why he almost quit, right?"

Carl paused a moment, and a thought occurred. "You know what? Now I'm not so sure that's why he quit. I read Warner claimed he never did receive a Porsche. John believed he was set up by some unknown people looking to either destroy his reputation, or who wanted the University of Colorado to look bad, or both. Colorado was placed on a five-year probation because of it. Do you think your father had something to do with it? Warner's parents hired a private investigator, then disappeared a short time later. Maybe that is the real reason John almost retired."

"Are you trying to tell me you think Warner's parents were killed?!"

"No, I'm guessing they were kidnapped."

"Kidnapped?! Why would someone do that?"

"To control John, that's why."

"You mean on the football field?"

"Yep, that's exactly what I mean!"

"Why wouldn't the kidnappers want cash as a ransom? After all, John Warner makes plenty of money."

"Accepting a ransom would be a one-time deal. Blackmail, on the other hand, would be a continuous transaction resulting in a much greater payout. To keep his parents alive, John may have followed a weekly script on the football field. Think about it, Bruce. You're a cop. Last week, the sure-handed Warner fumbled the ball that gave Seattle the win, which I'm sure made many gamblers very happy!"

Bruce finally made the connection. "So you believe John Warner is a puppet for the syndicate? And he's here at InterPlan to discuss his next role play on Sunday? That pretty much confirms Wally and Syd are key players with the mob, doesn't it?"

"I'm assuming that's a rhetorical question. Let's go back to the airport and get Jack. Seems our suspicions have come to fruition."

*****

"You're sure it was John Warner?" asked Jack. He, Carl, and Bruce were sitting at the cramped table inside the Winnebago at Palm Beach International airport. Jack suggested getting a suite at the Breakers Resort, which would be several thousand times more comfortable than the worn down motorhome, but Carl didn't want to take the risk. No one who stayed at the upscale Breakers paid in cash. Instead, everyone used their American Express Black Centurion or Chase Sapphire Reserve to show off their wealth. Right now, he was supposed to be dead, and dead people didn't use credit cards.

"There's not an ounce of doubt in my mind. And it's my opinion that John Warner is not building a house in Florida."

"The Rams are playing the Dolphins in Miami on Sunday," said Jack. "Perhaps he is a friend of Wally's who is just stopping by to say 'hi.' Did UNLV ever play Colorado in football? Maybe they met on the playing field and became friends, just like my son Jim did with Curt Anderson and George Markins."

Carl rolled his eyes. "You're grasping at straws, Jack. It's time the three of us face the inevitable—Grandpa Syd, Wally, and John Warner are part of a crime syndicate that is corrupting NFL games. John is probably being blackmailed, but we don't know for sure. So let's move on, okay? We need a plan, fellas!"

Jack moved to the fridge to check out the contents, then returned with several cheese curds in the palm of his hand—and two in his mouth. He didn't need to see the license plate to know the Winnebago came from Wisconsin. The sound of fresh Colby squeaking away on his palate was proof the camper had originated in the Dairy State.

Jack looked at Bruce, then at Carl. "I think I have an idea. We need to find a print shop that can whip up some business cards on the spot."

Chapter 49

"Hello, sir. My name is Wally Roseberg. And you are—?" Wally was trying to be pleasant, but he was in a meeting and didn't want to be disturbed.

"Giles. Giles Mumphrey." Jack was attempting to keep a straight face while trying his best to fake a British accent. There was no receptionist when he entered the InterPlan building and no architects at the dedicated CAD computers, which was odd for a Friday afternoon. But Randy Hansen was on vacation in Maine, and he had given all his employees a day off so they could have a long weekend. Wally came from a conference room in the back to greet him. "I own several casinos in England, and I would like to expand into the United States. There are so many bloody rules and regulations regarding sports gaming that I get dizzy trying to keep up! Anyway, you probably don't know much about sports gaming, so I won't waste my time telling you about all my troubles. But let me tell you, America is the place to be for betting on professional sports, and I'd like to build one right here in Florida."

Wally was startled. What a coincidence a potential customer would be inquiring about building a casino with a sportsbook while he was meeting with Syd West and John Warner regarding the same topic. He decided to probe. "Casinos in Florida are owned by Native American tribes. Perhaps you should think about Nevada or New Jersey. Would you like me to refer you to an architect in those states?"

"Ah, Mr. Roseberg, please allow me to correct you, sir. The Indian Gaming Regulatory Act of 1988 does not discriminate against who can own a casino on Native American land. Yes, it must be built within designated reservation boundaries, and its purpose should be to generate revenue for the tribes. I was thinking about constructing one in the Seminole Nation, perhaps on Lake Okeechobee. What are your thoughts, sir?"

"Why would you invest in a casino where the profits go to a Native American tribe? That doesn't sound very enterprising to me!"

That was the question Jack hoped Wally would ask. Now was the time to test the waters of his plan. He knew Syd West and John Warner were in the conference room, and the door was open. Jack needed to talk loud enough for them to catch what he was about to say.

"Okay, may I speak freely, Mr. Roseberg?" Jack's voice echoed down the hallway. Anyone within earshot would hear him clearly. "I would like to tell you something in strict confidence. If you turn me over to the authorities, I will simply deny ever meeting with you."

Wally gave him a puzzled look, then nodded. "Go ahead, Mr. Mumphrey. I have no reason to get myself involved with the law."

This was it—now or never. Could Jack convince Wally to buy his story? Or was it too outlandish to even try?

"The casinos I own in England are legit, Mr. Roseberg. However, the sports gaming is not quite on the up and up, if you know what I mean. I have found a way to cheat on soccer and cricket matches in Europe. I pay off officials and key players to make mistakes."

Jack waited for a response from Wally, but Wally said nothing. Their eyes were locked on each other. Jack continued.

"Anyway, I believe I could be successful doing the same thing in the United States. American football, for instance, seems a logical target. I think I could make a hefty profit on the side while the casino dedicates itself to the Seminole tribe's economic development. A win-win, right?! I won't go into details, Mr. Roseberg, because I know this is most likely well above your level of comprehension." Jack was hoping Wally would be offended and let his guard down. It didn't happen.

Feigning ignorance of what he just heard, Wally asked, "Why us? How did you find our architectural firm?"

"Luck of the draw, that's all. Because I was thinking about building in the Seminole Nation and on Lake Okeechobee, I flew into Palm Beach. When I landed, I Googled ***architects near me***, and your firm popped up as a five star. I only deal with the best, Mr. Roseberg!"

Wally was sure Syd West and John Warner heard every word of his conversation with Giles Mumphrey. He smiled and motioned to the conference room. "Please, Mr. Mumphrey, let me introduce you to two of my clients. You may have something in common with them."

"Oh, how so? Are they sports gamblers, too?"

"You might say that. Follow me."

Wally led Jack to the conference room. Syd and John stood to greet him. "Giles, this is Syd West and John Warner. Syd owns a sports marketing company, and John is an NFL star running back for the LA Rams. Syd and John, this is Giles Mumphrey from England."

Jack grasped their hands and shook vehemently. Then he stared at John and asked, "A running back, you say. Is that anything like a midfielder in the real game of football?!" Jack laughed loudly while John just smiled back.

Wally patted Jack softly on his shoulder, then said, "Why don't you folks get to know one another. I need to make a phone call and will be back in a few minutes."

Wally grabbed his cell phone off the table and left the room. Then he walked outdoors to make the call. He needed complete privacy.

*****

Wally returned to the conference room a half-hour later. He apologized for taking so long, then lied and told Jack he had just spoken to InterPlan owner Randy Hansen about his casino proposal.

Wally claimed Randy was very interested and wanted to meet with him as soon as he returned from Maine. In reality, Randy was preparing a transfer of ownership document for a lobster boat he just purchased from a ninety-five-year-old sailor in Bar Harbor. Randy purposely left his cell phone in the car so he wouldn't be disturbed.

Jack gave Wally his fake Giles Mumphrey business card with his burner cell phone number engraved. As he shook hands and departed, Jack said he looked forward to a long-term partnership with InterPlan. If fibbing were an Olympic sport, Wally and Jack would both receive gold medals!

Wally sat down at the conference table and looked soberly at Syd and John Warner. Then he stood back up and paced the room. It was apparent to Syd and John that something about Wally's phone call was troubling him.

"What is it, Wally?" asked Syd. "Who were you talking to?"

"Let's just say that we have a problem. There's no such person who owns a casino in England named Giles Mumphrey."

Chapter 50

"It's taken care of," said Rob Fornasiere with an edge to his voice. Sam Diggins was sitting across from him on the couch in Rob's office. "The Vikings will lose this Sunday. We have no other games to rig this week, so I've assigned our boys to US Bank Stadium. With seven corrupt officials in place, Minnesota doesn't stand a chance."

"They better lose, Rob, or you may want to take your wife and kids and find a new home somewhere on an obscure island." Sam Diggins thought he would probably need to move to that island, too, if the Vikings won. Burt Merriman wouldn't stand for two mess-ups in consecutive weeks. "This week is all about the big payoff—the Super Bowl. The Vikes' odds to even make the playoffs will be high if they start the season at zero and three, but they will be astronomical to become NFL champs. The last of our 360 operatives received their new phones a few hours ago. Each one has been instructed to wager big money on the Vikings to win the Super Bowl, regardless of their game's outcome with the Titans. But there is a difference of millions of dollars should they go to one and two instead of zero and three!"

"You're preaching to the choir, Sam. I know what's at stake. I've always known what was at stake if I couldn't deliver!"

"You were on the phone with Roger Goodell when I arrived. What did the commish want anyway?"

"He wanted me to fire Kevin Yustis. He watched the Rams-Seahawks game tape several times and thought Kevin's calls were unconscionable. Which they were, by the way!"

"Did you do it—fire him?"

"I didn't have much choice, Sam. The media was crucifying him and putting pressure on Goodell to do something. I talked to Burt. He bought Kevin a luxury yacht and told him to sail the world. The boss thought it was best not to keep him. The fans and press would scrutinize his every call from here on out, and that would put us at risk."

"Yes, but Yustis was one of our best! I hate to lose him."

"Sometimes we just change their names, but that is very risky. Chances are good a sports announcer would recognize the face. So, all our guys know they are temporary. SOTO would lose credibility if we kept them too long after they consistently made bad calls on the field. If we have them for half a season, we're very lucky."

"Well, Jake Shrum has lasted longer than that, which is fortunate!"

"Jake pretends to be friends with players and coaches. He schmoozes with them during the games, and even though they get upset with his calls, they don't make a big deal of it. They love the guy!"

There was nothing more to be said. Sam stood and walked to the door, then turned to face Rob. "We're all done with point spreads and over/unders, thanks to Carl West screwing us. Moneyline betting won't be up and running for two more weeks. We need the Titans to win this game so we can make a haul on the Super Bowl. Are we perfectly clear, Rob?"

Rob nodded his head, although his face was burning red with anger and frustration. As soon as Sam was gone, he checked the contacts on his cell and found who he was looking for. He punched the man's mobile phone number. Mike Kohlrusch answered on the first ring.

"What's up, Rob?"

"We need to meet."

*****

"Dad killed him, Curt!" Molly sobbed and set the wine glass on the table. She and her brother had been sitting on his porch in Eau Claire, talking and drinking as Friday night turned into Saturday morning. Four empty bottles of Caymus Cabernet absorbed the shimmering moonlight. "Carl was a good man who wouldn't hurt a flea. How did we get to this point?"

"Your husband stuck his nose where it didn't belong, Sis. But you don't know for sure it was our stepfather who ordered the hit. It could have been Sam Diggins. Either way, I'm going to miss Carl." The clouds had cleared, and the constellations glittered in the black sky. The full moon provided ample light for the porch. An autumn chill was in the air, but the wine had provided enough warmth for Molly and Curt to nix wearing a jacket.

"Why did we get ourselves involved in Burt's organization? I could have been a legit sportswriter for any newspaper in the country. And you could have been a psychologist making an honest living, maybe in a school system where you could have made a difference in kids' lives."

"Money, Mol. The curse of good people everywhere. Damn money, that's why! Dad waved that carrot in front of our noses when we were in high school, remember? Who in their right mind would turn down millions of dollars a year to be a school psychologist?! Knowing my luck, I would have landed a job in Arizona and ended up poisoned by a rattlesnake or something!"

"What do you think happened to your buddy, George Markins? You said he hasn't shown up for work all week, and his phone rings dead."

"I'm guessing that with us no longer coding with obituaries, he decided to get out while the getting was good. Probably moved to Texas—he always wanted to live on South Padre Island."

"Why would he leave the syndicate? I'm sure Burt could have placed him elsewhere."

Molly and Curt stopped chatting for a moment to reflect on their lives, both wishing they would have taken a different fork in the road with their careers. Then Molly continued, "The Gazette and the Dispatch have no idea they are being compromised. How did George ever get hired in the first place?"

"Burt was friends with George's father. As a favor, Burt had Giuseppe Benotti, the Italian soccer star, write a recommendation.

Guiseppe also threw in four tickets to the World Cup for the Gazette's sports editor in exchange for putting in a good word about George."

Molly shrugged. "It's never what you know—it's who you know!"

"Yep, you're right, Sis. But going back to George, I still can't figure out why he hasn't touched base with me."

"Do you think we should get out, too? Would our stepdad have us murdered if we slipped up?"

Curt leaned forward and took Molly's hand in his. "No more wine for you, Sis. The alcohol is decaying your brain!"

*****

Rob Fornasiere and Mike Kohlrusch were perched on stools at Vinny's Sports Bar and Grill watching Wisconsin pummel Notre Dame at a neutral site—Lambeau Field in Green Bay. It was doubtful folks from South Bend would deem any game played anywhere in the Dairy State outside of Madison as neutral! Crazed Badger fans smothered the tavern in red and white amongst a smattering of Kelly green Fighting Irish hopefuls. Being *ABC's Game of the Week*, millions of college football fans viewed the two top-ten teams as they clashed on the same gridiron made famous by Vince Lombardi, Bart Starr, and yes, even New Richmond's own Johnny Blood McNally. Surprisingly, the game was out of reach by the end of the first quarter. Rob was glad he had nothing to do with that!

Vinny's was set in a rural location four miles east of New Richmond and was jam-packed during weekend football games. Forget about finding a seat during the Thanksgiving break when hunters crowded the bar to tell tall tales about the thirty-six-point bucks they had killed with muzzleloaders that were now hanging from hooks at nearby Deer's Food Locker. It was amazing what Wild Turkey bourbon shots with Miller draft chasers would do to the jaws of normally sane men!

Reminiscing about the good old days, Mike said, "I used to play softball here quite often when this place was the Hitching Post. A photographer named Butch Norton sponsored our team. While everyone else was focused on winning the beer trophy, we usually brought home the first-place cup."

"I wish I were back in college," Rob stated somberly. "A do-over is all I want! I would rather have been a plumber!"

"Life is what it is, my friend. You're working for Burt Merriman to protect your family. We both know your wife, kids, and grandkids would be in grave danger if you backed out now. Look what they did to Jim Bowman."

"Not only Jim, but Sam Diggins had Carl West killed on Monday."

"What?! I hadn't heard that! Not Carl, he's a good man!"

"Was a good man, Mike. Was. But he found out about the coding and purposely switched an obituary around to trap the syndicate. They lost millions."

Mike set the beer glass on the bar and walked aimlessly to the restroom. He couldn't believe it! He had to find a way out of the organization that was blackmailing both him and Rob. Mike pounded the sink and took a long look at himself in the mirror, then returned to the barstool.

"How did this happen, Rob? Deep down, we're both good people."

"I didn't know what I was getting in to, Mike. It just happened! With all the money they were offering, it sounded great. But when I found out what they wanted me to do and the role I'd play, I refused to participate. That's when Sam Diggins showed me close up pictures of my wife and kids and told me I would never see them again if I didn't do what they wanted!" Rob guzzled the beer and asked the bartender for a refill. "I'm sorry, Mike, you already know my story. It just pisses me off, that's all!"

"I'm in the same boat, Rob. They needed me to falsify Jim Bowman's death certificate and say it was leukemia and not poisoning. Death by arsenic would have started a police investigation. With two guns aimed at my heart and head, they threatened to kill my wife and me if I didn't cooperate. I sent Teri away to a friend's house in Malibu, but I'm sure they would find her if I said something to the authorities. You don't mess with the Mafia!"

"You probably didn't know that I was the one who dropped Jim off at the Westfield Hospital the night he died. Sam Diggins made me tag along to his place in Hammond and watch as he forced Jim to drink the arsenic. Sam hotwired Jim's car and stole it, telling me to take him to the hospital myself. I knew Jim was still alive, and I hoped you could save him, but I figured the odds were slim based on how much he drank. Did he ever have a chance?"

"I tried to save him, Rob. I really did, but he was too far gone when he arrived. Had I saved his life, I planned to leave town, get Teri, and move to Mexico. But that didn't happen, and here I am!"

"You've done your job, Mike. So long as you don't report them to the FBI, why can't you pick up your wife and just live happily ever after?"

"Because the syndicate has one more assignment for me. They want me to falsify one more death certificate. If I do that and keep my mouth shut, I can go back to living a normal life."

"What the hell?! Who are they planning to terminate next?!"

"Burt Merriman has a son from a previous marriage. He found out the man is a cop—a deputy sheriff for St. Croix County. You might say Burt doesn't want an officer of the law in his family. Do you get my drift?"

In anger, Rob slammed his fist on the bar, but it happened at the same time Nakia Watson scored his third touchdown for the Badgers, so no one heard it. He leaned in close to Mike and declared, "We can't let them murder Burt's son! Enough is enough!"

"You're right, Rob. We need to find a way out, and do so without our families being at risk! I just don't know how."

"I have an idea. Let's go somewhere quieter."

The extra point was good. High fives everywhere!

Chapter 51

The enormous boos sounded like bombs exploding inside US Bank Stadium on Sunday. Every questionable call seemed to favor the visiting Titans, and the hometown crowd wasn't happy. A loss today would virtually end their beloved Vikings' chance to make the playoffs. Poor officiating had become the mantra for NFL announcers this season, and this game in Minneapolis was no exception.

Molly was in a daze as she feigned interest in the contest while sitting in the Dispatch's suite on the forty-yard line. Yesterday, she reluctantly reported Carl as missing to the St. Croix County Sheriff's Department. It was a formality she couldn't skirt because someone would soon inquire as to his whereabouts—be it his poker buddies, fellow golfers at the club, or his employer, the Gazette. Molly appeared distraught as she lied and said she believed Carl left her for some other girl. She hated to do it, but hopefully, it would keep the sheriff's department from pursuing a possible murder. A story like that would hit the newswires immediately. Being a prime suspect as spouses usually are, her cover at the Dispatch could be blown. She envisioned the headline:

NFL Great Billy West's Son Missing and Presumed Dead

After Molly's conversation with her brother on Friday night, she was convinced her husband had been killed by her boss, Sam Diggins, possibly under the orders of her stepfather, Burt Merriman. Although she didn't want to be at the stadium, the Dispatch required her to work in their suite during all home games. She was expected to interview coaches and players before and after the game to gather unique insight that would elevate her sports column above all others. Molly had tears in her eyes before the coin flip as she talked with Kirk Cousins on the sideline, and the Vikings' quarterback interrupted the dialogue to ask if she was okay.

Knowing the outcome was in the hands of Rob Fornasiere and had nothing to do with player skills, Molly wrote her Monday column as the game progressed, lambasting the organization for conducting a terrible draft and hiring incompetent coaches. Sam had explicitly ordered her not to mention the poor officiating and to title it exactly as he had demanded—four words Vegas bookies would see as they checked out local sports news before placing odds on NFL futures:

There's Always Next Year!

Molly had warned Sam about the risk of submitting a negative column attacking the Vikings' organization. She could lose favor with all her inside contacts, and the Dispatch might even fire her for collapsing bridges with Zygi's team. But Sam didn't see it the same way. Once the Vikings started their winning streak, Molly would write complementary articles and be back in their good graces. He just needed this one lousy article to help increase the unlikeliness of the Vikings reaching the Super Bowl in the eyes of the Vegas oddsmakers. After today, Molly's focus would be on tipping off the outrageous moneyline upsets for the syndicate's operatives.

The officials didn't even make a game of it. Sixteen flags were thrown on Minnesota players, and only three on Tennessee. The refs were careful to make only questionable calls—ones the announcers couldn't say with one hundred percent certainty weren't penalties when looking at the replays. But the Vikings' flags all stopped possible touchdown drives, while the Titans were penalized for minor violations when they had little chance to make a first down anyway, like illegal motion on third and fifteen or offsides on fourth and twenty. True fans of the NFL know holding calls or pass interference happens on every snap of the football. Good officials simply ignore minor infractions if they don't affect the play's outcome, and unbiased commentators usually keep quiet, knowing that only fifty percent of their listeners agree with them anyway.

The final score was forty-two to seven in favor of the Titans. But in the end, no one really cared all that much. Neither team seemed destined for the playoffs. Tennessee's victory was their first, and Minnesota had yet to notch something other than a goose egg in the win column.

Yes, Viking fans were getting restless. However, pro football memories would quickly be forgotten, replaced by title aspirations for the upcoming NBA and NHL seasons. The Timberwolves would soon be bouncing basketballs on the hardcourt at the Target Center, and the Wild would be taking to the ice at the Xcel Energy Arena in St. Paul.

Molly didn't bother to interview anyone after the game. She cried all the way back to New Richmond, then drowned her sorrows with a bottle of Zinfandel, passing out on the couch until she was awakened at midnight by an incessant chiming throughout the house. Molly thought about calling the police, but if whoever was outside really wanted to break in, they wouldn't be ringing her damn doorbell. And besides, she had forgotten to set the locks before falling asleep. All an intruder needed to do was turn the handle and walk in.

Molly opened the door a crack and recognized the two men standing on her porch. One was Carl's golf buddy, Dr. Mike Kohlrusch. The other was someone she once met at a café in Minneapolis where she was having lunch. He had been eating in a booth next to her with Sam Diggins. It was Rob Fornasiere, the owner of Sports Officials Training Organization, or SOTO for short. A man she now deplored!

"It's midnight, for God's sake!" exclaimed Molly as she stepped out to the porch. She had no plans to let her visitors enter the house. "What the hell do you want?!

"Our sincere apologies," replied Mike soberly. He then nodded at Fornasiere. "I think you know Rob. There is something we would like to discuss with you, and time is of the essence. But first, I'd like to offer my condolences for your loss. Rob told me what happened. Carl was a good friend and a wonderful person."

Rob dropped his head and nodded sadly. Molly noticed and was very confused. Rob was Sam Diggins's henchman, a murderer in his own right! Guilt by association, no less! How dare he show up at her house while she was mourning the loss of her husband?! And why was he with Mike Kohlrusch—someone everyone in the community loved and trusted?! This didn't make sense!

Molly pointed at Rob as she addressed the doctor. "Mike, take this man and get the hell out of here! I have nothing I want to discuss with him!"

Mike was going to reply, but Rob cut him off. "Molly, I'm not the person you think I am. We're here to put an end to the gambling corruption that I allowed to happen. I know you're wondering how I know Mike, and I'll be happy to explain. Please, can we come in and talk?"

"You've got ten minutes; then I call the police."

Chapter 52

Sports Analysis Calculations and Odds Corporation, SACOC for short, was based in Las Vegas with satellite offices in Reno, Atlantic City, Monte Carlo, and Macao. On Sunday nights in the fall, one group of mathematically sharp employees reviewed every NFL game played that day. In contrast, another group read online game summaries written by local sportswriters where the pro football franchises were located. As a contractor for the Las Vegas Bookmakers Association, SACOC's deadline for providing suggested opening odds for future pro football games was 8:00 a.m. on Mondays. Although no casino was required to use their probability statistics to create initial betting lines, every sportsbook did so because of SACOC's unequivocal accuracy. During the week, the odds would change based on how gamblers wagered, but SACOC's opening odds were usually spot on.

The research group that read local sports columns took great interest in Molly West's harsh criticism of the Minnesota Vikings. She led readers to believe the team's best hope would be to lose all their games and get the top pick in the 2021 draft. The Vikes were going nowhere this year, but the future could be better thanks to the quality of college prospects graduating next May.

Incredibly, the Vikings' odds to make the playoffs were set on Monday, September twenty-eighth, at 500 to one, and to win the Super Bowl, an astonishing 1000 to one! Burt Merriman was licking his chops! The trap had been set, and he saw nothing but dollar signs spinning in his head like a slot machine! This was going to be much more lucrative than he ever imagined!

At precisely 10:00 a.m. Pacific Time in various casinos throughout Las Vegas, Reno, and Atlantic City, sixty operatives placed $10,000 each on Minnesota to win the Super Bowl. Three hundred additional bets were placed simultaneously online, bringing the total wagered to $3,600,000. It was imperative that every bet was placed at the same time because the odds would drop significantly once the bookmaker's computers spit out data on how much had been gambled on the Vikings' future. But in the end, no bookie at any sportsbook even raised an eyebrow. To them, that was the easiest $10,000 they would have ever raked in for their casino! Only an idiot would bet on horrendous Minnesota to win the NFL Championship!

Burt was visioning the wild party he planned to throw after the Super Bowl on February seventh in Tampa! He will have just won $3.6 billion, which will be laundered through his corporation, Rankins, and its affiliate, Holmes Mortuary. Time to start thinking about where InterPlan could build his next home!

Now the ball was figuratively in Rob Fornasiere's court. The Vikings needed to win out and make the playoffs. Meanwhile, Rankins Corporation would continue its profitable ways by winning one moneyline bet each week. Enzo Esposito would select the games from his office at Holmes Mortuary in Prudhoe Bay, Molly West would code the game in her sports column, and Sam Diggins would oversee the entire operation. Newcomer Wally Roseberg would recruit corrupt athletes on each NFL team, but Rob was the key. Bad officiating had to be in place to make this happen.

What Rob didn't know was that this was his and SOTO's last season—their final ride into the sunset. Rankins would be dissolved, and the Holmes Mortuary would be torn down. Burt Merriman knew the FBI would eventually catch up with the illegal gaming scheme, and it was time to get out while the getting was good. He would send his stepchildren, Curt and Molly, to a Pacific island he owned to live out their lives. They would have no choice or say in the matter—he couldn't take the risk. And unfortunately, Rob would need to be permanently silenced, as would his wife, kids, and grandkids. Burt's henchman, Oliver Harwas, would take care of that minor detail.

*****

Curt Anderson reluctantly placed the required bet on the Vikings to win the Super Bowl, then dressed in the only suit he owned. To him, dressing up was overrated, but he needed something to wear at funerals and weddings. Five years ago, he purchased a flawed Joseph Abboud black herringbone from Men's Wearhouse, which was on sale for $89, thanks to an imperfection in the material that no one would notice. Today, he was attending Eve Smith's funeral in Withee. Eve had been his only client when he took over Doc Morgan's practice after he had died. With her taking a seat in heaven, Curt had no reason to make the weekly trip to the tiny community east of Eau Claire anymore. He had used the office as a front for his online gambling, but a few months ago, things changed, and he worked strictly from home using a new laptop that Rankins had given all their operatives. But he had developed a close relationship with the eighty-five-year-old and was sad to see her go. Eve had become like family to Curt, and she was someone he could talk to who had no connection to the mob. He couldn't say that about any of his other relatives or friends.

Curt's extended conversation with his sister on Saturday night made him stop and think about his career and life. After waking up in a cold sweat from a nightmare that seemed more real than the bed he was sleeping in, he decided he wanted out from underneath Burt and Sam's thumb. But the more he thought about what his stepfather had done to Carl, the more anxious he had become. Fear entrenched him, and he couldn't shake it. If he or Molly tried to leave the syndicate, would they end up dead in a ditch?!

For the first time since becoming an operative, Curt didn't make the same bet using his own money. It was against the Rankins's rules and one that could get him killed. Before Carl had been murdered, Curt thought he was untouchable—his stepdaddy ran the syndicate, after all! If caught, he would just apologize and tell Burt he would never do it again. Right?! Curt always believed it was better to ask for forgiveness than for permission.

Curt straightened his tie using the bathroom mirror and was headed for the car when his cell rang.

"What are you doing right now, Curt?" asked Molly with a hint of nervousness in her voice. Curt could make out the sound of men talking in the background.

"Going to a funeral, Sis. Why do you ask?"

"Can you come to the house? We need to chat."

"Not right now, Molly. I need to say farewell to perhaps the best friend I have."

"George Markins?! Is George dead?!"

"No, it's not George. It's a client named Eve, whom I have grown very fond of this past year." Curt could hear Molly give out a sigh of relief. "Why are you at home? It's Monday; shouldn't you be at work?"

"I called in sick. This is important, Curt. When can you be in New Richmond?"

"Maybe by two or three. I hear the voices of two guys in the background, Molly. Would you please tell me what's up?"

"A permanent way out of this mess we're in."

Chapter 53

John Warner rushed for 253 yards and gained another eighty-seven in the air as the LA Rams thrashed Miami fifty-six to three at Hard Rock Stadium on Sunday. He set a Rams' record with five touchdowns in a game. John was free to dominate the contest, and he did just that. The syndicate had no plans for him to fumble or make other blunders against the Dolphins. But Rob Fornasiere had warned him that from here on out, the mob was going to gamble on moneyline bets only, and he would be a big factor if the Rams were chosen to lose a game they should easily win.

*****

Late afternoon on Monday, Randy Hansen was back in the office after returning from Maine five pounds heavier. A plethora of lobster tails soaked in melted butter and Boston cream pies will do that to you. Randy overheard Wally Roseberg chatting with someone in the conference room. Thinking it might be a potential client, he started down the hallway but suddenly stopped when he heard Wally say something that sounded curious.

"Giles Mumphrey is CIA, or ex-CIA, I should say," stated Wally to Syd West, who had stopped by InterPlan at Wally's request on the way to the airport. Syd's long flight back to Reno was leaving at 4:00 p.m. "His real name is Jack Bowman, and he lives in Virginia."

"How did you find out?"

"The business card he gave me before he left. I had it analyzed for fingerprints. Not a very smart move for someone who worked for the CIA, wouldn't you agree?"

"Why would the CIA be involved? Are we being set up?" Syd was becoming more worried by the moment. He started pacing the room. "How do they know about us?"

Randy had heard enough! The mention of the CIA had startled him. He tried to enter the conference room calmly, but that was not meant to be. "Hi, I'm back," Randy said bluntly with an edge to his voice. He didn't give Wally a chance to respond. "I didn't mean to be spying, but I overheard your conversation about the CIA being involved in something. My curiosity has been peaked!" Randy approached Syd and offered a cold stare and an abrupt handshake. "And who are you, sir?"

"Syd West. Nice to meet you, I think."

"Syd West? I know that name. Wait a minute! Are you Billy West's father?"

"Yes, Randy, I am." Syd stared into Randy's stunned eyes.

"I recognized the name because I read about your lawsuit. You sued WMIA for negligence. You believe the drone that caused Billy's taxi to crash into that semi belonged to them, right?"

Syd nodded but decided it was best not to talk about his son's death. Wally walked to the door and closed it. Randy was in a state of confusion. Was Syd West here to receive architectural services for something he was building? Why was Wally talking to him about the CIA?

Wally eyed both men. "Randy, I need to tell you something in strict confidence. Syd, you need to cancel your flight back to Reno."

*****

When everyone was seated at the conference table, Wally began. "Randy, I'm not an architectural draftsman by trade, although I did take courses in college to become one. That's how I fooled you. No matter. I'm actually an undercover agent for the FBI."

"What?! Are you kidding me?!"

"Because InterPlan was contracted to build Burt Merriman's mansion in the Caymans, I used your firm to set up shop. Sorry, but I wasn't able to tell you. You'll understand why shortly."

"I better! You've got a lot of explaining to do!"

"Burt Merriman is an international crime syndicate boss. He is under investigation for illegal gaming. We believe, I should say we know, he has masterminded a scheme and is using the National Football League as his pawn. He has hired fraudulent officials and blackmailed players to manipulate point spreads, over/unders, and moneylines in games his operatives have bet on. I purposely befriended him while building his house in the Caymans, and he has since hired me to recruit dishonest athletes into his organization."

Randy was silent for a moment as he processed what Wally told him. He glanced at Syd and asked, "Why are you here? I thought you ran a huge sports marketing company."

"Yes, Randy, I do. However, I'm also a close friend of Burt Merriman—or I should say, I was a close friend. I thought he was just a wealthy restaurateur who owned many upscale eateries. He was a top-level sponsor for my company, West Enterprises, so of course, I wined and dined in his establishments. When I purchased the Reno Mountaineers' franchise in 2014, Burt wanted to become not just a close friend—but my best friend. I didn't know he was just using me to get inside information on the NFL! Then he—"

Syd stopped suddenly in midsentence and pounded his fists on the table.

Frustrated, Randy leaned in and asked, "Then he what?!"

"During the week before the Super Bowl, a man approached Billy after practice. He waved a gun in his face and threatened to kill his wife and son, and even me, if Billy didn't do what he was supposed to do."

"What was he asked to do?!" Randy was beside himself with agitation.

"Make sure the Mountaineers lost the Super Bowl! Billy didn't know him or who he worked for, but the man had telephoto pictures of us in our homes! I now realize he was Burt Merriman's right-hand man, but I didn't back then. Burt's bogus company, Rankins Corporation, had placed a million dollars in 2015 on Carolina to win the Super Bowl's moneyline wager. The odds were twelve to one against the Panthers, meaning Rankins would have pocketed twelve million!

"But Billy refused to cheat. His reputation and everything I had taught him about ethics, integrity, and sportsmanship were on the line. He wasn't going to bend his honor, something he would have to live with for the rest of his life. However, his family always came first, and he needed to ensure we would be safe if he disregarded the extortioner and won the game.

"Billy thought he found a way to protect us. An old college buddy of his, Ron Mauston, had become an executive assistant director for the FBI, so he told him about the threats to our family if he didn't throw the game for the Panthers. Billy described the man in detail, and Mauston emailed him a picture of a mob hitman on the ten most wanted list. His name was Oliver Harwas, and Billy confirmed he was the same person who intimidated him. Mauston assured Billy we would all be protected. He begged me to keep quiet because he didn't want to scare Carl.

"Then, I made the most regrettable mistake of my life!" Syd stood up, walked to the window, and gazed at the clouds. Tears were sliding down his cheeks. "One night before the Super Bowl, I was having dinner with Burt Merriman. I didn't know at the time he was associated with Oliver Harwas. And, of course, I didn't know he was the leader of a crime syndicate! So after too many drinks, I let the cat out of the bag. I told him that some man named Oliver was blackmailing Billy into making sure Reno lost the Super Bowl. Regrettably, I also told him Billy had called a friend in the FBI."

Randy knew where this conversation was going. "Let me guess. Burt Merriman had Ron Mauston killed?"

"Yes, two days after the Super Bowl. Not only Mauston but four other agents who worked for him! Anyone who Merriman thought may have knowledge of Rankins and the gambling scheme was executed! Had my son known five FBI agents were in grave danger, I'm sure he would have thrown the game."

"When did you find out about all of this?"

"Not until this summer."

"This summer?! What are you talking about?!"

"When Billy and Carol were killed on the way to the airport after the Super Bowl, I assumed, like an idiot, that it was an accident! So I sued WMIA. I thought their drone caused the driver to lose control. Rather naïve, I know! But what's worse is I didn't know then what I know now—that Burt Merriman had ordered them killed."

Randy began piecing everything together and then looked inquisitively at Wally.

"So, where do you come into the picture?"

"I quit school when I was twenty to join the FBI. After my training in Washington, DC, was complete, I was assigned to a task force investigating the death of Executive Assistant Director Ron Mauston and his agents. We found notes in Mauston's file cabinet with the name Burt Merriman on them. Ron had initiated a formal investigation into an alleged illegal gaming syndicate run by Merriman, but the evidence he left us was sketchy. Our task force probed into Merriman's life, but we were also following other possible suspects at the same time. No matter how long it took, the task force was determined never to make the execution of their own agents a cold case."

Something was puzzling Randy, but he couldn't pinpoint it. "You're not telling me everything. Like, for instance, why you two are here together in my office."

Wally fidgeted. He wasn't sure how much to tell Randy. After a long pause, he said, "Syd's grandson Carl was my best friend in high school. I wanted Syd to know we were closing in on Merriman."

"Wait a minute! Syd said he didn't know about Merriman until just this summer. Why did you wait so long to tell him? If his drone killed Billy and his wife, it was certainly information he should have known earlier. He was your best friend's grandfather, after all!"

"Randy, this whole thing is highly confidential. I wish I could tell you more, but I can't."

"Okay, have it your way. But I overheard you talk about an ex-CIA agent who disguised himself as Giles Mumphrey. You said you met with him while I was in Maine. Can you explain?"

"All I know is that Giles' real name is Jack Bowman. He may be an ex-agent who was lured into Burt's syndicate. The Mafia is known to try and recruit retired spies and gun experts with the carrot of extreme cash waving in their eyes!"

Randy was displeased by the metaphor. He stood and paced the room nervously. "This is all craziness! You know that, don't you, Wally?! And my architectural firm is smack dab in the middle! If this Jack Bowman fella knows you're working here, then am I to assume the rest of us and our families are in danger?"

"Perhaps, Randy. But I just learned about Bowman and wasn't prepared to tell you everything. Now that you know, I have a way to protect all your employees and their families."

"What's that? I'm listening!"

"Not only do I work as an undercover special agent for the FBI, but I also oversee the Witness Protection Program for the southeast United States. I think it would be wise to place everyone in protective custody until we put Burt Merriman away for good."

"Well, now, isn't that ironic. A week ago, Burt Merriman was my best client. Today he's my worst nightmare!"

"There's one more thing you should know, Randy, and I'm hesitant to tell you."

"Spit it out, Wally. Remember, you're still on my payroll!"

"I am only at liberty to tell you if you agree to go into the Witness Protection Program immediately. I need an answer now."

"You have got to be kidding me!"

Chapter 54

Bright and early on Tuesday morning, Wally called the number on the business card. No employees were at the InterPlan office, and none would be working there for quite some time. During the night, each of them and their families were hastily moved to various locations around the United States as part of the Federal Witness Protection Program.

On the second ring, a man's voice answered with one of the worst fake British accents Wally had ever heard. "Giles Mumphrey here. May I help you?"

"Hello, Mr. Mumphrey. This is Wally Roseberg at InterPlan Architecture in Tequesta. I spoke to our owner, Randy Hansen, and he is interested in building your casino on Lake Okeechobee. He would like for me to meet with you and go over the specifics and review our fees. If you approve, we could sign a contract today."

"Jolly good, it is!" exclaimed Giles. Wally rolled his eyes. Giles had to have flunked acting school! "When can we meet?"

"I'm available right now. Randy took the rest of the architects and his secretary on a retreat to Freeport. They should be somewhere in the Bermuda Circle sailing on the Balearia Bahamas Express as we speak."

"Ah, the deadly Triangle. Sounds ominous! Why didn't he take you?"

"Because of you, sir! He is confident I can handle all the preliminary details of your casino."

"And I think you can, too, Wally! I will be there in an hour or two."

"I look forward to it. See you soon!"

*****

The Winnebago was parked at Jonathan Dickinson State Park in nearby Jupiter. Its occupants were becoming restless. The motorhome's air conditioner was on its last leg and couldn't produce enough cool air to make the humid nights comfortable. The boys were tempted to drive down to Palm Beach and check into the Marriott on Singer Island but decided against it. Now, after Wally's call to Jack, an air of optimism had changed everyone's attitudes. They pulled out of the campground and turned south on Federal Highway, then parked a few minutes later at the Tequesta Shoppes Mall, the closest location to InterPlan that would accommodate a motorhome. From there, they would walk fifteen minutes to the architectural firm.

The three men decided to dress casually in shorts and deck shoes. Jack tucked a Glock 26 Gen 4 pistol inside a narrow holster belt, then covered it with a red polo shirt. Bruce slipped a Smith and Wesson M&P 40C into an elongated pocket of his baggy cargo pants. Carl shook his head and frowned at his cronies.

"Do you really need guns?" he asked with clear annoyance. "Wally Roseberg is a friend, and I don't want him injured—or God forbid, killed!"

"Your friend is deceitful and dangerous," declared Jack. "The weapons are only for our protection. Self-defense, if we need it."

Carl didn't reply. The three men paced rapidly on the sidewalk towards InterPlan. At the intersection of Tequesta Drive and Old Dixie Highway, Bruce and Carl turned south while Jack continued west to Cypress Drive. They would wait for him at Oceana Coffee Roasters, which was only a few blocks away.

As Jack approached the entrance to InterPlan, he took out his smartphone and booted up a special monitoring app used by the CIA to record conversations. Those conversations could also be heard live by anyone the user designated—in this case, Carl and

Bruce. The microphone was powerful enough to be heard clearly through fabric; thus, the cell could be stored in a pocket out of sight.

It was time to find out who Wally Roseberg really was.

*****

"Top o' the mornin' to ya, Mr. Roseberg!" Jack shook Wally's hand firmly as they greeted one another in the reception area.

"And the rest of the day to you, Mr. Mumphrey. Please call me Wally."

They walked to the conference room in silence. Jack wasn't sure how this meeting would play out, but he detected something was troubling Wally. Upon entering the room, Jack stopped on a dime and stared at a video camera sitting on a tripod at the end of the table. Wally moved to it and pushed a button. A red light came on, and Jack knew everything from here forward was being recorded. He stood at the opposite end of the table and gazed at the menacing video lens.

"What's the camera for?" Jack inquired.

"Randy Hansen asked me to record our conversation, seeing he couldn't be here today." Wally moved towards Jack's chair as if he were going to show courtesy and pull it out for him.

"Ah, yes! Most certainly. Well then, let's make haste, should we?"

He was about to sit down when Wally abruptly reached under Jack's polo with his right hand and grabbed the Glock from his holster. He pushed Jack into the seat with his left hand, then pointed the pistol at the back of his head.

"Oi!" exclaimed Jack, trying not to panic. He would need to come up with a quick explanation, yet he needed to stay in character. "Are ya a nutter, or what?! My God, this is not the best way to start a business deal, ya know!"

Wally ambled around Jack so he could look him in the face. The gun was now aimed directly at his forehead.

"Cut the crap, especially the fake British accent. No one I know from England would use an Irish greeting, as you did in the reception area. Now, Giles, I want the truth. You can start by explaining why you changed your name from Jack Bowman to Giles Mumphrey!"

*****

Bruce and Carl rushed out of the coffee shop and jogged towards the InterPlan building. They had heard on their cell phones the conversation that was taking place between Jack and Wally and knew it was time to intervene. Bruce and Carl were both completely baffled. How did Wally Roseberg know Jack's real name?

"Put the gun down, and we can talk like gentlemen," said Jack calmly, although his heart was racing. "I have no more weapons, and I'm too old to attack you with my feeble body!"

Wally extracted the bullet cartridge from the Glock, then handed the pistol back to Jack. "Okay, Jack Bowman. Please tell me for the record why an ex-CIA agent would be disguised as a British tycoon wanting to build a casino on Lake Okeechobee." Wally pointed at the video camera to emphasize the conversation was being recorded.

Jack didn't flinch. He had received years of training on how to remain calm in the face of adversity. But theories were swirling swiftly in his head as he tried to piece them together and think clearly. In Jack's mind, Wally must be a linchpin in Burt Merriman's criminal organization.

"First, how did you know my real name and that I was a retired CIA agent?" Jack was stalling for time. He knew Carl and Bruce were listening and would be here any second.

"I'll ask the questions, Jack. You'll give me the answers. Understand?"

"How about some coffee, Wally? I didn't get my caffeine fix this morning. I'm prepared to tell you everything, but some java would help me focus."

There was a drip coffeemaker on the counter by a sink in the corner of the room. Wally stepped over to it while keeping a close eye on Jack. If Bowman tried to make a run for it, he would stand no chance. Wally was confident in his own athletic prowess! He filled the water tank, slipped a filter into the holder, and scooped in several tablespoons of Folgers. Wally waited quietly while the coffee perked, and the pungent aroma encircled the room.

Suddenly, the conference room door burst open, and Bruce Merriman aimed his Smith and Wesson directly at Wally's heart. Wally didn't even wince or recoil. Instead, his mouth gaped open at the sight of the other man standing in the doorway.

"Well, I'll be damned! Carl West, what are you doing here, my friend?!"

*****

"Put the gun away," ordered Carl as he reached out and pushed Bruce's arms down to his side. Then he walked to Wally and embraced him in a bear hug. "It's been a long time, Rosey!"

Jack moved next to Bruce and watched the emotional scene unfolding. Both Wally and Carl had tears in their eyes. Then Carl stepped back and asked, "I was here looking for you a few weeks ago. Did you get my messages?"

Wally dropped his head momentarily and nodded, then looked seriously back at Carl. "Yes, I knew you were here, and mom told me you were trying to find me up in Jacksonville. As much as I wanted to see you, I couldn't."

"Why not?"

Wally glanced at Bruce and Jack, then motioned everyone to move to the conference table.

"Please, have a seat. I'll try and answer your questions the best I can, but there are some things I may not be able to tell you."

"Like what?!" demanded Jack. He pulled what appeared to be a newspaper article from his wallet, unfolded it, then slapped it down on the table in front of Wally. "Like, why you placed a fake obituary for yourself in a small-town newspaper in Wisconsin! And how the details of your false eulogy enabled nefarious criminals to rake in millions of dollars in an illegal gaming scheme! You and your Mafia connections have corrupted the National Football League by somehow finding unscrupulous players and officials to work with your organization—I'm assuming with the promise of riches! You're one bad apple, Wally Roseberg!"

Carl glared at Jack. He was caught in the middle. Wally was his best friend from high school, yet Jack had every right to grill him. One of his sons was dead, and the other serving a life prison sentence. But cooler heads needed to prevail if they were ever going to get to the bottom of this.

"Please, Jack, give him a chance to speak."

Wally looked at the three faces staring at him and could read everything from confusion to anger in their eyes. It was time for an explanation.

"Okay, but first, I need assurance that what I'm about to tell you will be strictly confidential."

Jack blurted out a sarcastic laugh. "You trust us to keep silent?! You're not in any position to make demands. So, no way I agree to keep quiet. Put it this way—consider this conversation a practice session for what you will be telling the FBI!"

"Once again, if you want me to speak, I need promises that you will tell no one. Carl is a lifelong friend. If he assures me what I say doesn't leave this room, I will explain freely."

Jack stood, leaned his face into Wally's, and stated sarcastically, "Sorry, Rosey, no can do. You're going down. We will be calling the FBI as soon as we're done."

"I can assure you that will do you no good," Wally replied calmly, yet firmly.

"And why not?"

"Because I'm an undercover special agent for the FBI."

Bruce and Jack glanced at one another while Carl stared at his old friend. Flabbergasted, Carl muttered, "Say what?"

Chapter 55

By noon, the anger and tension that enveloped the conference room earlier in the morning had disappeared. Carl, Jack, and Bruce could see Wally was on their side, and his goals were the same as their own—stop the corruption without exposing the NFL to irreversible negative publicity, and put Burt Merriman and his employees away for life. On the other hand, Wally now understood why Jack Bowman, an ex-CIA agent, had disguised himself as Giles Mumphrey, and why he had erroneously thought Jack was part of the illegal gaming operation.

Wally explained that the first he heard of his obituary being placed in the Gazette was when his mother told him, which she did shortly after Carl had shown it to her. But the obit became a strong lead for Wally, and it took some time before he realized that his name had been chosen at random from the White Pages directory—a cosmic mistake on the part of the syndicate.

The three-hour mixing of minds brought clarity to the Mafia's scheme. Jack and Carl laid out everything that had happened, from finding out Jim Bowman had been poisoned to Molly and Curt's involvement in the operation, and everything in between. Wally already knew about Rankins and Sam Diggins. Still, various details he hadn't investigated surprised him—like John Bowman's football lottery partnership with the fake Holmes Mortuary in Prudhoe Bay to his sacrificial march to prison to protect his brother. Wally also suspected SOTO was criminally involved, but he hadn't conducted a background check on either the company or Rob Fornasiere. Bruce provided information about his father, Burt Merriman, which helped profile the man they were targeting.

Until now, nothing was said about Syd West. Carl wasn't sure he was ready to hear that his grandfather was a crook, so he didn't ask. But finally, he needed to know the truth.

"My grandfather—," muttered Carl sheepishly, then paused. "Is my grandfather, Syd, involved with the mob? I know he was meeting with you a few days ago, and I know he is a friend of Burt Merriman. Does he know you are an undercover FBI agent? Or are you trying to trap him? Sorry, Wally, I just need to know if he's a good guy or a bad guy!"

Wally smiled at his old friend and placed a comforting hand on his shoulder. "I've known your grandfather all my life, as you well know. He is an upstanding, honest, and noble person, Wally. Just like your father! He is helping me bring Burt Merriman to justice, and like you and me, wants to do it in a way that the NFL can save face."

Carl let out a massive sigh of relief. This was the news he didn't think he would ever hear. He embraced Wally for the second time.

The group ordered pizza for lunch and committed to staying put at InterPlan until they developed a strategic plan. Carl wanted to call Molly, but the others cautioned him against it. By late afternoon, frustrations were mounting. The brainstorming session wasn't producing positive results.

In a moment of vexation, Jack slapped his hand on the table, then decided to release the anger building up inside him. He confronted Wally again. "This has nothing to do with what we're trying to accomplish, but there's something I need to know. I did a background check on you. What I found is that you're dead—a death certificate and the whole works! The obituary Carl placed in the Gazette may have been a coincidence, but I feel like there's something you're not telling us! You have no bank records and haven't filed a tax return for quite some time. I understand you're an undercover agent, but shoot, so was I, and I still had to file a damn tax return!"

Wally stood up and walked to the door without saying a word.

"Where are you going?" Jack demanded.

"I need a breath of fresh air to think. I'll be back soon."

After Wally left, the others began arguing. Carl was upset that Jack tried to alienate his good friend. Jack brushed it off and stated they needed to find a solution, regardless of whose feelings were hurt. Every possible idea mentioned by one of them was met with skepticism by another. Ten minutes later, Wally returned and sat down. The others could tell he wanted to say something but was hesitating.

"What is it?" Bruce asked brusquely. He was tired and cranky, as was everybody. "You want to speak, so just spit it out!"

Wally looked at each person, then said, "Jack was right. I do have a death certificate. Only my parents, Burt Merriman, and the InterPlan employees know I exist. I went off the grid as a requirement for my job. But now, I need to tell you something I've held back." He hesitated before continuing. "Not only am I an undercover agent for the FBI, but I'm in charge of the Witness Protection Program for the southeastern United States. I've placed Randy Hansen and all his employees in protective custody. They aren't on a retreat in the Bahamas."

"Why didn't you mention that to us earlier?!" asked Jack irately.

"Obviously, I'm sworn to silence to keep those folks from being in harm's way."

"So why are you telling us now?"

"Because I have a plan to end the corruption and lock Burt Merriman up for life. But it will be time-consuming and involve a great deal of risk. I'm not sure I want to endanger you."

"Risk?! Danger?! Oh, come on, Wally!" exclaimed Jack. "You think I haven't worked in perilous situations during my career with the CIA? And Bruce is a cop. Let's hear your plan!"

Wally got up again and paced the room. Telling them his idea would mean revealing a highly confidential secret, one that could jeopardize his career with the FBI. But worse, what he needed to disclose could backfire and fuel an emotional explosion. Wally looked up to the ceiling, perhaps hoping God would provide some guidance. Then he sat back down and divulged his secret and his plan.

The cat was out of the bag, and there was no turning back.

*****

On Friday, someone from the St. Croix County Sheriff's Department had leaked to a reporter for the St. Croix Press that Carl West, son of NFL Hall-of-Famer Billy West, was missing and presumed dead. Without calling Molly for confirmation, the newspaper published a story in their online addition. The article said Carl had split from Molly following an extramarital affair, and the sheriff's department suspected suicide.

Sitting at her desk in Minneapolis, Molly skimmed the online version of the Press during a coffee break. She did so daily to keep up with what was happening in her neck of the woods. When she read the article about Carl, she was overcome with rage! After one lousy week, the sheriff's department called it a suicide! Of course they did—that way, they could close the case quickly! When this was all over, and her stepfather was rotting in prison, she would sue the sheriff and the news publisher for every penny they had!

Molly's anger turned to grief as she thought about Carl. Why did she ever get involved with the syndicate?! Molly cried and tried to focus on her work but couldn't force herself to be productive. At noon, secretary Jan Willows buzzed her on the intercom. "Molly, you have Rob Fornasiere and Mike Kohlrusch here to see you. Should I show them in?

Molly stood up, wiped the tears from her cheeks, straightened her dress, and greeted the men at the door. Rob and Mike sat down, but Molly walked to the window and gazed out at downtown Minneapolis. If she started crying again, she didn't want them to see her.

"What is it?" Molly asked, somewhat curtly. Rob and Mike weren't her friends, and she wanted them to know it. "You told me on Monday you were coming up with an idea that could end this madness. But I haven't heard from you since."

"We have a plan, Molly. If you have a few minutes, we will lay it out for you."

"A few minutes? I've had enough 'work' for one week. Let's go down to Dan Kelly's Pub and grab a table in the back. We'll start our own Irish fest!"

*****

By the time happy hour rolled around, Rob, Mike, and Molly had consumed several Guinness Stout drafts, a few shots of Jameson whiskey, and a plate of corned beef sliders. They were now sipping dessert—Bailey's Irish Cream on the rocks.

Perhaps due to a high-level blood alcohol count, Rob and Mike's plan had made sense to Molly. It involved precarious actions on their parts, and the results were unpredictable. However, at this point, the reward outweighed the risk.

Molly would continue coding moneyline games each week in her sports column, and Rob would assign ignoble referees to officiate those contests. Yes, it was cheating, but they considered it necessary collateral damage for the end product they hoped to achieve. Rob's biggest challenge was to ensure the Vikings made it to the Super Bowl. If they fell short, their entire plan would be down the drain. And if that happened, Rob and his family would be facing dire consequences from Burt Merriman.

Mike Kohlrusch had connections in the pharmaceutical industry. In fact, he sat on the board of directors for Kiner Medical Innovations, a St. Paul-based drug company. This multibillion-dollar corporation rose to the top by mass-producing the first successful vaccine for the Coronavirus pandemic. Mike was a good friend of KMI's founder and CEO, Alex Kiner, who was very amenable to Kohlrusch's plan. Alex had rid the world of COVID-19, and he was more than willing to end corruption in the world of football!

Chapter 56

Sunday, October 4th, was an incredibly horrendous day in Houston. On Friday, Hurricane Zoe's eye had passed directly over Galveston and Trinity Bay, knocking out power from Beaumont to Katy and collapsing the I-10 bridge over Old River Lake. The city was now crawling with emergency first responders, electrical workers, and FEMA agents. A stay-at-home order was placed for the areas hardest hit. But it was a fall Sunday in the NFL, and that meant the games must go on come hell or high water, which in Houston that day, was literally both! Ironically, the Texans played in NRG stadium, and the faithful season ticket holders employed by the locally-based energy company would not be attending the game. They were busy restoring electricity to a large population of the Lone Star State.

Houston's airports, Intercontinental and Hobby, had shut down operations on Thursday night in advance of the storm and just reopened on Sunday morning. The Vikings flew their charter into Austin on Saturday, but the roads to Houston were closed, and they were forced to stay in the state capital. They could not find a place to practice, so they watched game films for a couple of hours in the hotel conference room. The Vikings bussed the 160 miles to Houston, but with unrooted trees, upside-down fishing boats, and couches ripped from homes blocking the roads, the trip took six hours. The Vikings arrived at NRG stadium a half-hour before game time and hustled onto the field forty-five seconds before the scheduled noon kickoff, which was also the required forfeit time for no-show teams. When owner, Zygi Wilf, heard that the Vikings' bus was stranded on Texas roads, he pleaded on the phone with Roger Goodell to postpone the game, but to no avail. Evidently, in the commissioner's eyes, the game was a meaningless necessity. Minnesota was zero and three, definitely not playoff contenders, and had no chance to beat the mighty Texans anyway. Postponing the game would cost the league millions of dollars in lost revenue!

The coin toss had occurred a few minutes before the Vikings took the field. The Texans won the toss and elected to receive, thinking they could make a fast start against the Vike's defense that had no warmups. They were right.

Houston's offense didn't even need to don their helmets until they had a double-digit lead. The Vikings' special teams were disastrously unprepared, and the opening kickoff resulted in a touchdown for the Texans. DeAndre Carter ran ninety-eight yards without a purple jersey coming within three yards of him! Then, on the ensuing kickoff, Vikings' return specialist, Ameer Abdullah, fumbled, and Houston's Tyrell Adams recovered the ball and galloped into the endzone. After a three and out on the Vikings' first possession from scrimmage, the score was fourteen to nothing when Texans' quarterback Deshaun Watson took his first snap from center. And to add insult to the Vikings' injury, the talented Watson ran eighty yards from scrimmage after the intended play, a quick pass over the middle, didn't emerge because the tight end tripped over his own feet.

The Texans were up twenty-four to zip at the end of the first quarter. Vikings' players sat dejectedly on the sideline with their heads down and helmets resting precariously in their laps. Rob Fornasiere was in a tizzy watching the game from his living room. If Minnesota lost, it would take a miracle to get them into the playoffs. He had a meeting scheduled with Burt Merriman and Sam Diggins on Monday morning—and it wouldn't be pretty!

But once the second quarter was underway, the duplicitous referees shifted into high gear and stole the show. The officiating became dreadfully terrible, much to the exasperation of the sports commentators and the hometown crowd. The fans weren't sure what was the biggest disaster taking place in southeast Texas—Hurricane Zoe or the debacle at NRG stadium! After Minnesota went ahead twenty-seven to twenty-four early in the fourth quarter, the boos could be heard all the way to Louisiana—and that was with the roof closed!

The Vikings were ecstatic as they boarded the plane for the flight to Minneapolis. Was their victory a result of a sudden mystic transcendence into football supremacy, or merely a total fluke? Evidently, the Vegas bookmakers decided on the latter. On Monday morning, the odds for them to make the playoffs, say nothing of the Super Bowl, remained unchanged. Rodney Dangerfield received more respect!

*****

"You called this meeting. It better be for a good reason." Burt Merriman locked eyes with Rob Fornasiere. "Minneapolis is not exactly on a direct route to Las Vegas from the Caymans."

"I assure you that you will be glad you came, Mr. Merriman."

Burt and Sam Diggins both turned their heads to glance at two men standing next to Rob's desk.

"And who are you, may I ask?"

Rob cut in. "Let me introduce you to my good friends. This is Dr. Mike Kohlrusch and Dr. Alex Kiner. And these are my associates, Burt Merriman and Sam Diggins."

Burt and Sam shook hands with Mike and Alex. Burt couldn't stop staring at Kiner. "Are you the same Alex Kiner who developed the COVID vaccine?"

"Yes, sir. It's considered my discovery, but it was a team of incredibly gifted scientists and researchers who deserve all the credit."

"Ah, humble, and a team player." Burt smiled and patted Alex on the shoulder while shaking hands once more. "I like that! Without you, there would be no football this year. No sports, actually. So, now may I ask, why are you here today?"

"Please, have a seat, gentlemen, and I'll explain."

The four men sat casually on the leather couch and chairs in Rob's office while Oliver Harwas, Burt's henchman and pilot, stood at the door.

"Mike is on the board of directors for Kiner Medical Innovations, and he has a business proposal I believe would be of great benefit to our organization."

Burt looked skeptically at Kohlrusch. Why would the most famous pharmaceutical company in the world want to do business with an illegal gaming operation that had ties to the Mafia? Did Rob tell these two men about Rankins without his permission?

"Go ahead, Dr. Kohlrusch," said Burt. "What is this proposal of yours?"

"As you know, the KMI vaccine eradicated the world of COVID-19. While our scientists were studying, researching, and testing the vaccine, they made an amazing discovery. To make a long story short, and to put it in layman's terms, they found a cure for pancreatic cancer."

Burt was no medical expert, but he did know that the survival rate for patients with pancreatic cancer was incredibly slim. This drug, or treatment, or whatever, was going to be another game-changer for KMI. Alex Kiner was going to be a shoo-in for the Nobel prize for medicine. What kind of business deal was he proposing?

"I'm listening," stated Burt, trying to keep from showing his excitement. He acted the same way when he bought cars, planes, and yachts. Never let the salesman think you're very interested. "What are you offering, and what do you want from me?"

"We need major investors to move this forward for FDA approval and marketing development. We need to build new research facilities, laboratories, and factories, plus hire patent lawyers, advertising, and salespeople, as well."

"How many investors are you acquiring?"

"As many as needed to raise $500 billion."

Burt got up from the chair and walked to the window. Dollar signs were clouding up his mind. A $500 billion investment in this company might net him $2 trillion.

"And if I were to invest the entire $500 billion, would that be exclusive?"

"Yes, of course. We would promise you that."

Burt thought for several minutes while everyone waited to hear what he had to say. Finally, he looked at Rob and asked, "Is there somewhere we can go to talk?"

Chapter 57

Rob led Burt to an unoccupied office and closed the door. Rob motioned for Burt to take a seat at the desk, but Burt shook his head no. He wanted to get right down to business.

"How sure are you that the Vikings will win the Super Bowl? I want an exact percentage, not wishful thinking!"

"We have plenty of corrupt officials currently on staff and much more waiting in the wings. I can place an entire crew at every Minnesota game. In all honesty, I can guarantee a one hundred percent success rate."

"What about the playoffs? Coaches have a say in who is picked to referee those games."

"Yes, but I conduct the survey. I can falsify the results without anyone knowing. If you don't mind me asking, what are you thinking? Do you intend to finance the entire KMI business proposal?"

"My short answer is yes. I believe this man, Alex Kiner, can provide me with a windfall profit, which is why I don't want to share a penny with other investors. Rob, I'm closing the shop after this year. Things have gotten out of hand with both Jim Bowman and Carl West going rogue. I'm getting out while the getting is good. You and Sam Diggins are welcome to continue the operation but without help from the Mafia. I will be dissolving Rankins Corporation."

Rob did his best to hold back a smile. Thank God! Perhaps now he could return to everyday life with his family! "Do you have $500 billion in cash lying around?"

"No, but I can get close to that figure by mortgaging my homes and restaurants."

"But it's going to take time for KMI to show profits. How long can you hang on before that money rolls in?"

"Well, now let me cut to the chase. I will max out personal loans to up the ante this week. I will have all our operatives triple their wagers on the Vikings to win the Super Bowl."

"That's risky, Mr. Merriman," offered Rob, tongue in cheek. "Placing all that money on a losing team might raise red flags with bookies. It could be dangerous."

Burt laughed. "And when was the last time you knew the Mafia to back down from danger?" Rob smiled reluctantly, then Burt's demeanor became serious. "You better make sure the Vikings win, Rob. Do you understand?"

*****

Rob and Burt rejoined Mike and Alex. Burt didn't hesitate—not even flinch. He got right to the point. "I'm prepared to invest $500 billion in your company at the current share price. However, I will need five months to raise the money. Are you able to agree to that offer?"

Playing hard to get, Mike asked for a private moment to confer with Alex. They both knew the reason for requesting a five-month delay was that the Super Bowl would be over, and Burt believed he would have plenty of cash. In other words, he fell for their guise—hook, line, and sinker!

Burt and Oliver waited in Minneapolis as KMI lawyers designed an unbreakable contract using Burt's residential properties, restaurants, and other business holdings as collateral. Burt's own lawyer was at home in New York and asked that the contract be faxed to him for review before signing. He cautioned Burt to wait a few days to think it over, but Burt would hear nothing of it. He would be contacting his operatives tonight, advising them to wager three times more on the Vikings than they had already placed last week.

At 11:05 p.m., Burt received a call from his lawyer, who had just read the contract. He stepped outside into the frosty Minneapolis night for privacy. It was just past midnight on the east coast, and his lawyer didn't mince words. "Are you nuts, Burt! Have you gone completely mad?!"

"With all the money I'm going to be making on this deal, I could buy every insane asylum in the US and staff them all with pretty girls who would be waiting on me hand and foot," said Burt sarcastically. "Not a bad way to go, wouldn't you say?"

"Get serious, Burt. This is a horrible deal. An extremely horrible deal! I've been your legal advisor since you got into this illegal gaming racket. I know your financial strength. You don't have enough cash to make this happen without some sort of windfall gambling profit. Who are you betting on this time?"

"The Vikings to win the Super Bowl."

"What?! You are totally insane! I know you have officials in your back pocket, but if you think those clowns from Minnesota can win the Super Bowl, I think I will be committing you today, my friend!"

"I assure you they will win. Now, unless you have more to add, I'm going to sign the contract."

"You are living a very comfortable life right now, Burt. Why take the risk? You don't need more money. The contract is one hundred percent lock tight. If you don't come up with the money in five months, you will lose everything!"

"My middle name is risk. And for your comment about not needing more money—get real! Who doesn't need more money?!"

Burt and his lawyer wished each other well, and twenty minutes later, it was a done deal. In five months, he would have more money than the gross national product of many countries.

*****

Burt's private Airbus A380 touched down at McCarran International Airport in Las Vegas at 5:00 a.m. He had tried to sleep on the three-hour flight, but that wasn't possible with his mind firing neurons in every direction. Burt had second thoughts about buying into KMI, but at this point, there was nothing he could do except move forward.

Wally Roseberg was waiting in the sportsbook at Caesars' Palace, drinking coffee and munching on a donut. He had flown in on Monday and wasn't happy that Burt had postponed their meeting until today. Then again, Wally had no idea the massive investment Burt had just gotten himself into, which was the reason for the delay.

"Sorry about moving our meeting around, Wally. Something came up yesterday. But, you probably cleaned out the poker tables in my absence!" Burt laughed, but Wally didn't even smile.

"I actually sat by the pool all day. Anyway, I've recruited one player on three teams so far. I'm trying to get a player from the other twenty-nine before Sunday, but I need to be careful. I'm researching every key player's personal life, trying to guess who needs extra cash the most and who may have had a history of small crimes or misdemeanors during college. No one else on the team can find out, or we'll be exposed. But, as you suggested, I'm offering a million dollars to each player we secure. It's difficult to turn down that much money in exchange for a simple fumble or stupid penalty."

"That's great, Wally, but things have changed. I need you first to find corrupt players on the Vikings' opponents, then work on the rest of the league later."

"The Vikings' opponents? May I ask why?"

"We're done with point spreads and over/unders. We have one moneyline upset game planned for each week. But, our big haul will be when Minnesota wins the Super Bowl. Are you following me?"

"I doubt I can find enough corrupt players to do that! Most likely, the Vikings would have to win the rest of their games to make the playoffs. Are you kidding me?!"

"Just do it, Wally. Find me dishonest players on the teams playing against Minnesota. The officials will be helping out substantially. This must work! Do you read me?"

"I'll get to work on it today, boss!" Wally got up to leave, and Burt stood up to shake hands. He looked earnestly into Wally's eyes, then patted him affectionately on the arm.

"You're my main man, Wally."

*****

Wally stepped out onto the mostly deserted Strip at 6:30 a.m. Soon, lucky and unlucky tourists, street musicians, and scantily clad women of every shape and size would be filling up the sidewalks from the Sahara to the Tropicana. But for now, Wally was alone with his thoughts. He had enough evidence to arrest Burt Merriman and put him in prison for the rest of his life. But the mob had ways of getting their people out of legal trouble, and Burt could possibly spend minimal, if any, time behind bars. As an FBI employee, Wally knew his duty was to tell his bosses what Carl had told him about Rankins and the illegal gaming operation. However, doing so would put the reputation of the NFL at risk, which was why he decided to instead move forward with the plan he, Carl, Jack, and Bruce had devised.

Wally came to Vegas to find out who the operatives were betting on in the Super Bowl. He needed that information for their scheme to be successful. Stunningly, Burt spilled the beans to him this morning, but even more shocking was the wager was on the Minnesota Vikings! However, the more he thought about it, the more it made sense. The Vikes were a 1,000 to one underdog to win it all, so Burt must be focused on them winning to rake in millions, maybe even billions! Wally now knew exactly what must be done to ensure his plan succeeded. He pulled out his cell phone and punched in the number.

"Hey, Carl. We're in luck. Burt told me his Super Bowl bet. It's the Minnesota Vikings. And I have the entire conversation recorded. We're in business!"

Chapter 58

As the 2020 season progressed, Burt was satisfied with his decision to no longer wager on point spreads and over/unders. Rob Fornasiere had been given notice by commissioner Roger Goodell that SOTO's contract would end after the Super Bowl if the consistency of officiating didn't improve. Burt didn't care about next year because this was his last season of illegal gaming. By selecting only one moneyline upset game each week and canceling point spreads and over/unders, the number of games needing bad referees was reduced—along with the chances of his organization getting caught. Rob knew that Burt had secured someone who would recruit unsavory players, but he didn't know who that man was.

Molly continued to code the moneyline games in her column each week, and Curt continued to work as an operative. The NFL officiating was terrible for each upset that was fixed, and they worried that SOTO's contract might end before the season was finished. Molly's hatred for Burt grew by the day as she tried to come to terms with Carl's death. Still, she needed to continue her pretense of loving her stepfather until the charade ended in February, and he was rotting away in prison or living on the streets penniless.

The Minnesota Vikings were on a winning streak, thanks to Rob's perfect placement of corrupt referees and Wally's assistance in finding dishonest players on opposing teams who would be willing to fumble for a million dollars. As soon as the season was over, Wally would have the shameless players and amoral officials arrested, and he prayed a judge would lock them up for life!

The Vikings beat the Lions in Detroit on January third to finish the regular season thirteen and three. They were the top seed in the

NFC and would receive a first-round bye in the playoffs. Minnesota would host the next two games at US Bank Stadium in Minneapolis. They were the talk of the town of every professional sports fan, not because they were that good, but because they were that lucky! Opponents fumbled the ball at the most inopportune times when Minnesota players didn't even hit them, and penalty calls went their way time and time again. Opposing coaches formally protested three of their games, but to no avail. Perhaps the worst football team on paper was now sitting at the top of the NFL!

Meanwhile, another strange thing was happening in the AFC. The Reno Mountaineers started the season at two and five, then traded their quarterback and $20 million to the LA Rams for running back John Warner. The next day, Bobby Smith, an eighteen-year-old quarterback from Truckee High School in California, tried out for the team at midseason and shocked the Mountaineer fan base by becoming the first undrafted, walk-on athlete who never played in college to start an NFL game. With Warner dominating the running game, Smith took to the air with pinpoint accuracy and finished the regular season with a 132.5 quarterback rating, highest by far in the league. Like the Vikings, the Mountaineers were also on a winning streak and entered the postseason with an eleven and five record, good enough for the third seed in the AFC.

Not wanting the publicity to go to his head, the Reno coaching staff prohibited their sensational quarterback from speaking to the press. In fact, they refused to release a picture of him. On the other hand, John Warner loved the spotlight, and no longer were sportswriters talking about his accepting a Porche from a college booster. Instead, the focus was on the unlikely possibility that two subpar teams at the beginning of the season could meet in the Super Bowl. The Vikings versus the Mountaineers would have many storylines should the impossible happen.

*****

On Sunday, January twenty-fourth of 2021, the impossible did indeed happen. Minnesota edged Dallas, twenty-one to twenty, thanks mostly to the Cowboys receiving twelve penalties for 145 yards, compared to the Vikings being flagged twice for only ten yards. But Dallas still should have won the game in the final seconds. They drove the ball to the Minnesota three-yard line, and quarterback Dak Prescott called their last time out with four seconds remaining. A chip-shot field goal would end the Vikings' winning streak and send the Cowboys to the Super Bowl. However, a most unfortunate and unlikely action happened next. Placeholder Barry Miller fumbled the snap, and Vikings' defensive end Yannick Ngakoue fell on the ball as time expired.

Coincidently, the sure-handed Miller was also the Cowboy's special teams captain and dominating return man who dropped a punt early in the game, leading to the Vikings' first touchdown. Minnesota would be making their first Super Bowl appearance since 1977. Barry Miller would be receiving a check from Wally Roseberg for $4 million. And Burt Merriman, who almost had a heart attack when the Cowboys lined up for the game-winning field goal, could now relax for two weeks before becoming perhaps the richest man in the world!

Meanwhile, Reno quarterback Bobby Smith threw for five touchdowns, and John Warner ran for another two as the Mountaineers destroyed the Baltimore Ravens, forty-nine to fourteen. But, unfortunately for Reno, Warner suffered a severe groin injury near the end of the third quarter, and experts in the medical profession doubted he would be ready to play in the Super Bowl. Warner's backup was average at best, which meant Reno would most likely take to the air to have a chance at winning the championship.

CBS was planning to send an army of reporters and cameramen to Tampa to prepare an hour-long pregame segment featuring the league's new, young superstar quarterback who never played in college. Mountaineers' coaches would not be able to prevent their teenage phenom from speaking to the press during the two weeks leading up to the Super Bowl. With all the fluff and fanfare, they just hoped he could remain poised during the big game.

But then, the worst thing that could happen to the Mountaineers occurred the day after the AFC playoff game—Bobby Smith took ill. He was diagnosed with the flu and ordered to bed rest at home in Truckee for the rest of the week to not expose the other players. A small unit from CBS was allowed to visit and interview Smith's parents. The crew got footage from Bobby's house, but they weren't allowed to see him. Instead, they were given his graduation picture and a few photos of him in action in high school so the network could do a background story for the pregame show. The virus persisted into the second week, and Reno practiced with their backup quarterback, Joe Barnes, taking all the snaps.

Along with discussing the impressive roster changes Reno made at midseason, sports reporters worldwide talked about the Vikings' rise from the depths of despair to the brink of their first NFL championship—and yes, all with the weekly array of bad calls and fortunate fumble recoveries. Football experts evaluated every player and every position matchup. In the end, analysts gave the Vikings a significant edge to win it all. Along with Warner possibly being sidelined, they weren't sure if Reno's rookie quarterback phenom would play either. If he did, they doubted he could lead his team to victory in the most prestigious global sports event next to the World Cup. After recuperating for two weeks without practicing, the young man would certainly be overcome with butterflies, stomach aches, and panic attacks. Anyway, Vegas bookies followed suit and made Minnesota fourteen-point favorites. A *Sports Illustrated* journalist joked about the colossal turnaround from the fourth week in the season when the Vikings' odds to win it all were 1,000 to one. He doubted anyone made that bet. Boy, was he wrong!

Perusing the weekly sports publication from his expansive deck overlooking the crisp blue Caribbean Sea, Burt Merriman grinned. The corners of his mouth seemed to stretch from ear to ear. He poured a shot of rum into his coffee and lifted his mug to cheer the seagulls as they scoured the ocean for a fishy breakfast.

Chapter 59

Sunday, February seventh, was a glorious day in Tampa, Florida—scattered clouds, soft winds, and a perfect seventy-two degrees at game time. Ten thousand seats had been added to Raymond James Stadium, bringing the total capacity to 75,618. The average ticket price was in the neighborhood of $4,500, but no one batted an eye. Attending a Super Bowl is a bucket list item for every diehard football fan in America.

Over one hundred million viewers would tune into CBS to watch either the game or the innovative commercials or just the halftime show. Twelve million pounds of potato chips would be consumed, as would nine million pounds of tortilla chips dipped into eight million pounds of guacamole. All that grease would be washed down with 325 million gallons of beer. Comparatively speaking, suds consumption would be 169 times greater than at Oktoberfest in Munich.

Using Rankins Corporation as a front, Burt Merriman won an auction bid for a suite on the fifty-yard line for $1 million. It held thirty guests, and Burt invited family, friends, and associates. Because Carl's grandfather, Syd West, was coming, Molly declined her invitation and told Burt that the Dispatch needed her to cover the Winter Carnival in St. Paul. Molly lied and said all the sportswriters were at the Super Bowl, and she drew the short straw and had to stay in the Twin Cities. Her brother, Curt, sat in the suite with his stepdad and pretended to be excited, even though he knew the game was fixed. Sam Diggins from the Minneapolis office and Enzo Esposito from the Prudhoe Bay office were there, as was Rob

Fornasiere from SOTO. Burt's architects were invited, but strangely, neither showed up.

Burt was baffled and disappointed that Wally Roseberg didn't come. He had done an exemplary job finding corrupt players that aided the Vikings' rise to glory. Burt was hoping to give him a bonus check for $1 million that was tucked away in his pocket.

Rookie quarterback Bobby Smith hadn't practiced the entire two weeks leading up to the Super Bowl and was listed as doubtful for the game. John Warner was ruled out but was in full uniform and planned to be the Mountaineers' loudest cheerleader. Warner was replaced on the roster by Joe Boone, a halfback who played on the Winnipeg Blue Bombers of the Canadian Football League. Due to Warner's injury, the Mountaineers were allowed to make an offer to anyone not under contract. Boone had retired a few weeks earlier and was able to sign with Reno as a free agent.

Boone's signing was a complete mystery to every sports reporter covering the game. He had only started four of the Bombers' games, and his stats were mediocre. Chances of him playing in the Super Bowl were slim, seeing Reno had two other halfbacks on the roster. But still, why Joe Boone?

When warmups were over, and both teams went back to their locker rooms for last-minute strategy prep, self-esteem hype, and to offer up a few prayers, Bobby Smith was nowhere to be seen. In fact, no one had seen him on a football field since the conclusion of the NFC championship game. Commentators Jim Nantz and Tony Romo were speculating that the young man who led the Mountaineers to the big game was too frustrated to even be on the sideline. Immaturity had gotten the best of him!

The Vikings were at full strength. All their dings and bruises had been healed during the two weeks prior to the Super Bowl, and they were raring to go. Burt Merriman was licking his chops. In four hours or so, he may well be on his way to becoming the world's wealthiest man.

Whispering to Rob, he asked, "Are the officials all in place?"

"Yes, sir," replied Rob with confidence. "No doubt about it!"

Then Syd West inserted, "And we have an ace in the hole working for us just to make sure."

"An ace in the hole? I like the sound of that. Who is it?"

"His name is Joe Boone, an obscure running back who signed this week from Winnipeg of the CFL. You can thank Wally Roseberg for bringing him on board."

Burt motioned for Syd to come closer. "You're a good man, Syd. And I'm not saying that because you're my best friend. This was your opportunity to win an NFL championship for your franchise, but instead, you chose to help me out. Your generosity will not go unnoticed, my friend." Burt winked at Syd, then shook hands firmly.

*****

Following the national anthem and the United States Air Force Thunderbirds' flyover, Raymond James Stadium was rocking! Reno won the coin toss and deferred to the second half. Without their star quarterback and running back, they hoped to rely on their sturdy defense to somehow win a game everyone said they couldn't.

The kickoff went through the end zone, and the Vikings would start from their own twenty-five-yard line. During a quick commercial break before the first snap from center, the crowd roared as if a touchdown had been scored. Not knowing why Reno fans were stomping their feet and hootin' and hollerin' at a decibel range that was off the charts, the Vikings' offense turned to see rookie sensation Bobby Smith emerge from the Reno locker room. With his helmet on and a football cradled in his arms, Smith jogged to the sideline, then began a soft toss with newly acquired halfback, Joe Boone.

Burt leaned forward in his seat and gazed at the Reno bench with a pair of powerful binoculars. He frowned, and his face turned red with anger. "I thought that damn kid was out for the game! Hell, he hasn't practiced for two weeks or even shown his face anywhere near Tampa!"

"Relax, Burt," said Sam Diggins complacently. "He's been bedridden for two weeks with the flu. It's doubtful he'll have enough energy to play. And even so, all seven refs are SOTO's finest! Right, Rob?"

"Yep, that's correct!" replied Fornasiere smugly.

"And Joe Boone will make sure there is a key turnover," stated Syd West confidently.

In a mild panic, Burt turned to Syd. "Are you sure your coaches know enough to play Boone?"

"Yes, yes, yes, Burt. Don't sweat it. I took care of everything!"

Burt leaned back, laid the binoculars on a table, and took a huge gulp of the Macallan Scotch on the rocks he'd been sipping since pregame warmups. He would break out the Moet and Chandon Imperial Brut champagne once the Vikings had secured the win. But for now, he was at peace knowing Rob Fornasiere and Syd West had his back.

*****

Minnesota's strategy was to control the time of possession, which would keep its defense fresh for the entire game. For the first play of the game, Head Coach Mike Zimmer called for a conservative run up the middle with star halfback Dalvin Cook. But quarterback Kirk Cousins saw the Reno defense stack the box with five down linemen and three linebackers, so he changed the call at the line of scrimmage. Why not start the game with a bang and throw a long bomb on the first play from scrimmage?

Wide receiver Adam Thielen had beaten the cornerback and safety down the right side and was open, but Cousin's pass was overthrown by five feet. Early game jitters, no doubt—Cousins is usually much more accurate than that. As Thielen and the defense began trotting back to the huddle, a yellow flag appeared close to the fifty-yard line, nowhere near where the play had finished. Safety Marcus Varden had been called for pass interference as he crossed over to help out cornerback Ray Tubbs. Replays from every angle showed that neither Varden nor Tubbs had made contact with Thielen, and even if they had, the ball was uncatchable. Mountaineers' coach Jerry Thomas was irate, as were the thousands of Reno fans in attendance. The ball was placed at the spot of the foul, and the Vikings had a first and ten at the Reno thirty-eight-yard line.

Commentators Jim Nantz and Tony Romo were beside themselves. The Vikings had been blessed by favorable penalties all season long, but how could this happen in the Super Bowl? Regardless if they were Vikings' or Mountaineers' fans, one hundred million television viewers could all see the pass interference flag was a bad call. Burt Merriman jumped up from his seat, high-fived Sam Diggins, then winked at Rob Fornasiere. Rob smiled back—half-heartedly.

Rob was pissed! He had instructed the referees to help out the Mountaineers, not the Vikings! What the hell were they doing?! If the Vikings won the game, his and Mike Kohlrusch's scheme would be a complete failure. Burt Merriman would walk away with a controlling interest in Kiner Medical Innovations and perhaps become the wealthiest man on the planet!

*****

Rob didn't know that Sam Diggins had breakfast this morning with his friend Jake Schrum, who was assigned to be the head linesman for the game. Jake told Sam that his crew would make sure the Mountaineers won, and they would try not to favor them so that it looked obvious to the fans. Sam was confused, then realized that Rob Fornasiere must have turned on Burt.

Trying to remain calm to avoid a suspicious reaction from the head linesman, Sam said, "No, Jake, we have a change of plans. You are to make sure the Vikings win—not the Mountaineers."

"I don't understand, Sam. I thought the bets were already placed. The Mountaineers are fourteen-point underdogs. I was assuming your organization bet heavily on the moneyline." Jake had no idea the mob had wagered months ago on the Vikings winning the Super Bowl.

Sam began to show his frustration. Lying with a straight face, he said, "Rob Fornasiere told me to tell you that we changed our bets this morning. The Vikings need to win. You got that?!"

Jake was taken back by his friend's tone of voice. He paused momentarily, then replied, "I'm not sure we can do that. Rob is our boss, and he needs to give the okay to me directly."

"I'm Fornasiere's boss, damn it! If you want to be paid, you will make sure the Vikings win. Do you understand me?!"

"Yep. Loud and clear, Sam!" After a tense moment of silence, Jake smiled and added, "Are we still friends?"

"Of course, Jake. Very much so!"

Sam shook hands, then made his way to the stadium. He decided not to tell Burt about Rob's doublecross until after the game. Sam wanted to see the look on Rob's face when the Vikings won the game, and whatever scheme Rob was planning had failed.

*****

Reno ran the ensuing kickoff back to their own twenty-eight-yard line, and the Mountaineer fans gave a standing ovation that lasted well past the commercial break. Rookie quarterback Bobby Smith was starting the game! From the line of scrimmage, Bobby barked a presnap cadence at the top of his lungs, but he could tell that his wide receivers and linemen had a difficult time hearing it. So he raised his arms and motioned for the crowd to quiet down a bit. A second later, a yellow flag flew from the side judge, and he jogged over to Jake Schrum to make the call.

"False start on number sixty-seven!" Jake exclaimed in his mic. Then he picked up the ball and moved it back to the twenty-three-yard line. Replays showed that number sixty-seven, the offensive tackle, had not moved nor even flinched once he was set. In the broadcast booth, Tony Romo shook his head but said nothing to the television viewers. He did not want to appear to be favoring the Mountaineers.

On the next play, newly acquired halfback Joe Boone took Smith's handoff and dropped the football in the backfield. No one had touched him! Vikings' nose tackle Shamar Stephen fell on the ball and covered it completely with his 313-pound belly. Burt Merriman paraded around the suite, high-fiving everyone in sight! Wally Roseberg had recruited the perfect player for the big game.

Burt looked over to Syd West and said, "I hope the coach doesn't pull him. I may need him again later!" Burt let out a burst of thunderous laughter, sat down, and finished off his third glass of Scotch.

"Oh, trust me, Burt, Joe Boone will keep playing. We invested too much to bench him now."

In unison, Jim Nantz and Tony Romo blurted, "Are you kidding me?!"

Chapter 60

Cardi B and Harry Styles weren't exactly a musically-matched duo made in heaven, but their mix of hip hop and Britpop had Raymond James Stadium rocking at halftime. Meanwhile, Rob Fornasiere excused himself from the suite and was striding to the elevator when Sam Diggins caught up and grabbed his shoulder. "Where are you going?" asked Sam.

Rob turned to face Sam and stuttered, "Ah, well, I, well, I'm headed, I mean heading, down to the official's locker room to check on my refs. I thought I'd see if they needed anything." Red with embarrassment, Rob had been caught off guard.

The Vikings were leading twenty-eight to nothing, and Alex Kiner had texted Rob eight times in the first half. Every text started the same way, "WTF!" The Mountaineers were penalized nine times for 135 yards, while the Vikings had yet to be flagged. Rob had planned to read the officials the riot act before Sam stopped him.

"Best you sit back down and watch the halftime show," stated Sam with a stern look in his eyes. "The officials are doing a bang-up job as it is. I'm sure they don't need anything!"

Rob could tell that Sam must have gotten to Jake Schrum before the game. He knew they were friends. If Jake told Sam that Rob wanted him to ensure a Reno victory instead of a Minnesota win, then Sam knew Fornasiere had turned on the organization. Rob could smell trouble.

As Cardi B and Harry took bows and walked off the stage hand-in-hand, the cleanup crews stormed in. They had five minutes to prepare the field for the second half. With the Vikings killing the Mountaineers, many viewers would be switching channels and wrapping up their parties. They would be looking forward to the 2021 NFL draft and hoping their team picked a future gamechanger who could lead them to the 2022 Super Bowl.

The halftime replays were dismal. Nantz and Romo couldn't help but focus on bad calls and Boone's terribly-timed fumble. Bobby Smith was a perfect sixteen for sixteen for 245 yards in the air, but too many penalties had nullified an incredible performance by the rookie sensation. This could be the first Super Bowl where a quarterback threw for 500 yards and lost the game—and maybe didn't even score!

Enzo Esposito was having a heart to heart conversation with Burt Merriman when Sam and Rob sat back down in the suite. "The sports commentators are sure fired up about the bad calls, Burt. I'm wondering if we should call off the dogs a bit."

Burt shot a puzzled look at Enzo. "What do you mean?"

"This is the Super Bowl. There are at least twenty more cameras on the field than regular-season games and even the playoffs. Fans are seeing every call from every angle. The announcers are going crazy, and the Mountaineers' faithful are too."

"What are you suggesting, Enzo?"

"I think you should send Rob down there and tell them to just ref the second half fairly to avoid continual scrutiny. There's no way the Vikings' defense will give up twenty-eight points in thirty minutes anyway. They're just too good. They'll win the game and shut up Nantz and Romo. The constant jabber about poor officiating will go away."

Burt thought about it for a moment, then glanced at Sam and Rob to get their opinions. "What do you guys think?"

Rob quickly replied, "Enzo is right. We can't take the risk of a protested Super Bowl game. I'll get down there and let them know."

Sam stood up and pushed Rob back in his seat. "No, no, Rob. I'll do it. I need a break anyway, and it's probably best that I tell your crew. They know I'm your boss, after all." No one saw the stern glare that Sam gave Rob.

As the officials were walking through the tunnel, Sam stopped them. In a soft voice so nobody else could hear, Sam said, "Make good calls for the second half, boys. You're being way too obvious, and the announcers are having a field day with the replays of your penalties. In other words, make the right calls. However, if the Mountaineers mount a comeback by some chance, you need to change direction again and ensure that the Vikings win. Do you all understand me?"

The refs looked at one another and nodded. Jake grinned smugly at Sam and said, "We got your back, boss!"

*****

The Vikings' kickoff sailed through the uprights, and Reno had the ball at the twenty-five to start the second half. Joe Boone was back on the field for the first time since fumbling the football on the Mountaineers' first possession. Syd West had gone to the locker room at halftime and instructed Coach Thomas to give Joe another chance. Thomas didn't bat an eye. Whatever Syd wanted, Syd got.

Bobby Smith called for a buck sweep to begin the second half. He took the snap and faked a trap to fullback Mike Meadows. Billy then lateralled the ball to Boone, and a split second later, Joe was off to the races! He broke three tackles on his gallop to the end zone and flattened free safety Anthony Harris with a stiff-arm before storming past the goal line. Once there, he gently handed the pigskin to the referee and huddled with his teammates, thanking them for the excellent blocks. There was no dancing, spinning the ball, or even a Lambeau Leap. Joe Boone was the epitome of good sportsmanship.

Burt Merriman gazed at Syd West with a frown. "What the hell, Syd. What was that all about?"

"Oh, come on, Burt. If Joe didn't show some good stuff, everyone would wonder why we signed him as a free agent. If that happened, the organization could be exposed. You know that!"

Burt nodded a semi-approval. He didn't like the fact that the second half had barely started, and Reno was back within three scores at twenty-eight to seven. But Syd was right. Soon a fortune would be his, and the last thing he needed was a postgame investigation.

Minnesota wasted no time regaining its momentum. They marched down the field, ate up eight minutes off the clock, and scored a touchdown when Cousins kept the ball for a quarterback sneak on third down from the Mountaineers' one-yard line. Then, on the ensuing kickoff, Reno's Ed Mackenzie looked like he would run one back for 101 yards, but kicker Dan Bailey caught him at the fifty and knocked the ball out of his arms. Minnesota recovered on their own forty-seven, then killed another five minutes on the clock before kicking a chip-shot field goal. With the score thirty-eight to seven at the end of the third quarter, Minnesota's lead appeared insurmountable.

Quarterback Bobby Smith, who was sixteen of sixteen in the first half, hadn't thrown a pass in the second half. In fact, Reno's offense hadn't even touched the ball since Joe Boone's seventy-five-yard scamper to start the third quarter. But things changed quickly.

After Mackenzie knelt in the end zone for a touchback, the ball was placed on the twenty-five-yard line. Smith looked like he was going to run another buck sweep. He faked the handoff to Meadows, then faked a lateral to Boone, drawing all sorts of attention from the Vikings' defense. Bobby then stepped back and threw a perfect pass to wide receiver Vince Coffman who was streaking down the sideline uncovered. Minnesota had bit on the fake lateral, and Coffman was wide open for an easy seventy-five-yard touchdown. The two-point conversion was successful, making the score thirty-eight to fifteen.

No one guessed that Reno would attempt an onside kick this early in the game, which turned out to be a horrible mistake on the part of the Vikings' special teams. The kick bounced high in the air, and the Mountaineers recovered on Minnesota's forty-eight-yard line. Once again, Bobby Smith wasted no time. The Vikings, who just moments ago thought the game was entirely in hand, were caught off guard when Smith dropped back and sent four receivers downfield in a crossing pattern that confused Minnesota's defensive backs. With an incredibly soft touch, Smith placed the ball in Rod Persons' outstretched arms on the five, and the Mountaineers' tailback waltzed into the end zone. Minnesota was so stunned that they only had nine men on the field for the two-point conversion, which resulted in an easy pass play to the tight end, Dave Hammer. And just like that, Reno was now back in the game with the score thirty-eight to twenty-three. The odds of successful back-to-back onside kicks were slim to none, so the Mountaineers decided to rely on their defense to step up.

Minnesota moved the ball to the Reno thirty-one-yard line, but Dan Bailey's field goal attempt was wide right, and the Mountaineers took over at the thirty-eight. However, the good news for the Vikings was that they used up six minutes on the clock.

Bobby Smith was now eighteen of eighteen for 378 yards and two TDs. The young quarterback was well on his way to shattering every Super Bowl record ever held. However, he could care less. What good was a 500-yard passing day if his team lost the game? Reno had the ball once again, but the clock had dwindled down to 7:59.

Minnesota brought in six defensive backs and went into a prevent defense, taking away Bobby Smith's chance to throw another long bomb. But Smith played it smart and threw several short passes in the middle. He knew his team needed only two scores, and they had all three timeouts remaining. If he could get a touchdown, the defense could use the timeouts to get the ball back.

Eight plays later, Bobby threw another touchdown pass to tight end Hammer, and once again, the two-point conversion was good. He now was an amazing twenty-six of twenty-six for 440 yards, but all that mattered was Reno was now within one score—thirty-eight to thirty-one. There was 2:08 left on the game clock, and if Reno's defense could step up, they would have one last chance to pull out a victory from the depths of despair! How unfortunate for the television viewers who had turned off their TVs before the chips and beers were gone!

Burt Merriman hadn't seen the comeback. When the Vikings went ahead thirty-eight to seven, he left the suite to make phone calls to every restaurant he owned. Burt instructed each one to provide free champagne to every dining customer when the Super Bowl ended. He didn't tell his managers why; he said it was just a good public relations move.

Burt about collapsed with shock when he returned to the suite with a little over two minutes remaining. Reno was within a touchdown! How the hell did that happen?! He was about to say something to Sam Diggins, but Sam cut him off. "Don't sweat it, boss. I know what you're thinking. Our refs won't let it happen. I told them to officiate fairly the second half but not to let Reno win. Trust me. They won't let us down!"

Burt looked around but didn't see who he was looking for to get more assurance. "Where's Fornasiere?"

Suddenly, Sam became very anxious. He had been so focused on watching the comeback unfold that he didn't realize Rob was gone. But there was no way that traitor could get to the refs now! Or was there?! Sam picked up his binoculars and scanned the field. Rob wasn't anywhere to be seen. Under his breath, Sam muttered, "The SOB escaped, damn it!"

"What did you say?" asked Burt. "I couldn't hear you."

"Nothing, Burt. All the Vikings need is a first down, and the game is over. Our officials will make that happen. Just wait and see."

Not only had Rob disappeared, but so had Syd West. Everyone in the suite assumed he wanted to be with his team to console them after the loss. Everyone was wrong.

Sam walked nonchalantly to the back row and found Burt's henchman, Oliver Harwas, munching popcorn, sipping a beer, and watching the game with a good deal of interest. As a young man, he had attended Super Bowl IX at Tulane Stadium and cheered for his beloved Steelers as their Steel Curtain defense had dismantled the Vikings, sixteen to six. Now, even though his boss would be furious,

Oliver silently wished the Mountaineers would tie it up and send the game to overtime just for giggles. But, of course, he would want the Vikings to prevail. A loss would be financially devastating to Burt, and he would be left without a job.

Speaking quietly but sternly, Sam whispered, "Oliver, you need to find Rob Fornasiere and keep him on a leash until I can speak to the bastard after the game."

"Why?" What's Rob done?"

"It's none of your business! Just find him and hold him until I can get there! Do you understand?!"

"Where did he go?"

"I have no idea, damn it! Just find him, okay!"

Reno opted not to try another onside kick. Instead, they would rely on their defense to make one last stop. Unfortunately, the first play from scrimmage didn't invoke a lot of confidence in their believers. Dalvin Cook ran fifteen yards on the first play. The Mountaineers chose not to call a timeout.

Minnesota had the ball first and ten from their own forty. The two-minute warning sounded. Reno's defense would have one last opportunity.

*****

The Mountaineers' defense held firm on the next three plays as Vikings' coach Mike Zimmer chose to run the ball to prevent an interception. Minnesota fans in attendance booed when he had Kirk Cousins take a knee on third down and five instead of having Cook try to run for a first down. Zimmer didn't want to risk a turnover—either by interception or fumble. After a booming punt, Reno took over at their own six-yard line. The Mountaineers had one minute and thirty-five seconds to go ninety-four yards with no timeouts. Was their rookie sensation up to the task, or would he melt in the clutch? Everyone was on their feet, not only in Raymond James Stadium but in household dens around the world!

Once again, the Vikings lined up in a prevent defense, but this time brought eight defensive backs into the game. Three down linemen would pressure the young and somewhat inexperienced quarterback to throw a duck into tight coverage. But Bobby Smith remained cool as he stepped into the huddle to call several plays. The Vikings would be expecting short down and outs to stop the clock by running out of bounds. Smith had no plans to do any such thing.

From a shotgun position, Bobby took the snap and scrambled around in the end zone. Knowing his wide receivers would be covered, he was looking for Joe Boone to get open coming out of the backfield. Bobby dodged the rushers with fakes and quick reversals as he gave Boone a few more seconds. A safety now would end the game.

Joe faked a hook at the twenty-five-yard line while Bobby faked a pass to him, and two defensive backs fell for the ruse. Boone raced upfield and caught Bobby's perfectly placed football at the Reno forty-one, then miraculously held on to it as the Vikings' Harrison Smith crushed him to the ground. The Mountaineers hustled the best they could to the line of scrimmage, but many precious seconds ticked off the clock. The next snap occurred precisely at the one-minute mark.

With pinpoint accuracy, Smith threw to an array of receivers in the middle of the field. Minnesota didn't seem to care—they were protecting the sidelines and the end zone. Anything in the middle would just eat up the clock. With ten seconds remaining, Bobby threw an eleven-yard pass for a first down at the Vikings' four-yard line. He hurried his team to the scrimmage line and spiked the ball to stop the clock with three seconds left. That was his first and only incomplete pass of the entire game!

Bobby Smith was now thirty-five of thirty-six for 536 yards. But that would mean absolutely nothing if this one last pass didn't hit paydirt! Burt Merriman's face was red as a beet with anger. The refs let this one get too close! Minnesota now called their first timeout of the half. They changed coverage and lined up man to man with four rushers and a middle linebacker, but they left five defensive backs in the game. It was time to get inside the rookie's head!

Bobby took the snap in a shotgun and looked to hit Dave Hammer on a quick pass, but saw Vikings' middle linebacker Eric Kendricks step towards his tight end. Bobby knew he couldn't thread the needle, so he pulled the ball back and scrambled to his left. Coach Mike Zimmer was stunned—any other rookie would have attempted that pass! Shoot, even Brett Favre would have attempted that pass! What was up with this rookie that no one had ever heard of at the beginning of the season?!

After scrambling back to his right, Bobby's offensive linemen could no longer hold their blocks. There were now five purple jerseys chasing Smith towards the sidelines with a defensive back moving in for the kill. That's when Bobby stopped on a dime, turned quickly, and rifled the ball across the field to the left corner of the end zone where Joe Boone, who had lined up in a tailback position, was standing all by himself. Touchdown, and no time left on the clock!

The noise in Raymond James Stadium was maddening. The dolphins swimming in Tampa Bay could hear the roar. Burt Merriman stormed up to a table in the back of the suite, grabbed a bottle of Moet and Chandon Imperial Brut champagne, and threw it at the wall. Enzo Esposito's shirt was drenched with sweat, and his legs were shaking. Sam Diggins walked over to Burt to reassure him that the Vikings would still win.

Down now by only one point, thirty-eight to thirty-seven, Reno shocked the entire sports universe by lining up for another two-point conversion. Everyone assumed they would kick the extra point and take the game to overtime. But Coach Jerry Thomas had other ideas. Minnesota quickly called their second time out. One final play. It was all or nothing!

Thinking pass all the way, the Vikings had challenged their defense to one last immense effort—mano a mano. And it would have worked if Bobby Smith had not crossed them up. He took the snap, dropped back, then ran a quarterback draw up the middle and scored virtually untouched! The crowd screamed and yelled as the scoreboard flashed thirty-nine to thirty-eight in favor of Reno. Burt Merriman was about to lose it when he saw the yellow flag fly through the air from the line judge.

"False start, number two. The quarterback abruptly moved his head to get the defense to jump. That's a five-yard penalty. Replay the down."

"What?!" exclaimed Tony Romo and Jim Nantz, once again in unison, but this time at the top of their lungs.

"You've got to see the replay!" shouted Tony. "This is incredible!"

From every angle possible, not one sliver of an abrupt or quick movement could be detected during Bobby's cadence. Yes, he moved his head from side to side to survey the defense, but absolutely nothing out of the normal.

Fans were booing loudly, and some were throwing empty bottles at the officials. Three unruly men wearing no shirts and displaying the Mountaineers' logo tattoed on their chests jumped the fence and rushed out onto the field. They were heading in the line judge's direction when fifteen security officers caught up and tackled them.

Head linesman, Jake Schrum, cleared the area for the safety of everyone involved. But the boos became louder and more items were tossed onto the field. Enough was enough. Bad calls had aided Minnesota's march to the Super Bowl, and everyone knew it. NFL fans were not going to let them win the championship the same way!

Burt Merriman and Sam Diggins moved to the big screen TV in the suite and listened precariously as the announcers demanded Commissioner Goodell to fire every referee in the league. He should clean house and start over!

After a twenty-minute delay, Jake Schrum stepped to a microphone to address the crowd in Raymond James Stadium. "Fans, this is a one-time warning. Per league rules regarding endangerment of players and other personnel, if you cannot act with the high level of sportsmanship expected and required, we will be forced to conclude this contest immediately. If so, the game will end with the final score thirty-eight to thirty-seven in favor of the Minnesota Vikings."

That ignited an explosive uproar from the crowd, and even more litter was flung onto the field. Jake Schrum was about to toss one last yellow flag, which would signal the end of the game, when Roger Goodell hustled over and stopped him. "No, Jake, not in the Super Bowl. We're going to see this one through to a fair conclusion. Now get out there and play ball!"

"There will be a damn investigation after this one!" declared Burt vociferously to everyone in the suite.

"Let them investigate!" replied Sam. "After the game, we collect our winnings and shut down SOTO before the league starts snooping around. Tell our operatives to look for another job because we're closing shop! Give them huge bonus checks to keep their mouths shut. Move your money to an offshore account and lawyer up! It's doubtful that you will ever be caught!"

"Doubtful! I want more of an assurance than that!"

"Okay, okay. I'm one hundred percent certain our scheme will be successful! How does that sound?!" Burt nodded, and they sat back down in their seats.

Surely the game was going to overtime. Now that the penalty moved the Mountaineers back to the seven-yard line, they would simply kick an extra point and try to win it in sudden death, right? That's what Jake Schrum figured. His mind was a mixed flurry of scenarios for his crew to implement to ensure a Vikings' victory. But then, the unexpected happened. Reno was once again going for two.

The Mountaineers set up with a nine-man front, and Joe Boone was the lone running back behind Bobby Smith, who lined up directly behind center. Strangely, this would not be a shotgun attempt. However, Minnesota was convinced that a pass play was inevitable. There was no way Reno would try another quarterback draw from the seven.

But what was this?! Linebacker Kendricks sensed something wasn't right. Reno had shifted two tight ends onto the left side. He immediately signaled for the Vikings' last timeout. Let the guessing game begin—would the Mountaineers come back out in the same alignment or try something different?

To the delight of the Vikings' defensive coordinator, Adam Zimmer, Reno chose to stay in the same formation. He had guessed right. Unfortunately, Adam didn't know what Bobby Smith had up his sleeve.

Totally disregarding the play called by Coach Thomas, Bobby clearly communicated to his teammates in the huddle what he wanted to do. Some were confused—they had never practiced the play—but they were entirely confident in their quarterback. He had performed miracles all game long! They marched back to the line of scrimmage and waited for Bobby's cadence. It was as if this last play was unfolding in slow motion.

Bobby took the snap, rolled left, and tossed a lateral to Joe Boone. Joe took two steps to his left, then unexpectedly stepped back. Meanwhile, Bobby had reversed to his right and was making his way to the end zone as Joe looked to throw back to him. But cornerback Holton Hill wasn't to be fooled, and he was on Smith like glue as Bobby crossed the end line. Joe was about to be crushed, so he ran backward and to his right, then saw Bobby slip towards the middle. Joe gunned the ball to where his quarterback was heading. Bobby dove and caught the ball as a pile of purple jerseys crushed him to the ground. Final score—Reno thirty-nine, Minnesota thirty-eight.

There it was! Justice had prevailed! The Mountaineers had completed another incredible Super Bowl comeback for the second time in their brief history. The first was due to Billy West's heroics against Carolina in 2015. This time it was thanks to rookie superstars Bobby Smith and Joe Boone, neither of whom were on the roster on day one! Once again, the Mountaineers' fans were going wild as the dejected Vikings' fans sat in their seats in stunned silence. Burt Merriman was livid, cussing madly and stomping the floor—until back judge Frank Komento waved his arms and ruled that the pass was incomplete. The scoreboard changed once more—it now read Minnesota thirty-eight, Reno thirty-seven.

"Are you kidding me?!" bellowed Tony Romo into the mic. "Not again! Oh my God, there's going to be a riot in Raymond James Stadium!"

Chapter 61

Word got out to those who had turned off their TVs early that the Mountaineers were staging a massive comeback. Rumor had it that Reno was on the verge of winning their second Super Bowl in six years. Molly had been watching the game at home in New Richmond, munching on potato chips and drowning her sorrows with wine, beer, and anything left in the liquor cabinet. There was a soft knock on the door, and she reluctantly got up to answer it. She was wearing her wooly winter PJs and had scrubbed the makeup off her face several hours ago. Molly didn't care—her life had become a miserable nightmare with no light at the end of the tunnel.

She pulled the door gently, then fainted. Seconds later, Molly opened her eyes, and she was on the floor—cradled in the arms of her husband. Carl was squeezing and rocking her and kissing her forehead. She gazed into his eyes, too stunned to know what to say.

Carl had been listening to the game on the Winnebago's radio as he drove on a desolate interstate highway through Wisconsin. In the icy-cold Midwest, not many folks left the comforts of their fireplaces and dens on Super Bowl Sunday. Carl carried Molly to the couch, and the young couple cuddled as they watched the end of the game. He promised to tell Molly everything, but the game's outcome was critical to their future, and they both gazed at the TV with enormous interest as Head Linesman Jake Schrum made his way to the replay camera on the sideline.

*****

The honor of the National Football League for those who played, officiated, and were diehard fans was now beyond repair! It was no longer bent—it was broken. Unruly fans had charged onto the field toward the referees after they saw the line judge call the pass incomplete. The Florida State Patrol, who had arrived at the park to assist with postgame traffic, was called into the stadium with their guns in hand. What a disaster!

The outcome of the game rested squarely in Schrum's deceitful hands. CBS slow-motion replays from every angle showed that Bobby Smith clearly had possession of the ball. In fact, it never touched the ground. Smith had rolled on his back as he caught the pass from Boone, and he held firmly onto the pigskin as the Vikings' defense tried in vain to strip the ball away. Schrum now had a choice to make—change the call, which would right the error, or leave the call as is and walk away a very rich man, thanks to the Rankins Corporation. His life was in danger regardless of the decision! Might as well take the money and run!

As he approached the camera, Rob Fornasiere stepped in front of it and motioned for Schrum to stop. Schrum was aghast! What the hell was Fornasiere doing here?! All eyes, those in the stadium and viewers glued to their TVs from home, were on them. Then, Commissioner Roger Goodell walked up and stood next to Rob.

"Stay put, Schrum!" ordered Goodell. "Fornasiere will make the final call of this game!"

Schrum was confused with multiple thoughts zigzagging through his brain. He stood completely still as Rob went under the hood of the camera. What difference will it make? Rob works for Rankins and will make sure the Vikings win!

In less than a minute, Rob came out from under the hood and whispered to Roger Goodell. The commissioner nodded, grabbed a mic, then strutted to midfield, where security guards and state patrolmen had formed a human circle around him. The national guard was on its way.

Goodell addressed the crowd. "First, I apologize for everything that has happened today, and I assure you all that things will be fixed in the very near future! The integrity of professional football will not be compromised on my watch! I asked the Sports Officials Training Organization director to make the final call for this Super Bowl. Although many of you will not be happy, it is the correct decision.

"Number Two of the Reno Mountaineers caught the football while diving through the air and immediately corralled it while lying on his back. The ball never touched the ground. Therefore, the incomplete pass has been changed, and the two-point conversion is good. The Reno Mountaineers have won Super Bowl LV by a score of thirty-nine to thirty-eight."

Within seconds of Goodell making the final call, FBI agents stormed the playing field and arrested all seven referees. The postgame entertainment had been canceled, and a few minutes later, the stunned crowd began filing out. Meanwhile, another team of FBI agents entered the Rankins Corporation suite and handcuffed Sam Diggins, Enzo Esposito, Curt Anderson, and several others.

Burt Merriman cussed and threatened the agents for apprehending his employees. But he wondered why they hadn't cuffed him. A few seconds later, he got his answer.

Dressed in his full St. Croix County deputy uniform, Bruce Merriman pointed his pistol at Burt's chest. He was well out of his jurisdiction, but the FBI had given him special permission to make the arrest. "Put your arms behind you, Dad, so Agent Owens can cuff you! And do us all a favor when you finally leave prison in a coffin—rot in hell, okay?!"

*****

Postgame onfield interviews were scrubbed. All players, coaches, and other team personnel were hustled to the locker rooms for their safety. Because there were no players congratulating one another to film, CBS chose to cover the melee inside the stadium. One camera crew was assigned to Reno's locker room in hopes of getting an interview with the game's dual MVPs—Bobby Smith and Joe Boone. However, neither could be found anywhere.

Although the atmosphere outside wasn't pretty, the Mountaineers were ecstatically celebrating their monumental comeback to win the NFL championship! Bottles of champagne were uncorked and poured over heads, and almost every player was taking a selfie to preserve the moment forever!

Due to the unfortunate circumstances that had occurred near the end of the game, Commissioner Goodell had moved the trophy ceremony into a secure area of the hallway. All fans loitering on the playing field were ushered out of the stadium by police; however, anyone willing to sit peacefully in their seat could watch the trophy ceremony on the vast HD scoreboard. Millions more were still watching from home.

Goodell presented Head Coach Jerry Thomas and Owner Syd West with the Vince Lombardi trophy, and together, they raised the sterling silver pedestal and engraved football high over their heads. As a man of the utmost integrity, Vince would be in awe of the Mountaineers' comeback but deeply disturbed by the dishonorable officiating. Syd West wasn't sure if he was more thrilled by winning his second Super Bowl—or by knowing that Burt Merriman would finally receive the justice he deserved.

When Goodell was about to present Bobby Smith and Joe Boone with the co-MVP trophy, they were not with the team. However, Bobby and Joe were watching the ceremony from a distance—strangely, with their helmets still on. Bobby had not been photographed the entire season without his helmet. Curiously, the prize rookie quarterback never removed his helmet during the Super Bowl, either. Same with Joe Boone. There were no photos of him without his helmet on since arriving from the Canadian Football League!

Syd got back on the microphone and motioned for Bobby and Joe to come to the front. Both were hesitant but finally came forward. Syd gave both players a massive bearhug, then raised the mic to his mouth.

"Commissioner Goodell and sports fans around the world, I want to introduce two fine gentlemen and two astonishing football players. They are men of incredible honor—two heroes who I am proud to be standing with today! Without them, I would not be here accepting the Vince Lombardi trophy. I would ask them now to remove their helmets. This will be a moment that will never be forgotten in the annals of sports history!"

Commissioner Goodell raised an eyebrow, confused as to where Syd was going with this. The crowd in their seats at Raymond James stadium fell silent, wondering what the Mountaineers' owner was trying to say. In New Richmond, Wisconsin, Molly reached for the remote and turned up the volume. Carl smirked and lovingly rubbed Molly's back. Soon she and the entire world would know the truth.

Joe Boone unsnapped his helmet first and slipped it off. Syd smiled and said, "This man's name is not Joe Boone, and he never played in the CFL. His name is Wally Roseberg, and he's a dear friend of my family." Syd then nodded at Bobby and motioned for him to remove his helmet.

In awe, the cameraman's mouth dropped wide open. He flinched, making the video feed a bit shaky. Syd didn't need to say another word. The entire planet recognized the face of the man wearing jersey number two. And it wasn't Bobby Smith.

It was Billy West.

Chapter 62

Billy and Carol rented a condo on Sanibel Island for the rest of February while they debriefed with the FBI and interviewed with the media. Carl's reunion with his dad and mom had occurred back in September, the day after he, Jack Bowman, and Bruce Merriman cornered Wally at InterPlan in Tequesta. Carl fainted when Wally told him that his parents were alive and in the Witness Protection Program.

Carl's get-together with his dad and mom had been heart-rending yet poignant. At first, he was angry they would leave him to think they were dead, but he finally understood that Billy and Carol did so to protect him. It didn't take long for Carl to forgive and forget—he was just thrilled to have his parents back in his life.

He prayed the same thing for his wife.

Minutes after Billy removed his helmet on TV for the world to see, the FBI stormed the West's home in New Richmond and arrested Molly. She was taken to the FBI holding cell in Brooklyn Center, Minnesota, and booked on multiple counts of racketeering. The charges were so extensive and extraordinarily profound that even Wally couldn't get Molly released. Her brother Curt was in a cell next to her. Grandpa Syd moved in with Carl at his home in New Richmond to offer moral support.

The FBI raid at his house had been emotionally devastating, and Carl thought he would lose his wife forever. When he showed up on Super Bowl night, Molly was relieved that Carl was alive and well but upset he hadn't contacted her months ago. She thought Burt's thugs had killed him. Carl explained to Molly that he wasn't sure she was working for the crime syndicate or not, which was the reason he pretended to be dead.

Syd and Carl visited Molly every day. It was during those visits when both plots to bring down Burt Merriman were revealed. Molly told about meeting Mike Kohlrusch, Alex Kiner, and Rob Fornasiere, and how she backed their scheme to set up Burt to financially collapse once Minnesota lost the game. Carl told Molly about meeting Jim Bowman's father, and how he was an ex-CIA agent who happened to be the mysterious man in the Chevy SUV following him around when they moved to New Richmond. He described his RV ride to Florida with Bruce Merriman and finding Wally and Syd at InterPlan. At that time, Carl discovered that his parents were still alive and placed in the Witness Protection Program.

Syd West's lawyers worked vigorously to negotiate a deal for Molly and Curt with the US Attorney General, but William Barr was in no hurry. Finally, on March second, Syd's granddaughter-in-law and Curt were released in exchange for turning state's evidence against their stepfather, Burt Merriman. It would be a pleasure!

Curt's testimony resulted in the arrest of every one of Burt's gambling operatives, both the online gamers and those who worked the casinos in person. He didn't know them, but they were easily traced once Curt explained the codes.

Sam Diggins and Enzo Esposito admitted guilt and testified against Burt and the mob in exchange for leniency. Burt shook his head in disgust as his two longtime associates turned on him. But in a surprise move, the judge refused to grant their plea deal after the evidence had been presented. "You will never again see the light of day outside a federal prison!" barked the enraged magistrate of the court. The attorneys on both sides of the table were in shock. How could the judge nullify a contractual plea bargain?

Sam's beautiful home on the St. Croix River, along with his massive sailboat, was sold at an auction, with the proceeds benefitting Gambler's Anonymous, an international fellowship of people who have compulsive gambling problems. Holmes Mortuary in Prudhoe Bay was converted into a cultural exchange facility for the indigenous Eskimo tribes on the North Slope.

*****

One month following the shocking conclusion to Super Bowl LV, Billy West put an end to television, radio, and YouTube interviews. He believed the American public had a right to know what happened six years ago and where he and his wife had been hiding since he received his first Super Bowl ring. But Billy never relished the spotlight, and he believed that his son Carl's best friend, Wally Roseberg, deserved to be the hero anyway. Not only had Wally demonstrated spectacular football savvy on the playing field after only practicing for two weeks, he was the one who put an end to Burt Merriman's illegal gaming operation.

To save the integrity of the NFL, which was what Billy West had wanted more than anything, it was imperative that Wally continue working as an architect—and avoiding the media. He could not risk sports reporters snooping around and blowing his FBI cover. Someday he might consider playing full-time in the NFL; however, at this moment, he wanted to continue serving his country as a federal agent. Eventually, Wally would resign from InterPlan, but for now, he designed homes. And Randy Hansen was thrilled to death. As soon as the word got out that the Super Bowl hero was an architect who worked for him, his business soared through the roof!

Wally's refusal to speak to the press was frustrating for sportswriters. This was a human interest story times ten! The only other player to go from rags to riches overnight was Kurt Warner. Kurt stocked groceries before walking on the field and becoming a two-time league MVP. Reporters tried to extract background information from Wally's parents, but all they got from them was that Wally had been an exceptional athlete who played high school ball with Carl West. And yes, because of their son's companionship, Batya and Gershom were friends with Carl's dad and mom. To this day, Wally's parents don't know he works for the FBI. They still believe InterPlan Architects employ him. Wally hasn't spent a nickel of the money he earned on false pretenses. He has invested his paychecks and plans to return it all to InterPlan once his stint is up. Meanwhile, Randy was pleased and excited to have one of his architects secretly turn into a temporary pro football star. He wished he could do the same!

Chapter 63

"Dad and Mom, I'd like you to meet my wife, Molly."

A month ago, Carl never thought he would be saying those words outside of a federal prison. Thanks to Grandpa Syd's lawyers' relentless efforts, Molly was free and clear of all charges relating to racketeering. So, too, was her brother Curt. Knowing Billy and Carol West had never met their daughter-in-law, Syd held a welcome home party at his cabin near Lake Tahoe. The relentless Papparozzi couldn't stalk them in the gorgeous house nestled deep in the woods under a canopy of pine trees. When the party was over, the whole group would partake in some serious Lahontan cutthroat trout fishing in the deep, blue lake.

Billy, Carol, Molly, Curt, Carl, and Wally laughed and socialized on the deck while getting to know one another. Besides never having met Carl's parents, Molly had not met Carl's best friend, Wally, either. Syd said he was picking up a few surprise guests at the Reno airport and would be back soon. Three hours later, he returned and introduced Mike Kohlrusch, Alex Kiner, and Rob Fornasiere. Their talk evoked a variety of emotions, and the discussions lasted well into the night, finally fading with the break of dawn.

*****

"It was Wally's crazy idea, not mine," laughed Billy. "How he thought a forty-eight-year-old washed-up has-been could return to the NFL and lead Reno to the Super Bowl is beyond me! That gamble could have backfired, leaving Burt Merriman a wealthy man, and the NFL's integrity lost for years to come."

"The risk was worth the reward," replied Wally, smiling at his best friend's dad, then addressing everyone. "Every time I visited Billy in the Witness Protection Program, we tossed the football around and even played pickup games with other FBI agents, all who were stars in high school or college. At least that was their egocentric claim to fame! Anyway, I could tell Billy was still a top-notch athlete and was in incredible shape. Besides that, Billy simply knew how to win!"

"When did you find out Burt had wagered a fortune on Minnesota to win the championship?" asked Mike Kohlrusch. He was fascinated that Wally and Syd were plotting against Burt while he, Alex, Molly, and Rob were doing the same thing.

"September. I befriended Burt while building his house in the Caymans. He hired me to find dishonest players to help the swindling officials ensure the outcomes of moneyline games. That's when Burt told me about the Vikings' bet. We were getting close to having enough evidence to throw the book at Merriman, but we were trying to find a way to keep it out of the press. Syd and I concocted a solution and thought it had a good chance of success. Burt was going to make sure Minnesota won the Super Bowl, so we needed to find a team to beat them. It was a no-brainer using Reno as that team. Syd was their majority owner, and besides that, Billy was still under an eight-year contract he signed in 2015. There was no rule in the NFL saying a player couldn't play under a different name than what was on his contract!"

"There was also no rule stating that a player could play under a false name," smirked Syd. "That was a loophole that will probably be taken care of next year. My greatest challenge was making sure Reno's players and coaches didn't leak the news that Billy was taking over the helm at quarterback. He was still in the Witness Protection Program, and if the word got out, his life would be in danger. I had the entire team sign a contract to that effect, offering stock options in my sports marketing company to guarantee their silence. They were all thrilled to have Billy on board, and they believed he could lead them to a championship!"

Wally continued, "Yes, that was true. Reno was a good team as it was—and Billy was the shot of confidence that put their eyes on the prize. However, they needed an upgrade to have a chance to make it to the Super Bowl. Fortunately, Syd was able to trade for all-star running back John Warner. Teamed together, John and Billy would be a formidable duo in the backfield. Seeing we were hiding Billy, and everyone outside of our locker room thought he was dead, we had to find a real person willing to loan out his name. If we just used a fictitious name, snooping reporters would expose the truth as soon as they tried to get background information, or a playing history, for the fake name."

"So, how in the world did you ever pull that off?!" chuckled Mike.

"Syd happened to be a hunting buddy of Truckee High School Coach Milt Boyer, and he told his pal about the illegal gaming operation and his plans to put an end to Burt Merriman. Milt was shocked to know that Billy West was very much alive, but he promised to keep it a secret. The coach and Syd met with Bobby Smith and his parents, asking them to participate in the charade. Bobby wouldn't have to do anything but hide out for a few months. All Syd needed was for Billy West to use Bobby's name, and in return, Syd gave Bobby's family $1 million. The entire time that Billy pretended to be Bobby Smith, he was never photographed without his helmet!"

"When did you decide to play, Wally?"

"It certainly wasn't my idea! When John Warner went down with an injury, it was Billy who talked me into replacing him. To this day, I think he was totally out of his mind!"

"Absolutely not!" responded Billy. "You are phenomenally strong, with quickness that is second to none! I had no doubts about your ability to play at a high level!"

"I searched to find a retired Canadian Football League player who would agree to let his name be used and keep the ruse a secret," inserted Syd. "Because of all the media attention, an American player might raise a lot of questions. Joe Boone fit the bill and was also paid

$1 million. His teammates and coaches had no idea that it wasn't him—Wally never removed his helmet either! To make it legal under NFL policy, he changed his real name to Wally Joe Boone Roseberg!"

Everyone at the party laughed out loud. Carl chuckled, "So, I guess I'll start calling you WJBR!"

Wally smiled, "I guess so, CW."

At that point, Billy got up and stepped away from the group. He leaned on a deck post, staring off into the dark forest where long shadows were forming from the full moon. The snow was melting thanks to an early spring thaw, but the night air was chilly. His family and newfound friends stopped talking, wondering what was bothering him.

Carl walked to Billy and asked, "What's the matter, Dad? What are you thinking about?"

"I'm thinking about the season, and I'm thinking we made a serious mistake helping the Vikings get to the Super Bowl. Sadly, we shattered the game's honor when we allowed teams that shouldn't have won to win. "

Wally joined Carl at the deck post and placed his arms on Billy's shoulders. "We didn't shatter the honor of the NFL. We may have bent it a little, but we did so for the long-term benefit of everyone who ever played the game."

Epilogue

Bruce Merriman sat in the front row next to his half-brother, Curt Anderson. Molly and Carl stood in the back of the tiny room—they didn't need a close-up view of what was about to happen. Five reporters were allowed to watch; however, their cameras and cell phones were confiscated when they walked through security. Warden Barry Reddish was at his post next to the wall phone, which was a hotline to the Governor. Outside, death row advocates and adversaries either cheered or protested in the steamy Florida air next to Raiford's state prison.

The curtain opened, and all eyes gaped at Burt Merriman. His arms and legs were strapped to the electric chair, and the electrode gel that had been applied to his freshly shaved head shimmered in the low light. Two executioners had taken positions on each side of the Mafia mogul. Burt waived the reading of the warrant.

Using a natural sea sponge taken from the saturated saline solution container, the executioners soaked every area of Burt's body where an electrode was attached. Then the PA switch was flipped in the execution room and the witness gallery. Warden Reddish asked if Burt had any final words.

Speaking remorsefully, Burt said, "I'd like to tell my kids that I'm sorry. I never meant to harm you." Burt then decided to end on a sarcastic note. "Stay out of trouble—it could be the death of you!"

The chin strap and headpiece assembly were attached to a high voltage lead. Witnesses waited nervously, wondering if the phone would ring. It didn't. There would be no stay of execution from the governor's office. Warden Reddish announced that the execution process should commence.

The primary executioner engaged the switches. The automatic cycle began, and 2,300 volts shot into Burt's body for eight seconds; followed by a second cycle of 1,000 volts for twenty-two seconds; and a final burst of 2,300 volts for eight seconds. A faint puff of smoke could be seen emanating from Burt's ears and nose. Molly turned away, covered her eyes, and sobbed. Bruce vomited on the floor. Burt was pronounced dead at 10:07 a.m. on July second of 2022.

*****

Burt was found guilty of the murder of eight FBI agents following the conclusion of the 2015 Super Bowl game in Miami. After Alex Kiner sued Burt for full payment on the loan agreement that he signed in the fall of 2020, Burt was forced to declare bankruptcy. Kiner Medical Innovations assumed all of Burt's assets: his homes, his restaurants, and his cars, boats, and airplanes. With nothing left, Burt didn't bother fighting his death row sentence. No appeals—he just wanted to die quickly. And it was the fastest trial to execution ever in the history of the United States!

Although the judge disallowed plea bargains from Sam Diggins and Enzo Esposito, he did allow deals for every one of Burt's operatives in exchange for leniency. And while the operatives provided an abundance of evidence, it was Billy, Syd, Wally, and Rob Fornasiere who were the star witnesses in Burt's trial. With reporters swarming the courtroom, the fascinating story of what happened to Billy and Carol West could finally be told.

*****

Billy had been approached by an unknown man wielding a semiautomatic pistol following practice before the 2015 Super Bowl. Waving the gun in Billy's face, the intimidator had threatened to kill him and his family if Billy didn't agree to fumble, throw an interception, or whatever it took to ensure that the Carolina

Panthers won the championship. To demonstrate that he meant business, the man showed Billy close up photos of Carol, Carl, and Syd relaxing in his backyard. Billy was aghast!

When he got home, he told his wife and father about the confrontation, but nothing was said to Carl. He didn't want his son to worry. Billy then phoned Ron Mauston, a friend who worked for the FBI, and described the man who threatened him. Mauston emailed Billy a picture of one of the FBI's ten most wanted criminals, and sure enough, it was the same person! His name was Oliver Harwas, and he was a hitman for the Mafia. But at that time, the FBI hadn't made a connection between Harwas and Burt Merriman; thus, Burt's name was never mentioned to Billy, Carol, or Syd.

Billy was distraught with anxiety. At first, he planned to throw the game for the Panthers. Family was more important to him than football! But the integrity of the NFL was on the line. Would Bart Starr, Terry Bradshaw, or Joe Montana purposely have caused their teams to lose as part of an illegal gambling scheme?

Ironically, Syd and Merriman had become friends years earlier, but Syd never knew Burt headed up an illegal gaming crime syndicate until last summer. And to make matters worse, Syd dined with Burt before the Super Bowl, and he inadvertently told him about the threats to Billy. He said that his son had called his FBI buddy, Ron Mauston. So Burt ordered a hit on Mauston and four agents who worked for him! The executions occurred two days after the Super Bowl.

With forty-eight hours to go before game time, Billy met with Ron Mauston at the FBI headquarters in Miami, the city where the Super Bowl was to be played. Billy wanted assurance that the FBI could guarantee his family wouldn't be harmed if he chose to go for the win. Ron said he could keep them safe if Billy and Carol agreed to enter the Witness Protection Program, but he cautioned Billy that they would need to stay in the program until Oliver Harwas was arrested. And, they would not be able to tell anyone, including Carl and Syd. Reluctantly, Billy agreed. He hoped and prayed his father would watch over Carl's well-being and care for him during their absence.

Billy West's incredible pass to Corey Simes won Super Bowl XLIX for the Reno Mountaineers. Billy dropped to his knees to thank God for making the throw perfect. But he also asked him to take care of Carl until he and his son could be reunited.

Ron Mauston had an FBI agent pick Billy and Carol up in a fake taxi and drive towards the airport. They were hustled out of the car at a concealed intersection and jumped quickly into Mauston's SUV. Because Mauston assumed that television crews or Papparozzi would be filming the MVP's departure from the stadium, two special agents, one male and one female, replaced the Wests in the back seat. A third agent was the cab driver. Once the taxi arrived at the airport, the decoy was supposed to continue. The special agents would act like a married couple about to head home from vacation, and the people filming would be left to wonder what happened to Billy and Carol.

But after Billy defied Harwas's threats, Burt Merriman ordered his henchman to cause an accident that would kill the Wests. A year earlier, Oliver shot down a WMIA news drone that had flown too close to his home in Miami Beach. He copied the serial number and engraved it onto his own drone, thinking someday he could use it criminally and then blame the local news media. Harwas carried the small flying machine in his trunk at all times. It was his idea to fly the drone and run the hero and his wife off the road. It would be untraceable! Unfortunately, it was the three FBI agents who were killed in the line of duty.

Billy and Carol were devastated to hear that Mauston and four of his agents had been murdered. A short time later, they were in complete shock when their son's high school friend, Wally Roseberg, replaced Mauston. They cried when Wally told them about the deaths of the undercover cab driver and the two impersonators who helped them to escape.

*****

Wally dropped out of college at UNLV to work for the FBI. Within a short time, he was promoted to become the Southeast Region's Witness Protection Program director. It wasn't until he replaced Ron Mauston that Wally found out Billy and Carol West were in the program. Following up on Mauston's cases led him to Burt Merriman and the illegal gaming operation. Wally guaranteed Billy and Carol that he would work tirelessly until the FBI had enough evidence to shut down Burt Merriman for good. Billy pleaded with Wally to find a way to arrest Merriman without destroying the NFL's reputation.

When he heard that Burt was about to build a mansion in the Caymans, Wally wanted to find a way to get closer to him. That's when he began his disguise as an architect. Fortunately, he had enough drafting skills to fool Randy Hansen into hiring him.

*****

Rob Fornasiere was found guilty of aiding and abetting a federal crime. He was sentenced to ten years of probation and ordered to shut down the Sports Officials Training Organization immediately. Rob started the company with the full intention of training and placing the highest quality referees and umpires into professional sports contests. But that aspiration ended abruptly the night his wife and kids were kidnapped at gunpoint by men working for Sam Diggins. They were held in an abandoned warehouse until Rob agreed to use SOTO for Burt Merriman's illegal gaming operation. Once his family was released, Rob knew they were being watched closely and at any time could be killed. He had no choice but to play along in Burt's scheme.

The judge wanted to let Rob off scot-free after listening to the testimony from him and his wife. After all, Rob blew the whistle and called the FBI and Roger Goodell in the second half of the Super Bowl. But in the strangest move ever in the United States legal system's history, Rob refused to be pardoned. He insisted on receiving some sort of punishment for not telling the FBI sooner and trusting that they could keep his family safe. When asked why he would live the rest of his life with a felony conviction, he simply replied, "To teach my sons to live by the law—and do the right thing."

*****

Because Holmes Mortuary, a subsidiary of Rankins Corporation, was located in Prudhoe Bay, Alaska, the FBI determined that Sam Diggins and Enzo Esposito would be tried at the US District Court in Anchorage. The day Sam and Enzo were to be processed at the Federal Correctional Institute in Sheridan, Oregon, John Bowman was being released. His father, Jack, bear-hugged his son tightly, then walked arm-in-arm to Dad's black Chevy Tahoe. Jack and John noticed a van had just stopped at the prison's intake doors and paused to watch as two men in leg shackles and handcuffs emerged.

John pointed, "That's Enzo Esposito, the man who tricked me into the fake football lottery in Prudhoe Bay!"

Jack responded, "And that's Sam Diggins, the man who had your brother killed! Quite a coincidence that they're entering the gates of this prison for the rest of their life at the same time you're going home."

Just then, two gunshots crackled and echoed from a patch of greenery behind the parking lot. Jack and John dove to the ground instinctively and covered the back of their heads. They looked up to see prison guards rushing towards the van. Sam and Enzo were lying facedown in a pool of their own blood. Any appeals that the two crooks hoped to make while in Sheridan's correctional facility would now have to be done with the devil.

Oliver Harwas climbed down from the Oregon White Oak tree, 977 yards from the frantic scene that he had caused. He placed the McMillan Tac-50 sniper rifle in the Dodge Charger SRT Hellcat trunk, hustled into the driver's seat, then floored the accelerator, smoking the asphalt with burnt rubber from his squealing tires.

Barring slow-moving RVs and semis hauling logs on Highway 18, he would be back on his yacht in Lincoln City in less than an hour.

Oliver had successfully fulfilled Burt's final request—one last eternal desire made from death row the day before the execution.

"End them!" ordered Burt. "Damn traitors!"

AUTHOR'S NOTE

Writing a novel in 2020 was a challenge. Yes, COVID-19 gave me more time to compose, but the distractions were abundant, as were the new rules applied to daily routines. A pragmatic approach to picking up the mail included rubbing down letters with Clorox wipes. Suddenly, in the midst of the unknown, everything we took for granted was upended. Optimism and pessimism were in a battle for the human soul!

I started *Bend of Honor* two weeks before the NBA shut down and March Madness teetered on the brink of postponement. I survived April with five-dollar rolls of toilet paper, ten-dollar generic hand sanitizers, and cloth masks sewn by our Canadian friend, Joanne Thompson. Weekly date night dinner and movies became faded memories.

Our son and daughter moved in with us in May—following their self-imposed quarantines to keep us safe. We watched every Netflix documentary while the kids sat at a distance. They worked in separate rooms each day, and we were all thankful they still had a job that could be done online. In June, our son returned to Brooklyn and our daughter to Milwaukee as the pandemic turned America and the rest of the world into a rollercoaster of uncertainty.

We canceled a bucket-list trip to Scotland and a road trip to Seattle to see our grandkids. How do you explain to a three-year-old and a one-year-old that Papa and Grandma can't visit them? And when we finally got the chance to see William and Charlotte in August, we played with them from six-feet away.

Protests, wildfires, and an unconscionable murder of a black man by a police officer in Minneapolis racked the headlines while the relentless Coronavirus took a backseat in the news. The travel and hospitality industries were on the verge of bankruptcy, and workers from every walk of life were being laid off or let go permanently. A country whose leaders believed strongly in capitalism gladly accepted socialistic stimulus checks from the government.

As the election neared, a divided nation of blue and red hindered the enjoyment of watching TV. Hateful and misleading advertisements from both parties inundated the airwaves, and social media tested the limits of civility. Would November third change all that? Could we ever unify this nation as we did before the Revolutionary War, during the Apollo 11 landing on the moon, or after that fateful day in September of 2001?

As of today, over 331,600 fellow Americans have perished as a result of the virus. I say ***fellow*** because ending this mess will require harmony, compassion, and working together whether you like it or not. So, now I conclude my *Author's Note.* It's time to move on to the editing process: correcting errors, fixing the parts that are difficult to understand, and polishing up the story to make it better.

Let's hope our country begins its own editing process.

ACKNOWLEDGMENTS

Because I would undoubtedly forget someone, I'll offer a group hug to all who touched my life while growing up in New Richmond, Wisconsin. Thanks to my family, friends, teachers, coaches, and citizens of that beautiful community in the great Midwest! You were my inspiration.

For the most part, the cities, towns, buildings, businesses, and street names are genuine in this novel and were used only to enhance the region's authenticity. And speaking of genuine, some of the *Bend of Honor* characters are veritable, living, breathing human beings! Those who have read *Seminole Bend* and *Gila Bend* know that I choose to grant the wishes of readers who would like to see their names in print. Okay, so that's a bit of a stretch—some of you asked to be in my book, others were reluctant warriors! So here it goes, my alphabetical list of real-life characters. You are truly bona fide aristocrats, plebians, and gentlefolk of our world!

Curt Anderson was my school psychologist while I was a principal in Arizona. As characterized in the book, he actually graduated from the University of Wisconsin-Eau Claire and is a diehard Packers' fan, just like me! After too many Miller Lites watching Green Bay beat up on Philly, he asked to be accurately portrayed in my novel. I did my best!

Rob Fornasiere and I go back to our college days. His wife, Ruth, and my wife were roommates and close friends. He played baseball for the University of Wisconsin-LaCrosse and had a tremendous career coaching the Minnesota Golden Gophers team. While hiking the Superstition Mountains in Arizona, Rob agreed to be a main character in the book. Because I was his trail guide and ride home, his options were limited. Need I say more?

Randy Hansen is my big brother. I needed an architect in Florida to make the story complete, and lo and behold, he fit the bill perfectly. He is a designer extraordinaire for all of the Gold Coast and even agreed to remodel our home twice in exchange for daily breakfast at the Waffle House. Being a diehard Vikings fan, I'm sure Randy was disappointed that I chose to have them lose the Super Bowl.

Oliver Harwas is back again!. You may recall that his character was Oliver Harfield in *Seminole Bend.* Because he was portrayed as a terrorist in that book, he begged for redemption in *Bend of Honor.* Granting his wishes, I downgraded him to a simple Mafia hitman. Okay, the reality is that Oliver is the total opposite of a bad guy—he's a good and honorable man! Athletically, he struggles in a sand trap, has flown headfirst off a mountain bike several times, and sunk a kayak or two. But if he doesn't stop making ridiculous bets with me, Oliver may never find his way out of my novels!

Mike Kohlrusch is a New Richmond native, high school friend, well-respected pharmacist, and most importantly, a really great guy. His wife Teri recruited him for a part in the novel, then offered lifetime pontoon rides on Bear Trap Lake if I made him a hero instead of a villain. Fortunately for Mike, I can be bought!

Mary Reppe, also a New Richmond native, has been a friend since before kindergarten. I had a sneaking suspicion she would enjoy being a CIA agent. And to ensure that her identity remained a secret, which is what you do for spies, I didn't tell her she was a character in the book until it had been written. Surprise!

Linda Schultz is my sister. I'm sure she was jealous that her husband Gene was immortalized in *Gila Bend*, so I needed to make amends in this novel. After all, she was the only person who subscribed to my weekly five-cent newsletter that I published in fourth grade. Thanks to her, I made my first dollar!

John Warner taught sixth grade at the school where I was principal. He is an exceptional educator who has dedicated his life to children. John's friendly and caring personality rubs off on everyone—a real, living, Facebook smiley-face emoji! His dream has always been to be a football star, and now he is—albeit in a fiction novel. Get ready, John, for the long line of autograph hounds knocking on your door!

I tapped into family skills to finalize this project, so a special thanks goes out to Marc (advertising), Luke (creative design), Shea (marketing), and my wife, Meg, who edited the first rough draft and provided exceptional advice.

ABOUT THE AUTHOR

Tom Hansen is a native of New Richmond, Wisconsin. He has lived in or traveled to seventy-two countries and all fifty states and is currently an Arizona resident. Tom has dedicated most of his life to the field of education as a teacher (Dhahran, Saudi Arabia, Okeechobee, Florida, and Orlando, Florida), principal (Hazel Green, Wisconsin and Mesa, Arizona), educational consultant (State of Arizona), college professor and administrative director (Scottsdale, Arizona). This is his third novel.

APPENDIX ONE: CAST OF CHARACTERS
Alphabetized by Last Name & Chapter First Appeared in Book

FIRST	LAST	REFERENCE	CH
Curt	Anderson	Molly's brother, a psychiatrist in Eau Claire, WI	2
Molly	Anderson	Meets Carl West in college and becomes his wife	2
Jalen	Biggs	Night custodian at General Hospital	19
Jack	Bowman	Father of Jim Bowman	38
Jim	Bowman	Obit consultant before Carl; Died in car accident	3
John	Bowman	Brother of Jim Bowman; Petroleum engineer in Alaska	5
Nanouk	Brown	FBI agent in Fairbanks	39
Hugh	Cicero	Sports columnist who Molly replaced at Dispatch	6
Ann	Colter	Receptionist at InterPlan Architecture (Wally's job)	14
Drew	Cullens	WMIA news anchor	23
Sam	Diggins	Assistant Funeral Director for Holmes Mortuary	8
Henry	Ellis	Custodian at Bolles HS where Carl attended school	10
Enzo	Esposito	Works for Rankins in Prudhoe Bay, Alaska	38
Rob	Fornasiere	Director of Sports Officials Training Organization	22
Randy	Hansen	Architect and owner of InterPlan (Wally's job)	14
Oliver	Harwas	Top assistant to "the boss" of the crime syndicate	30
Betty	Johnson	Receptionist nurse at General Hospital	19
Alex	Kiner	Founder & CEO of Kiner Medical Innovations	55
Mike	Kohlrusch	Physician, and head of the Cancer Treatment Center	19
George	Markins	Human Resources for EC Gazette	3
Ron	Mauston	FBI Executive Assistant Director	53
Bruce	Merriman	Burt's son; St. Croix County deputy sheriff	21
Burt	Merriman	Wealthy restaurant owner; Anderson's stepfather	3
Barry	Miller	Special team captain for Dallas Cowboys	58
Miles	Milton	Back judge for NFL	12
Doc	Morgan	Psychiatrist who supervised Curt's internship	3
Marla	Owens	Day manager at Heritage Court Assisted Living Ctr	4
Ken	Peterson	Professional oddsmaker for ESPN	10
Mary	Reppe	CIA agent and colleage of Jack Bowman	38
Max	Rivers	Soccer coach at UW-Eau Claire	3
Batya	Roseberg	Wally Roseberg's mother	13
Gershom	Roseberg	Wally Roseberg's father	13
Wally	Roseberg	Carl West's best friend from high school	9
Linda	Schultz	Administrator of Woodlawn Cliffs Rest Home	21
Jake	Shrum	Head linesman for NFL	12
Eve	Smith	Wealthy widow; Doc Morgan's only patient	3
John	Warner	LA Rams halfback who was NFL's leading rusher	32
Billy	West	NFL Quarterback & Future Hall-Of-Famer	1
Carl	West	Son of Billy West (NFL QB); Obituary Writer	1
Syd	West	Carl West's Grandfather; Wealthy NFL Owner	1
Jan	Willows	Molly's secretary at the Dispatch	22
Tom	Yary	Young man in hospital whose wife is in labor	19
Kevin	Yustis	Back judge for NFL	32

www.ingramcontent.com/pod-product-compliance
Lightning Source LLC
Chambersburg PA
CBHW020605310726
48979CB00008B/1351/J

* 9 7 8 1 7 3 2 8 1 8 2 5 5 *